YEAR'S BEST FANTASY

⊰ 3 ⊱

**EDITED BY DAVID G. HARTWELL
AND KATHRYN CRAMER**

An Imprint of HarperCollins*Publishers*

EOS
An Imprint of HarperCollins*Publishers*
10 East 53rd Street
New York, New York 10022-5299

Copyright © 2003 by David G. Hartwell and Kathryn Cramer
ISBN: 0-06-052180-5
www.eosbooks.com

First Eos paperback printing: July 2003

Eos Trademark Reg. U.S. Pat. Off. And in Other Countries, Marca Registrada, Hecho en U.S.A.
HarperCollins® is a trademark of HarperCollins Publishers Inc.

Printed in the U.S.A.

10 9 8 7 6 5 4 3 2 1

To Elizabeth Constance Cramer Hartwell, to
whom everything is new

Contents

Acknowledgments

We would like to acknowledge the help provided by the print and online reviewers of short fiction, especially in Locus, locusmag.com, and tangentonline.com. There is more vigorous dialog now about short fiction in the fantasy field than there has been in years, because of the growing number of opinionated and experienced reviewers.

Introduction

It was an especially good year for fantasy short fiction in 2002, and we wish this book could have been twice as long so we could have fit in a bunch of longer stories that are just as good as the ones collected here. It was an exceptional year for children's and young adult fiction, as well. The publishers had geared up for a year in which there would be no new *Harry Potter* novel (and to follow up on the huge success of the film of *The Fellowship of the Ring*). Everyone knew there is an audience for good children's/young adult fantasy, and many tried to satisfy it, including a goodly number of successful writers, from Clive Barker and Neil Gaiman to Isabel Allende and Michael Chabon, as well as less familiar names such as Nancy Farmer and Cornelia Funke. Readers are going to be catching up on 2002 for some time to come because there was so much that was so good, and in such unusual places. Perhaps the best anthology of original stories was *The Green Man*, edited by Ellen Datlow and Terri Windling, also a young adult publication.

So welcome to the third volume of the *Year's Best Fantasy*, representing the best of 2002. Like the earlier volumes in this series, this book provides some insight into the fantasy field now, who is writing some of the best short fiction published as fantasy, and where. But it is fundamentally a collection of excellent stories for your reading pleasure. We follow one general principle for selection: this book is full of fantasy—every story in the book is clearly that and not primarily something else. We (Kathryn Cramer and David G. Hartwell) edit the *Year's Best Science Fiction* in paperback from Eos as a companion volume to this one—look for it if you enjoy short science fiction, too.

In this book, and this anthology series, we use the broadest definition of fantasy (to include wonder stories, adventure fantasy, supernatural fantasy, satirical and humorous fantasy). We believe that the best-written fantasy can stand up in the long run by any useful literary standard in comparison to fiction published out of category or genre, and furthermore, that out of respect for the genre at its best we ought to stand by genre fantasy and promote it in this book. Also, we believe that writers publishing their work specifically as fantasy are up to this task, so we set out to find these stories, and we looked for them in the genre anthologies, magazines, and small press pamphlets. Some fine fantasy writers will still be missing. A fair number of the best fantasy writers these days write only novels, or if they do write short fiction, do so only infrequently, and sometimes it is not their best work.

This was a notable year for short fiction anthologies, as well as for the magazines both large and small. The last SF and fantasy magazines that are widely distributed are *Analog, Asimov's, F&SF,* and *Realms of Fantasy.* And the electronic publishers kept publishing, sometimes fiction of high quality, in spite of the fact that none of them broke even or made money at it. We are grateful for the hard work and editorial acumen of the better electronic fiction sites, such as SciFiction, Strange Horizons, Fantastic Metropolis, and Infinite Matrix, and hope they survive.

The small presses remained a vigorous presence this year. We have a strong short fiction field today because the small presses, semiprofessional magazines (such as *Fantastic, Weird Tales,* and *Horror Garage*), and anthologies are printing and circulating a majority of the high-quality short stories published in fantasy, science fiction, and horror. The U.S. is the only English-language country that still has any professional, large-circulation magazines, though Canada, Australia, and the UK have several excellent magazines.

The semi-prozines of our field mirror the "little magazines" of the mainstream in function, holding to professional editorial standards and publishing the next generation of writers, along with some of the present masters. We encourage you to subscribe to a few of your choice. You will find the names of many of the most prominent ones in our story notes.

In January of 2003, as we write, professional fantasy and science fiction publishing as we have always known it is still concentrated in nine mass market and hardcover publishing lines (Ace, Bantam, Baen, DAW, Del Rey, Eos, Roc, Tor, and Warner), and those lines are publishing fewer titles in paperback. But they do publish a significant number of hardcovers and trade paperbacks, and all the established name writers at least appear in hardcover first. The Print-on-Demand field is beginning to sort itself out, and Wildside Press and its many imprints look to be the umbrella for many of the better publications, including original novels and story collections.

This was a very strong year for original anthologies. Among the very best were *The Green Man*, edited by Ellen Datlow and Terri Windling; *Leviathan 3*, edited by Jeff VanderMeer and Forrest Aguirre; *Conjunctions 39*, edited by Peter Straub; *Embrace the Mutation*, edited by Bill Sheehan; *Dark Terrors 6*, edited by Stephen R. Jones, and the *DAW 35th Anniversary Anthology: Fantasy*, edited by Sheila Gilbert and Betsy Wollheim. One noticeable trend evident in some of these is toward non-genre, or genre-bending, or slipstream fantastic fiction. There were a number of quite good original anthologies and little magazines devoted to stories located outside familiar genre boundaries, yet more related to genre than to ordinary contemporary fiction—and marketed to a genre readership.

It was also a good year for novellas and novelettes in the genre, though, sadly, we do not have the space in this book to include more than a couple. There were dozens of good ones, and we would have liked to include many of them.

We repeat, for readers new to this series, our usual disclaimer: this selection of fantasy stories represents the best that was published during the year 2002. It would take two or three more volumes this size to have nearly all of the best—though even then, not all the best novellas.

We try to represent the varieties of tones and voices and attitudes that keep the genre vigorous and responsive to the changing realities out of which it emerges. This is a book about what's going on now in fantasy. The stories that follow show, and the story notes point out, the strengths of the evolving genre in the year 2002.

David G. Hartwell & Kathryn Cramer
Pleasantville, NY

Her Father's Eyes

Kage Baker

*Kage Baker [http://members.tripod.com/~MrsCheckerfield/]
lives in Pismo Beach, California. She is known primarily as
a science fiction writer, especially for her series of stories
and novels about The Company, an organization from the
future that sends agents back in time to retrieve lost artifacts, such as priceless art treasures. Her collection of stories in that setting—Black Projects, White Knights: The
Company Dossiers—was published to substantial critical
acclaim in 2002. She has attracted additional notice in the
last few years for fantasy stories. Last year her story
"What the Tyger Told Her" appeared in our Year's Best
Fantasy 2. Her first fantasy novel, The Anvil of the World,
is published in 2003. She worked for some years for the
Living History Centre and says, "Twenty years of total im-
mersion research in Elizabethan as well as other historical
periods has paid off handsomely in a working knowledge
of period speech and details."*

*Her attention to period detail is certainly evident in
"Her Father's Eyes." This story was published in Asimov's,
where most of her short fiction has appeared. A girl child
and her parents—her father just back from military service—are riding a train in the late 1940s, and she sits next
to a little boy who is in the custody of an evil couple who
are not really his parents. There are perhaps echoes of
Hans Christian Andersen's great fairy tale "The Snow
Queen."*

It was so long ago that fathers were still gaunt from the war, their awful scars still livid; so long ago that mothers wore frocks, made fancy Jell-O desserts in ring molds. And that summer, there was enough money to go for a trip on the train. She was taken along because she had been so sick she had almost died, so it was a reward for surviving.

She was hurried along between her parents, holding their hands, wondering what a *dome coach* was and why it was supposed to be special. Then there was a gap in the sea of adult legs, and the high silver cars of the train shone out at her. She stared up at the row of windows in the coach roof, and thought it looked like the cockpits in the bombers her father was always pointing out.

Inside it was nicer, and much bigger, and there was no possible way any German or Japanese fighter pilots could spray the passengers with bullets; so she settled into the seat she had all for herself. There she watched the people moving down on the platform, until the train pulled out of the station.

Then her parents exclaimed, and told her to look out the wonderful dome windows at the scenery. That was interesting for a while, especially the sight of the highway far down there with its Oldsmobiles and DeSotos floating along in eerie silence, and then, as they moved out into the country, the occasional field with a real horse or cow.

The change in her parents was more interesting. Out of uniform her father looked younger, was neither gloomy nor sarcastic but raucously happy. All dressed up, her mother was today as serene and cheerful as a housewife in a magazine advertisement. They held hands, like newlyweds, cried out in rapture at each change in the landscape, and told her repeatedly what a lucky little girl she was, to get to ride in a dome coach.

She had to admit they seemed to be right, though her gaze kept tracking nervously to the blue sky framed by the dome, expecting any minute steeply banking wings there, fire or smoke. How could people turn on happiness like a tap, and pretend the world was a bright and shiny place when they knew it wasn't at all?

The candy butcher came up the aisle, and her father bought her a bag of mint jellies. She didn't like mint jellies but ate them anyway, amazed at his good mood. Then her mother took her down the car to wash the sugar from her face and hands, and the tiny steel lavatory astonished and fascinated her.

From time to time the train stopped in strange towns to let people off or on. Old neon signs winked from brick hotels, and pointed forests like Christmas trees ran along the crests of hills, stood black against the skyline. The sun set round and red. While it still lit the undersides of the clouds, her parents took her down to the dining car.

What silent terror, at the roaring spaces between the cars where anyone might fall out and die instantly; and people sat in the long room beyond, and sipped coffee and ate breaded veal cutlets as calmly as though there were no yawning gulf rushing along under them. She watched the diners in awe, and pushed the green peas round and round the margin of her plate, while her parents were chatting together so happily they didn't even scold her.

When they climbed the narrow steel stair again, night had fallen. The whole of the coach had the half-lit gloom of an aquarium, and stars burned down through the glass. She was led through little islands of light, back to her seat. Taking her place again she saw that there were now people occupying the seats across the aisle, that had been vacant before.

The man and the lady looked as though they had stepped out of the movies, so elegant they were. The lady wore a white fur coat, had perfect red nails; the man wore a long coat, with a silk scarf around his neck. His eyes were like black water. He was very pale. So was the lady, and so was their little boy who sat stiffly in the seat in front of them. He wore a long coat too, and gloves, like a miniature grownup. She decided they must be rich people.

Presently the Coach Hostess climbed up, and smilingly informed them all that there would be a meteor shower tonight. The elegant couple winked at each other. The little girl scrambled around in her seat, and peering over the back, asked her parents to explain what a meteor was. When she understood, she pressed her face against the cold window glass, watching eagerly as the night miles swam by. Distant lights floated in the darkness; but she saw no falling stars.

Disappointed, cranky and bored, she threw herself back from the window at last, and saw that the little boy across the aisle was staring at her. She ignored him and addressed her parents over the back of the seat:

"There aren't either any meteors," she complained.

"You're not looking hard enough," said her father, while at the same time her mother said,

"Hush," and drew from her big purse a tablet of lined paper and a brand-new box of crayons, the giant box with rows and rows of colors. She handed them over the seat back and added, "Draw some pictures of what you saw from the windows, and you can show them to Auntie when we get there."

Wide-eyed, the little girl took the offerings and slid back into her seat. For a while she admired the pristine green-and-yellow box, the staggered regiments of pure color. All her crayons at home lived in an old coffee can, in a chaos of nub ends and peeled paper.

At last she selected an Olive Green crayon and opened the tablet. She drew a cigar shape and added flat wings. She colored in the airplane, and then took the Sky Blue and drew on a glass cockpit. With the Black, she added stars on the wings and dots flying out the front to signify bullets.

She looked up. The little boy was staring at her again. She scowled at him.

"Those are nice," he said. "That's a lot of colors."

"This is the really big box," she said.

"Can I draw too?" he asked her, very quietly, so quietly

something strange pulled at her heart. Was he so quiet because he was scared? And the elegant man said:

"Daniel, don't bother the little girl," in a strange resonant voice that had something just the slightest bit wrong about it. He sounded as though he were in the movies.

"You can share," she told the little boy, deciding suddenly. "But you have to come sit here, because I don't want to tear the paper out."

"Okay," he said, and pushed himself out of his seat as she moved over. The elegant couple watched closely, but as the children opened the tablet out between them and each took a crayon, they seemed to relax and turned their smiling attention to the night once more. The boy kept his gloves on while coloring.

"Don't you have crayons at home?" she asked him, drawing black doughnut-tires under the plane. He shook his head, pressing his lips together in a line as he examined the Green crayon he had taken.

"How can you not have crayons? You're rich," she said, and then was sorry she had said it, because he looked as though he were about to cry. But he shrugged and said in a careless voice,

"I have paints and things."

"Oh," she said. She studied him. He had fair hair and blue eyes, a deep twilight blue. "How come you don't look like your mommy and daddy?" she inquired. "I have my daddy's eyes. But you don't have their eyes."

He glanced over his shoulder at the elegant couple and then leaned close to whisper, "I'm adopted."

"Oh. You were in the War?" she said, gesturing at her airplane. "Like a bomb was dropped on your house, and you were an orphan, and the soldiers took you away?"

"No," he said. He put back the Green crayon, took a Brick Red one instead and drew a house: a square, a triangle on top, a chimney with a spiral of smoke coming out of it. He drew well. "I don't think that's what happened."

She drew black jagged lines under the plane, bombed-out wreckage. She drew little balloon heads protruding from the rubble, drew faces with teardrops flying from the eyes.

"This is what happened to the war orphans," she explained. "My daddy told me all about them, and I could see it when he told me. So that didn't happen to you?"

"Nope," he replied, drawing a window in the house. It was a huge window, wide open. It took up the whole wall. He put the Brick Red crayon back in its tier carefully, and selected the Gray crayon. "The War is over now, anyway."

"Everybody thinks so," she replied, glancing uneasily up at the dome. "But my daddy says it isn't really. It could come back any time. There are a lot of bad people. Maybe those people got you from an orphanage."

The boy opened his mouth, closed it, glanced over his shoulder. "No," he whispered. "Something else happened to me. Now I'm their little boy. We came tonight so they could see the meteors from a train. They never did that before. They like trying out new things, you see."

With the Gray crayon, he drew the figure of a stick-man who towered over the house, walking away from the window. He gave it a long coat. He drew its arms up like Frankenstein's monster, and then he drew something in its arms: a white bundle. He put away the Gray crayon, took out the Pink and added a little blob of a face to the bundle.

"See," he said, "That's—"

"What are you drawing, Daniel?" said the elegant lady sharply. The little boy cringed, and the little girl felt like cringing too.

"That's a man carrying wood into his house for the fireplace, Mother," said the little boy, and grabbing the Brown crayon he drew hastily over the bundle in the man's arms, turning it into a log of wood. The little girl looked at it and hoped the lady wouldn't notice that the man in the picture was walking *away* from the house.

"I'm going to be an artist when I grow up," the little boy said. "I go to a studio and they make me take lessons. A famous painter teaches me." He sketched in a row of cylinders in brown, then took the Green crayon and drew green circles above the cylinders. "That's the forest," he added in an undertone. He took the Dark Blue and drew a cold shadow within the forest, and sharp-edged stars above it.

"Is he taking the baby to the forest?" she whispered. He just nodded. When he had drawn the last star he folded the page over, and since she had used up all the room on her page she did not complain, but took the Olive Green crayon again. She laboriously drew in stick-figure soldiers while he watched.

"What are you going to be when you grow up?" he asked.

"A waitress at the dinette," she replied. "If I don't die. And a ballerina."

"I might be a dancer too, if I don't die," he said, reaching for the Gray crayon. He began to draw cylinders like oatmeal boxes, with crenellations: a castle. She took the Black crayon and drew bayonets in the soldiers' hands, remarking:

"Boys aren't ballerinas."

"Some boys have to be," he said morosely, drawing windows in the castle walls. "They have to wear black leotards and the girls wear pink ones. Madame hits her stick on the ground and counts in French. Madame has a hoof on one foot, but nobody ever says anything about it."

"That's strange," she said, frowning as she drew the soldiers bayoneting one another. She glanced over at his picture and asked: "Where's the king and queen?"

He sighed and took the Blue Violet crayon. On the top of one tower he drew an immense crowned figure, leaving the face blank. He drew another crowned figure on the other battlement. "May I have the Black, please?"

"You're *polite*," she said, handing it to him. He drew faces with black eyes on the crowned figures while she took the Red crayon and drew a flag on the ground. She drew a red circle with rays coming off it to the edges of the rectangle, and then drew red dots all over the flag.

"What's that?" he asked.

"That's the blood," she explained. "My daddy has that flag at home. He killed somebody for it. When he told me about it I could see that, too. What did your daddy, I mean, that man, do in the War?"

"He sold guns to the soldiers," said the boy. He drew

bars across the windows in the castle and then, down in the bottommost one, drew a tiny round face looking out, with teardrops coming from its eyes.

The little girl looked over at his picture.

"Can't he get away?" she whispered. He shook his head, and gulped for breath before he went on in a light voice:

"Or I might be a poet, you know. Or play the violin. I have lessons in that too. But I have to be very, very good at something, because next year I'm seven and—"

"Have you drawn another picture, Daniel?" said the elegant man with a faint warning intonation, rising in his seat. Outside the night rolled by, the pale lights floated, and the rhythm of the iron wheels sounded faint and far away.

"Yes, Father," said the boy in a bright voice, holding it up, but with his thumb obscuring the window with the face. "It's two people playing chess. See?"

"That's nice," said the man, and sat down again.

"What happens when you're seven?" the little girl murmured. The boy looked at her with terror in his eyes.

"They might get another baby," he whispered back. She stared at him, thinking that over. She took the tablet and opened it out: new fresh pages.

"That's not so bad," she told him. "We've had two babies. They break things. But they had to stay with Grandma; they're too little to come on the train. If you don't leave your books where they can tear the pages, it's okay."

The boy bowed his head and reached for the Red Orange crayon. He began to scribble in a great swirling mass. The girl whispered on:

"And you're rich, not like us, so I bet you can have your own room away from the new baby. It'll be all right. You'll see."

She took the Sky Blue crayon again and drew in what looked at first like ice cream cones all over her page, before she got the Olive Green out and added soldiers hanging from them. "See? These are the parachute men, coming to the rescue."

"They can't help," said the little boy.

She bit her lip at that, because she knew he was right. She thought it was sad that he had figured it out too.

The boy put back the Red Orange, took both Red and Yellow and scribbled forcefully, a crayon in either fist. He filled the page with flame. Then he drew Midnight Blue darkness above it all and more sharp stars. He took the Black and drew a little stick figure with limbs outstretched just above the fire. Flying? Falling in?

"I'm almost seven," he reiterated, under his breath. "And they only like new things."

"What are you drawing now, Daniel?" asked the lady, and both children started and looked up in horror, for they had not heard her rise.

"It's a nice big pile of autumn leaves, Mother," said the little boy, holding up the tablet with shaking hands. "See? And there's a little boy playing, jumping in the leaves."

"What a creative boy you are," she said throatily, tousling his hair. "But you must remember Mr. Picasso's lessons. Don't be mediocre. Perhaps you could do some abstract drawings now. Entertain us."

"Yes, Mother," said the little boy, and the girl thought he looked as though he were going to throw up. When the lady had returned to her seat she reached over and squeezed his hand, surprising herself, for she did not ordinarily like to touch people.

"Don't be scared," she whispered.

In silence, he turned to a fresh pair of pages. He took out a Green crayon and began to draw interlocking patterns of squares, shading them carefully.

She watched him for a while before she took the Silver and Gold crayons and drew a house, with a little stick figure standing inside. Then she took the Olive Green and drew several objects next to the figure.

"That's my bomb shelter, where I'm safe from the War," she explained. "But you can be in it. And that's your knapsack, see it? I made it with big straps for you. And that's your canteen so you can be safe afterward. They're colored like what soldiers have, so you can hide. And this is the most important thing of all." She pointed. "See that? That's a map. So you can escape."

"I can't take it," he said in a doomed voice.

"That's all right; I'll give it to you," she said, and tore the page out. Folding it up small, she put it into his coat pocket.

Moving with leisurely slowness, he put back the Green crayon. Then, holding his hands close to his chest, he pulled off one of his gloves and took the folded paper out. He thrust it into an inner pocket, glancing over his shoulder as he did so. Nobody had noticed. Hastily he pulled the glove back on.

"Thank you," he said.

"You're welcome," she replied.

At that moment gravity shifted, the steady racketing sound altered and became louder, and there were three distinct bumps. Nobody in the car seemed to notice. Many of the grownups were asleep and snoring, in fact, and did no more than grunt or shift in their seats as the train slowed, as the nearest of the lights swam close and paused outside the window. It was a red blinking light.

"Ah! This is our stop," said the elegant man. "Summerland. Come along, Daniel. I think we've seen enough of the Dome Car, haven't you?"

"Yes, Father," said the boy, buttoning his coat. The elegant lady yawned gracefully.

"Not nearly as much fun as I thought it would be," she drawled. "God, I hate being disappointed. And bored."

"And you bore so easily," said the man, and she gave him a quick venomous glance. The little boy shivered, climbing out of his seat.

"I have to go now," he explained, looking miserable.

"Good luck," said the little girl. The lady glanced at her.

"I'm sure it's past your bedtime, little girl," she said. "And it's rude to stare at people."

She reached down her hand with its long scarlet nails as though to caress, and the little girl dodged. Two fingertips just grazed her eyelid, and with them came a wave of perfume so intense it made her eyes water. She was preoccupied with blinking and sneezing for the next minute, unable to watch as the family walked to the front of the silent car and descended the stair.

But she held her palm tight over her weeping eye and got up on her knees to peek out the window. She looked down onto no platform, no station, but only the verge of the embankment where trees came close to the tracks.

There was a long black car waiting there, under a lamp that swung unsteadily from a low bough. The elegant couple was just getting into the front seat. The little boy was already in the car. She could see his pale face through the windows. He looked up at her and gave a hopeless kind of smile. She was impressed at how brave he was. She thought to herself that he would have made a good soldier. Would he be able to escape?

The train began to move again. People woke up and talked, laughed, commented on the meteor shower. She sat clutching her eye, sniffling, until her mother got up to see if she had fallen asleep.

"Did you get something in your eye?" her mother asked, her voice going sharp with worry.

The little girl thought a moment before answering.

"The rich lady's perfume got in it," she said.

"What rich lady, honey? Don't rub it like that! Bill, hand me a Kleenex. Oh, what have you done to yourself now?"

"The lady with the little boy. They sat there. They just got off the train."

"Don't lie to your mother," said her daddy, scowling. "Those seats have been empty the whole trip."

She considered her parents out of her good eye, and decided to say nothing else about it. By the time she was bundled off the train, wrapped against the dark and cold in her daddy's coat, her eye had swollen shut.

It was red and weeping for days, even after they'd come home again, and her vision in that eye remained blurred. She was taken to an eye doctor, who prescribed an eyepatch for a while. The eyepatch was useful for pretending she was a pirate but did not help, and made her walk into walls besides.

She knew better than to tell anyone about the things she

saw out of the other eye, but she understood now why the boy had wanted so badly to escape. She thought about him sometimes, late at night when she couldn't sleep and the long lights of passing cars sent leaf-shadows crawling along her wall.

She always imagined him running through a black night country, finding his way somehow through the maze of wet cobbled alleys, hiding from the Nazis, hiding from worse things, looking for the dome coach so he could escape; and he became clearer in her head as she thought about him, though that always made the headaches come. She would pull the covers over her head and try to hold on to the picture long enough to make the train arrive for him.

But somehow, before he could slip into the safety of the station, bright morning would blind her awake. Sick and crying, she would scream at her mother and knock her head against the wall to make the pain go away.

In the end the doctor prescribed glasses for her. She started kindergarten glaring at the world through thick pink plastic frames, and no one could persuade her she was not hideous in them.

Want's Master

Patricia Bowne

Patricia Bowne, who published this story under the nom-de-plume A. B. Ming, lives in Milwaukee, Wisconsin, and is a zoologist and an associate professor at Alverno College. She says, "My writing career has centered around academia, my first adult exercise in fiction being an undergraduate term paper in which I tried to convince my World Literature professor that The Pirates of Penzance *was a parody of* Hamlet. *My interest in fiction continued into graduate school, where I wrote much of a never-to-be-assembled science fiction novel on the backs of ATM receipts. It wasn't until I left university and realized how much I missed its excitement, its diversity, and its sheer silliness that I was motivated to create the Royal Academy of Osyth, a setting that has kept me interested enough to write multiple stories and two novels. My academic career centers around fish, and ichthyologically inclined readers will find fish names in my fiction (mainly as the names of demons)." Her first story, "A World They Never Made," appeared in 2002 in* The Leading Edge, *with her real name in the table of contents.*

"Want's Master," her second published story, appeared in Tales of the Unanticipated. *It is a tale of love and magic, in a university setting.*

When William Harrison Gracile came in to work at four-thirty in the afternoon looking as if he had aged twenty years overnight, his suit hanging loose on a wizened frame, his secretary wished him good day and went back to her typing. Gracile was offended. He had never been late to work before; he had never come in with a hair out of place. He deserved better from his secretary, he thought. She should make shocked noises, ask after his health, give unsought advice; she should stop him, as he went into his office. "I'm sorry," she should say, "I don't want to intrude, but . . ."

"Oh, by the way," said his secretary, "a package came for you. I put it on your desk."

A package was exciting, even to someone of an age and station that begged for unsolicited, meaningless packages. This could be the one from someone who mattered, the one filled with treasure rather than with advertising information. Indeed, it was too small a box to contain flyers. The package was the size to hold jewelry, perhaps a tie tack with some charity's logo on it or a refrigerator magnet . . . but it was wrapped in brown paper and addressed by hand in a clear, old-fashioned, feminine script. When Gracile opened it he found a sheet of paper wrapped around the box within.

"A thank-you for last night," was written on it in the same hand. "I'm sure you'll know what to do with it." The note was unsigned. Gracile opened the box and it was a tie tack, indeed; a silver tie tack, with a moonstone set in it. A muted rainbow swirled through the stone, restless and demanding. He looked the paper over for watermarks or clues and examined the box carefully, and then he leaned over the tie tack—absurd, such caution for a tiny piece of silver—and touched it with one finger. And if his secretary

14

had been there, even she must have been perturbed to see her employer become in an instant twenty years younger, thirty pounds heavier. When Gracile turned to look out the window he saw his outline reflected over the Royal Academy's buildings and fall leaves, the outline of a man in his prime. He closed the box and put it in his pocket.

When William Harrison Gracile had joined the Royal Academy of the Arcane Arts and Sciences as Development Officer, he had insisted on an office overlooking the campus. He had told the president that an enchanter couldn't work without an eyrie. "What the eye doesn't see," Gracile had said, "the heart doesn't yearn after." And as yearning after things was his job, that had been argument enough.

When Gracile stood at the window with his back turned to the City and the suburbs behind it, he looked north into the past. Far to his left lay the undeveloped part of the ley-line, the river of magic that tumbled down a chasm at each end of the Osyth plateau and filled the valleys below with mists and wonder. Built squarely on the ley-line, to west and east of Gracile's gaze, the two great castles of the Academy—Magic's fairy-tale palace and Wizardry's squat gray towers—glared at one another with arrow-slit eyes, remembering the magewars of old. Outbuildings clustered around them, clambered up their walls, pushing to get near the line. Between the castles rose the gargantuan modern complex of Sorcery's towers and teaching hospital. The three schools lay in a narrow band along the line, piled high over its power, and beyond them Gracile could see the tops of trees and the tiniest bit of roof of the low Alchemy building.

When he looked across the quad to that reef of buildings, Gracile did not see the modern Academy and its staff. He saw the magicians of old, sallying forth down the ley-line with staff and pack. Wizards in their red gowns clustered around half-finished buildings, girders lifting into place at their command; black-clad sorcerers slipped past, their satchels full of nameless items . . . it was easy for him to believe, then, that the Academy needed a new Wizardry Center. A field station for Celestial Mechanics. Six dozen dryad traps. New gold plating in the pentarium, and the moat around the Magic Building dredged. He could believe these things so much that his very longing for the perfect Academy would cast its spell over alumnae, donors, legislators. That was enchantment.

When it was dark, the window turned into a mirror. Gracile could check himself and do touch-ups, making sure his nose was as straight and his eyes as gray as they should be, that he was still the picture of a successful administrator in his early forties. He could spy on whoever was entering his office and know their names before he turned around. Even in June, it was dark enough by eight for him to see the Vice President for Finance come through the door and turn to close it. The VP Finance was a sturdy man, red-faced and white-haired, with a great beak of a nose. His reflection looked more solid than Gracile's own.

"Are you ready?" Gracile asked.

"No. Well, I am, but you're not. The Dean of Wizardry wants to see you before the meeting."

"No," said Gracile, in dismay. "Are you letting him talk to the trustees?"

"The only way I can keep him out of the trustees' meeting is to let him talk with you," said the VP Finance.

Gracile refocused his eyes and looked across campus at the Magic Building's towers. "The more I see of him, the less I want to get him a building," he said. "You know that."

"Don't get temperamental on me, Bill. You have to have all the arguments before you see the trustees. They have to be able to say you presented them with evidence. I can't have the Dean of Wizardry going around telling people you never heard the arguments in favor of this building, but you convinced the trustees anyway."

"Yeah, I'm only supposed to do that to donors," said Gracile. "Well, show him in. Get it over with."

The Dean of Wizardry was nothing like the red-robed powers of Gracile's fancy. Talking to him was like being eaten by a long slow snake, the kind that moved you down its throat with infinitesimal sideways motions of its jaws, so that your head was swallowed and dissolved while your feet still dangled outside. In less than ten minutes, Gracile had to convince the board of trustees that he could raise millions for the man's building project; yet with every word the Dean of Wizardry inflicted on him, Gracile's enthusiasm for the task dwindled. He looked out the window, therefore, and thought about how much he wanted the Dean of Wizardry to be quiet, to go away, to fall off the tower to a flat and silent death. He thought about how much he wanted to go home and sit under the tree in his back yard, drink a beer and read the evening paper. He fortified himself with these images, and when he finally left for the board meeting there was all about him the glamour of unfulfilled desire, the slightly haunted beauty that made people associate him with high and noble causes.

The trustees met in a warded boardroom. They wore personal wards as well, and these always amused Gracile. No ward was proof against enchantment, which drew its strength from human longings; and the trustees had plenty of these, after five hours of meetings.

"We agree, the old Wizardry Building is out of date," said the President of the Board. "But even if the wizards built it themselves, we can't commit the Academy to this kind of outlay for materials without a significant initial donation. Even a challenge grant would give us something to start with."

"A silent fund-raising campaign," said Gracile. "Then we can start a general drive in the fall."

"That soon? Do you have any donors in mind?"

"Always," smiled Gracile, a man who knew what he was doing. A man to be trusted. "Just say the word, and I can have a meeting with one before the week's out." How straightforward! Trust me, said Gracile's steady gaze, his businesslike gray suit. It was Gracile's job to make magic seem respectable, and he did it well. He looked just enough younger than the trustees to make them feel pleasantly superior, inclined to let the boy try his hand. Trust me, said his posture, his patience, his eager silence. Trust me, so I can go home and read my paper. So I can put my briefcase down in the hall, hang my coat up, take off my shoes and loosen my tie. Pour a beer into a tall cool glass and take that first sip, feel it foam across my tongue . . .

"Ahh," said the president of the Board of Trustees, "I think that's reasonable, don't you?"

"Don't try to charm a charmer," said Mrs. Szince. "I've studied enchantment since you were a gleam in your father's eye, young man. Sugar or lemon?"

"Sugar, of course." Gracile had never been in Mrs. Szince's home before. The house built of dreams, people called it—at least, people who'd never been invited in. While she poured tea he scanned the room, looking for any signs of illusion. The Szinces were the richest family in Osyth; dreams from the Szince factory were in every drugstore, next to the sleep aids, but it was a questionable industry. Selling dreams was rather like selling narcotics. Gracile had expected the house to betray some lapse of taste.

The room was coral-colored, full of sunlight, its colors and fabrics worn soft. Tall windows looked into a garden glowing with roses. A fire burned in the fireplace beside them, its flames almost transparent in the light. It all set off Mrs. Szince perfectly, making her look twenty years younger than she really was, a gentle and dignified lady. Her hair was silver, her skin soft and pale and powdery. What did it feel like? Gracile wondered. Was her glamour strong enough to fool touch as well as sight?

"I wouldn't think of trying any cheap tricks on you," said Gracile. "I know when I'm outclassed." He smiled an honest smile and thought his hair into just the suggestion of a forelock, his head into just the suggestion of a bashful nod, his tweeds into just the suggestion of a loyal outdoorsman, rough and honest. Mrs. Szince gave him a sharp look.

"You may think I don't know what you're up to, but I do," she said. "Not that I'm not enjoying it—while you're at it, flatter my looks and tell me why I should buy bricks and boards for these low-class wizards, who aren't even intelligent enough to recognize how low-class they are. That dean did not impress me at all." She bent forward confidentially. Her eyes sparkled.

The room's colors looked even softer through the steam from Gracile's teacup; it was a calm place, a place where one could lie at ease and listen to the wind in the garden. Looking at the fire, he could imagine the best of fall outside, leaves the color of those flames blowing past the glass on a wind the color of steam. He would like to see that, and to see cold spring rains beating against the windows and turn away from them to this warm corner.

"While you're at it," said Mrs. Szince, "tell me why you've taken up with those people at the Academy. You can't make me believe they appreciate you."

"I'd prefer it if you told me why you're asking," said Gracile, leaning back. "Do I detect an offer?"

"Indeed you do. My late husband's company needs a lobbyist. Besides myself, of course."

"I've never considered it," said Gracile. "I've never thought about selling dreams." This was a time-honored enchanter's technique, the lie direct, and Gracile knew he did it beautifully; the statement and the look, both serious enough to be taken as true but a little more intense than truth warranted. Done properly, it left the hearer no choice but to believe or to join the enchanter in a closed circle of the People Who Knew what was being said. Trust me, it said. Only you and I know what's really going on here.

Mrs. Szince looked back at him through the steam, and her white hair gleamed. She was erect and slender in her old-fashioned green gown, such as enchanters wore when they were creatures of mystery, Gracile thought. The clothing of a time when people asked enchantment to carry them out of themselves, to show them something they would remember and long for all the rest of their lives. If he only reached out, that skin would feel like velvet, or something even finer. Her eyes were the color of dark honey.

"What a lovely liar you are," she said. "Does anyone at the Academy respect you for it? Well, charm me, young man. Charm me out of my money, for a bunch of silly wizards who think charming donors is beneath them. You'll get them the money, and they'll say 'Thank goodness he's willing to do it, because I could never lower myself; but then, enchanters have no standards.'"

The fire made a whispering sound, and a bird sang. I can't hear any engines, Gracile thought—a miracle, here in the city. This was what it sounded like a hundred years ago. Here in this room, a hundred years ago, enchanters would have gathered. They would have spun marvels. They would not have made enchantment respectable. They would not have worn suits, or flattered businessmen.

"Do you think modern enchanters have no standards?"

"I think modern enchanters have no imagination," said Mrs. Szince. "People as a group have no imagination. It's small loss for most of them. But enchanters are meant for greater things. What a pity, that we let people like that dean of wizardry dream for us. What do you dream of, Mr. Gracile?"

"I would never set my dreams up against a professional's," Gracile said smoothly. Mrs. Szince sat back and watched him, and he watched the fire and thought about answering her question.

I dream of momentary things, he might have said to her. Of things seen in a flash and gone when you turn around; the golden bird, flown out of sight before you can quite see it. Sparks, flying upward through twilight air; the green flash you might see cross the sky, once in a lifetime, just at that moment when the sun sets into the sea. Gracile dreamed of falling stars, and the smooth circles on water after a fish has jumped, and all the beautiful things that go away. It isn't restful, to dream such dreams. A night spent chasing them is wasted.

"We all dream of home," said Mrs. Szince. "We dream of a place where what we are is right, where what we can do is the right thing. Don't think it's easy, making dreams. People come to me for what they can't imagine about themselves—people who've been told they're wrong so often, they can't even imagine being right."

"People can be fools, even in dreams," said Gracile.

"Not in my dreams," said Mrs. Szince. "It's a big world, Mr. Gracile. There's room in it for all of us. We can all find our place in it, if we can once see ourselves truly." And this, too, was an enchanter's trick, though it could only be used when the victim was already mazed, confused. This rhetorical assertion, that only a churl could protest against but that only a fool could believe. Manners demanded that the listener submit to the enchanter's will, join the circle of those who agreed to be agreeable . . .

"No," said Gracile, struggling to his feet. "There are people without a place in the world. But you and I are not among them. You have your company, and I have the Academy."

Mrs. Szince smiled. "My," she said. "What a very complicated statement." But Gracile knew better than to explore himself under her guidance. The old lady's spell was thick around him, here in her home. The room's soft colors, the whispering flames, Mrs. Szince herself, were like dreams of color and flame and woman as they ought to be. Gracile stood in front of the fire and it was all he could do to keep himself calm and unafraid and respectable.

"You're too good for me," he said. "I was a fool to think I could cozen you. But they're expecting me back at the Academy for a lunch meeting, to tell them how much money I got from the philanthropic Mrs. Szince."

"Oh, must you go? A pity," said Mrs. Szince. "I'd so like to see what's under that glamour. Come again, Mr. Gracile. I'll go easier on you, next time. Perhaps you'll have something happier to tell them at the Academy."

Gracile found he could walk away, more firmly with every step. The room behind him would become another flash of memory, to be longed for but never possessed, to be thought of when he needed to face the trustees again . . . but lying to himself was not Gracile's talent, and with every step he felt Mrs. Szince behind him, ready to welcome him if he would only turn, go to her, bury his face in that soft skin and hair, and want no more.

"We need to talk about the new building fund," said the VP Finance.

"Oh, don't," sighed Gracile. The VP Finance opened his eyes wide.

"I thought I was going to have to tell you it was that bad," he said.

"I know my job," said Gracile. "It may not seem like it at the moment, but I do."

He liked the VP Finance and never tried to charm him. A man needed someone he could go out for a drink with. Gracile and the VP Finance went downtown, far away from the Academy and the Faculty Club. Gracile liked being surrounded by businessmen, grownups. He liked the thick linen and heavy silver, the way men's faces were reflected in crystal and china.

"Unless you have something up your sleeve, we're not going to be able to start the general campaign on schedule," said the VP Finance. He looked around the room as though one of its inhabitants might be the ace up Gracile's sleeve. "If you're planning a surprise announcement at the Donor's Ball, do my ulcers a favor and tell me now."

"No surprises," said Gracile. The VP Finance sighed.

"I don't want to tell you your business—"

"But you're going to anyway."

They drank in silence for a while.

"What made you so sure you could get the money this fast?"

"Mrs. Szince," said Gracile. "I thought I could get it all from Mrs. Szince. Go ahead, laugh."

"Why should I laugh? She gives away lots of money."

"Because she's an enchantress," said Gracile. "Why do you think I kept away from her last year? She's better than I am. I got cocky."

"So she turned you down?"

"She was charming. Too charming. If I go back into that house, I won't come out."

"Ohh," said the VP Finance, and grinned. "A magewar!"

"You can't have a war with only two people," Gracile pointed out. "And this one's already been fought and lost."

The VP Finance looked across the room with a dreamy expression. "I'm amazed," he said. "Who'd ever have thought Mrs. Szince was dangerous? That sweet old woman." Gracile looked at his friend and sighed. Mrs. Szince hosted large parties. Probably every man in the room had been in her house, was in her thrall.

"She wants me to help her sell dreams," he said.

"Oh, I can imagine! The legislature's within an inch of declaring her stuff an addictive drug," said the VP Finance. "But if she can enchant you, she should be able to handle the legislators." He shook himself. "Well, so she's out. You'll just have to work the other donors."

"I don't know what I want to do," said Gracile.

"You want to raise the money for this building. After that, you can go work for Mrs. Szince, if that's what—"

"I could work for her now, if that's what I wanted! It's not that simple."

The VP Finance spread his hands and creased his round face into a question. "So tell me," he said.

"I want to work for her," said Gracile. "But when I am working for her, what's there for me to want? When you've gotten what you want, you're not much of an enchanter anymore."

The VP Finance frowned. "You get what you want all the time."

"No, I get what you want." Gracile swept his arm out in a gesture that meant the VP Finance, the Academy, Osyth, the world. "What I want—I don't go there. I steer clear of that."

"Doesn't sound like you'd be much use to Mrs. Szince, then."

"Oh, I don't know about that. I'd want to please her . . . she'd want me to keep enchanting people . . . it could become very complicated," said Gracile. He finished his drink and put the glass down hard. They sat for a few moments looking at the table, and then the VP Finance pushed his own drink over to Gracile. Gracile drank it.

"Who's the girl in gold?" Gracile didn't really want to know. But she was striking, a girl in a champagne-colored frock, with a head full of gold curls. She stood by the window in the Hotel Eleuthra's penthouse ballroom, looking out into the evening light. Was she a donor, growing disgusted with the Academy as she stood there alone? Or was she from the Academy, neglecting her duties? Gracile didn't care. It was just restful to look at something all gold against a calm autumn evening, all blue. The sun poured in the windows beside her, blocks of glowing air leaning through the glass.

"Who's the girl in gold?" he asked the Alumnae Officer. She craned her neck.

"Faculty," she said. "Magister Hoth, from Demonology. Not doing very well, is she?"

"Perhaps I should go talk to her," said Gracile. If faculty came to fund-raisers, they were supposed to help raise funds. One demonologist looking superior could undo a lot of Gracile's charm. Although this evening, Gracile had charm to spare. He'd raised a lot of money this evening. People who'd already given to the Academy; people who'd already given all they thought they could afford; people who'd already given all they really could afford, he raised money from them all. The man running the cloakroom had given him a few bills, just to be a part of whatever it was that Gracile wanted so much.

What Gracile wanted so much was dancing with the VP Finance at the other end of the room. Mrs. Szince was silver and gray, mysterious as moonlight. He'd thought she might lose power outside her home, but she was at her most beautiful, and she was flirting with the VP Finance. She whispered to him and laughed a low, charming laugh at his replies. She rested her hand on his sleeve, on his lapel; she leaned her silver head on his bosom when they danced, and the VP Finance gazed over it into the distance with a rapt expression, noble and protective.

Gracile looked at the pair and felt his glamour flame. He was beautiful, passionate, inconsolable. What could the donors do, any of them, except give him what little they had?

"She's a lecher," said the Alumnae Officer.

"What?"

"Magister Hoth. I suppose mere donors are small beer to her, after spending her days with incubi."

"Meow," said Gracile, and they both laughed. Purple shadows were darkening behind the girl in gold, and the last rays of sunlight slanted across the corner of the ball-room to gild her an avid, brazen flame-yellow. She turned and looked straight into the light, her eyes wide and un-afraid.

"I thought I should let you know—no, I shouldn't. Forget it."

A remark like that is effective, even for gaining the attention of a Development Officer in the middle of a fund-raising event. Gracile turned all his glamour toward the speaker. It was Magister Hoth, not as golden as she had been in the sunset. Late at night, under the ballroom's lights, she was the color of pale champagne.

"What?"

"This is conflict of interest," she said. "Damn."

"How can we have a conflict of interest? We're here for the same thing." Gracile looked closer and discovered she was very angry. Some drunken donor had probably groped her or made rude jokes about lechery. He gave her his full attention, the kind that made hardened businessmen reach for their checkbooks. "If anything unsuitable has hap-pened, I want it dealt with as much as you do," he said. "You can trust me."

"It doesn't matter whether I can trust you or not," she said. "I've called the police."

Gracile's habit, whenever moved to shout "WHAT!",

was to stand perfectly still for a moment and then take two steps back while looking mild and thoughtful. "I see," he said gently. "What have you called them to do, and why?"

"One of your guests is carrying an illegal incubus. I saw it in the washroom."

"Oh, my goodness," said Gracile. "First, are you sure it's illegal?"

"I know what I'm talking about," she said sharply. "I'm Vice-President and a founding member of the Alliance for Ethical Lechery. Keeping an incubus is nothing less than sexual slavery. I'm only telling you about this so we can get this woman arrested with the least disruption."

"Which woman would that be?" asked Gracile, but he already knew. He stood taller as Magister Hoth searched the room. I knew I was as good as any enchanter living, he thought. It took an incubus to charm me. They were among the most powerful demons, those spirits of lust. An enchantress holding an incubus captive, drawing strength from its longings—what would be her limits? And I walked away from her, thought Gracile. She had all that going for her, and I was still able to walk away.

"Over there," said Hoth. "The woman in silver."

Gracile looked across the room at the woman in silver. Mrs. Szince, so beautiful, so powerful, so seductive. He stared for a minute, cataloguing her strengths. They made this triumph all the greater.

"Are the police coming up here?" he asked.

"No. I told them I'd get her down to the front lobby."

"That will be my job," said Gracile. "You did the right thing. I can get her down there without causing a fuss, and we'll have this taken care of before the other guests start to leave. You go down and talk with the police. Give me five minutes." Hoth had barely walked away when Gracile was doing what he'd wanted to all evening. He cut in on the VP Finance and took Mrs. Szince away.

She laughed, a low sound of triumph, shaking in his arms.

"You never came back," she said.

"You were entirely too much for me, ma'am," said Gracile. "May we speak in private?"

"Of course."

"Not here," said Gracile. "Not even on this floor."

Mrs. Szince laughed again. "I like you," she said. "You don't waste my time."

"I don't have any time to waste, myself," said Gracile. He stopped dancing; she took his arm and swayed, slender against his side. She was like a tree in moonlight. When she smiled up at him she could have been fifty, or fifteen. And Gracile could have taken her down the East elevator to the lobby and the police or the West one, that led to the back parts of the hotel and out into the alley . . . he walked east and saw all the donors they passed take that catch of breath you take when your everyday life snags for a second on something wondrous. Romance didn't end with youth, he saw them thinking. They would have given Gracile more money, just for showing them this.

"Where are we going?" Mrs. Szince murmured.

"To the lobby," said Gracile. He watched the numbers change, and felt her leaning on his arm. At floor twenty-five, he had to speak.

"The police are in the lobby," he said. "They're doing some kind of sweep of the district for illegal incubi."

Floor twenty—floor eighteen—

"How interesting," said Mrs. Szince. "Do you know, I fear I've forgotten my wrap." Floor ten—

"I thought it was an interesting coincidence," said Gracile. "Given that you'd called me about it. In fact, I invited the academy's lecher to this party so we could deal with it properly. You'll be glad to know that she's an expert on illegal incubi."

Mrs. Szince was very still, as still as moonlight. "Excuse me?"

"It must be very distressing to pay so much for something and then find out it's illegal," he said. "You did the right thing in coming to me. The police will have to take your statement about who sold it to you, but you can hand the incubus over to us. I know you wouldn't want to remain in possession of it any longer than you have to." The floors chimed—floor three, mezzanine—

"My dear boy! You are a challenge, after all," said Mrs. Szince. "You can't imagine how much I appreciate that. It's lonely to think one is the last. The field has so declined from the days of the great dreamlords. Too many of us are mere hirelings, nowadays. We waste our talents on the mundane things." The door chimed.

"Perhaps we can start over," said Gracile. "I fear we began on uneven ground."

"What an intriguing concept," said Mrs. Szince. "As if it were a game . . . I've always viewed enchantment as an art, myself. One does the best one can, with whatever comes to hand." The lobby was before them, two men in the black uniforms of Osyth Police talking to Hoth, and Mrs. Szince was opening her purse and smiling at them all. "Mr. Gracile," she said, "has been so helpful. I believe this is what you've been looking for?"

Gracile had his first look at the incubus, swirling in a moonstone two inches across. It was beautifully set in silver, an art nouveau brooch of sinuous naked bodies and water plants. Both policemen looked at it with respect and apprehension as Patsy Hoth reached out to take it. She closed her hand over the gem, and Gracile realized that she was more beautiful than Mrs. Szince had ever been.

"I'll have to take it back to the Academy," she told the police. "The standard procedure is to let it out into a rabbit colony so it can feed. After that, it'll be able to get away on its own."

"Yeah, I know the drill," said the shorter policeman. He had blond hair in a ponytail, and a loop of gold chain through one ear. "What about this lady?"—indicating Mrs. Szince in a way she could not have often been indicated. He might as well have said, "this old bag."

"Mrs. Szince brought the incubus here tonight to hand it over to us," Gracile said. "You're just here to witness the formalities; we hardly want to be possessing an illegal incubus ourselves, after all."

"What?" said Hoth, looking up. Gracile turned all his attention toward Mrs. Szince.

"I'll have them call your car," he said. "Excuse me for a moment." Hoth was at his elbow as soon as he walked toward the bellman's desk.

"You're letting her go!"

"You heard her story," he said. "You saw her give up the incubus. We don't have a leg to stand on."

"Oh, sure. And she has enough money to buy the academy."

"If you don't like donors, keep out of development. Your car's coming around," said Gracile, turning back to Mrs. Szince. The open door sucked all three of them out into the night, toward the waiting car. He didn't want to see her go, to have this victory ended. Mrs. Szince smiled at him, gracious in defeat.

"Never imagine," she said, "that I don't appreciate what you've done for me tonight." She reached out to pat his sleeve in farewell. She still was a lovely old lady, a wise woman, silk and velvet, even without the incubus—something shone in the air in front of him, a sparkle of powder, and he heard Hoth yell, saw her drop the gem as it burst into a dazzle. When his vision cleared Mrs. Szince was gone. Taillights at the corner might have been her car, might not.

"What is it?" Gracile picked up the brooch. Its stone was moon-colored, the rainbow glints gone. He offered it to Hoth, but she ignored him and clutched her hands to her middle.

"She let it out," she groaned. She doubled over and cried out, a harsh sound he had never heard before.

"Are you all right? How far is the hospital?" Gracile asked.

"No," gasped Hoth. "No hospital. I'm fine." Gracile put a hand on her arm and gasped himself. It was nothing he had ever felt before, when they touched; pure desire, that almost shut off the mind. He felt his glamour flare again. He was beautiful, powerful, invincible. If I'd felt like this a minute ago, Mrs. Szince would have funded the whole building, he thought, and at that moment a cab pulled up.

"Get in," he said, pushing Hoth down into the cab's back seat, and she pulled him after her, clutched his coat, rubbed against him.

"Where to?" asked the cab driver, turning half around. "You just want me to drive?"

"Get out of here," said Gracile. "Around the block. Anywhere." He turned back to Hoth, and she pulled his head down and kissed him. He kissed back, but the cab turned a sharp corner and they slipped apart. The desire diluted as quickly as it had come. "What is this?" he asked, and Hoth laughed up at him. She was a pale blur, half-lying across the seat. They passed a streetlight and it lit up her face, excited and shining.

"Sex," she said. "It's called sex."

"But it isn't real," said Gracile, bracing himself against the back of the driver's seat. Hoth laughed again and reached up, putting a hand on the back of his neck. He felt her fingernails brush the short ends of hair, her fingers opening and the warm part of her hand touching his skin, and then that power was filling him again and the delight of using it was the only thing that mattered.

It must have been twenty years since Gracile had looked at his true face. He knew he had done it when his last classmate retired. He had looked at the beginning of old age, then, and sworn at it, and thought about things he wanted until his glamour was strong enough to cover that face. Ever since, he had put the glamour on in bed before getting up. But this morning he was in bed with a woman, a golden woman lying too close for him to see her clearly, and he could not call up any longing, could not think of anything he wanted to change.

He felt his sunken cheeks, pinched them up into bristly folds. She'll never sleep with you again if she sees your real face, he thought. She'll hate you. But the folds didn't tighten under his fingers, and then he was afraid, cold-sweat afraid, of—he didn't know what.

Gracile snuck out of his own bed, silent as a schoolboy creeping out before breakfast. His bare feet knew every crack in the floor and every shift in the pattern of sunlight and shadow that carpeted the hall under the window. He looked out into the golden elm, his heart bouncing in his chest, just as a swirl of leaves spun down from it. They said you could see the dryad of the tree in such a whirlwind of leaves. They said you could rush into the eddy and clasp it to yourself . . . Gracile watched it fall to the ground, choking down thought and panic, and went on to the bathroom.

This was himself, this stranger looking out of his mirror. Beneath his glamour, he had grown old. Gray hair and stubble. Lines—the deep creases around eyes and mouth that puzzle whoever looks at the old man. What expressions do they echo? Was this a man who smiled or scowled? Impossible to tell what this face had been doing, hidden away by itself. Its eyes were washed out, its skin tough and bristly. And as he squinted at himself in the mirror, wondering whether it was blurred by mist or farsightedness, the bathroom door opened. Living alone, he never locked it. Patsy Hoth walked in.

"I—Oh!" she said, shocked twice—by walking in on someone, and by what she had walked in on. "Excuse me," and she was gone.

"Wait!" said Gracile, and looked into the mirror again, just for a second, seeing what she must have seen in that second. Old. Decrepit. A geezer. He pulled the door open, acting faster than he could think, and what he said almost surprised him. "You must be Will's friend," he said, and Hoth's retreating back stopped. "I'm his father," said Gracile. "Bill, senior."

"He doesn't usually bring women home," said Gracile. "You're the first in—oh, years. I was still living with his mother, then. She was still alive." He had never said such a thing before. The public Gracile was a bachelor, with a hint of mysterious heartbreak in his past.

"I'm sorry," said Hoth.

"Don't be. That was a long time ago. But how about you—are you and Will serious?"

"Us? No," said Hoth. "It was an accident. An incubus." She looked into her coffee. "It was my own fault," she said. "If I'd had my field kit, I could have let it out with no harm done."

"You didn't take your field kit to a donors' ball? What were you thinking of?" chaffed Gracile. It was morning outside, bright and merry, slipping carelessly away into day. He ate bacon and eggs and to hell with his cholesterol.

"Is your family from Osyth?" she asked, and again Gracile had that strange feeling, the disorientation of having to make up a new life.

"No," he said. "I was born in the country outside Selanto. We moved here after the war." He said this delicately, not sure it would hold his weight, but it did. It was the truth, after all. The truth! He could tell her about his real life, he thought suddenly. The things that had meant so much to him—the farm, the family. Growing up. The war, his wife. All the things that had never happened to Will, that a man in his forties could never admit to knowing. He found himself talking, babbling like any lonely old man. Like an old man who had jumped off a cliff, who needed to say all he knew before he hit bottom. She listened, drinking coffee, and he couldn't tell whether she was interested or polite, and he didn't care.

"You remind me of a girl I met in the war," he said. "She had a head of curls like that—and I think she was magic, as well, because she never got hurt. The whole village was bombed away, except their one house." He sighed. "I've had a full life. It's Will I worry about. He hardly ever meets a nice girl."

"I'm a lecher," said Hoth. "I have to be a nice girl. If you give them an inch, the lab gets out of control. So I don't carry on affairs."

"It's too bad . . ."

"We hardly even know each other. It was just an accident."

"Most magicians," said Gracile, "won't hang around with enchanters."

"I don't see why not. These distinctions are stupid . . ."

"But."

"Well—I would always wonder if I was being charmed."

Gracile leaned forward, propped his bristly chin in his shaky hands. "D'you drink? D'you worry you might get intoxicated?"

"It's not quite the same."

"It is. The world—it's always moving," said Gracile. "You can hold on and and try to keep everything under control, or you can let go and fly with it. You kids have never had a war. Things pick you up and take you with 'em. That's what life really is, not this sitting in one spot like a barnacle."

"What happened to the girl in the house?" asked Hoth, changing the subject.

"Eh?"

"You were just telling me. The house that didn't get bombed." Gracile told her the rest of his story about war, cold and muddy, and one house standing untouched among ruins. He told her about how warmth and light feel to a man coming in from war, and about the way song can rise up around a blue plate on the mantelpiece, and how beautiful a woman is when she gets up barefoot at midnight, wrapped in a ragged sheet. When she leans against a door frame and looks at a dead land and says, "Nothing ever really ends. The important things go on." Hoth listened like a child, forgetting her coffee.

"But what happened to her?"

"I told you. The important things don't end."

Hoth sighed, and then sharpened. "Was that enchantment? Are you putting a spell on me?"

"Not that I know of," said Gracile dryly. "And I think I would know."

He had meant to send her off by herself in a cab, but they were friends by then. They rode downtown together and said goodbye at the Hotel Eleuthra. He put his thin old arms around her, and gave her a father's kiss on the hair.

"Will should be home by midnight," he said. "Call him."

"Don't get your hopes up," she said. "He didn't even leave a note."

"I'll give him hell!" said Gracile. "I didn't bring him up to act like that." As soon as she was gone into the parking garage, he went into a florist's. He had roses and a note sent to her office. I must want something to come of this, he thought; but the face that looked back from the cooler doors was still an old man's.

Gracile spent the day in open spaces around Osyth, not afraid of being recognized. He watched birds and beasts, sat in Westpark looking out over the edge of the plateau, walked along the ley-line where it ran toward the Academy, overgrown with hawthorn, alder, fairy rings and mandrake. He walked for miles, until he wanted to sit down. Wanted dinner. Wanted a beer, and to go home and find someone waiting for him, waiting to hear his stories . . . at the outskirts of the Academy he looked into a window and saw an echo of his younger self, and headed in to his office.

"A package came for you," said his secretary.

A package too small for flyers or promotional videotapes, a package the size to hold jewelry; and even before he touched it, he felt Mrs. Szince's breath on it. A package full of wonders. A package of treasure, of longings . . . for what greater treasure is there, Gracile thought as he stood over the open box, what greater treasure is there than the dream of treasure? He touched it with one finger—absurd, such caution for a tiny piece of silver—and felt the trapped spirit's hunger surge through him. And in that instant, the old man was gone. He had spent one day in the open, one day looking at the world without longing and letting it look at him, and now he was gone. He was put away, with all his memories, closed away as firmly as the box in Gracile's pocket.

Gracile stood at the window looking at the Academy lit from one side, shadows pooling between the buildings, with his own silhouette laid over them all, as solid and unchanging as any of them. He looked for a long time, until the campus lights came on below and he could see himself clearly in the glass, watching unchanged as suns and seasons faded away, and then he went back to his desk. He set the box on his blotter and put away the note and wrapping paper in a desk drawer, and then he picked up the phone and dialed.

"Magister Hoth's lab," said a student voice. "She's not in—may I take a message?"

"This is William Harrison Gracile," he said. "Tell her Mrs. Szince has sent me another incubus for her to release. And tell her—tell her my father would like to see her again."

October in the Chair

Neil Gaiman

*Neil Gaiman [www.neilgaiman.com], who lives near Min-
neapolis, Minnesota, is a world-famous comics writer, and
an excellent writer of fantastic fiction whose popularity has
been growing in recent years. His comic book* Sandman *is
the primary basis for his reputation to date. According to his
website,* "Sandman *the comic sold over a million copies a
year. The collections have sold several million copies in paperback and hardback, and remain in print."* The Los Ange-
les Times *described it as "The greatest epic in the history of
comic books" and "the best monthly comic book in the
world." He is a charismatic public figure in the fantasy and
horror fields, and a snappy dresser. However, 2002 was the
year that he blossomed as a fiction writer, after years of
moderate success, with the bestselling novel* American Gods
and the distinguished young adult novel Coraline. *His previous complicated publishing history includes* Angels and Visitations *(1993), a hardcover small press collection of his
short fiction, prose, and journalism, issued to celebrate ten
years as a professional writer. Before that, he was co-author,
with Terry Pratchett, of* Good Omens, *a humorous fantasy
novel, and was best known for his humorous works,*
Ghastly Beyond Belief *(1985) and* Don't Panic *(1987), and,
as editor, a book of poetry,* Now We Are Sick *(1991).*

"October in the Chair" appeared in Conjunctions: 39
*(see also the stories by Hopkinson and Miéville later in this
book). It is an homage to Ray Bradbury's fantasy stories
and quite engaging in its own right.*

—For Ray Bradbury

October was in the chair, so it was chilly that evening, and the leaves were red and orange and tumbled from the trees that circled the grove. The twelve of them sat around a campfire roasting huge sausages on sticks, which spat and crackled as the fat dripped onto the burning applewood, and drinking fresh apple cider, tangy and tart in their mouths.

April took a dainty bite from her sausage, which burst open as she bit into it, spilling hot juice down her chin. "Beshrew and suck-ordure on it," she said.

Squat March, sitting next to her, laughed, low and dirty, and then pulled out a huge, filthy handkerchief. "Here you go," he said.

April wiped her chin. "Thanks," she said. "The cursed bag-of-innards burned me. I'll have a blister there tomorrow."

September yawned. "You are *such* a hypochondriac," he said, across the fire. "And such *lan*guage." He had a pencil-thin mustache, and was balding in the front, which made his forehead seem high, and wise.

"Lay off her," said May. Her dark hair was cropped short against her skull and she wore sensible boots. She smoked a small brown cigarillo, which smelled heavily of cloves. "She's sensitive."

"Oh puhlease," said September. "Spare me."

October, conscious of his position in the chair, sipped his apple cider, cleared his throat, and said, "Okay. Who wants to begin?" The chair he sat in was carved from one large block of oak wood, inlaid with ash, with cedar, and with cherrywood. The other eleven sat on tree stumps equally spaced about the small bonfire. The tree stumps had been worn smooth and comfortable by years of use.

37

"What about the minutes?" asked January. "We always do minutes when I'm in the chair."

"But you aren't in the chair now, are you, dear?" said September, an elegant creature of mock solicitude.

"What about the minutes?" repeated January. "You can't ignore them."

"Let the little buggers take care of themselves," said April, one hand running through her long blond hair. "And I think September should go first."

September preened and nodded. "Delighted," he said.

"Hey," said February. "Hey-hey-hey-hey-hey-hey-hey. I didn't hear the chairman ratify that. Nobody starts till October says who starts, and then nobody else talks. Can we have maybe the tiniest semblance of order here?" He peered at them, small, pale, dressed entirely in blues and grays.

"It's fine," said October. His beard was all colors, a grove of trees in autumn, deep brown and fire orange and wine red, an untrimmed tangle across the lower half of his face. His cheeks were apple red. He looked like a friend, like someone you had known all your life. "September can go first. Let's just get it rolling."

September placed the end of his sausage into his mouth, chewed daintily, and drained his cider mug. Then he stood up and bowed to the company and began to speak.

"Laurent DeLisle was the finest chef in all of Seattle; at least, Laurent DeLisle thought so, and the Michelin stars on his door confirmed him in his opinion. He was a remarkable chef, it is true—his minced lamb brioche had won several awards, his smoked quail and white truffle ravioli had been described in the *Gastronome* as 'the tenth wonder of the world.' But it was his wine cellar . . . ah, his wine cellar . . . that was his source of pride and his passion.

"I understand that. The last of the white grapes are harvested in me, and the bulk of the reds: I appreciate fine wines, the aroma, the taste, the aftertaste as well.

"Laurent DeLisle bought his wines at auctions, from private wine lovers, from reputable dealers: he would insist on a pedigree for each wine, for wine frauds are, alas, too common, when the bottle is selling for perhaps five, ten, a hundred thousand dollars, or pounds, or euros.

"The treasure—the jewel—the rarest of the rare and the *ne plus ultra* of his temperature-controlled wine cellar was a bottle of 1902 Château Lafitte. It was on the wine list at $120,000, although it was, in true terms, priceless, for it was the last bottle of its kind."

"Excuse me," said August politely. He was the fattest of them all, his thin hair combed in golden wisps across his pink pate.

September glared down at his neighbor. "Yes?"

"Is this the one where some rich dude buys the wine to go with the dinner, and the chef decides that the dinner the rich dude ordered isn't good enough for the wine, so he sends out a different dinner, and the guy takes one mouthful, and he's got, like, some rare allergy and he just dies like that, and the wine never gets drunk after all?"

September said nothing. He looked a great deal.

"Because if it is, you told it before. Years ago. Dumb story then. Dumb story now." August smiled. His pink cheeks shone in the firelight.

September said, "Obviously pathos and culture are not to everyone's taste. Some people prefer their barbecues and beer, and some of us like—"

February said, "Well, I hate to say this, but he kind of does have a point. It has to be a new story."

September raised an eyebrow and pursed his lips. "I'm done," he said abruptly. He sat down on his stump.

They looked at each other across the fire, the months of the year.

June, hesitant and clean, raised her hand and said, "I have one about a guard on the X-ray machines at La Guardia Airport, who could read all about people from the outlines of their luggage on the screen, and one day she saw a luggage X ray so beautiful that she fell in love with the person, and she had to figure out which person in the line it was, and she couldn't, and she pined for months and months. And when the person came through again she knew it this time, and it was the man, and he was a wizened old Indian man and she was pretty and black and, like twenty-five, and she knew it would never work out and she let him go, because she could also see from the shapes of his bags on the screen that he was going to die soon."

October said, "Fair enough, young June. Tell that one."

June stared at him, like a spooked animal. "I just did," she said.

October nodded. "So you did," he said, before any of the others could say anything. And then he said, "Shall we proceed to my story, then?"

February sniffed. "Out of order there, big fella. The man in the chair only tells his story when the rest of us are through. Can't go straight to the main event."

May was placing a dozen chestnuts on the grate above the fire, deploying them into patterns with her tongs. "Let him tell his story if he wants to," she said. "God knows it can't be worse than the one about the wine. And I have things to be getting back to. Flowers don't bloom by themselves. All in favor?"

"You're taking this to a formal vote?" February said. "I cannot believe this. I cannot believe this is happening." He mopped his brow with a handful of tissues, which he pulled from his sleeve.

Seven hands were raised. Four people kept their hands down—February, September, January, and July. ("I don't have anything personal on this," said July apologetically. "It's purely procedural. We shouldn't be setting precedents.")

"It's settled then," said October. "Is there anything anyone would like to say before I begin?"

"Um. Yes. Sometimes," said June, "sometimes I think somebody's watching us from the woods and then I look and there isn't anybody there. But I still think it."

April said, "That's because you're crazy."

"Mm," said September, to everybody. "She's sensitive but she's still the cruelest."

"Enough," said October. He stretched in his chair. He cracked a cobnut with his teeth, pulled out the kernel, and threw the fragments of shell into the fire, where they hissed and spat and popped, and he began.

There was a boy, October said, who was miserable at home, although they did not beat him. He did not fit well, not his family, not his town, nor even his life. He had two older brothers, who were twins, older than he was, and who hurt him or ignored him, and were popular. They played football: some games one twin would score more and be the hero, and some games the other would. Their little brother did not play football. They had a name for their brother. They called him the Runt.

They had called him the Runt since he was a baby, and at first their mother and father had chided them for it.

The twins said, "But he *is* the runt of the litter. Look at *him*. Look at *us*." The boys were six when they said this. Their parents thought it was cute. A name like "the Runt" can be infectious, so pretty soon the only person who called him Donald was his grandmother, when she telephoned him on his birthday, and people who did not know him.

Now, perhaps because names have power, he was a runt: skinny and small and nervous. He had been born with a runny nose, and it had not stopped running in a decade. At mealtimes, if the twins liked the food they would steal his; if they did not, they would contrive to place their food on his plate and he would find himself in trouble for leaving good food uneaten.

Their father never missed a football game, and would buy an ice cream afterward for the twin who had scored the most, and a consolation ice cream for the other twin, who hadn't. Their mother described herself as a newspaper-woman, although she mostly sold advertising space and subscriptions: she had gone back to work full-time once the twins were capable of taking care of themselves.

The other kids in the boy's class admired the twins. They had called him Donald for several weeks in first grade, until the word trickled down that his brothers called him the Runt. His teachers rarely called him anything at all, although among themselves they could sometimes be heard to say that it was a pity the youngest Covay boy didn't have the pluck or the imagination or the life of his brothers.

The Runt could not have told you when he first decided to run away, nor when his daydreams crossed the border and became plans. By the time he admitted to himself that he was leaving he had a large Tupperware container hidden beneath a plastic sheet behind the garage, containing three Mars bars, two Milky Ways, a bag of nuts, a small bag of licorice, a flashlight, several comics, an unopened packet of beef jerky, and thirty-seven dollars, most of it in quarters. He did not like the taste of beef jerky, but he had read that explorers had survived for weeks on nothing else, and it was when he put the packet of beef jerky into the Tupperware box and pressed the lid down with a pop that he knew he was going to have to run away.

He had read books, newspapers, and magazines. He knew that if you ran away you sometimes met bad people who did bad things to you; but he had also read fairy tales, so he knew that there were kind people out there, side by side with the monsters.

The Runt was a thin ten-year-old, with a runny nose, and a blank expression. If you were to try to pick him out of a group of boys, you'd be wrong. He'd be the other one. Over at the side. The one your eye slipped over.

All through September he put off leaving. It took a really bad Friday, during the course of which both of his brothers sat on him (and the one who sat on his face broke wind, and laughed uproariously) to decide that whatever monsters were waiting out in the world would be bearable, perhaps even preferable.

Saturday, his brothers were meant to be looking after him, but soon they went into town to see a girl they liked. The Runt went around the back of the garage and took the Tupperware container out from beneath the plastic sheeting. He took it up to his bedroom. He emptied his schoolbag onto his bed, filled it with his candies and comics and quarters and the beef jerky. He filled an empty soda bottle with water.

The Runt walked into the town and got on the bus. He rode west, ten-dollars-in-quarters worth of west, to a place he didn't know, which he thought was a good start, then he got off the bus and walked. There was no sidewalk now, so when cars came past he would edge over into the ditch, to safety.

The sun was high. He was hungry, so he rummaged in his bag and pulled out a Mars bar. After he ate it he found he was thirsty, and he drank almost half of the water from his soda bottle before he realized he was going to have to ration it. He had thought that once he got out of the town he would see springs of fresh water everywhere, but there were none to be found. There was a river, though, that ran beneath a wide bridge.

The Runt stopped halfway across the bridge to stare down at the brown water. He remembered something he had been told in school: that, in the end, all rivers flowed into the sea. He had never been to the seashore. He clambered down the bank and followed the river. There was a muddy path along the side of the riverbank, and an occasional beer can or plastic snack packet to show that people had been that way before, but he saw no one as he walked.

He finished his water.

He wondered if they were looking for him yet. He imagined police cars and helicopters and dogs, all trying to find him. He would evade them. He would make it to the sea.

The river ran over some rocks, and it splashed. He saw a blue heron, its wings wide, glide past him, and he saw solitary end-of-season dragonflies, and sometimes small clusters of midges, enjoying the Indian summer. The blue sky became dusk gray, and a bat swung down to snatch insects from the air. The Runt wondered where he would sleep that night.

Soon the path divided, and he took the branch that led away from the river, hoping it would lead to a house, or to a farm with an empty barn. He walked for some time, as the dusk deepened, until, at the end of the path, he found a farmhouse, half tumbled down and unpleasant-looking. The Runt walked around it, becoming increasingly certain as he walked that nothing could make him go inside, and then he climbed over a broken fence to an abandoned pasture, and settled down to sleep in the long grass with his schoolbag for his pillow.

He lay on his back, fully dressed, staring up at the sky. He was not in the slightest bit sleepy.

"They'll be missing me by now," he told himself. "They'll be worried."

He imagined himself coming home in a few years' time. The delight on his family's faces as he walked up the path to home. Their welcome. Their love. . . .

He woke some hours later, with the bright moonlight in his face. He could see the whole world—as bright as day, like in the nursery rhyme, but pale and without colors. Above him, the moon was full, or almost, and he imagined a face looking down at him, not unkindly, in the shadows and shapes of the moon's surface.

A voice said, "Where do you come from?"

He sat up, not scared, not yet, and looked around him. Trees. Long grass. "Where are you? I don't see you."

Something he had taken for a shadow moved, beside a tree on the edge of the pasture, and he saw a boy of his own age.

"I'm running away from home," said the Runt.

"Whoa," said the boy. "That must have taken a whole lot of guts."

The Runt grinned with pride. He didn't know what to say.

"You want to walk a bit?" said the boy.

"Sure," said the Runt. He moved his schoolbag, so it was next to the fence post, so he could always find it again.

They walked down the slope, giving a wide berth to the old farmhouse.

"Does anyone live there?" asked the Runt.

"Not really," said the other boy. He had fair, fine hair that was almost white in the moonlight. "Some people tried a long time back, but they didn't like it, and they left. Then other folk moved in. But nobody lives there now. What's your name?"

"Donald," said the Runt. And then, "But they call me the Runt. What do they call you?"

The boy hesitated. "Dearly," he said.

"That's a cool name."

Dearly said, "I used to have another name, but I can't read it anymore."

They squeezed through a huge iron gateway, rusted part open, part closed into position, and they were in the little meadow at the bottom of the slope.

"This place is cool," said the Runt.

There were dozens of stones of all sizes in the small meadow. Tall stones, bigger than either of the boys, and small ones, just the right size for sitting on. There were some broken stones. The Runt knew what sort of a place this was, but it did not scare him. It was a loved place.

"Who's buried here?" he asked.

"Mostly okay people," said Dearly. "There used to be a town over there. Past those trees. Then the railroad came and they built a stop in the next town over, and our town sort of dried up and fell in and blew away. There's bushes and trees now, where the town was. You can hide in the trees and go into the old houses and jump out."

The Runt said, "Are they like that farmhouse up there? The houses?" He didn't want to go in them, if they were.

"No," said Dearly. "Nobody goes in them, except for me. And some animals, sometimes. I'm the only kid around here."

"I figured," said the Runt.

"Maybe we can go down and play in them," said Dearly.

"That would be pretty cool," said the Runt.

It was a perfect early October night: almost as warm as summer, and the harvest moon dominated the sky. You could see everything.

"Which one of these is yours?" asked the Runt.

Dearly straightened up proudly, and took the Runt by the hand. He pulled him over to an overgrown corner of the field. The two boys pushed aside the long grass. The stone was set flat into the ground, and it had dates carved into it from a hundred years before. Much of it was worn away, but beneath the dates it was possible to make out the words DEARLY DEPARTED WILL NEVER BE FORG.

"Forgotten, I'd wager," said Dearly.

"Yeah, that's what I'd say too," said the Runt.

They went out of the gate, down a gully, and into what remained of the old town. Trees grew through houses, and buildings had fallen in on themselves, but it wasn't scary. They played hide-and-seek. They explored. Dearly showed the Runt some pretty cool places, including a one-room cottage that he said was the oldest building in that whole part of the country. It was in pretty good shape, too, considering how old it was.

"I can see pretty good by moonlight," said the Runt. "Even inside. I didn't know that it was so easy."

"Yeah," said Dearly. "And after a while you get good at seeing even when there ain't any moonlight."

The Runt was envious.

"I got to go to the bathroom," said the Runt. "Is there somewhere around here?"

Dearly thought for a moment. "I don't know," he admitted. "I don't do that stuff anymore. There are a few outhouses still standing, but they may not be safe. Best just to do it in the woods."

"Like a bear," said the Runt.

He went out the back, into the woods which pushed up against the wall of the cottage, and went behind a tree. He'd never done that before, in the open air. He felt like a wild animal. When he was done he wiped himself with fallen leaves. Then he went back out the front. Dearly was sitting in a pool of moonlight, waiting for him.

"How did you die?" asked the Runt.

"I got sick," said Dearly. "My maw cried and carried on something fierce. Then I died."

"If I stayed here with you," said the Runt, "would I have to be dead too?"

"Maybe," said Dearly. "Well, yeah. I guess."

"What's it like? Being dead."

"I don't mind it," admitted Dearly. "Worst thing is not having anyone to play with."

"But there must be lots of people up in that meadow," said the Runt. "Don't they ever play with you?"

"Nope," said Dearly. "Mostly, they sleep. And even when they walk, they can't be bothered to just go and see stuff and do things. They can't be bothered with me. You see that tree?"

It was a beech tree, its smooth gray bark cracked with age. It sat in what must once have been the town square, ninety years before.

"Yeah," said the Runt.

"You want to climb it?"

"It looks kind of high."

"It is. Real high. But it's easy to climb. I'll show you."

It was easy to climb. There were handholds in the bark, and the boys went up the big beech tree like a couple of monkeys, like pirates, like warriors. From the top of the tree one could see the whole world. The sky was starting to lighten, just a hair, in the east.

Everything waited. The night was ending. The world was holding its breath, preparing to begin again.

"This was the best day I ever had," said the Runt.

"Me too," said Dearly. "What are you going to do now?"

"I don't know," said the Runt.

He imagined himself going on, walking across the world, all the way to the sea. He imagined himself growing up and growing older, bringing himself up by his bootstraps. Somewhere in there he would become fabulously wealthy. And then he would go back to the house with the twins in it, and he would drive up to their door in his wonderful car, or perhaps he would turn up at a football game (in his imagination the twins had neither aged nor grown) and look down at them, in a kindly way. He would buy them all—the twins, his parents—a meal at the finest restaurant in the city, and they would tell him how badly they had misunderstood him and mistreated him. They would apologize and weep, and through it all he would say nothing. He would let their apologies wash over him. And then he would give each of them a gift, and afterward he would leave their lives once more, this time for good.

It was a fine dream.

In reality, he knew, he would keep walking, and be found tomorrow, or the day after that, and go home and be yelled at and everything would be the same as it ever was, and day after day, hour after hour, until the end of time he'd still be the Runt, only they'd be mad at him for leaving.

"I have to go to bed soon," said Dearly. He started to climb down the big beech tree.

Climbing down the tree was harder, the Runt found. You couldn't see where you were putting your feet, and had to feel around for somewhere to put them. Several times he slipped and slid, but Dearly went down ahead of him, and would say things like "Just a little to the right now," and they both made it down just fine.

The sky continued to lighten, and the moon was fading, and it was harder to see. They clambered back through the gully. Sometimes the Runt wasn't sure that Dearly was there at all, but when he got to the top, he saw the boy waiting for him.

They didn't say much as they walked up to the meadow filled with stones. The Runt put his arm over Dearly's shoulder, and they walked in step up the hill.

"Well," said Dearly. "Thanks for stopping by."

"I had a good time," said the Runt.

"Yeah," said Dearly. "Me too."

Down in the woods somewhere a bird began to sing.

"If I wanted to stay—?" said the Runt, all in a burst. Then he stopped. *I might never get another chance to change it*, thought the Runt. He'd never get to the sea. They'd never let him.

Dearly didn't say anything, not for a long time. The world was gray. More birds joined the first.

"I can't do it," said Dearly eventually. "But *they* might."

"Who?"

"The ones in there." The fair boy pointed up the slope to the tumbledown farmhouse with the jagged broken windows, silhouetted against the dawn. The gray light had not changed it.

The Runt shivered. "There's people in there?" he said. "I thought you said it was empty."

"It ain't empty," said Dearly. "I said nobody lives there. Different things." He looked up at the sky. "I got to go now," he added. He squeezed the Runt's hand. And then he just wasn't there any longer.

The Runt stood in the little graveyard all on his own, listening to the birdsong on the morning air. Then he made his way up the hill. It was harder by himself.

He picked up his schoolbag from the place he had left it. He ate his last Milky Way and stared at the tumbledown building. The empty windows of the farmhouse were like eyes, watching him.

It was darker inside there. Darker than anything.

He pushed his way through the weed-choked yard. The door to the farmhouse was mostly crumbled away. He stopped at the doorway, hesitating, wondering if this was wise. He could smell damp, and rot, and something else underneath. He thought he heard something move, deep in the house, in the cellar, maybe, or the attic. A shuffle, maybe. Or a hop. It was hard to tell.

Eventually, he went inside.

Nobody said anything. October filled his wooden mug with apple cider when he was done, and drained it, and filled it again.

"It was a story," said December. "I'll say that for it." He rubbed his pale blue eyes with a fist. The fire was almost out.

"What happened next?" asked June nervously. "After he went into the house?"

May, sitting next to her, put her hand on June's arm. "Better not to think about it," she said.

"Anyone else want a turn?" asked August. There was no reply. "Then I think we're done."

"That needs to be an official motion," pointed out February.

"All in favor?" said October. There was a chorus of "Ayes." "All against?" Silence. "Then I declare this meeting adjourned."

They got up from the fireside, stretching and yawning, and walked away into the wood, in ones and twos and threes, until only October and his neighbor remained.

"Your turn in the chair next time," said October.

"I know," said November. He was pale, and thin lipped. He helped October out of the wooden chair. "I like your stories. Mine are always too dark."

"I don't think so," said October. "It's just that your nights are longer. And you aren't as warm."

"Put it like that," said November, "and I feel better. I suppose we can't help who we are."

"That's the spirit," said his brother. And they touched hands as they walked away from the fire's orange embers, taking their stories with them back into the dark.

Greaves, This Is Serious

William Mingin

William Mingin lives in central New Jersey, where he runs a small book-exporting company. He has published poetry and fiction in the small press, and over 70 essays, articles, and book reviews (reviews for the St. Petersburg [Fl.] Times, The Annual Review of Science Fiction and Fantasy, *and* Publishers Weekly*). He attended Clarion West and writing courses taught by Carol Emshwiller and Shawna McCarthy. "I've got English degrees from Yale and Princeton, if you want to go back that far," he says. But he has published only a few short stories to date. From what we have read, we hope for more, soon. His works are literate and embedded in a deep knowledge of fantastic literature, as well as literature in general.*

"Greaves, This Is Serious" appeared in Tales of the Unanticipated. *It is number seven in a series of short short stories called 1001 Deaths, others of which have been published there. It is a short literary parody of the Jeeves stories of P. G. Wodehouse, and a fantasy with the effect of a neat shot of whiskey.*

Greaves oozed into the bedchamber bearing what I took to be that tonic for the nerves of which, with his uncanny brain-power, he knew the young master had a desperate need. The man is little shy of genius. He *lives* on fish.

"Greaves," the selfsame young master—I—croaked out, "is it day again already?"

"Yes, sir. In fact, we are well into the post meridian, sir."

"And is that which you hold the precious restorative cup of your concoction?"

"Yes, sir. I was sure that you would want it, sir."

"I do. Bring it 'round."

He brought the odd mixture—egg, tomato juice, Worces-tershire sauce, and Heaven knows what else—ambrosia, eye of newt, and butterscotch pudd, for all I, young Ferdi-nand Brewster, cared—and I downed it. There followed a sudden, threatening stillness; the next moment the Fellow Upstairs was back at the old stand, and all was right with the world—or at least, with long-suffering self.

"Greaves, in the depths of my painful hibernation, did I hear someone ringing for entry?"

"Yes, sir. Mrs. Dodgson, sir."

"Aunt Adele? And you kept her from the Inner Sanctum? Stout work, Greaves."

"Indeed, sir, I can take only partial credit for the happy result; most belongs to the intense disgust which Mrs. Dodgson presently holds for you. She would not see you at present, she said, if you crawled to her domicile on your knees, sir."

"Right ho! How did I work this magic, Greaves?"

"Perhaps her errand would enlighten you, sir. Mrs. Dodgson requested me to remind you when, as she put it, 'he finally rouses himself from his alcoholic stupor,' that you owe her £20 for standing your bail."

"Bail? As bad as all that, eh?"

"Yes, sir. Evidently, sir, you—as you put it last night—'chucked biggish stones' at the window of a government ministry while singing songs that were not, perhaps, suitable for all listeners."

"I say! Dashed sticky business, that, eh, what? I'm jolly well out of it."

"I am afraid, sir, that you will have to appear before a tribunal at some juncture. Although I am sure that someone in your position, and with a clean record, will merely have a fine to pay, sir."

"You don't mean to tell me I gave them *my* name, do you?"

"Evidently you could not remember any name, sir, including your own, so that the constabulary was forced to—ahem—go through your pockets to ascertain it."

"Distinctly rummy! Speaking of which—what was in those drinks you provided yestereve?"

"In the drinks of most of the company, sir, a light mixture of champagne and various liqueurs. In yours, a mixture of champagne and, as you so aptly say, rum, containing alcohol in a proportion of slightly higher than 75%."

"150 proof?"

"151, sir, to be precise."

"That was a bit much on your part, Greaves, I must say. Were you trying to render the young master *non compos*? I'll have a devil of a time now trying to carry on the wretched political career Aunt Adele was trying to construct for me."

"Yes, sir. I believe you now have no future in politics. Mrs. Dodgson seemed also of this persuasion, and instructed me to convey her sentiment that you are, and I quote, 'a worthless idler, a waste of a human form, a trifler, a blood-sucker, a drone.'"

"All rather ripe," I said, reflecting gloomily. And then came the light. "Wait—you say my political career is finished, and my Aunt says she will shun me, for the foreseeable f., like the proverbial p.?"

"Yes, sir."

"And all I have to pay for this excellent result is a fine and a rapidly vanishing badness of the head?"

"Yes, sir."

"Greaves, you *are* a genius! An unmitigated wonder! I must say, I can't see why you shouldn't go down in legend and song!"

"Thank you, sir. I am most gratified to hear you say so."

"Send the £20 round to my Aunt, and when you do—take another twenty for yourself. You've earned it."

"Thank you, sir." Greaves went to the dresser to find the required sums among the bills scattered thereon and

I set my teacup down. "Good of you to rally round, Greaves," I said, with the frank appreciation that, when all is said and done, *noblesse oblige*. "Awfully, sportingly Feudal. Imagine Aunt Adele setting me up to run that charity wheeze—I mean, unwed mothers! I blush to think! Hundreds of droopy, weepy females, giving yours truly the old fish eye, I'm sure. The look of silent reproach, don't you know, and so undeserved! To say nothing of the squalling offspring!"

"I'm sure Mrs. Dodgson had in mind only an administrative position, sir, and not actual—ahem—'hands-on-care.' "

"What then? Just another job, wouldn't you say?"

"Precisely why I thought it unsuitable, sir."

"Well, good thing the place was all wood. I suppose the insurance will let them build again, what?"

"Unfortunately, sir, the edifice in question, being located in rather—ahem—questionable environs, was uninsurable."

"Ah, well. I suppose they'll find someplace else to run that blighted hole. Hmm, Greaves. . . ."

"Yes, sir?"

"What *is* holding up the eggs and b.?"

"I am going just now to collect them, sir."

"Good job," I said, finishing the day's first Bohea. I had hardly set down the cup before Greaves

* * *

bowed his thanks. I went on: "Your protuberant brain has sized up the situation, engineered the solution, and carried it through with the executive skill of a generalissimo."

He bowed again. "Thank you, sir. One does one's best to give satisfaction, sir."

"Satisfaction isn't the half of it; life-saving, I call it. If it hadn't been for the master plan, deftly executed, I might before the end of the coming June have been forced to tread the strewn orange blossoms, or the rose petals, or whatever it is one strews at weddings, with Catalina Glimpet"—one of the soupiest young females, I must say, of whom I ever had the misfortune to make the acquaintance. She had the perpetual look of a mollusk bearing a burden of unspoken sorrow. "Do you realize, Greaves, that she wanted a brood of six? Or *eight*? And that I was to work in Daddy's business—leather tanning, or import-export, or banana ripening rooms, or whatever wheeze they prosecute at the family stand—taking on more and more responsibility, until yours truly would have been running the whole ignoble enterprise?"

We Brewsters are of unimpeachable courage and resource, but the linkage of "responsibility" with "more and more" gave this scion of the old tree absolute chattering chills.

"Yes, sir. I thought it most unsuitable, sir."

"How did you come up with the idea? So simple, so effective! Just took the handbrake off?"

"Yes, sir. I knew the young lady in question was given to a swim at that particular hour of the day. The happy position of the motorcar, the gentle but unimpeded slope, the vehicle's inertia, sure to carry it across the dock—"

"Thank Heaven for your knowledge of practical physics! Well, given the happy outcome, I suggest an invigorating and celebratory 'whiskey and,' Greaves, rather lightish on the 'and.'"

"Yes, sir. Right away, sir."

I took the glass from Greaves and raised it to the lips with a "God bless Catalina Glimpet, the poor blister, wherever she may be!," downed it, then turned and

"I say, Greaves," I began as he brought me the day's first re-vivifying cup of Oolong, to be followed in not too tardy a fash, one hoped, by the matutinal eggs and b., "I say—"

Which I had said once already. I paused to marshal the thoughts. We Brewsters are nothing if not the Field Marshals, as it were, of our thoughts, disciplined troops of logic and ratty-o—ratial—erm—what was the word that Poe chappie used?

"I say, Greaves," I said for the third and, one hopes, final time in this narrative, plunging ahead now, into the breach, my marshaled thoughts doing double-time to keep up, "do we ever do anything—erm—else?"

"Else, sir?"

"Else—different—other?"

"In what way, sir?"

I tsked at the fellow. I mean, I hauled off and *tsked* at him—and I meant it to *sting*. Could a fellow with such a bulge of brainy matter really fail to understand even *one* of these three simple terms?

But no matter. I marshaled the aforementioned thoughts where he could review the troops. "Different, Greaves, don't you see? Other than what we have been doing. Oh, you know what I mean—something useful—perhaps getting a job—marriage—raising children—as an adult person does. If not a paying job, then perhaps running some worthy philanthropic institution. All the activities we've been trying to avoid."

Greaves, in the true Feudal spirit, does not lightly gainsay the Master, so he shook his head with some regret and said, "No, sir. In that sense, we do not do anything 'different,' as you say. Things will always remain just as they are."

I suppose for the moment I didn't pay full attention to the man, as I was pursuing the vaguest of thoughts, like the memory of a dream brought to mind by seeing someone sporting the same color spats they'd worn in the dream *op. cit.* "Dash it all, Greaves, but sometimes I could swear by my dear Aunt Penelope that I did things like that once—or I was supposed to, anyhow, wanted to, perhaps, sloughed them off a bit and all that—wasted the precious shining hours. Well, now, here's a ripe bit of flapdoodle—mustn't laugh at the young master—"

"Not at all, sir."

"But I could swear I once was someone else, before I came here and did these damned silly things we do, over and over and over."

Greaves waited in respectful s. The Brewster brain was humming on—no, damn the Brewster brain. I had a thought and spat it out before it could vanish.

"Greaves," I said, going chill all over, despite the warmth of the breakfast beverage, which was served, of course, at the perfect temp., "have I died? And is being this"—I motioned, judiciously, with the cup toward Self—"my punishment? To be this trifling silly ass forever? To never—never *touch* anyone again?"

The fellow nodded slightly, if gravely, and said, "Yes, sir. Very good, sir. The punishment is not fully consummated until one comes to realize it, sir." Then, finally, something *was* different. Despite his word, Greaves laughed—and kept on laughing.

"Enough to give one the absolute pip," I muttered—not because I wanted to, but because I couldn't utter anything else. Then, at the full realization of my predicament, I emitted a hollow g.

Shift

Nalo Hopkinson

Nalo Hopkinson [www.sff.net/people/nalo] was born in the Caribbean and lives in Toronto. She studied with Judith Merril in Canada, and attended the Clarion East writing workshop in 1995. She is on the steering committee of the Carl Brandon Society, which promotes the involvement of people of color in speculative fiction. After publishing a few short stories, her first novel, Brown Girl in the Ring (1998), established her reputation as an important new fantasy writer. Her second novel, Midnight Robber, was published in 2000, and her short story collection, Skin Folk, in 2002. Her third novel, The Salt Roads, will appear in 2003. Hopkinson edited the anthologies Whispers from the Cotton Tree Root: Caribbean Fabulist Fiction (2000) and Mojo: Conjure Stories (2003). She says, "I write speculative fiction. For anyone who doesn't know the term, it's fiction in which impossible things happen. It includes magic realism, fantasy, science fiction and horror."

"Shift" appeared in Conjunctions: 39, the large special issue of that distinguished literary quarterly, edited by Peter Straub and devoted to "the New Fabulists." The Neil Gaiman story, above, and the China Miéville story later in this book are also from that fine collection. Hopkinson here plays sophisticated fantastic games with Shakespeare's characters from The Tempest—Ariel, Caliban, and Sycorax.

Down,
Down,
Down,
To the deep and shady,
Pretty mermaidy,
Take me down.
—AFRICAN-AMERICAN FOLK SONG

"Did you sleep well?" she asks, and you make sure that your face is fixed into a dreamy smile as you open your eyes into the morning after. It had been an awkward third date; a clumsy fumbling in her bed, both of you apologizing and then fleeing gratefully into sleep.

"I dreamed that you kissed me," you say. That line's worked before.

She's lovely as she was the first time you met her, particularly seen through eyes with color vision. "You said you wanted me to be your frog." *Say it, say it,* you think.

She laughs. "Isn't that kind of backward?"

"Well, it'd be a way to start over, right?" You ignore the way that her eyes narrow. "You could kiss me," you tell her, as playfully as you can manage, "and make me your prince again."

She looks thoughtful at that. You reach for her, pull her close. She comes willingly, a fall of little blonde plaits brushing your face like fingers. Her hair's too straight to hold the plaits; they're already feathered all along their lengths. "Will you be my slimy little frog?" she whispers, a gleam of amusement in her eyes, and your heart double-times, but she kisses you on the forehead instead of the mouth. You could scream with frustration.

"I've got morning breath," she says apologetically. She means that you do.

"I'll go and brush my teeth," you tell her. You try not to sound grumpy. You linger in the bathroom, staring at the whimsical shells she keeps in the little woven basket on the counter, flaunting their salty pink cores. You wait for anger and pique to subside.

"You hungry?" she calls from the kitchen. "I thought I'd make some oatmeal porridge."

So much for kissing games. She's decided it's time for breakfast instead. "Yes," you say. "Porridge is fine."

Ban . . . Ban . . . ca-ca-Caliban . . .

You know who the real tempest is, don't it? The real storm? Is our mother Sycorax; his and mine. If you ever see her hair flying around her head when she dash at you in anger; like a whirlwind, like a lightning, like a deadly whirlpool. Wheeling and turning round her scalp like if it ever catch you, it going to drag you in, pull you down, swallow you in pieces. If you ever hear how she gnash her teeth in her head like tiger shark; if you ever hear the crack of her voice or feel the crack of her hand on your backside like a bolt out of thunder, then you would know is where the real storm there.

She tell me say I must call her Scylla, or Charybdis.

Say it don't make no matter which, for she could never remember one different from the other, but she know one of them is her real name. She say never mind the name most people know her by; is a name some Englishman give her by scraping a feather quill on paper.

White people magic.

Her people magic, for all that she will box you if you ever remind her of that, and flash her blue, blue y'eye-them at you. Lightning *braps* from out of blue sky. But me and Brother, when she not there, is that Englishman name we call her by.

When she hold you on her breast, you must take care never to relax, never to close your y'eye, for you might wake up with your nose hole-them filling up with the salt sea. Salt sea rushing into your lungs to drown you with her mother love.

Imagine what is like to be the son of that mother.

Now imagine what is like to be the sister of that son, to be sister to that there brother.

There was a time they called porridge "gruel." A time when you lived in castle moats and fetched beautiful golden balls for beautiful golden girls. When the fetching was a game, and you knew yourself to be lord of the land and the veins of water that ran through it, and you could graciously allow petty kings to build their palaces on the land, in which to raise up their avid young daughters.

Ban . . . ban . . . ca-ca-Caliban . . .
When I was small, I hear that blasted name so plenty I thought it was me own.

In her bathroom, you find a new toothbrush, still in its plastic package. She was thinking of you then, of you staying overnight. You smile, mollified. You crack the plastic open, brush your teeth, looking around at the friendly messiness of her bathroom. Cotton, silk, and polyester panties hanging on the shower-curtain rod to dry, their crotches permanently honey-stained. Three different types of deodorant on the counter, two of them lidless, dried out. A small bottle of perfume oil, lid off so that it weeps its sweetness into the air. A fine dusting of baby powder covers everything, its innocent odor making you sneeze. Someone *lives* here. Your own apartment—the one you found when you came on land—is as crisp and dull as a hotel room, a stop along the way. Everything is tidy there, except for the wastepaper basket in your bedroom, which is crammed with empty pill bottles: marine algae capsules; iodine pills. You remind yourself that you need to buy more, to keep the cravings at bay.

Caliban have a sickness. Is a sickness any of you could get. In him it manifest as a weakness; a weakness for cream. He fancy himself a prince of Africa, a mannish Cleopatra, bathing in mother's milk. Him believe say it would make him pretty. Him never had mirrors to look in, and with the mother we had, the surface of the sea never calm enough that him could see him face in it. Him would never believe me say that him pretty already. Him fancy if cream would only touch him, if him could only submerge himself entirely in it, it would redeem him.

Me woulda try it too, you know, but me have that feature you find among so many brown-skin people; cream make me belly gripe.

Truth to tell, Brother have the same problem, but him would gladly suffer the stomach pangs and the belly-running for the chance to drink in cream, to bathe in cream, to have it dripping off him and running into him mouth. Such a different taste from the bitter salt sea milk of Sycorax.

That beautiful woman making breakfast in her kitchen dives better than you do. You've seen her knifing so sharply through waves that you wondered they didn't bleed in her wake.

You fill the sink, wave your hands through the water. It's bliss, the way it resists you. You wonder if you have time for a bath. It's a pity that this isn't one of those apartment buildings with a pool. You miss swimming.

You wash your face. You pull the plug, watch the water spiral down the drain. It looks wild, like a mother's mad hair. Then you remember that you have to be cautious around water now, even the tame, caged water of swimming pools and bathrooms. Quickly, you sink the plug back into the mouth of the drain. You'd forgotten; anywhere there's water, especially rioting water, it can tattle tales to your mother.

Your face feels cool and squeaky now. You mouth is wild cherry-flavored from the toothpaste. You're kissable. You can hear humming from the kitchen, and the scraping of a spoon against a pot. There's a smell of cinnamon and nutmeg. Island smells. You square your shoulders, put on a smile, walk to the kitchen. Your feet are floppy, reluctant. You wish you could pay attention to what they're telling you. When they plash around like this, when they slip and slide and don't want to carry you upright, it's always been a bad sign. The kisses of golden girls are chancy things. Once, after the touch of other pale lips, you looked into the eyes of a golden girl, one Miranda, and saw yourself reflected back in her moist, breathless stare. In her eyes you were tall, handsome, your shoulders powerful and your jaw square. You carried yourself with the arrogance of a prince. You held a spear in one hand. The spotted, tawny pelt of an animal that had never existed was knotted around your waist. You wore something's teeth on a string around your neck and you spoke in grunts, imperious. In her eyes, your bright copper skin was dark and loamy as cocoa. She had sighed and leaped upon you, kissing and biting, begging to be taken. You had let her have what she wanted. When her father stumbled upon the two of you, writhing on the ground, she had leaped to her feet and changed you again; called you monster, attacker. She'd clasped her bodice closed with one hand, carefully leaving bare enough pitiful juddering bosom to spark a father's ire. She'd looked at you regretfully, sobbed crocodile tears, and spoken the lies that had made you her father's slave for an interminable length of years.

You haven't seen yourself in this one's eyes yet. You need her to kiss you, to change you, to hide you from your dam. That's what you've always needed. You are always awed by the ones who can work this magic. You could love one of them forever and a day. You just have to find the right one.

You stay a second in the kitchen doorway. She looks up from where she stands at the little table, briskly setting two different-sized spoons beside two mismatched bowls. She smiles. "Come on in," she says.

You do, on your slippery feet. You sit at the table. She's still standing. "I'm sorry," she says. She quirks a regretful smile at you. "I don't think my cold sore is quite healed yet." She runs a tongue tip over the corner of her lip, where you can no longer see the crusty scab.

You sigh. "It's all right. Forget it."

She goes over to the stove. You don't pay any attention. You're staring at the thready crack in your bowl.

She says, "Brown sugar or white?"

"Brown," you tell her. "And lots of milk." Your gut gripes at the mere thought, but milk will taint the water in which she cooked the oats. It will cloud the whisperings that water carries to your mother.

Nowadays people would say that me and my mooncalf brother, we is "lactose intolerant." But me think say them mis-name the thing. Me think say is milk can't tolerate we, not we can't tolerate it.

So: he find himself another creamy one. Just watch at the two of them there, in that pretty domestic scene.

I enter, invisible.

Brother eat off most of him porridge already. Him always had a large appetite. The white lady, she only passa-passa-ing with hers, dipping the spoon in, tasting little bit, turning the spoon over and watching at it, dipping it in. She glance at him and say, "Would you like to go to the beach today?"

"No!" You almost shout it. You're not going to the beach, not to any large body of water ever again. Your very cells keen from the loss of it, but She is in the water, looking for you.

"A true. Mummy in the water, and I in the wind, Brother," I whisper to him, so sweet. By my choice, him never hear me yet. Don't want him to know that me find him. Plenty time for that. Plenty time to fly and carry the news to Mama. Maybe I can find a way to be free if I do this one last thing for her. Bring her beloved son back. Is him she want, not me. Never me. "Ban, ban, ca-ca-Caliban!" I scream in him face, silently.

"There's no need to shout," she says with an offended look. "That's where we first saw each other, and you swam so strongly. You were beautiful in the water. So I just thought you might like to go back there."

You had been swimming for your life, but she didn't know that. The surf tossing you crashing against the rocks, the undertow pulling you back in deeper, the waves singing their triumphant song: *She's coming. Sycorax is coming for you. Can you feel the tips of her tentacles now? Can you feel them sticking to your skin, bringing you back? She's coming. We've got you now. We'll hold you for her. Oh, there'll be so much fun when she has you again!*

And you had hit out at the water, stroked through it, kicked through it, fleeing for shore. One desperate pull of your arms had taken you through foaming surf. You crashed into another body, heard a surprised "Oh," and then a wave tumbled you. As you fought in its depths, searching for the air and dry land, you saw her, this woman, slim as an eel, her body parting the water, her hair glowing golden. She'd extended a hand to you, like reaching for a bobbing ball. You took her hand, held on tightly to the warmth of it. She stood, and you stood, and you realized you'd been only feet from shore. "Are you all right?" she'd asked.

The water had tried to suck you back in, but it was only at thigh height now. You ignored it. You kept hold of her hand, started moving with her, your savior, to the land. You felt your heart swelling. She was perfect. "I'm doing just fine," you'd said. "I'm sorry I startled you. What's your name?"

Behind you, you could hear the surf shouting for you to come back. But the sun was warm on your shoulders now, and you knew that you'd stay on land. As you came up out of the water, she glanced at you and smiled, and you could feel the change begin.

She's sitting at her table, still with that hurt look on her face.

"I'm sorry, darling," you say, and she brightens at the endearment, the first you've used with her. Under the table, your feet are trying to paddle away, away. You ignore them. "Why don't we go for a walk?" you ask her. She smiles, nods. The many plaits of her hair sway with the rhythm. You must ask her not to wear her hair like that. Once you know her a little better. They look like tentacles. Besides, her hair's so pale that her pink scalp shows through.

Chuh. *I'm sorry, darling.* Him is sorry, is true. A sorry sight. I follow them out on them little walk, them Sunday perambulation. Down her street and round the corner into the district where the trendy people-them live. Where those cunning little shops are, you know the kind, yes? Wildflowers selling at this one, half your wages for one so-so blossom. Cheese from Greece at that one, and wine from Algiers. (Mama S. say she don't miss Algiers one bit.) Tropical fruit selling at another store, imported from the Indies, from the hot sun places where people work them finger to the bone to pick them and box them and send them, but not to eat them. Brother and him new woman meander through those streets, making sure people look at them good. She turn her moon face to him, give him that fuck-me look, and take him hand. I see him melt. Going to be easy to change him now that she melt him. And then him will be gone from we again. I blow a grieving breeze oo-oo-oo through the leaves of the crab apple trees lining that street.

She looks around, her face bright and open. "Isn't it a lovely day?" she says. "Feel the air on your skin." She releases your hand. The sweat of your mingled touch evaporates and you mourn its passing. She opens her arms to the sun, drinking in light.

Of course, that white man, him only write down part of the story. Him say how our mother was a witch. How she did consort with monsters. But you know the real story? You know why them exile her from Algiers, with a baby in her belly and one at her breast?

She spins and laughs, her print dress opening like a flower above her scuffed army boots. Her strong legs are revealed to midthigh.

Them send my mother from her home because of the monster she consort with. The lord with sable eyes and skin like rich earth. My daddy.

An old man sitting on a bench smiles, indulgent at her joy, but then he sees her reach for your hand again. He scowls at you, spits to one side.

My daddy. A man who went for a swim one day, down, down, down, and when he see the fair maid flowing toward him, her long hair just a-swirl like weeds in the water, her skin like milk, him never 'fraid.

As you both pass the old man, he shakes his head, his face clenched. She doesn't seem to notice. You hold her hand tighter, reach to pull her warmth closer to you. But you're going down, and you know it.

When my mother who wasn't my mother yet approach the man who wasn't my father yet, when she ask him, "Man, you eat salt, or you eat fresh?" him did know what fe say. Of course him did know. After his tutors teach him courtly ways from since he was small. After his father teach him how to woo. After his own mother teach him how to address the Wata Lady with respect. Sycorax ask him, "Man, you eat salt, or you eat fresh?"

And proper proper, him respond, "Me prefer the taste of salt, thank you please."

That was the right answer. For them that does eat fresh, them going to be fresh with your business. But this man show her that he know how fe have respect. For that, she give him breath and take him down, she take him down even farther.

You pass another beautiful golden girl, luxuriantly blond. She glances at you, casts her eyes down demurely, where they just happen to rest at your crotch. You feel her burgeoning gaze there, your helpless response. Quickly you lean and kiss the shoulder of the woman you're with. The other one's look turns to resentful longing. You hurry on.

She take him down into her own castle, and she feed him the salt foods she keep in there, the fish and oysters and clams, and him eat of them till him belly full, and him talk to her sweet, and him never get fresh with her. Not even one time. Not until she ask him to. Mama wouldn't tell me what happen after that, but true she have two pickney, and both of we shine copper, even though she is alabaster, so me think me know is what went on.

There's a young black woman sitting on a bench, her hair tight peppercorns against her scalp. Her feet are crossed beneath her. She's alone, reading a book. She's pretty, but she looks too much like your sister. She could never be a golden girl. She looks up as you go by, distracted from her reading by the chattering of the woman beside you. She looks at you. Smiles. Nods a greeting. Burning up with guilt, you make your face stone. You move on.

In my mother and father, salt meet with sweet. Milk meet with chocolate. No one could touch her while he was alive and ruler of his lands, but the minute him dead, her family and his get together and exile her to that little island to starve to death. Send her away with two sweet-and-sour, milk chocolate pickney; me in her belly and Caliban at her breast. Is nuh that turn her bitter? When you confine the sea, it don't stagnate? You put milk to stand, and it nuh curdle?

Chuh. Watch at my brother, there, making himself fool-fool. Is time. Time to end this, to take him back down. "Mama," I whisper. I blow one puff of wind, then another. The puffs tear a balloon out from a little girl's hand. The balloon have a fish painted on it. I like that. The little girl cry out and run after her toy. Her father dash after her. I puff and blow, make the little metallic balloon skitter just out of the child reach. As she run, she knock over a case of fancy bottled water, the expensive fizzy kind in blue glass bottles, from a display. The bottles explode when them hit the ground, the water escaping with a shout of glee. The little girl just dance out of the way of broken glass and spilled water and keep running for her balloon, reaching for it. I make it bob like a bubble in the air. Her daddy jump to one side, away from the glass. He try to snatch the back of her dress, but he too big and slow. Caliban step forward and grasp her balloon by the string. He give it back to her. She look at him, her y'eye-them big. She clutch the balloon to her bosom and smile at her daddy as he sweep her up into him arms.

The storekeeper just a-wait outside her shop, to talk to the man about who going to refund her goods.

"Mother," I call. "Him is here. I find him."

The water from out the bottles start to flow together in a spiral.

You hear her first in the dancing breeze that's toying with that little girl's balloon. You fetch the balloon for the child before you deal with what's coming. Her father mumbles a suspicious thanks at you. You step away from them. You narrow your eyes, look around. "You're here, aren't you?" you say to the air.

"Who's here?" asks the woman at your side.

"My sister," you tell her. You say "sister" like you're spitting out spoiled milk.

"I don't see anyone," the woman tells you.

"El!" you call out.

I don't pay him no mind. I summon up one of them hot, gusty winds. I blow over glasses of water on café tables. I grab Popsicles *swips!* out from the hands and mouths of children. The Popsicles fall down and melt, all the bright colors; melt and run like that brother of mine.

Popsicle juice, café table water, spring water that break free from bottles; them all rolling together now, crashing and splashing and calling to our mother. I call up the whirling devils. Them twirl sand into everybody eyes. Hats and baseball caps flying off heads, dancing along with me. An umbrella galloping down the road, end over end, with an old lady chasing it. All the trendy Sunday people squealing and running everywhere.

"Ariel, stop it!" you say.

So I run up his girlfriend skirt, make it fly high in the air. "Oh!" she cry out, trying to hold the frock down. She wearing a panty with a tear in one leg and a knot in the waistband. That make me laugh out loud. "Mama!" I shout, loud so Brother can hear me this time. "You seeing this? Look him here so!" I blow one rassclaat cluster of rain clouds over the scene, them bellies black and heavy with water. "So me see that you get a new master!" I screech at Brother.

The street is empty now, but for the three of you. Everyone else has found shelter. Your girl is cowering down beside the trunk of a tree, hugging her skirt about her knees. Her hair has come loose from most of its plaits, is whipping in a tangled mess about her head. She's shielding her face from blowing sand, but trying to look up at the sky above her, where this attack is coming from. You punch at the air, furious. You know you can't hurt your sister, but you need to lash out anyway. "Fuck you!" you yell. "You always do this! Why can't the two of you leave me alone!"

I chuckle, "Your face favor jackass when him sick. Why you can't leave white woman alone? You don't see what them do to you?"

"You are our mother's creature," you hiss at her. In your anger, your speech slips into the same rhythms as hers. "Look at you, trying so hard to be 'island,' talking like you just come off the boat."

"At least me nah try fe chat like something out of some Englishman book." I make the wind howl it back at him. "At least me remember is boat me come off from!" I burst open the clouds overhead and drench the two of them in mother water. She squeals. Good.

"Ariel, Caliban; stop that squabbling or I'll bind you both up in a split tree forever." The voice is a wintry runnel, fast-freezing.

You both turn. It's Sycorax. Your sister has manifested,

has pushed a trembling bottom lip out. Dread runs cold along your limbs. "Yes, Mother," you both say, standing sheepishly shoulder to shoulder. "Sorry, Mother."

Sycorax is sitting in a sticky puddle of water and melted Popsicles, but a queen on her throne could not be more regal. She has wrapped an ocean wave about her like a shawl. Her eyes are open-water blue. Her writhing hair foams white over her shoulders and the marble swells of her vast breasts. Her belly is a mounded salt lick, rising from the weedy tangle of her pubic hair, a marine jungle in and out of which flit tiny blennies. The tsunami of Sycorax's hips overflows her watery seat. Her myriad split tails are flicking, the way they do when she's irritated. With one of them, she scratches around her navel. You think you can see the sullen head of a moray eel, lurking in the cave those hydra tails make. You don't want to think about it. You never have.

"Ariel," says Sycorax, "have you been up to your tricks again?"

"But he," splutters your sister, "he . . ."

"*He* never ceases with *his* tricks," your mother pronounces. "Running home to Mama, leaving me with the mess he's made." She looks at you, and your watery legs weaken. "Caliban," she says, "I'm getting too old to play surrogate mother to your spawn. That last school of your offspring all had poisonous stings."

"I know, Mother. I'm sorry."

"How did that happen?" she asks.

You risk a glance at the woman you've dragged into this, the golden girl. She's standing now, a look of interest and curiosity on her face. "It's your fault," you say to her. "If you had kissed me, told me what you wanted me to be, she and Ariel couldn't have found us."

She looks at you, measuring. "First tell me about the poison babies," she says. She's got more iron in her than you'd thought, this one. The last fairy-tale princess who'd met your family hadn't stopped screaming for two days.

Ariel sniggers. "That was from his last ooman," she says. "The two of them always quarreling. For her, Caliban had a poison tongue."

"And spat out biting words, no doubt," Sycorax says. "He became what she saw, and it affected the children they made. Of course she didn't want them, of course she left; so Grannie gets to do the honors. He has brought me frog children and dog children, baby mack daddies and crack babies. Brings his offspring to me, then runs away again. And I'm getting tired of it." Sycorax's shawl whirls itself up into a waterspout. "And I'm more than tired of his sister's tale tattling."

"But Mama . . . !" Ariel says.

" 'But Mama' nothing. I want you to stop pestering your brother."

Ariel puffs up till it looks as though she might burst. Her face goes anvil-cloud dark, but she says nothing.

"And you," says Sycorax, pointing at you with a suckered tentacle, "you need to stop bringing me the fallout from your sorry love life."

"I can't help it, Mama," you say. "That's how women see me."

Sycorax towers forward, her voice crashing upon your ears. "Do you want to know how *I* see you?" A cluster of her tentacle tails whips around your shoulders, immobilizes you. That *is* a moray eel under there, its fanged mouth hanging hungrily open. You are frozen in Sycorax's gaze, a hapless, irresponsible little boy. You feel the sickening metamorphosis begin. You are changing, shrinking. The last time Sycorax did this to you, it took you forever to become man enough again to escape. You try to twist in her arms, to look away from her eyes. She pulls you forward, puckering her mouth for the kiss she will give you.

"Well, yeah, I'm beginning to get a picture here," says a voice. It's the golden girl, shivering in her flower-print dress that's plastered to her skinny body. She steps closer. Her boots squelch. She points at Ariel. "You says he's colorstruck. You're his sister, you should know. And yeah, I can see that in him. You'd think I was the sun itself, the way he looks at me."

She takes your face in her hands, turns your eyes away from your mother's. Finally, she kisses you full on the mouth. In her eyes, you become a sunflower, helplessly turning wherever she goes. You stand rooted, waiting for her direction.

She looks at your terrible mother. "You get to clean up the messes he makes." And now you're a baby, soiling your diapers and waiting for Mama to come and fix it. Oh, please, end this.

She looks down at you, wriggling and helpless on the ground. "And I guess all those other women saw big, black dick."

So familiar, the change that wreaks on you. You're an adult again, heavy-muscled and horny with a thick, swelling erection. You reach for her. She backs away. "But," she says, "there's one thing I don't see."

You don't care. She smells like vanilla and her skin is smooth and cool as ice cream and you want to push your tongue inside. You grab her thin, unresisting arms. She's shaking, but she looks into your eyes. And hers are empty. You aren't there. Shocked, you let her go. In a trembling voice, she says, "Who do you think you are?"

It could be an accusation: *Who* do you *think* you are? It might be a question: Who do *you* think you are? You search her face for the answer. Nothing. Your mother and your sib both look as shocked as you feel.

"Hey," says the golden girl, opening her hands wide. Her voice is getting less shaky. "Clearly, this is family business, and I know better than to mess with that." She gathers her little picky plaits together, squeezes water out of them. "It's been really . . . interesting, meeting you all." She looks at you, and her eyes are empty, open, friendly. You don't know what to make of them. "Um," she says, "maybe you can give me a call sometime." She starts walking away. Turns back. "It's not a brush-off; I mean it. But only call when you can tell me who you really are. Who you think you're going to become."

And she leaves you standing there. In the silence, there's only a faint sound of whispering water and wind in the trees. You turn to look at your mother and sister. "I," you say.

A Book, by Its Cover

P.D. Cacek

P.D. Cacek[www.pdcacek.com] lives in Pennsylvania. The winner of awards for her short fiction, P.D. Cacek is the author of a collection, Leavings, *two humorous vampire novels,* Night Prayers, *and its sequel,* Night Players, *and a contemporary werewolf novel set in Denver, Colorado,* Canyons. *A lifelong lover of the supernatural, Cacek has begun work on what she calls her New Hope Quartet—a series of nontraditional gothic ghost novels set in New Hope, Pennsylvania. She is currently working on the second in the series, entitled* Reflections through Beveled Glass. *Cacek's nonfiction articles on New Hope, and its ghosts, can be seen on-line at www.newhopepa.com.*

"A Book, by Its Cover" was published in Shelf Life, *a $75 limited-edition fantasy anthology on the theme of books and bookselling that was one of the best anthologies of the year, though not widely circulated. It is the story of a bookstore owner, Reb Shendelman, and his young neighbor, Yavin. Yavin suspects him of something evil in the aftermath of Kristallnacht, that night in Nazi Germany in the 1930s when violent anti-semitic riots swept the country, windows were broken and property destroyed or looted, many books were burned, and many Jews were beaten or killed.*

A cloud passed in front of the sun and the already pale light faded to the color of bone. Snow was coming, but not one of the people scurrying along the street, bundled against the cold as they hurried from one shop to another, seemed to notice. Or care. All of them acted as if the day and the light and the approaching snow was normal, part of the ordinary.

And he hated them, all of them, for that—for not noticing what the world had become.

He couldn't understand why they didn't see and how they could continue to shop and pray and go on with the day to day business of living, as if the future still existed.

Because he knew better. He had seen the end of the future the day his grandfather had sewn the two yellow triangles together to make the star on his coat. The future was finite now and he seemed to be the only one who knew it.

Yavin Landauer pulled the old frock coat's collar tighter against his neck and watched a man in a fedora and camel-hair overcoat, the color of honey, walk hand-in-hand with a boy of nine or ten in knickers and jacket and cap all of soft gray wool. The cheap cotton stars looked out of place on the expensive material, material that Yavin could almost feel the texture of even from across the street. His grandfather had obtained a few bolts of wool much like that just a few weeks before. . . .

He shook the memory away before it could take root and glared at the man and boy. They were laughing as they walked, the man pointing at things in those shop windows that had somehow, miraculously, escaped the bricks and bullets and bats of the brown-shirted Wulf packs. But even if a window or two had been spared, each building in the ghetto had been marked by the pack. *Juden.* In yellow paint across each lentil, instead of lamb's blood—insurance that

76

the Angel of Death would not pass over them this time.

Yavin let his hand drop from the collar to trace the edge of the star. His grandfather had been careful, the star's center was directly over his heart. When the future ended for Yavin, it would be quick.

Not like the little boy across the street. His future would end in shock and surprise because his father, like so many others, didn't notice the change in the light of the world. It was cruel and a part of Yavin wanted to shout at the man, but he didn't. He huddled deeper in the fire-blackened doorway of what had been his grandfather's tailor shop as the man and boy entered Reb Shendelman's bookshop. He closed his eyes. Took a deep breath and smelled snow riding the back of charred wood.

It had been almost three months since *Kristallnacht*, the Night of Broken Glass, and still the stench of the fire was as strong as the memory of his grandfather running out into the street when the first torch shattered the shop's front window. Yavin had stayed inside, hidden and safe, he thought, until the fire began to consume the bolts of cloth. It was only then, when the fire came at him, that he fled—out the small window at the back of the shop and down the narrow alley until he could circle back to the main street.

And by then his grandfather was dead, a sacrifice to the new god who ruled Germany.

Yavin had hidden in the shadows and watched the pack of brown-shirted Wulfs as they laughed and clapped each other on the shoulders. One of the boys, Karl, had been his best friend . . . once . . . when only the night sky wore stars.

Once. Upon a time.

The sunlight brightened suddenly and Yavin opened his eyes, blinking as the first fat flakes of snow began to fall. There were fewer people on the street—finally, they noticed.

Yavin leaned back against the only home he'd ever known and rubbed the cold out of his nose as the man in the honey-colored coat left the bookstore. His hat was pulled low over his eyes and he was clutching a brown-paper wrapped parcel to his chest. A book, what else would one buy at a bookshop?

Except from a bookshop that had no books?

Rolling his shoulders under the coat, Yavin stared at the object in the man's hands. It was square and *looked* like a book wrapped in paper . . . but it couldn't be, he'd seen what the Wulfs had done that night. The fire that had gorged itself on the bolts of cloth in his grandfather's shop was nothing more than a small camp fire compared to the inferno that brightened the night sky in front of the bookshop. Hundreds, maybe thousands of books were fed to the flames while Reb Shendelman, ancient for as long as Yavin had known him, howled and cried and tore at his clothes.

The old man had wept for his books, but not once so much as glanced at the body that was sprawled on the ground only a few feet away. And when he finally said Kaddish, it was for the books alone.

Karl and the others had thought that was funny, that an old man should become so distraught over a few words and ideas, so they let him live.

With only a small beating.

The man in the honey-colored coat stumbled on a patch of ice and dropped the paper-wrapped bundle into the snow. The sound that came from his lips sent a chill up Yavin's spine that had nothing to do with the cold. Whatever it was, he thought as he watched the man brush the damp snow off the wrapping, it had to be very valuable. Reb Shendelman could have managed to hide some of the more expensive and rare volumes. That would make sense . . . and explain why the man seemed so upset.

Where was the boy?

Yavin frowned as he glanced up and down the street. He'd forgotten the boy as he watched the father, but there was no sign of the child on the street. A gust of wind swirled into the doorway, powdering him with snow. The little boy was probably already home by now, his father sending him ahead so he wouldn't be caught in the storm. Telling him to stay warm and not catch cold . . . lying to him by pretending there was a future that wanted them.

Shivering, Yavin reached up and touched the charred remains of the mezuzah that had done nothing to protect them from the Wulfs.

The man in the honey-colored coat came back just before sunset, holding the hand of a little girl. Dressed all in white, the yellow star on her coat dancing as she skipped through the unswept drifts, she looked like an angel made of snow.

Yavin nibbled along one edge of the roll he had begged from a neighbor and watched the little girl giggle up at the man. She didn't look hungry and Yavin hated her, a little, for that. Food had always been provided for him without thought, now it had become something that was always in his mind and belly.

Just like the future, or, rather, the lack of it . . . always there, always grumbling. Always.

For some.

Hand in hand, the man walked the little girl into the bookshop.

The roll was a memory on Yavin's tongue and his stomach was still grumbling when the door of the bookshop opened again and the man in the honey-colored coat left. The brim of his fedora was pulled low over his eyes and, like the day before, he clutched a brown-paper wrapped bundle to his chest. The little girl in white wasn't with him.

Yesterday there had been a boy, today a girl.

Something besides hunger growled in Yavin's belly as he left the protection of the soot-covered shadows and crossed the icy cobblestones. And only fell twice.

The man looked up from beneath the hat's brim when Yavin stepped onto the sidewalk directly in front of him. There were tears frozen on the man's lower lashes and a look on his face that almost made Yavin stumble again. It was a book. Yavin could see one corner of it through a tear in the brown wrapping, a book bound in white satin, the thick pages edged in gold. It was the sort of book that would cost a great deal of money, especially now, even for a man in a camel-hair coat, the color of honey.

Yavin felt his shrunken stomach turn over as he looked up at the man.

"What have you done?"

The man blinked as if waking from a deep sleep and shook his head, stepped to one side, tightening his grip on the book.

"I don't know what you're talking about. Leave me alone."

"What have you done with the little girl?"

"I don't know what you're talking about." The man said. "There's no little girl here."

Yavin pointed to the walk behind the man. There were two sets of footprints in the snow—one large, one small. Both sets led to the bookshop, but only one set, the one belonging to the man, left.

"She is safe," the man's voice was almost as silent as the falling snow. "Please, I must get this onto the train. A woman has promised to take this to England for me. Please, I have to hurry."

He was talking about the book, not the little girl. Yavin stepped back, the soles of his shoes almost sliding out from under him again as the man rushed past. He could hear the man mumbling to himself.

"Why didn't I listen before this? She will be safe, dear Gott, please . . . with her brother, please. I should have come sooner, but who thought . . . who would have thought . . . Mein gott, bitter, let me get there in time."

Yavin felt his heart stop when the man looked back—but not at him. At the bookshop.

"Hurry, there's not much time left."

When the momentary death passed, Yavin made himself turn and look at the shop. It was so quiet the sound of his own breathing pounded against the inside of his brain.

The bookstore sat hunched and still at the end of the street, aloof but miserable like a once pampered cat that had been forgotten and left out in the snow. Anyone passing would think the building was deserted, just another shop that had been abandoned. Or left ownerless. There were no lights showing through the cracks in the boards that covered the broken front window and the snow had already covered the scorched spot on the street. In an hour or less, there'd be no evidence that anyone had visited the shop that day. Or the day before that.

Would a man sell his children for books? No . . . no . . .

One book, one child.

One child that no longer needed to be cared for or fed, for one book, hollowed out and filled with what? Forged documents? Money? A pair of scissors to cut yellow stars from coats?

The future, without limits.

A man might offer anything for that.

The flesh on Yavin's fingers stung as he curled his hands into fists and followed the shallow tracks back to the bookshop. He only stumbled once and that was when he reached for the doorknob and looked up. There had been a brass marker there, generations old, that once read *Shendelman's Books* in Hebrew and German. Now it was unreadable. Yavin had watched Karl in the glow of the fire, strike the sign again and again with a hammer while the other Wulfs chanted: *Juden. Juden. Juden.*

There used to be a small brass bell that jingled every time the door opened—he remembered that, remembered the sound of it echoing through the huge room filled with books as Karl raced him to see who would be first into the shop. Karl always won and now the bell was gone and only the squeal of unoiled hinges announced him.

To the room of empty shelves.

Yavin tried not to listen to the hollow thud of his shoes against the dust-streaked floor.

His grandfather had always encouraged him to be a scholar, and so only saw merit in those obscure volumes of archaic text that were the size of a crate of whitefish. Each night, for an hour, Yavin would wade through the didactic mire . . . and each day, with Karl, tucked into a corner out of the way of customers, he would rediscover old friends.

Don Quixote. The plays of Shakespeare. Jules Verne. Shelly. Stoker.

Gone forever.

"I've wondered when you'd decide to come across the street, Yavin Landauer."

The soles of Yavin's shoes squeaked as he whirled toward the pale shape that hovered near the back wall. Yavin was no longer a child, so the first images in his mind were not of ghosts or Dybbuks, but of brown-shirts and black swastikas.

"What is it? Are you all right?"

Yavin's heart was pounding against his ribs, like a prisoner trying to escape a cell, when Reb Shendelman stepped out of the shadows. The old man was thinner than Yavin remembered and his feet dragged across the floor as if lifting them was too much effort. He was still wearing the coat he'd had on the night of the fire—the torn pocket fluttered like a broken bird's wing with each shambling step.

"Yavin, what is it? Come, let me get you something to eat."

Drool filled his mouth and his belly rumbled so loudly it sounded like thunder at the mention of food. "No! I won't take anything from you."

"What take? I give it. Besides, we're friends, no?"

Yavin looked down at the floor and saw the outline of a child's shoe in the dust. "No."

"No?" Reb Shendelman asked. "Then we are enemies?"

Yavin nodded.

"Ah." The old man mimicked his nod. "Can I ask why? No? Then all right. It will be strange after so many years, but if we are enemies, then we are enemies. So, enemy, come and eat. I have potato and cabbage soup and some black bread. Come. We can discuss being enemies later."

"What was inside the book, Reb Shendelman?"

Confusion flickered over the old man's face as he lifted his arms toward the empty shelves. "What book? I have no books, Yavin. You saw what they did."

"I saw . . . but I also saw the man and the little girl today," Yavin said, wanting to shout but barely able to whisper. "And the man and boy yesterday. I know what you're doing, Reb Shendelman. I know."

"No," the old man said as he waved Yavin toward the small back room, "you don't, but you will. Come, I'll explain while you eat."

It took three bowls of the thin, but wonderful soup before Yavin stopped shivering and his belly remembered what it felt like to be full. And through it all, Reb Shendelman kept quiet.

. . . which, now that Yavin was finished, was a good thing. If the old man had tried to tell him the . . . fairy tale while he'd been eating, Yavin might have laughed so hard the soup would have come back up.

A child might have believed what the old man was saying, but Yavin didn't. He *was* a man, after all.

"I think it was because this building has always been a bookshop. With that many books, it almost makes sense, doesn't it? That the thoughts and ideas of those books could become something . . . real, no?"

Yavin stopped mopping up the dregs of the soup with a narrow crust of black bread to shrug, not that it was noticed. Reb Shendelman was looking out into the empty shop, rocking slowly back and forth over his clasped hands.

"Men can die, Yavin, but not ideas, never ideas. Do you understand?"

Yavin stuffed the softened crust into his mouth to avoid answering. Again the old man didn't notice, he kept talking as though the silence was an answer in itself.

"It isn't that hard a thing to accept . . . not when you think of all the thoughts and ideas and words contained in those books. Generations of books, lining these very shelves. How do we learn, Yavin, do you know? How is what we read transformed into a memory that we can keep forever, huh? There was so much knowledge here on these shelves for so long it must have been easy for some of it to seep into the wood . . . to become part of the store itself.

Such an easy thing, when you stop and wonder about it. Thoughts and ideas can't die, but they can build, one upon the other until all the knowledge of the universe creates a life of its own.

"Wasn't Adam begun as just a thought in the All Mighty's mind? Adam became a man from a single thought . . . so what is it for a building, within whose walls contained so many thoughts, to become a shapeless thing endowed with life, but not body?"

The bread caught in Yavin's throat and almost choked him.

"A Golem?" he squeaked when he was finally able to draw breath. "You're saying that this building is a Golem?"

"Yoh, a Golem . . . one constructed of thoughts and ideas, housed in a body of stone and mortar and wooden shelves. A Golem of creation, not destruction."

"And fed with the blood of children?"

"What are you talking about?"

Yavin tossed the empty bowl back onto the small table between them and shook his head. He'd seen his grandfather shake his head like that whenever the truth was stretched too far and about to unravel.

"The children who are bartered for those very special books you sell, Reb Shendelman. Do you keep them for the Nazis or do you kill them yourself so your invisible Golem can live? One book per child seems fair . . . but you'll give me a book without payment, won't you? Unless you want everyone to know what you've been doing."

Again, the old man's reaction was not what Yavin expected. Reb Shendelman stood up and walked to the empty shelves, ran his hands gently against the worn wood and nodded.

"One book per child . . . or one man or one woman."

"What?"

"Emmanuel Wiesel was the first. You remember Reb Wiesel, yoh?"

Yavin leaned back in his chair and hoped he looked apathetic. Of course he remembered the fishmonger. Who inside the ghetto didn't know the man who worked from before dawn to after dark, hauling fish, cleaning fish, selling fish . . . and who smelled so much of fish he was the beloved of every cat within a five-mile radius? Yavin also remembered the day his shop failed to open. The ghetto cats had been mourning him for almost a year now.

Reb Shendelman sighed as he turned around.

"They were waiting for him in his shop, three soldiers with guns for one man who smelled of herring. Someone warned him, so he came here. To hide or maybe just to say good-bye. When soldiers come, few of us have the luxury to say good-bye. But instead he started talking about his favorite book. *Ethics*, by Spinoza. Can you believe that? But what do I know from philosophers?"

"Here," he said, spreading his hands out in front of him. "This is where it happened.

"It was Friday, late, just before Shabbos and I was about to close when Wiesel rushed in. I had turned off the lights and I couldn't light a candle, so we just stood there, in the dark, and I listened while he talked about Spinoza. One minute he was explaining the philosopher's idea that evil was only part of the Lord God's perfection and the next?"

Yavin saw Reb Shendelman's hands begin to shake and felt a similar vibration roll across his shoulders.

"It was dark, so at first, I thought he had fallen or passed out, but when I ran to where he'd been standing all I found was a book. *Ethics*, by Baruch Spinoza. A beautiful book, bound in leather with thick parchment pages edged in gold, the title embossed in gold leaf. But the thing is, Yavin," the old man said, "I had no such book in the shop and I couldn't even have produced a thing of such beauty even if I had the materials. It was warm to the touch, like living flesh against my hands. Do you understand what I am saying, Yavin?"

Yavin felt his head shake slowly back and forth without any effort on his part.

"No, that is the problem with miracles . . . they are usually too miraculous for man to understand. I didn't believe it either, so I stand there, with this wondrous book in my hand and suddenly I remember Wiesel and I call out to him, 'Emmanuel Wiesel,' and then he is standing in front of me as if he'd never moved with my hands on his arms. He looked startled and rubbed his eyes, told me that he had been dreaming about sitting in Spinoza's workshop, watching the man grind lenses while they discussed monistic theory."

Reb Shendelman suddenly clapped his hands and Yavin jumped. "But it wasn't a dream, Yavin. The Golem of the shop had somehow transformed Wiesel the fishmonger into the book he loved the best. You see?

"I thought about the soldiers who had come for him and thought, in my ignorance, that I had been shown the way to save him, so we spoke more about Spinoza and this time I watched the miracle happen. There was no sound, Yavin, no stirring of the air. It was so peaceful. I placed him on the shelf with the other books and that night I spoke to the Golem over the Shabbos candles and not the All Mighty. I thought I could save them. A word here, a whisper there . . . people disappear from the ghetto all the time."

The smile faded from the old man's face.

"I never thought they would burn my books."

"That's why you were saying Kaddish that night," Yavin asked. "Wasn't it?"

Reb Shendelman nodded and Yavin couldn't hold the laughter in any longer. He could hear the soup slosh and gurgle inside his belly, which made him laugh even harder. The old man shrugged and began moving along the rows of empty shelves.

"Of course," he said, "you don't believe me, why should you? I know how impossible it sounds, Yavin, but all miracles are unless you see them first-hand."

Reb Shendelman stopped when he came to the far corner of the room, his hands dabbing at the still air. "This is where you two liked to sit, isn't it? Right here, yes? Yes . . . there used to be a chair here, and an old ottoman where my wife used to sit when she sewed. You and your friend, Karl . . . I remember. The two of you would sit here reading for hours. Let me think. What was your favorite book? I know it wasn't the work of Spinoza . . . what was it?"

Reb Shendelman's hands stopped moving and Yavin found himself leaning forward, hoping the old man would remember and hating himself for hoping that. What did it matter if the old man could remember which book had been his favorite? That was a lifetime ago, in a different world. To think about it or anything now seemed pointless, more than pointless . . . it was evil.

But even so, when the old man smiled and clapped his hands, Yavin felt his heart flutter.

"*Around the World in Eighty Days*. Yes?"

And Yavin nodded his head, ashamed and relieved that someone, at least, would remember that about him.

"Your grandfather, may he find everlasting peace, used to ask what you read . . . so I told him books on kashruth law. A small lie, but it made him happy." Reb Shendelman nodded as he walked toward Yavin. "He was a good man, but one of narrow imagination. You, on the other hand—"

The old man stopped when he was still an arm's length away and took a deep breath.

"You had the imagination of a true dreamer who could see beyond the hardness of this world and into what might be. Can you still do that, Yavin? Can you see Professor Phileas Fogg in his beautiful London flat? Can you see him accepting the challenge to go around the world . . . the entire world, Yavin, in only eighty days? Can you see him, Yavin? Can you see the world as Mr. Jules Verne wrote it? You can, if you try. Try, Yavin . . . see it . . . see . . . it. . . ."

"*Monsieur Passepartout.*"

Yavin staggered and grabbed the gangplank's rope handrail as he caught his breath. The air was hot and thick with the scent of brine. Water sprayed against his cheek and Yavin looked down to see the ocean lapped calmly against the barnacle-bedecked hull of a ship that had seen better days. He could see where someone had tried to patch the worm-holes and painted over them with tar. It was a miracle that the ship still floated, let alone that its captain could think it still sea-worthy enough to take out of port.

"*Monsieur Passepartout!*"

A gull cried and Yavin jerked his head up to follow its passage—stark white against the pale lavender twilight sky—over the lines of the bowsprit. There was a name on the bow, blocky wooden letters, faded by sun and wind and sea: General Grant.

It was the name of the ship . . . the large sea-going paddlewheel steamer bound from Yokohama to San Francisco with Phileas Fogg, Jean Passepartout and—

"*Monsieur Passepartout, do you ignore me purposely?*"

"*What?*"

Yavin clung to the rope as he turned toward the slightly shrewish tone. A woman, lovely and young, glared down at him. One hand grasped the ivory knob of a lace parasol, the other was tucked daintily against the tiny waist of her cream-colored traveling dress. A large hat, with ostrich plumes of a color Yavin had never seen in nature, sat firmly upon the mass of black curls. Towering above her hat and plumes and lovely face was the main of the three masts, rigged for full sail, that would aid the General Grant in maintaining the breakneck speed of twelve miles an hour and so cross the great Pacific Ocean in only twenty-one days.

Just like in the book.

Yavin laughed out loud. Until he saw the look on the woman's face.

And remembered who she was.

"You're Aouda. The girl who was going to be burned alive when the old rajah of Bundelcund died. I know you. Phileas Fogg saved you from the 'suttee' because he'd been early getting through the Indian forest and had time. That's what he said to Sir Francis Cromarty, he said he had the time to save you. You are Aouda, aren't you?"

"I am," the woman said with a heave of her fashionably confined bosom, "and you, Monsieur Passepartout, are impudent! I shall complain most earnestly to Mr. Fogg about your lack of courtesy."

"I'm afraid," a soft voice said behind Yavin, "that we

don't have the time for any reprimands at this moment. It will have to wait until after we have sailed, but rest assured, Passepartout, we shall discuss this matter. When there is time, of course."

Yavin turned around and gazed into the bearded, tranquil and enigmatic face of Phileas Fogg. He was just as Jules Verne had described him.

"Passepartout," Phileas Fogg said, "why do you look at me like that?"

"I'm Passepartout?" Yavin asked, giggling as if his belly was filled by a million tiny bubbles. "I'm Jean Passepartout?"

Phileas Fogg raised one perfectly arched eyebrow. "Passepartout, are you quite—"

"—all right, Yavin?"

Yavin found himself on the floor, staring up at Reb Shendelman.

"What did you do?" Yavin yelled as he scooted away from the old man until his spine encountered an empty bookshelf. "Leave me alone! You're some kind of mesmerist."

But the old man shook his head. "No, I'm just the seller of books, Yavin. It was the Golem that transformed you. Did you enjoy it?"

"There was nothing to enjoy!" His fear kept him shouting and Yavin could hear his voice echo back and forth through the empty store. "It was a dream . . . an illusion. It can't happen. It didn't happen!"

"What didn't happen, Jew?"

Karl came out of the darkness at the front of the store like the marauding Wulf-cub he'd become, silent and gray. His hungry, bright blue eyes never left Yavin's face as he crossed the room. Standing equal distance between Yavin and the old man, Karl snapped to attention and raised his right arm in stiff salute to his new god. Against the white of his armband, the black swastika looked like a giant spider.

"Heil Hitler!"

"Not in this shop, boy," Reb Shendelman said and was

rewarded with a slap across his face. *For his impudence,*
Yavin thought, remembering the word Aouda had used in
his dream.

Karl . . . his one-time friend . . . was sneering at Reb
Shendelman and wiping his hand against one leg of his uniform shorts, as if it had become corrupted by the mere
touch of Jewish flesh.

"You think just because we let you live the last time, old
man, that your life is somehow sacred?" Karl chuckled with
a sound Yavin remembered from the times they sat, huddled together, in the bookstore. "You're only alive because
you made us laugh when we burned your books. Poor old
Jew, crying over all those stupid books. We laughed about it
for days and days."

"Stop it, Karl," Yavin said, forgetting for a moment, but
only a moment, that they were no longer friends. He remembered the moment Karl's sneer found him.

"You dare tell me to stop, Landauer?" His lost friend
asked. "You have gotten brave since I last saw you . . . hiding in the shadows while your grandfather tried to be a hero.
He was as stupid as this old man here, but he didn't make us
laugh. Are you going to make me laugh, Landauer, or can I
just shoot you like a dog and put you out of your misery?"

The spider on Karl's arm twitched as he pulled a gun,
bright and shiny and too big for his hand, from the holster
hanging from his waist.

"I only came in here to see if there were any more books
to burn," Karl said as he leveled the muzzle at Yavin's face.
"They made such a fine fire last time, but now I think this
will be more fun."

"What was your favorite book, Karl?"

Yavin turned and looked at the old man at the same time
Karl did. There was a drop of blood in one corner of his
mouth that glistened like a dusty ruby in the dim light when
he spoke.

"What was your favorite book," Reb Shendelman asked
again before Karl could answer. "I can't remember which
book it was, but I remember it frightened you."

"It did not!" The gun twitched in Karl's hand as he

swung it toward the old man. "Books don't frighten me."

But the old man nodded. "This one did. I remember how you jumped once when I came with a plate of cookies for you and Yavin. You remember, don't you, Yavin?"

Yavin didn't remember anything at the moment.

"Yes," Reb Shendelman nodded, "now I remember. It was *Dracula*, by Bram Stoker. That is a very frightening book. Even I couldn't read it."

"What are you talking about?" Karl lifted his head as the muzzle of the gun drooped toward the floor. "That silly book didn't scare me at all. I read it a dozen times."

"What's your favorite part, Karl?" The old man asked and Yavin felt his stomach clench. "I was also so frightened when Jonathan Harker was in the coach along the Borgo Pass . . . I almost put the book down. Mein Gott, when he looks up and notices how excited the other passengers are because night is falling. Do you remember that part, Karl? Do you remember how the coach must have felt—how Harker described it as swaying like a boat on a stormy sea? Do you remember how the passengers offered him gifts and blessings and how they made the sign of the cross to guard against the evil to come? Do you see it, Karl? Do you? Yes, you do, I know you do. See it . . . see the Carpathians rising against the twilight sky . . . see it . . . see it, Karl."

The scream that had built in Yavin's throat as Karl's body began to shrink and fold in on itself—over and over and over—left his mouth as a soft hushing of air as he watched the old man bend down and slowly pick up the thick, black leather-bound volume from the floor. It didn't have gold leaf or gild edges, but the title was embossed in red, the color of fresh blood.

"He's . . ." Yavin licked his lips and tasted salt. "He's dead?"

Reb Shendelman shook his head and gently brushed his hand along one edge of the book before placing it on a shelf. It looked very lonely there all by itself.

"No, he's . . . only dreaming the story. We can't stay here, Yavin. His friends will come looking for him and I don't want you to be here when they burn this book."

"Reb Shendelman, you can't let them!"

"I can't stop them, Yavin. But what I can do, is get you out of this hell . . ."

"Reb Shendelman, please."

"Sha, Yavin. Listen to me. Do you know what my favorite part is in *Around the World in Eighty Days*? It's when they are all going up the Hudson River in America on that little boat. I have family in America . . . someplace called Upstate New York along that same river. What was the name of that boat, Yavin?"

"The *Henrietta*, Yavin answered and felt a numbing warmth began to grow in his belly.

"Ah, yoh, the little 'Henrietta' sailing past the lighthouse that marked the beginning of the river and the end of the ocean . . . the end of one world and the beginning of another. Do you see the lighthouse, Yavin? Do you see him, Phileas Fogg, walking up to the bridge because the captain is nowhere to be found? Do you see him? See it, Yavin . . . see it . . . see . . . it . . ."

"Passepartout," Phileas Fogg said to Yavin as he took the boat's wheel. "I fear Captain Speedy is still not enthusiastic about this diversion to Liverpool, so I ask that you keep him well tended . . . but, above all, well kept in his quarters."

"Of course, sir," Yavin said while carefully pouring the amber-colored tea into three dainty china cups—one for Mr. Phileas Fogg, one for Mademoiselle Aouda and the last for himself. "I shall see to his needs, have no fear."

"I never fear," Phileas Fogg said with a nod, "it is too time consuming. Now, if my calculations are correct, and there is nothing to say they aren't, the Henrietta should be more than able to make the three thousand mile crossing from New York to Liverpool in nine days, which would put us on good English soil again on the 21st of December—the Solstice, I believe."

Hanukkah, Yavin thought, but didn't say anything except, "One lump or two?"

* * *

"Wake up, Yavin."

Yavin opened his eyes, rubbing them against the bright yellow light that filled the small room. The room only looked small because it was filled with books—wall-to-wall and floor to ceiling, and encircling a narrow window through which Yavin saw a wide river bordered by high, rocky cliffs. A lighthouse, like the one the *Henrietta* had passed on her way to the sea, blinked at him from a high overlook across the river.

Reb Shendelman was standing over him, smiling in the bright yellow light.

"I was . . . dreaming."

"I know," Reb Shendelman said, "and now those dreams can come true."

Somewhere in My Mind
There Is a Painting Box

Charles de Lint

Charles de Lint [www.charlesdelint.com] lives in Ottawa, Ontario, with his wife Mary Ann Harris, an artist and musician. Together they perform Celtic and traditional music. De Lint popularized urban fantasy—fantasy set in the real world rather than an invented otherworld—in the 1980s with such books as Moonheart, and continues to tell tales of his trademark city, Newford. He's been a full-time writer for eighteen years. He has also written a monthly book review column for F&SF, and is a perceptive advocate of good fantasy fiction. His collections, Waifs and Strays (2002), his first Young Adult collection, and Tapping the Dream Tree, his fourth Newford collection and fiftieth book, came out in 2002. A Handful of Coppers is forthcoming in 2003, and is the first of a projected series collecting all his early stories. Spirits in the Wires is his next novel, and A Circle of Cats will be a hardcover picture book for children.

"Somewhere in My Mind There Is a Painting Box" is from the Young Adult fantasy anthology The Green Man, which is possibly the best anthology of the year, in a very strong year for fantasy anthologies. It is the story of landscape painters who accidentally find the way into fairyland, told from the point of view of a girl who finds one of their painting boxes twenty years later.

Such a thing to find, so deep in the forest: A painter's box nested in ferns and a tangle of sprucey-pine roots, almost buried by the leaves and pine needles drifted up against the trunk of the tree. Later, Lily would learn that it was called a pochade box, but for now she sat bouncing lightly on her ankles admiring her find.

It was impossible to say how long the box had been hidden here. The wood panels weren't rotting, but the hasps were rusted shut and it took her a while to get them open. She lifted the lid and then, and then . . .

Treasure.

Stored in the lid, held apart from each other by slots, were three 8 × 10 wooden panels, each with a painting on it. For all their quick and loose rendering, she had no trouble recognizing the subjects. There was something familiar about them, too—beyond the subject matter that she easily recognized.

The first was of the staircase waterfall where the creek took a sudden tumble before continuing on again at a more level pace. She had to fill in detail from her own memory and imagination, but she knew it was that place.

The second was of a long-deserted homestead up a side valley of the hollow, the tin roof sagging, the rotting walls falling inward. It was nothing like Aunt's cabin on its sunny slopes, surrounded by wild roses, old beehives, and an apple orchard that she and Aunt were slowly reclaiming from the wild. This was a place that would only get sun from midmorning through the early afternoon, a dark and damp hollow, where the dew never had a chance to burn off completely.

The last one could have been painted anywhere in this forest but she imagined it had been done down by the creek, looking up a slope into a view of yellow birches, beech, and

95

sprucey-pines growing dense and thick as the stars overhead, with a burst of light coming through a break in the canopy.

Lily studied each painting, then carefully set them aside on the ground beside her. There was the hint of another picture on the inside lid itself, but she couldn't make out what it was supposed to be.

The palette was covered in dried paint that, like the inside lid, almost had the look of a painting itself, and lifted from the box to reveal a compartment underneath. In the bottom of the box were tubes of oil paint, brushes, and a palette knife, a small bottle of turpentine and a rag stained with all the colors the artist had been using.

Lily turned the palette over and there she found what she'd been looking for. An identifying mark. She ran a finger over the letters that spelled out an impossible name.

Milo Johnson.

Treasure.

"Milo Johnson," Aunt repeated, trying to understand Lily's excitement. At seventeen, Lily could still get as wound up about a new thing as she had when she was a child. "Should I know that name?"

Lily gave her a "you never pay attention, do you?" look and went to get a book from her bookshelf. She didn't have many, but those she did have had been read over and over again. The one she brought back to the kitchen table was called *The Newford Naturalists: Redefining the Landscape*. Opening it to the first artist profiled, she underlined his name with her finger.

Aunt read silently along with her, mouthing the words, then studied the black-and-white photo of Johnson that accompanied the profile.

"I remember seeing him a time or two," she said. "Tramping through the woods with an old canvas knapsack on his back. But that was a long time ago."

"It would have to have been."

Aunt read a little more, then looked up.

"So he's famous then," she asked.

"Very. He went painting all through these hills and he's got pictures in galleries all over the world."

"Imagine that. And you reckon this is his box?"

Lily nodded.

"Well, we'd better see about returning it to him."

"We can't," Lily told her. "He's dead. Or at least they say he's dead. He and Frank Spain went out into the hills on a painting expedition and were never heard from again."

She flipped toward the back of the book until she came to the smaller section devoted to Spain's work. Johnson had been the giant among the Newford Naturalists, his bold, dynamic style instantly recognizable, even to those who might not know him by name, while Spain had been one of a group of younger artists that Johnson and his fellow Naturalists had been mentoring. He wasn't as well known as Johnson or the others, but he'd already been showing the potential to become a leader in his own right before he and Johnson had taken that last fateful trip.

It was all in the book which Lily had practically memorized by now, she'd read it so often.

Ever since Harlene Welch had given it to her a few years ago, Lily had wanted to grow up to be like the Naturalists—especially Johnson. Not to paint exactly the way they did, necessarily, but to have her own individual vision the way that they did. To be able to take the world of her beloved hills and forest and portray it in such a way that others would see it through her eyes, that they would see it in a new way and so understand her love for it and would want to protect it the way that she did.

"That was twenty years ago," Lily added, "and their bodies weren't ever recovered."

Twenty years ago. Imagine. The box had been lying lost in the woods for all that time.

"Never thought of painting pictures as being something dangerous," Aunt said.

"Anything can be dangerous," Lily replied. "That's what Beau says."

Aunt nodded. She reached across the table to turn the box toward her.

"So you plan on keeping it?" she asked.

"I guess."

"He must have kin. Don't you think it should go to them?"

Lily shook her head. "He was an orphan, just like me. The only people we could give it to would be in the museum and they'd just stick it away in some drawer somewhere."

"Even the pictures?"

"Well, probably not them. But the painting box for sure . . ."

Lily hungered to try the paints and brushes she'd found in the box. There was never enough money for her to think of being able to buy either.

"Well," Aunt said. "You found it, so I guess you get to decide what you do with it."

"I guess."

Finder's keepers, after all. But she couldn't help feeling that this find of hers—especially the paintings—belonged to everyone, not just some gangly backwoods girl who happened to come upon them while out on a ramble.

"I'll have to think on it," she added.

Aunt nodded, then got up to put on the kettle.

The next morning Lily went about her chores. She fed the chickens, sparing a few handfuls of feed for the sparrows and other birds that were waiting expectantly in the trees nearby. She milked the cow and poured some milk into a saucer for the cats that came out of the woods when she was done, purring and winding in between her legs until she set the saucer down. By the time she'd finished weeding the garden and filling the woodbox, it was midmorning.

She packed herself a lunch and stowed it in her shoulder satchel along with some carpenter's pencils and a pad of sketching paper she'd made from cutting up brown grocery bags.

"Off again, are you?" Aunt asked.

"I'll be home for dinner."

"You're not going to bring that box with you?"

She was tempted. The tubes of paint were rusted shut, but she'd squeezed the thin metal of their bodies and found that the paint inside was still pliable. The brushes were good, too. But her using them didn't seem right. Not yet, anyways.

"Not today," she told Aunt.

As she left the house she looked up to see a pair of dogs coming tearing up the slope toward her. They were the Shaffers' dogs, Max and Kiki, the one dark brown, the other white with black markings, the pair of them bundles of short-haired energy. The Shaffers lived beside the Welchs, who owned the farm at the end of the trail that ran from the county road to Aunt's cabin—an hour's walk through the woods as you followed the creek. Their dogs were a friendly pair, good at not chasing cows or game, and showed up every few days to accompany Lily on her rambles.

The dogs danced around her now as she set off through the orchard. When she got to the Apple Tree Man's tree—that's what Aunt called the oldest tree of the orchard—she pulled out a biscuit she'd saved from breakfast and set it down at its roots. It was a habit she'd had since she was a little girl, like feeding the birds and the cats while doing her morning chores. Aunt used to tease her about it, telling her what a good provider she was for the mice and raccoons.

"Shoo," she said as Kiki went for the biscuit. "That's not for you. You'll have to wait for lunch to get yours."

They climbed up to the top of the hill and then went into the woods, the dogs chasing each other in circles while Lily kept stopping to investigate some interesting seed pod or cluster of weeds. They had lunch a couple of miles further on, sitting on a stone outcrop that overlooked the Big Sinkhole, a two- or three-acre depression with the entrance to a cave at the bottom.

Most of the mountains around Aunt's cabin were riddled with caves of all shapes and sizes. There were entrances everywhere, though most only went a few yards in before they ended. But some said you could walk from one end of the Kickaha Hills to the other, all underground, if you knew the way.

Lunch finished, Lily slid down from the rock. She didn't feel like drawing today. Instead she kept thinking about the painting box, how odd it had been to find it after its having been lost for so many years, so she led the dogs back to that part of the woods to see what else she might find. A shiver went up her spine. What if she found their bones?

The dogs grew more playful as she neared the spot where she'd come upon the box. They nipped at her sleeves or crouched ahead of her, butts and tails in the air, growling so fiercely they made her laugh. Finally Max bumped her leg with his head just as she was in midstep. She lost her balance and fell into a pile of leaves, her satchel tumbling to the ground, spilling drawings.

She sat up. A smile kept twitching at the corner of her mouth but she managed to give them a pretty fierce glare.

"Two against one?" she said. "Well, come on, you bullies. I'm ready for you."

She jumped on Kiki and wrestled her to the ground, the dog squirming with delight in her grip. Max joined the tussle and soon the three of them were rolling about in the leaves like the puppies the dogs no longer were and Lily had never been. They were having such fun that at first none of them heard the shouting. When they did, they stopped their rough-housing to find a man standing nearby, holding a stick in his upraised hand.

"Get away from her!" he cried, waving the stick.

Lily sat up, so many leaves tangled in her hair and caught in her sweater that she had more on her than did some of the autumned trees around them. She put a hand on the collar of either dog, but, curiously, neither seemed inclined to bark or chase the stranger off. They stayed by her side, staring at him.

Lily studied him for a long moment, too, as quiet as the dogs. He wasn't a big man, but he seemed solid, dressed in a fraying broadcloth suit with a white shirt underneath and worn leather boots on his feet. His hair was roughly trimmed and he looked as if he hadn't shaved for a few days. But he had a good face—strong features, laugh lines around his eyes and the corners of his mouth. She didn't think he was much older than her.

"It's all right," she told the man. "We were just funning."

There was something familiar about him, but she couldn't place it immediately.

"Of course," he said, dropping the stick. "How stupid can I be? What animal in this forest would harm its Lady?" He went down on his knees. "Forgive my impertinence."

This was too odd for words, from the strange behavior of the dogs to the man's even stranger behavior. She couldn't speak. Then something changed in the man's eyes. There'd been a lost look in them a moment ago, but also hope. Now there was only resignation.

"You're just a girl," he said.

Lily found her voice at that indignity.

"I'm seventeen," she told him. "In these parts, there's some would think I'm already an old maid."

He shook his head. "Your pardon. I meant no insult."

Lily relaxed a little. "That's all right."

He reached over to where her drawings had spilled from her satchel and put them back in, looking at each one for a moment before he did.

"These are good," he said. "Better than good."

For those few moments while he looked through her drawings, while he looked at them carefully, one by one, before replacing them in her satchel, he seemed different once more. Not so lost. Not so sad.

"Thank you," she said.

She waited a moment, thinking it might be rude of her to follow a compliment with a question that might be considered prying. She waited until the last drawing was back in her satchel and he sat there holding the leather bag on his lap, his gaze gone she didn't know where.

"What are you doing here in the woods?" she finally asked.

It took a moment before his gaze returned to her. He closed the satchel and laid it on the grass between them.

"I took you for someone else," he said, which wasn't an answer at all. "It was the wild tangle of your red hair—the leaves in it and on your sweater. But you're too young and your skin's not a coppery brown."

"And this explains what?" she asked.

"I thought you were Her," he said.

Lily could hear the emphasis he put on the word, but it still didn't clear up her confusion.

"I don't know what you're talking about," she said.

She started to pluck the leaves out of her hair and brush them from her sweater. The dogs lay down, one on either side of her, still curiously subdued.

"I thought you were the Lady of the Wood," he explained. "She who stepped out of a tree and welcomed us when we came out of the cave between the worlds. She wears a cloak of leaves and has moonlight in Her eyes."

A strange feeling came over Lily when he said "stepped out of a tree." She found herself remembering a fever dream she'd once had—five years ago when she'd been snake bit. It had been so odd. She'd dreamed that she'd been changed into a kitten to save her from the snake bite, met Aunt's Apple Tree Man and another wood spirit called the Father of Cats. She'd even seen the fairies she'd tried to find for so long: foxfired shapes, bobbing in the meadow like fireflies.

That dream had seemed so real.

She blinked away the memory of it and focused on the stranger again. He'd gotten off his knees and was sitting cross-legged on the ground, a half dozen feet from where she and the dogs were.

"What did you mean when you said 'us'?" she asked.

Now it was his turn to look confused.

"You said this lady showed 'us' some cave."

He nodded. "I was out painting with Milo when—"

As soon as he mentioned that name, the earlier sense of familiarity collided with her memory of a photo in her book on the Newford Naturalists.

"You're Frank Spain!" Lily cried.

He nodded in agreement.

"But that can't be," she said. "You don't look any older than you do in the picture in my book."

"What book?"

"The one about Milo Johnson and the rest of the Newford Naturalists that's back at the cabin."

"There's a book about us?"

"You're famous," Lily told him with a grin. "The book says you and Mr. Johnson disappeared twenty years ago while you were out painting in these very hills."

Frank shook his head, the shock plain in his features.

"Twenty . . . years?" he said slowly. "How's that even possible? We've only been gone for a few days . . ."

"What happened to you?" Lily asked.

"I don't really know," he said. "We'd come here after a winter of being cooped up in the studio, longing to paint in the landscape itself. We meant to stay until the black flies drove us back to the city but then . . ." He shook his head. "Then we found the cave and met the Lady. . . ."

He seemed so lost and confused that Lily took him home.

Aunt greeted his arrival and introduction with a raised eyebrow. Lily knew what she was thinking. First a painting box, now a painter. What would be next?

But Aunt had never turned anyone away from her cabin before and she wasn't about to start now. She had Lily show Frank to where he could draw some water from the well and clean up, then set a third plate for supper. It wasn't until later when they were sitting out on the porch drinking tea and watching the night fall that Frank told them his story. He spoke of how he and Milo had found the cave that led them through darkness into another world. How they'd met the Lady there, with Her cloak of leaves and Her coppery skin, Her dark, dark eyes and Her fox-red hair.

"So there is an underground way through these mountains," Aunt said. "I always reckoned there was some truth to that story."

Frank shook his head. "The cave didn't take us to the other side of the mountains. It took us out of this world and into another."

Aunt smiled. "Next thing you're going to tell me is you've been to Fairyland."

"Look at him," Lily said. She went inside and got her book, opening it to the photograph of Frank Spain. "He doesn't look any older than he did when this picture was taken."

Aunt nodded. "Some people do age well."

"Not this well," Lily said.

Aunt turned to Frank. "So what is it that you're asking us to believe?"

"I'm not asking anything," he said. "I don't believe it myself."

Lily sighed and took the book over to him. She showed him the copyright date, put her finger on the paragraph that described how he and Milo Johnson had gone missing some fifteen years earlier.

"The book's five years old," she said. "But I think we've got a newspaper that's no more than a month old. I could show you the date on it."

But Frank was already shaking his head. He'd gone pale reading the paragraph about the mystery of his and his mentor's disappearance. He lifted his gaze to meet Aunt's.

"I guess maybe we were in Fairyland," he said, his voice gone soft.

Aunt looked from Lily's face to that of her guest.

"How's that possible?" she said.

"I truly don't know," he told her.

He turned the pages of the book, stopping to read the section on himself. Lily knew what he was reading. His father had died in a mining accident when he was still a boy, but his mother had been alive when he'd disappeared. She'd died five years later.

"My parents are gone, too," she told him.

He nodded, his eyes shiny.

Lily shot Aunt a look, but Aunt sat in her chair, staring out into the gathering dusk, an unreadable expression in her features. Lily supposed it was one thing to appreciate a fairy tale but quite another to find yourself smack dab in the middle of one.

Lily was taking it the best of either of them. Maybe it was because of that snake bite fever dream she'd had. In the past five years she still woke from dreams in which she'd been a kitten.

"Why did you come back?" she asked Frank.

"I didn't know I was coming back," he said. "That world . . ." He flipped a few pages back to show them reproductions of Johnson's paintings. "That's what this other world's like. You don't have to imagine everything being more of itself than it seems to be here like Milo's done in these paintings. Over there it's really like that. You can't imagine the colors, the intensity, the rich wash that fills your heart as much as it does your eyes. We haven't painted at all since we got over there. We didn't need to." He laughed. "I know Milo abandoned his paints before we crossed over and to tell you the truth, I don't even know where mine are."

"I found Mr. Johnson's box," Lily said. "Yesterday—not far from where you came upon me and the dogs."

He nodded, but she didn't think he'd heard her.

"I was walking," he said. "Looking for the Lady. We hadn't seen Her for a day or so and I wanted to talk to Her again. To ask Her about that place. I remember I came to this grove of sycamore and beech where we'd seen Her a time or two. I stepped in between the trees, out of the sun and into the shade. The next thing I knew I was walking in these hills and I was back here where everything seems . . . paler. Subdued."

He looked at them.

"I've got to go back," he said. "There's no place for me here. Ma's gone and everybody I knew'll be dead like her or too changed for me to know them anymore." He tapped the book. "Just like me, according to what it says here."

"You don't want to go rushing into anything," Aunt said. "Surely you've got other kin, and they'll be wanting to see you."

"There's no one. Me and Ma, we were the last of the Spains that I know."

Aunt nodded in a way that Lily recognized. It was her way of making you think she agreed with you, but she was really just waiting for common sense to take hold of you so that you didn't go off half-cocked and get yourself in some kind of trouble you didn't need to get into.

"You'll want to rest up," she said. "You can sleep in the barn. Lily will show you where. Come morning, everything'll make a lot more sense."

He just looked at her. "How do you make sense out of something like this?"

"You trust me on this," she said. "A good night's sleep does a body wonders."

So he followed her advice—most people did when Aunt had decided what was best for them.

He let Lily take him down to the barn where they made a bed for him in the straw. She wondered if he'd try to kiss her, and how she'd feel if he did, but she never got the chance to find out.

"Thank you," he said and then he lay down on the blankets.

He was already asleep by the time she was closing the door.

And in the morning he was gone.

That night Lily had one of what she thought of as her storybook dreams. She wasn't a kitten this time. Instead she was sitting under the Apple Tree Man's tree and he stepped out of the trunk of his tree just like she remembered him doing five years ago. He looked the same, too, a raggedy man, gnarled and twisty, like the boughs of his tree.

"You," she only said and looked away.

"That's a fine welcome for an old friend."

"You're not my friend. Friends aren't magical men who live in a tree and then make you feel like you're crazy because they never show up in your life again."

"And yet I helped you when you were a kitten."

"In the fever dream when I *thought* I was a kitten."

He came around and sat on his haunches in front of her, all long gangly limbs and tattered clothes and bird's nest hair. His face was wrinkled like the dried fruit from his tree.

He sighed. "It was better for you to only remember it as a dream."

"So it wasn't a dream?" she asked, unable to keep the eagerness from her voice. "You're real? You and the Father of Cats and the fairies in the field?"

"Someplace we're real."

She looked at him for a long moment, then nodded, disappointment taking the place of her momentary happiness.

"This is just a dream, too, isn't it?" she said.

"This is. What happened before wasn't."

She poked at the dirt with her finger, looking away from him again.

"Why would it be better for me to remember it as a dream?" she asked.

"Our worlds aren't meant to mix—not anymore. They've grown too far apart. When you spend too much time in ours, you become like your painter foundling, forever restless and unhappy in the world where you belong. Instead of living your life, you lose yourself in dreams and fancies."

"Maybe for some, dreams and fancies are better than what they have here."

"Maybe," he said, but she knew he didn't agree. "Is that true for you?"

"No," she had to admit. "But I still don't understand why I was allowed that one night and then no more."

She looked at him. His dark eyes were warm and kind, but there was a mystery in them, too. Something secret and daunting that she wasn't sure she could ever understand. That perhaps she shouldn't want to understand.

"What you do is important," he said after a long moment, which wasn't much of an answer at all.

She laughed. "What *I* do? Whatever do I do that could be so important?"

"Perhaps it's not what you do now so much as what you will do if you continue with your drawing and painting."

She shook her head. "I'm not really that good."

"Do you truly believe that?"

She remembered what Frank Spain had said after looking at her drawings.

These are good. Better than good.

She remembered how the drawings had, if only for a moment, taken him away from the sadness that lay so heavy in his heart.

"But I'm only drawing the woods," she said. "I'm drawing what I see, not fairies and fancies."

The Apple Tree Man nodded. "Sometimes people need fairies and fancies to wake them up to what they already have. But sometimes a good drawing of a real thing does it better."

"So is that why you came to me tonight?" she asked. "To tell me to keep doing something I'm going to go on doing anyway?"

He shook his head.

"Then why did you come?"

"To ask you not to look for that cave," he said. "To not go in. If you do, you'll carry the yearning of what you find inside yourself forever."

What the Apple Tree Man had told her all seemed to make perfect sense in last night's dream. But when she woke to find Frank gone, what had made sense then didn't seem to be nearly enough now. Knowing she'd once experienced a real glimpse into a storybook world, she only found herself wanting more.

"Well, it seems like a lot of trouble to go through," Aunt said when Lily came back from the barn with the news that their guest was gone. "To cadge a meal and a roof over your head for the night, I mean."

"I don't think he was lying."

Aunt shrugged.

"But he looked *just* like the picture in my book."

"There was a resemblance," Aunt said. "But really. The story he told—it's too hard to believe."

"Then how do you explain it?"

Aunt thought for a moment, then shook her head.

"Can't say that I can," she admitted.

"I think he's gone to look for the cave. He wants to go back."

"And I suppose you want to go looking for him."

Lily nodded.

"Are you sweet on him?" Aunt asked.

"I don't think I am."

"Can't say's I'd blame you. He was a good-looking man."

"I'm just worried about him," Lily said. "He's all lost and alone and out of his own time."

"And say you find him. Say you find the cave. What then?"

The Apple Tree Man's warning and Aunt's obvious concern struggled against her own desire to find the cave, to see the magical land that lay beyond it.

"I'd have the chance to say good-bye," she said.

There. She hadn't exactly lied. She hadn't said everything she could have, but she hadn't lied.

Aunt studied her for a long moment.

"You just be careful," she said. "See to the cow and chickens, but the garden can wait till you get back."

Lily grinned. She gave Aunt a quick kiss, then packed herself a lunch. She was almost out the door when she turned back and took Milo Johnson's painting box out from under her bed.

"Going to try those paints?" Aunt asked.

"I think so."

And she did, but it wasn't nearly the success she'd hoped it would be.

The morning started fine, but then walking in these woods of hers was a sure cure for any ailment, especially when it was in your heart or head. The dogs hadn't come to join her today, but that was all right. She could be just as happy on her own here.

She made her way down to that part of the wood where she'd first found the box, and then later Frank, but he was nowhere about. Either he'd found his way back into fairyland, or he was just ignoring her voice. Finally she gave up and spent a while looking for this cave of his, but there were too many in this part of the forest and none of them looked—no, none of them *felt* right.

After lunch, she sat down and opened the painting box.

The drawing she did on the back of one of Johnson's three paintings turned out well, though it was odd using her pencil on a wood panel. But she'd gotten the image she wanted: the sweeping boughs of an old beech tree, smooth-barked and tall, the thick crush of underbrush around it, the forest behind. It was the colors that proved to be a problem. The paints wouldn't do what she wanted. It was hard enough to get each tube open, they were stuck so tight, but once she had a squirt of the various colors on the palette it all went downhill from there.

The colors were wonderfully bright—pure pigments that had their own inner glow. At least they did until she started messing with them and then everything turned to mud. When she tried to mix them she got either outlandish hues or colors so dull they all might as well have been the same. The harder she tried, the worse it got.

Sighing, she finally wiped off the palette and the panel she'd been working on, then cleaned the brushes, dipping them in the little jar of turpentine, working the paint out of the hairs with a rag. She studied Johnson's paintings as she worked, trying to figure out how he'd gotten the colors he had. This was his box, after all. These were the same colors he'd used to paint these three amazing paintings. Everything she needed was just lying there in the box, waiting to be used. So why was she so hopeless?

It was because painting was no different than looking for fairies, she supposed. No different than trying to find that cave entrance into some magic elsewhere. Some people just weren't any good at that sort of thing.

They were both magic, after all. Art as well as fairies. Magic. What else could you call how Johnson was able to bring the forest to life with no more than a few colors on a flat surface?

She could practice, of course. And she would. She hadn't been any good when she'd first started drawing either. But she wasn't sure that she'd ever feel as . . . inspired as Johnson must have felt.

She studied the inside lid of the box. Even this abstract pattern where he'd probably only been testing his color mixes had so much vibrancy and passion. She leaned closer for a better look and found herself thinking about her Newford Naturalists book, about something Milo Johnson was supposed to have said. "It's not just a matter of painting *en plein air* as the Impressionists taught us," the author quoted Johnson. "It's just as important to simply *be* in the wilds. Many times the only painting box I take is in my head. You don't have to be an artist to bring something back from your wilderness experiences. My best paintings don't hang in galleries. They hang somewhere in between my ears—an endless private showing that I can only attempt to share with others through a more physical medium."

That must be why he'd abandoned this painting box she'd found. He'd gone into fairyland only bringing the one in his head. She didn't know if she could ever learn to do that.

She sighed and was about to get up and go when she thought she heard something—an almost-music. It was like listening to ravens in the woods when their rough, deep-throated croaks and cries all but seemed like human language. It wasn't, of course, but still, you felt *so* close to understanding it.

She lifted her head to look around. It wasn't ravens she heard. It wasn't anything she knew, but it still seemed familiar. Faint, but insistent. Almost like wind chimes or distant bells, but not quite. Almost like birdsong, trills and warbling melodies, but not quite. Almost like an old fiddle tune, played on a pipe or a flute, the rhythm a little ragged, or simply a little out of time like the curious jumps and extra beats in a Kickaha tune. But not quite.

Closing the painting box, she stood. She slung her satchel from her shoulder, picked up the box, and turned in a slow circle. The sound was stronger to the west, away from the creek and deeper into the forest. A ravine cut off to the left and she followed it, pushing her way through the thick shrub layer of rhododendrons and mountain laurel. Hemlocks and tulip trees rose up the slopes on either side with a thick understory of redbud, magnolia, and dogwood.

The almost-music continued to pull her along—distant, near, distant, near, like a radio signal that couldn't quite hang on to a station. It was only when she broke through into a small clearing, a wall of granite rising above her, that she saw the mouth of the cave.

She knew immediately that this had to be the cave Frank had been looking for, the one into which he and Milo Johnson had stepped and so disappeared from the world for twenty years. The almost-music was clearer than ever here, but it was the bas-relief worked into the stone above the entrance that made her sure. Here was Frank's Lady, a rough carving of a woman's face. Her hair was thick with leaves and more leaves came spilling out of her mouth, bearding her chin.

Aunt's general warnings, as well as the Apple Tree Man's more specific ones, returned to her as she moved closer. She lifted a hand to trace the contours of the carving. As soon as she touched it, the almost-music stopped.

She dropped her hand, starting back as though she'd put a finger on a hot stove. She looked around herself with quick, nervous glances. Now that the almost-music was gone, she found herself standing in an eerie pocket of silence. The sounds of the forest were muted, as the music had been earlier. She could still hear the insects and birdsong, but they seemed to come from far away.

She turned back to the cave, uneasy now. In the back of her mind she could hear the Apple Tree Man's voice.

Don't go in.

I won't. Not all the way.

But now that she was here, how could she not at least have a look?

She went as far as the entrance, ducking her head because the top of the hole was only as high as her shoulder. It was dark inside, too dark to see in the beginning. But slowly her eyes adjusted to the dimmer lighting.

The first thing she really saw were the paintings.

They were like her own initial attempts at drawing—crude, stick figures and shapes that she'd drawn on scraps of paper and the walls of the barn with the charred ends of sticks. Except, where hers had been simple because she could do no better, these, she realized as she studied them more closely, were more like stylized abbreviations. Where her drawings had been tentative, these held power. The paint or chalk had been applied with bold, knowing strokes. Nothing wasted. Complex images distilled to their primal essences.

An antlered man. A turtle. A bear with a sun on its chest, radiating squiggles of light. A leaping stag. A bird of some sort with enormous wings. A woman, cloaked in leaves. Trees of every shape and size. Lightning bolts. A toad. A spiral with the face of the woman on the entrance outside in its center. A fox with an enormous striped tail. A hare with drooping ears and small deer horns.

And more. So many more. Some easily recognizable, others only geometric shapes that seemed to hold whole books of stories in their few lines.

Her gaze traveled over the walls, studying the paintings with growing wonder and admiration. The cave was one of the larger ones she'd found—easily three or four times the size of Aunt's cabin. There were paintings everywhere, many too hard to make out because they were lost in deeper shadows. She wished she had a corn shuck or lantern to throw more light than what came from the opening behind her. She longed to move closer, but still didn't dare abandon the safety of the entranceway.

She might have left it like that, drunk her fill of the paintings and then gone home, if her gaze hadn't fallen upon a figure sitting hunched in a corner of the cave, holding what looked like a small bark whistle. She'd made the same kind herself from the straight smooth branches of a chestnut or a sourwood tree.

But the whistle was quiet now. Frank sat so still, enveloped in the shadows, that she might never have noticed him except as she had, by chance.

"Frank . . . ?" she said.

He lifted his head to look at her.

"It's gone," he said. "I can't call it back."

"The other world?"

He nodded.

"That was you making that . . . music?"

"It was me doing something," he said. "I don't know that I'd go so far as to call it music."

Lily hesitated a long moment, then finally stepped through the entrance, into the cave itself. She flinched as she crossed the threshhold, but nothing happened. There were no flaring lights or sudden sounds. No door opened into another world, sucking her in.

She set the painting box down and sat on her ankles in front of Frank.

"I didn't know you were a musician," she said.

"I'm not."

He held up his reed whistle—obviously something he'd made himself.

"But I used to play as a boy," he said. "And there was always music there, on the other side. I thought I could wake something. Call me to it, or it to me."

Lily raised her eyes to the paintings on the wall.

"How did you cross over the first time?" she asked.

He shook his head. "I don't know. That was Milo's doing. I was only tagging along."

"Did he . . . did he make a painting?"

Frank's gaze settled on hers.

"What do you mean?" he asked.

She pointed to the walls. "Look around you. This is *the* cave, isn't it?"

He nodded.

"What do you think these paintings are for?" she asked. When he still didn't seem to get it, she added, "Perhaps it's the paintings that open a door between the worlds. Maybe this Lady of yours likes pictures more than She does music."

Frank scrambled to his feet and studied the walls as though he was seeing the paintings for the first time. Lily was slower to rise.

"If I had paint, I could try it," he said.

"There's the painting box I found," Lily told him. "It's still full of paints."

He grinned. Grabbing her arms, he gave her a kiss, right on her lips, full of passion and fire, then bent down to open the box.

"I remember this box," he said as he rummaged through the paint tubes. "We were out painting, scouting a good location—though for Milo, any location was a good one. Anyway, there we were, out in these woods, when suddenly Milo stuffs this box of his into a tangle of tree roots and starts walking. I called after him, but he never said a word, never even turned around to see if I was coming.

"So I followed, hurrying along behind him until we finally came to this cave. And then . . . then . . ."

He looked up at Lily. "I'm not sure what happened. One moment we were walking into the cave and the next we had crossed over into that other place."

"So Milo didn't paint on the wall."

"I just don't remember. But he might not have had to. Milo could create whole paintings in his head without ever putting brush to canvas. And he could describe that painting to you, stroke for stroke—even years later."

"I read about that in the book."

"Hmm."

Frank had returned his attention to the paints.

"It'll have to be a specific image," he said, talking as much to himself as to Lily. "Something simple that still manages to encompass everything a person is or feels."

"An icon," Lily said, remembering the word from another of her books.

He nodded in agreement as he continued to sort through the tubes of paint, finally choosing a color: a burnt umber, rich and dark.

"And then?" Lily asked, remembering what the Apple Tree Man had told her in her dream. "Just saying you find the right image. You paint it on the wall and some kind of door opens up. Then what do you do?"

He looked up at her, puzzled.

"I'll step through it," he said. "I'll go back to the other side."

"But why?" Lily asked. "Why's over there so much better than the way the world is here?"

"I . . ."

"When you cross over to there," Lily said, echoing the Apple Tree man's words to her, "you give up all the things you could be here."

"We do that every time we make any change in our lives," Frank said. "It's like moving from one town to another, though this is a little more drastic, I suppose." He considered it for a moment, then added, "It's not so much *better* over there as different. I've never fit in here the way I do over there. And now I don't have anything left for me here except for this burn inside—a yearning for the Lady and that land of Hers that lies somewhere on the other side of these fields we know."

"I've had that feeling," Lily said, thinking of her endless search for fairies as a child.

"You can't begin to imagine what it's like over there," Frank went on. "Everything glows with its own inner light."

He paused and regarded her for a long moment.

"You could come," he said finally. "You could come with me and see for yourself. Then you'd understand."

Lily shook her head. "No, I couldn't. I couldn't walk out on Aunt, not like this, without a word. Not after she took me in when no one else would. She wasn't even real family, though she's family now." She waited a beat, remembering the strength of his arms, the hard kiss he'd given her, then added. "You could stay."

Now it was his turn to shake his head.

"I can't."

Lily nodded. She understood. It wasn't like she didn't have the desire to go herself.

She watched him unscrew the paint tube and squeeze a

long worm of dark brown pigment into his palm. He turned to a clear spot on the wall, dipped a finger into the paint and raised his hand. But then he hesitated.

"You can do it," Lily told him.

Maybe she couldn't go. Maybe she wanted him to stay. But she knew enough not to try to hold him back if he had to go. It was no different than making friends with a wild creature. You could catch them and tie them up and make them stay with you, but their heart would never be yours. Their wild heart, the thing you loved about them . . . it would wither and die. So why would you want to do such a thing?

"I can," Frank agreed, his voice soft. He gave her a smile. "That's part of the magic, isn't it? You have to believe that it will work."

Lily had no idea if that was true or not, but she gave him an encouraging nod all the same.

He hummed something under his breath as he lifted his hand again. Lily recognized it as the almost-music she'd heard before, but now she could make out the tune. She didn't know its name, but the pick-up band at the grange dances played it from time to time. She thought it might have the word "fairy" in it.

Frank's finger moved decisively, smearing paint on the rock. It took Lily a moment to see that he was painting a stylized oak leaf. He finished the last line and took his finger away, stepped back.

Neither knew what to expect, if anything. As the moments dragged by, Frank stopped humming. He cleaned his hands against the legs of his trousers, smearing paint onto the cloth. His shoulders began to slump and he turned to her.

"Look," Lily said before he could speak.

She pointed to the wall. The center of the oak leaf he'd painted had started to glow with a warm, green-gold light. They watched the light spread across the wall of the cave, moving out from the central point like ripples from a stone tossed into a still pool of water. Other colors appeared, blues and reds and deeper greens. The colors shimmered, like they were painted on cloth touched by some unseen wind, and then the wall was gone and they were looking through an opening in the rock. Through a door into another world.

There was a forest over there, not much different than the one they'd left behind except that, as Frank had said, every tree, every leaf, every branch and blade of grass, pulsed with its own inner light. It was so bright it almost hurt the eyes, and not simply because they'd been standing in this dim cave for so long.

Everything had a light and a song and it was almost too much to bear. But at the same time, Lily felt the draw of that world like a tightening in her heart. It wasn't so much a wanting, as a need.

"Come with me," Frank said again.

She had never wanted to do something more in her life. It was not just going to that magical place, it was the idea of being there with this man with his wonderfully creative mind and talent. This man who'd given her her first real kiss.

But slowly she shook her head.

"Have you ever stood on a mountaintop," she asked, "and watched the sun set in a bed of feathery clouds? Have you ever watched the monarchs settled on a field of milkweed or listened to the spring chorus after the long winter's done?"

Frank nodded.

"This world has magic, too," Lily said.

"But not enough for me," Frank said. "Not after having been over there."

"I know."

She stepped up to him and gave him a kiss. He held her for a moment, returning the kiss, then they stepped back from each other.

"Go," Lily said, giving him a little push. "Go before I change my mind."

She saw he understood that, for her, going would be as much a mistake as staying would be for him. He nodded and turned, walked out into that other world.

Lily stood watching him go. She watched him step in among the trees. She heard him call out and heard another man's voice reply. She watched as the doorway became a swirl of colors once more. Just before the light faded, it seemed to take the shape of a woman's face—the same woman whose features had been carved into the stone outside the cave, leaves in her hair, leaves spilling from her mouth. Then it was all gone. The cave was dim once more and she was alone.

Lily knelt down by Milo Johnson's paint box and closed the lid, fastened the snaps. Holding it by its handle, she stood up and walked slowly out of the cave.

"Are you there?" she asked later, standing by the Apple Tree Man's tree. "Can you hear me?"

She took a biscuit from her pocket—the one she hadn't left earlier in the day because she'd still been angry for his appearing in her dream last night when he'd been absent from her life for five years. When he'd let her think that her night of magic had been nothing more than a fever dream brought on by a snake bite.

She put the biscuit down among his roots.

"I just wanted you to know that you were probably right," she said. "About my going over to that other place, I mean. Not about how I can't have magic here."

She sat down on the grass and laid the paint box down beside her, her satchel on top of it. Plucking a leaf from the ground, she began to shred it.

"I know, I know," she said. "There's plenty of everyday magic all around me. And I do appreciate it. But I don't know what's so wrong about having a magical friend as well."

There was no reply. No gnarled Apple Tree Man stepping out of his tree. No voice as she'd heard in her dream last night. She hadn't really been expecting anything.

"I'm going to ask Aunt if I can have an acre or so for my own garden," she said. "I'll try growing cane there and sell the molasses at the harvest fair. Maybe put in some berries and make preserves and pies, too. I'll need some real money to buy more paints."

She smiled and looked up into the tree's boughs.

"So you see, I can take advice. Maybe you should give it a try."

She stood up and dusted off her knees, picked up the painting box and her satchel.

"I'll bring you another biscuit tomorrow morning," she said.

Then she started down the hill to Aunt's cabin.

"Thank you," a soft, familiar voice said.

She turned. There was no one there, but the biscuit was gone.

She grinned. "Well, that's a start," she said and continued on home.

The Pyramid of Amirah

James Patrick Kelly

James Patrick Kelly [www.jimkelly.net] is well known and an award winner for his science fiction stories, but in fact he has written novels, short stories, essays, reviews, poetry, plays, and planetarium shows. He writes a column on the Internet for Asimov's Science Fiction Magazine, with which his fiction is closely associated, and his audio plays are a regular feature on Scifi.com's Seeing Ear Theater. He informs us that he is currently one of fourteen councilors appointed to the New Hampshire State Council on the Arts and also serves on the board of directors of the New England Foundation for the Arts. His collections include Strange But Not a Stranger (2002) and Think Like a Dinosaur and Other Stories (1997), and his novels include Wildlife (1994) and Look Into the Sun (1989).

"The Pyramid of Amirah" appeared in F&SF, and is one of Kelly's occasional fantasy stories. Kelly said in an interview (at www.SCIFI.com), "Whenever I write a story that supposes that God exists, I have to imagine that Her ways are mysterious—and therefore scary—indeed. God is the ultimate alien." This story is about a teenage girl who has been chosen as a human sacrifice. It reminds us that there are many stories in scripture that are scary and disturbing.

Sometimes Amirah thinks she can sense the weight of the pyramid that entombs her house. The huge limestone blocks seem to crush the air and squeeze light. When she carries the table lamp onto the porch and holds it up to the blank stone, shadows ooze across the rough-cut inner face. If she is in the right mood, they make cars and squirrels and flowers and Mom's face.

Time passes.

Amirah will never see the outside of her pyramid, but she likes to imagine different looks for it. It's like trying on new jeans. They said that the limestone would be cased in some kind of marble they called Rosa Portagallo. She hopes it will be like Betty's Pyramid, red as sunset, glossy as her fingernails. Are they setting it yet? Amirah thinks not. She can still hear the dull, distant *chock* as the believers lower each structural stone into place—twenty a day. Dust wisps from the cracks between the stones and settles through the thick air onto every horizontal surface of her house: the floor, Dad's desk, windowsills and the tops of the kitchen cabinets. Amirah doesn't mind; she goes over the entire house periodically with vacuum and rag. She wants to be ready when the meaning comes.

Time passes.

The only thing she really misses is the sun. Well, that isn't true. She misses her Mom and her Dad and her friends on the swim team, especially Janet. She and Janet offered themselves to the meaning at Blessed Finger Sanctuary on Janet's twelfth birthday. Neither of them expected to be chosen pyramid girl. They thought maybe they would be throwing flowers off a float in the Monkey Day parade or collecting door to door for the Lost Brothers. Janet shrieked with joy and hugged her when Mrs. Munro told them the news. If her friend hadn't held her up, Amirah might have collapsed.

Amirah keeps all the lights on, even when she goes to bed. She knows this is a waste of electricity, but it's easier to be brave when the house is bright. Besides, there is nobody to scold her now.

"Is there?" Amirah says, and then she walks into the kitchen to listen. Sometimes the house makes whispery noises when she talks to it. "Is there anyone here who cares what I do?" Her voice sounds like the hinges of the basement door.

Time passes.

They took all the clocks, and she has lost track of day and night. She sleeps when she is tired and eats when she is hungry. That's all there is to do, except wait for the meaning to come. Mom and Dad's bedroom is filled to the ceiling with cartons of Goody-goody Bars: Nut Raisin, Cherry Date, Chocolate Banana, and Cinnamon Apple, which is not her favorite. Mrs. Munro said there were enough to last her for years. At first that was a comfort. Now Amirah tries not to think about it.

Time passes.

Amirah's pyramid is the first in the Tri-City area. They said it would be twenty meters tall. She had worked it out afterward that twenty meters was almost seventy feet. Mom said that if the meaning had first come to Memphis, Tennessee, instead of Memphis, Egypt, then maybe everything would have been in American instead of metric. Dad had laughed at that and said then Elvis would have been the First Brother. Mom didn't like him making fun of the meaning. If she wanted to laugh, she would have him tell one of the Holy Jokes.

"What's the first law of religion?" Amirah says in her best imitation of Dad's voice.

"For every religion, there exists an equal and opposite religion," she says in Mom's voice.

"What's the second law of religion?" says Dad's voice.

"They're both wrong." Mom always laughs at that.

The silence goes all breathy, like Amirah is holding seashells up to both ears. "I don't get it," she says.

She can't hear building sounds anymore. The dust has stopped falling.

Time passes.

When Amirah was seven, her parents took her to Boston to visit Betty's Pyramid. The bus driver said that the believers had torn down a hundred and fifty houses to make room for it. Amirah could feel Betty long before she could see her pyramid; Mom said the meaning was very strong in Boston.

Amirah didn't understand much about the meaning back then. While the bus was stopped at a light, she had a vision of her heart swelling up inside her like a balloon and lifting her out the window and into the bluest part of the sky where she could see everything there was to see. The whole bus was feeling Betty by then. Dad told the Holy Joke about the chicken and the Bible in a loud voice and soon everyone was laughing so hard that the bus driver had to pull over. She and Mom and Dad walked the last three blocks and the way Amirah remembered it, her feet only touched the ground a couple of times. The pyramid was huge in a way that no skyscraper could ever be. She heard Dad tell Mom it was more like geography than architecture. Amirah was going to ask him what that meant, only she realized that *she* knew because *Betty* knew. The marble of Betty's pyramid was incredibly smooth but it was cold to the touch. Amirah spread the fingers of both hands against it and thought very hard about Betty.

"Are you there, Betty?" Amirah sits up in bed. "What's it like?" All the lights are on in the house. "Betty?" Amirah can't sleep because her stomach hurts. She gets up and goes to the bathroom to pee. When she wipes herself, there is a pinkish stain on the toilet paper.

Time passes.

Amirah also misses Juicy Fruit gum and Onion Taste Tots and 3DV and music. She hasn't seen her shows since Dad shut the door behind him and led Mom down the front walk. Neither of them looked back, but she thought Mom might have been crying. Did Mom have doubts? This still bothers Amirah. She wonders what Janet is listening to these days on her earstone. Have the Stiffies released any new songs? When Amirah sings, she practically has to scream or else the pyramid swallows her voice.

"Go, go away, go-go away from me.

Had fun, we're done, whyo-why can't you see?"

Whenever she finishes a Goody-goody bar, she throws the wrapper out the front door. The walk has long since been covered. In the darkness, the wrappers look like fallen leaves.

Time passes.

Both Janet and Amirah had been trying to get Han Biletnikov to notice them before Amirah became pyramid girl. Han had wiry red hair and freckles and played midfield on the soccer team. He was the first boy in their school to wear his pants inside out. On her last day in school, there had been an assembly in her honor and Han had come to the stage and told a Holy Joke about her.

Amirah cups her hands to make her voice sound like it's coming out of a microphone. "What did Amirah say to the guy at the hot dog stand?"

She twists her head to one side to give the audience response. "I don't know, what?"

Han speaks again into the microphone. "Make me one with everything." She can see him now, even though she is sitting at the kitchen table with a glass of water and an unopened Cherry Date Goody-goody bar in front of her. His cheeks are flushed as she strides across the stage to him. He isn't expecting her to do this. The believers go quiet as if someone has thrown a blanket over them. She holds out her hand to shake his and he stares at it. When their eyes finally meet, she can see his awe; she's turned into President Huong, or maybe Billy Tiger, the forward for the Boston Flash. His hand is warm, a little sweaty. Her fingertips brush the hollow of his palm.

"Thank you," says Amirah.

Han doesn't say anything. He isn't there. Amirah unwraps the Goody-goody bar.

Time passes.

Amirah never gets used to having her period. She thinks

she isn't doing it right. Mom never told her how it worked and she didn't leave pads or tampons or anything. Amirah wads toilet paper into her panties, which makes her feel like she's walking around with a sofa cushion between her legs. The menstrual blood smells like vinegar. She takes a lot of baths. Sometimes she touches herself as the water cools and then she feels better for a while.

Time passes.

Amirah wants to imagine herself kissing Han Biletnikov, but she can't. She keeps seeing Janet's lips on his, her tongue darting into his mouth. At least, that's how Janet said people kiss. She wonders if she would have better luck if she weren't in the kitchen. She climbs the stairs to her bedroom and opens the door. It's dark. The light has burned out. She pulls down the diffuser and unscrews the bulb. It's clear and about the size of a walnut. It says:

"Whose lifetime?" she says. The pile of Goody-goody wrappers on the front walk is taller than Dad. Amirah tries to think where there might be extra light bulbs. She pulls the entire house apart looking for them but she doesn't cry.

Time passes.

Amirah is practicing living in the dark. Well, it isn't entirely dark; she has left a light on in the hallway. But she is in the living room, staring out the picture window at nothing. The fireplace is gray on black; the couch across the room swells in the darkness, soaking up gloom like a sponge.

There are eight light bulbs left. She carries one in Mom's old purse, protected by an enormous wad of toilet paper. The weight of the strap on her shoulder is as reassuring as a hug. Amirah misses hugs. She never puts the purse down.

Amirah notices that it is particularly dark at the corner

where the walls and the ceiling meet. She gets out of Dad's reading chair, arms stretched before her. She is going to try to shut the door to the hallway. She doesn't know if she can; she has never done it before.

"Where was Moses when the lights went out?" she says.

No one answers, not even in her imagination. She fumbles for the doorknob.

"Where was Mohammed when the lights went out?" Her voice is shrinking.

As she eases the door shut, the hinges complain.

"Where was Amirah went the lights went out?"

The latch bolt *snicks* home but Amirah keeps pressing hard against the knob, then leans into the door with her shoulder. The darkness squeezes her; she can't breathe. A moan pops out of her mouth like a seed and she pivots suddenly, pressing her back against the door.

Something flickers next to the couch, low on the wall. A spark, blue as her dreams. It turns sapphire, cerulean, azure, indigo, all the colors that only poets and painters can see. The blue darts out of the electrical outlet like a tongue. She holds out her hands to navigate across the room to it and notices an answering glow, pale as mothers' milk, at her fingertips. Blue tongues are licking out of every plug in the living room and Amirah doesn't need to grope anymore. She can see everything, the couch, the fireplace, all the rooms of the house and through the pyramid walls into the city. It's one city now, not three.

Amirah raises her arms above her head because her hands are blindingly bright and she can see Dad with his new wife watching the Red Sox on 3DV. Someone has planted pink miniature roses on Mom's grave. Janet is looking into little Freddy Cobb's left ear with her otoscope and Han is having late lunch at Sandeens with a married imagineer named Shawna Russo and Mrs. Munro has dropped a stitch on the cap she is knitting for her great-grandson Matthias. At that moment everyone who Amirah sees, thousands of believers, *tens* of thousands, stop what they are doing and turn to the pyramid, *Amirah's* pyramid, which has been finished for these seventeen years but has never meant anything to anyone until now. Some smile with recognition; a few clap. Others—most of them, Amirah realizes—are now walking toward her pyramid, to be close to her and caress the cold marble and know what she knows. The meaning is suddenly very strong in the city, like the perfume of lilacs or the suck of an infant at the breast or the whirr of a hummingbird.

"Amirah?" Betty opens the living room door. She is a beautiful young girl with gray hair and crow's feet around her sky blue eyes. "Are you there, Amirah?"

"Yes," says Amirah.

"Do you understand?"

"Yes," Amirah says. When she laughs, time stands still.

Our Friend Electricity

~~~~

Ron Wolfe

Ron Wolfe [www.hawkpub.com/wolfe.htm] lives in Little Rock, Arkansas, and is a feature writer and cartoonist for the Arkansas Democrat-Gazette. *He published a novel,* Death's Door, *in 2000, one of three written in collaboration with John Wooley. He said in an interview, "I've been writing fiction, usually with some sort of fantasy element, for about the past five years. The real start was my involvement with a writers' group called the Robert B. Leslie Foundation (named for the writer of pulp magazine mystery stories and author of the immortal line: 'My roscoe sneezed, "Kerchow! Kerchow!"') Also, I'd like to think that, growing up in North Platte, Nebraska, I caught the spirit of showmanship from the town's most famous resident, Buffalo Bill." In recent years he has appeared in Asimov's and in F&SF, where this story was published.*

"Our Friend Electricity" is reminiscent of the most ambitious and literate pulp fiction, of the fiction of Theodore Sturgeon and Ray Bradbury, in its clarity, precision, and deep romantic sensibility. "Of course," he says, "any carnival story owes something to Bradbury. It's his playground, and I sneaked in."

*I loved Tori. Tori loved Coney Island. The moral is
such an old one, maybe you know it already.
Don't take any wooden nickels.*

⌐ 1

Our first time at Coney, I guessed Tori liked slumming. Anything Tori liked was fine with me. Especially when we got
there, it was fine with me. The place did something for her,
made her the ballerina of the boardwalk.

Every wisp of a breeze, every movement she made that
day played in her summer dress the color of white sand. She
whirled and her hair streamed in waves of blond, bright as
glass in the morning sun. She breathed in the salt air as it
mingled with the smells of cotton candy and sea weed and
spoilage, and her eyes were like fireworks of green and gold
sparks.

"See, we *are* having fun, Brad," she said. "Didn't I tell
you? Run, silly, catch me!" I ran, and I caught.

Coney's old parachute drop haunted the beach like a dim
metal ghost in the salt haze. The roller coaster was broken.
The Wonder Wheel turned its sad, slow revolutions as if it
were grinding time to a fine dust. But then, I looked at Tori.
She loved it, every bit of it.

We ate "Hygrade Frankfurters" from a stand with
painted pictures of sausages and pizza and ice cream cones
that looked like freak show attractions, and Tori loved it.

We saw women with white and yellow snakes and tat-
toos, and men with nipple rings; and some hunched figure
in a filthy ski parka; and a straw-haired girl in a nothing
bikini, just standing there, hands clasped between her
breasts in the way she must have learned singing in church;

and the Latina woman with the tragic face, the wet eyes, trying to win a goldfish in a ring-toss game.

Cheers and organ music reached us from the new baseball stadium. I imagined a different crowd there: families, boys with baseball heroes, girls with the clean look of suburban shopping malls. Tori wouldn't go there.

"It's awful," she said the only time she even glanced toward the stadium, where the Brooklyn Cyclones were winning.

The score didn't matter. I don't know baseball. The Cyclones won just being there, Brooklyn's first professional baseball team since the Dodgers left forty-five years ago. They meant change.

"I want the old—the real Coney Island. Don't you?" Tori said, pulling me toward a shooting gallery. I didn't need the reminder of guns.

Old and real is where the fun is all worn out, and marked down, and sold broken with sharp edges to people who can't have anything better. But Tori loved it, and so all I saw was Tori.

"Did you know? I have a talent, Brad. A super secret, psychic talent," she said, making the "s" sounds in "super secret psychic" a conspiratorial whisper.

"You could fool me," I said. We'd met yesterday.

"You tell me the name of the last girl you cared about even a little. I'll tell you how much she really meant to you."

My tongue caught.

"Please?"

"Tori, it was a long time—"

"Just her first name. What could a name hurt? You'll be surprised how good I am."

"Anna," I said.

Tori took a soft breath, as if breathing in "Anna," who had taught me how to thumb wrestle and to sort my laundry colors, and whose cheeks had blushed when she laughed.

"It wasn't all that serious," Tori said, "but, oh!—she broke your heart. They all break your heart."

I swallowed and tried to smile as if she'd told a joke, and then did smile, I think, at the flattery that beautiful women trampled through my life—a parade of heartbreakers. I needed Tori's healing touch, yes, almost a mother's touch, tracing my face, as if to check me for a fever.

"It's just a game, Brad, silly," she said. "You try it. Ask me."

"I will. Later," I lied.

We aimed squirt guns into the red-rimmed mouths of plastic clowns, each of us trying to be the first to pop a balloon. Tori brushed my left arm. Crowding me to the right was some withered brown mummy who had shed his ancient wrappings for a pair of red-striped Speedos, and then a kid who looked like he might kill somebody if he lost.

My pistol was sad to the touch. Nearly all the once-shiny black paint had worn off the grip, and the metal beneath was a dull blue-gray, the color of a bad sky. But Tori aimed well, and her laugh was so high and sweet, I swear even the old guy and the kid threw the contest. They wanted her to win like I did. They wanted to see, like I did, what winning would do for her smile. We all got the prize that day.

And then, I asked her.

"His name?" She worked the teddy bear she'd won like a puppet, making the bear's head nod as if in greeting to me. "Skip," she said. "The bear's name is Skip, too."

Skip, I thought, and I'm no more psychic than a sidewalk, but something came to me. I swore I'd never play this game again.

"Skip had money," I said, "lots of money, and he knew how to throw it around."

"Could be," Tori said, and she made the bear say it, too, "He might have been rich. *I'm a rich, rich bear. But I was a long, long time ago*. How did you know?"

"Skip . . . ," I said. "Skipper, skipper of a yacht, makes him rich Skipper."

"The gentleman wins the bear," Tori said, tucking Skip under my right arm, and then taking my left arm herself, a cool touch of possession. She taught me how to promenade the boardwalk.

Casey would waltz
With a strawberry blonde,
And the band played on

⌐ 2

We met cute. Doesn't everybody?

I'd been browsing through the sale shelves and boxes in front of the Strand bookstore, 12th and Broadway, that Friday evening. I was working my way from the one dollar books to the forty-eight-centers.

It was down there among the most sadly forsaken—the ones you had to stoop to, literally—that I found the first book I'd ever candied and cudgeled through publication years ago as Brad Vogler, Boy Editor. It was a science-fiction paperback called *Crimson Cosmos*.

Then: "Yeww!" she said, our moment of introduction.

My line of sight rose from the book's clotted red cover to a surprise glimpse down the neckline of Tori's white shell top (lacy white bra; front catch; first sight of the pendant she always wore, a white disk in a silver mounting), and all in a rush: neck-lips-eyes. Ice blue eyes in this light.

She didn't see me at all; she was leaning toward me, staring at the book cover. I felt like I'd been caught with a dead frog in my hand, just when a barefoot boy finds out nothing matters but girls.

"Are you buying that?" she said.

No, I yearned to answer, but I couldn't.

I remembered how it felt to write the letter of acceptance for that book, the first I'd ever bought. My letter told a fifty-five-year-old newspaper sports reporter in Denton, Texas, that he had sold his novel, his first. I believed I had discovered the next Robert Heinlein, if not the next Norman Mailer, and he thought he had uncovered the next John Campbell.

It turned out that all we had found in each other was another paperback book with stock art for the cover: blood oozing down like a sloppy coat of Sherwin Williams, and a couple of flat yellow eyes staring out of the red. But the author had gathered nerve and got married on the strength of that sale, and rounded out his belated brood with two girls adopted from China. He still wrote—high school football scores and "Merry Christmas" in the family photo card he sent me every year. And I couldn't say no, so I said something crazy.

"I've read it, but I'll buy it for you."

"Really?" she said, or maybe, "Really!" or "Reall-lly. . . ." or Latin or dolphin talk. I just knew I was being sized up.

I paid with a five-dollar bill. Forgot the change. Some eons of floating time later, I woke up having coffee with her, our fingers almost touching across the little table. Talking. Still talking over empty cups.

She liked white in the summer, red in the winter; oatmeal sprinkled with Red Hots, and she didn't like earrings. Mostly, she asked about me.

I felt so right with her, I didn't try to sound interesting. Maybe I came off coherent.

Listening, Tori withdrew a silver case from her white purse, and a card from the case. The case was inscribed with initials in script, TCS. The card had nothing but her name on it, as if I'd ever forget Tori Christine Slayton.

She added her phone number to the card with a silver pen, slid it to me, and our hands brushed and lingered, mine slightly over hers.

"Can I call you tomorrow?" I said.

"No. Meet me tomorrow."

"Anywhere."

"Brad, silly—" A bit of a smile crossed Tori's face, quick as a butterfly. Then, mock-serious, she said, "You mean that? *Anywhere*? All right, I dare you."

She took back the card, turned it over to plain white and wrote something tiny on the back. She folded the card twice, so I couldn't see what she'd written, and placed it in my hand, folding my fingers over the hard-edged little package with a squeeze.

"No fair peeking," Tori said. "Read it tomorrow morning. Meet me there. We'll have fun, I promise."

I went strictly by the rules, afraid of breaking the magic spell if I didn't. In the morning, I read the card and caught the subway, a line I'd never ridden before, to a place I'd never been before. But I'd heard of it. Everybody's heard of Coney Island.

Tori was waiting for me in front of the Headless Woman sideshow. ("Still alive. See her living body without a head. Alive!")

And that was our first time at Coney.

I'll be with you
When the roses bloom again

～ 3

Roses. I sent her white roses on Monday. She called; I called; she called. We had lunch on Wednesday, a quick bite.

She had a small antiques shop on the Upper West Side— high end, American Federal furniture and some Victorian, she said. She was antiques, and me?—in a way I hadn't told her yet, I was collectibles. The comparison was close enough to make me uncomfortable.

We arranged to meet again Friday after work in front of the Strand. "Dress up for me, won't you?" Tori said. It seemed to be a hint.

Thursday, I laid out the best of my two summer suits, the white one that made me wonder how Tom Wolfe kept his so clean.

Friday, I had the night planned as well as I could. So much about her made thoughts drift away. Her perfume: I fancied it was made of champagne and cinnamon. The way she said my name, the way she played with it, making it sound like an ice cream flavor. The way people watched us, talking when they thought we couldn't hear.

". . . *Vogue*, I'm sure of it." ". . . stare at her, at least close your mouth . . ." ". . . Grace Kelly. . . ."

Those same eyes, finding me, blinked and narrowed with itchy guesses. *He* must be . . . her brother. Her boss. *He* must be rich, but he sure doesn't look it.

I clean up all right, fair shape for a desk job, and thirty-seven isn't so old. But Tori is twenty-five, twenty-six, close to that, and nobody ever took me to be such great company until she did.

I had this idea of a movie at the Angelika, and then dinner in the Village, candles and spumoni. I was full of love songs, old ones that I must have half-heard sometime and filed away, just in case I ever felt like grinning like a street loon.

Ida, sweet as apple
Ci-hi-hi-der

⌒ 4

Tori had warned me she might be late; she expected some buyers who liked to haggle at the last minute.

Waiting, I made up stories about Brad the Mad. Every now and then, Brad the Mad escaped from the insane asylum, but the police knew where to find him. Whenever he broke loose, Brad the Mad dressed up in a white suit and stood in front of the Strand Bookstore, waiting for the woman who was only a delusion.

Tori arrived moments before I conjured up police sirens. She looked laser bright. Somehow, she'd guessed I would wear white, her color, and her dress was a whipped-cream white linen with a silver chain around the waist, silver bracelets, ornately of antique design; white silk scarf, heels. The moon-white pendant was ivory. It was faintly carved: "*Elephas*. . . ."

"I guess you like the look," Tori said. I'd been staring.

I rushed into my dinner-and-a-movie plan as if the combination might amaze her.

"Could we do the movie another time?" she said. "I've missed you, Brad. I just want your attention."

The candles and spumoni part held up, and I caught a break on the waiter. He was gay, and he left us alone.

"So," Tori said, "Mr. Important Book Editor, you still haven't told me enough about your job."

I wished I were a handsome photo on a dust jacket, riding princely over an author's bio full of lies. He flipped crêpes, he topped trees.

"English major from Lincoln, Nebraska, seeks literary career," I said, trying not to shrug. "Braves the big city, finds job as editor with fly-by-night science-fiction and mystery publisher. . . ."

"*Crimson Cosmos,*" Tori said. She lifted her wineglass, a toast. Her fingernails showed silver edges.

"You've read it?" I said.

"No, but it's my favorite book." And that smile again, fire and innocence.

"The meteoric rise continues," I said, "a career arc that takes our hero from rockets and murders, to cookbooks, and then grade school science texts—"

She questioned with an eyebrow. "You know what I like about you?" Tori said. "You have smart eyes. You haven't found your niche yet, but you will."

"—*Our Friend Electricity*, thank you, please hold your applause. And now, I'm at Recollections Publishing. I do price guides for nostalgic babyboomers."

"Like?—"

"*Jungle Fever: A Collector's Guide to Tiki.*"

"Oh, no!"

"Tiki music, tiki dolls, even snow globes. I don't get it, but there were GIs coming home after World War Two, already feeling nostalgic about the South Pacific. And now, their kids are collecting old tiki stuff all over again. But I don't feel nostalgia for much of anything." I caught the mistake. "But I like antiques."

Tori laughed. "Oh, Brad, silly, you do not. I don't blame you. Antiques aren't nostalgia, antiques are investment. You can love an antique and not like it in the least."

I splashed the last of our bottle, a French Chardonnay that Tori had chosen, into our glasses, and raised mine.

"To the brand new," I said, already planning a second bottle I couldn't afford to keep the table and the company.

Her expression drifted, blanked for a moment. Her eyes seemed to mist, but it might have been a trick of the candle-light.

"I have to go," Tori said, half rising. My face must have slid into my lap like slush.

"Oh my, I said that all wrong, didn't I?" She reached across the table to touch my nose, a playful flick. Her finger softly traced a smile across my lips. "Brad, silly. Let me try it again. We should go."

And now, she had neon inside her, excitement that flick-ered and caught with the words, "Coney Island! We could, still."

My dumb grin seemed to encourage her.

"Tonight. We had such fun the last time, Brad, let's do it, let's go. Now. Can we?"

I may have yammered something about the subways be-ing bad at night. But Tori had the answer: She had a car. She knew ways to Coney Island, and we could be there in no time.

We whisked down the street to her car, if that's what you'd call it, parked at the curb between a red Mustang and some blocky sort of coupe.

Tori's car was a low, sculpted swoop of black metal and polished wood. Street lights played laser tag over the hood. Then, metal gave way to the cherry coach, made tight like an admiral's skiff. It was open-topped, brass- and copper-trimmed, upholstered in leather, and the wheels were wire-rim. The Great Gatsby could have wrestled for the keys to Tori's car with Deckard from *Blade Runner*.

I set foot on the running board. The car welcomed me like a butler with muscle. The seat had been tailored to me.

"It's a Panhard and Levassor Sport," Tori said, pulling into the street. "1914. Like it?"

"What's it doing outside the museum?"

She drove fast, as I should have guessed she would, and she knew the streets, how to work the lanes, how to keep moving.

I must have looked pale as my suit.

"It's some of the original chassis, but then a lot of restoration," Tori said. "Not a faithful restoration at all, though. The engine is something else, and it has protections built into it that aren't even close to the market, some that probably aren't legal. Watch your fingers."

The car seemed to repel other traffic. Even Pakistani cab drivers were afraid to come near it, scared of scratching it.

"Don't worry. It's not mine," Tori said. "I borrowed it from one of my customers—part of the deal for an eighteenth-century bedroom set he just had to have. I meet some interesting people."

Next thing I knew, we were sailing over the Brooklyn Bridge, the wind whipping Tori's hair like white fire; and then onto the Queens Expressway. We hit 70, 75, 80. Tori's white scarf streamed, it pulled loose, and I turned to see it go soaring like a ghost into the night. I reached as if I should have caught it, Tori laughing, and me laughing; and I pulled off my necktie and let that go, too.

Mermaid Avenue welcomed us with its offers of saltwater taffy, beer, and body-piercing, pawn shops, gun shops. Dim lights shone in old windows above the striped and rusted awnings.

A gaunt woman stopped to watch us from the sidewalk. Her hair was dyed orange, and she wore a black plastic trash bag twisted elegantly across her shoulders like a feather boa. To her, we were the aliens. I was Bug-eyed Brad from Planet Starbucks.

Bug-eyed Brad scans the ruins for life as he knows it, life that bags the trash, that fixes broken windows. But he is the stranger in a strange land of knives and needles. He expects to be eaten.

". . . Giuliani saying he wants to make Coney Island

'something very special again,' can you believe it?" Tori said. "It's special the way it is. Special the way it was. Oh, look!—"

We passed the remains of a shabby little candy store. Inside, the shelving and fixtures had been pushed to the center, giving the painters room to work. Already, it had the promise of something the mayor would approve.

But Tori had seen something else, and we turned toward the crawling lights of the old amusement park.

Coney Island was a different world in the dark, too bright and too shadowed. It left me straining to recognize anything I'd seen before. A mist of raindrops fell and passed, cleansing no part of the night.

Tori parked facing the roller coaster. High over us, the big letters read "Cyclone" in a way that chilled me like a cold smile: The letters looked eaten away, so many bulbs were dead. But Tori loved it, and I was high from the car ride. We ran like Mouseketeers into Disneyland.

The roller coaster was shut down again, or still, but Tori coaxed me onto the Wonder Wheel.

"You can see *everything* from the top," she promised.

At the top, our metal cage groaned and swung over a nightscape more speckled than lit with yellow bulbs and red neon. The rides below us looked tiny and meaningless. We faced toward a jumbled rim that appeared to be housing projects, mostly dark. But the air smelled fresh.

"Feel better up here?" Tori said, holding my arm, leaning tightly against me. I nodded. "I knew you would," she said.

Her pendant seemed almost to glow. An elephant was carved into the ivory, the creature's trunk lifted, and the words read, *"Elephas non timet."*

Tori smiled as if pleased that I'd noticed. She scooped the pendant lightly in her fingers, holding it toward me. " 'The elephant does not fear,' " she said. "It's an ancient saying. The elephant's trunk raised that way means good luck. Long life. Wisdom."

"It looks old."

"Not so very, around 1900. A century is nothing to an elephant."

"So!—all this, and she's an elephant expert, too. What else?"

"Maybe you'll find out," Tori said, as the Ferris wheel descended us into the smells of hot grease and machine oil.

We took the funhouse ride into its hell of plywood demons and painted flames, and Tori loved it. We joined a drunken clot of teenagers on a whirligig called the Calypso. I came off with a spattered stripe of something blue and sticky across my left sleeve.

"Here, this way, this way!" Tori said, pulling me. "Let's see how good you are at Skee-Ball."

The Skee-Ball setup was between a couple other games that had their metal shutters pulled down, scrawled with spray-painted gang signs. We had Skee-Ball to ourselves, just us and the sour yellow glow that spilled over the row of games, and the attendant. He slumped on a dangerously tilted stool at the entrance, head fallen to his chest, asleep or dead.

I fished a quarter to drop in the slot that was nicked and dented from all the wasted coins that had gone through it. Nine balls clacked down the chute. Tori bounced on her toes like a little girl trying to see the top of her birthday cake, and I tried to catch the mood.

We took turns. She rolled a ball, and then I did, and I learned how she played: Anything I scored above a ten was good for a baby hug. The score was eight balls and three little hugs, and I knew how it might feel to hold her.

Tori poised the last ball. She glanced at the pink prize tickets that had curled out of the battered machine as we scored. I dreaded waking the attendant to redeem them.

"Here's the prize I want," she said, turning the hard wooden ball in her hands like it was made of phantom quartz, like it was telling her secrets.

"You'd have to steal it," I said.

"Maybe you'd steal it for me."

She gave me the ball, wrapping my hesitant fingers around it, and cupping her cool hands over mine. "It's old, it's very old," she said. "I think it's old as the park. I think it remembers all the hands that have touched it, just like we're doing. Hundreds, thousands, lives and lives and lives, and every touch leaves something. Every touch tells something."

I may have flinched. Tori's grip tightened. Her breath came warm, close to my face.

"What do you love about a book, Brad? That it can hold lives? Well, so can this, only real ones."

She let go, and I saw the ball; it was the decrepit brown of age and skin oil, nicked, scratched, dented flat in a couple places.

". . . *he* doesn't care," Tori said, eying the big-bellied attendant. He had a Yankees ball cap pulled low. His dark glasses suggested he had been asleep since daylight. He had on a red T-shirt, and a baggy clown's pair of farm overalls with the ragged legs cut off to make shorts.

"Just hold the ball close against your leg, away from him, and we'll walk away. Please, Brad?"

I hadn't stolen since college. Petty shoplifting had been a brief, edgy craze in my sophomore year. You'd ask the check-out clerk what time it was, and in the moment it took her to look at the wall clock behind her, you'd snitch a pack of Dentyne. You'd buy a roll of waxed paper, and she'd never notice that you'd dropped two slim jars of olives down the cardboard tube. You'd try for the cigarettes, even though you didn't smoke—

I was good, and I was caught. A dumb thrill nearly cost my degree. Now, I freak when I've bought something that accidentally sets off the store alarm.

But we passed the attendant. "Shhhhh!" Tori hushed too loudly. He never stirred.

We were outside the Skee-Ball game.

We were steps away; we were gone.

I gave the ball a tiny flick. It smacked my hand like a soft kiss. I don't know what roused him.

The attendant roared a curse behind us. "Oh my, oh my, that bad boy's mad! . . ." Tori warned lightly, as if in answer to an amusing dare. She kicked off her high heels to run. I had no choice.

We tore, dodging fat men and slow men and blue jeans, belly buttons, baby carriages, we ran kicking trash, our hands clasped. Her excitement shot me like a current, jolting the fear out of me.

This was like another ride to Tori, like the Calypso only faster. But something gripped me. Caught me at the neck. The attendant locked a thick arm around me, holding me back, dragging me down. I lost Tori. He smelled of whiskey and vomit. My knees hit the asphalt, and he was on top of me.

He moved to pin my arms and shoulders. I knew this position from grade school: I was going to take a beating in the face. No teacher was going to pull him off me. He drizzled me with sweat and saliva, trying to capture my right arm. My fist clenched the ball.

I swung at him, catching him hard on the temple with a crack that I only hoped was the ball breaking. But the ball didn't break. He fell beside me, rolling, howling.

I pulled to my feet. He made it to his hands and knees, head down, as if he suddenly had decided to study bugs on the ground. With his left hand, he clasped his head. Blood welled between his fingers. A slow drop. A drop, a drop. A stain.

For a moment, it seemed that blood was falling all around me. A real rain had begun. Tori shook me, and she caught my hand again, led me and ran with me through the rain and the yells that cracked like thunder, and nobody stopped us.

Once we hit the expressway, she slowed below the limit. She let the rain wash me. She swerved off to a gas station, where she pulled up the car's top. She brought me a Coke.

"See, we *are* having fun, Brad," she said, drenched and muddied and altogether the most beautiful blessing I'd ever imagined.

I found something in my hand. The ball. The damned, wonderful ball. I tossed it to her. She was a good catch, too.

"Yours, I believe," I said.

Wait till the sun shines, Nellie,
And the clouds go drifting by

~ 5

We drove to my apartment in the East Village, listening to cool jazz on the Panhard and Levassor's Bose FM stereo. A parking space was waiting for us. It was that kind of night.

"I have something for you, too," Tori said. She snapped open the glove box, withdrawing some object she kept hidden.

I saw yet another Tori then, one hesitant with a gift, afraid to go through with it, anxious that I wouldn't like it. What she might have done that I wouldn't like, if a street fight didn't count as a problem, I had no wild idea.

"Here—" She showed me the copy of *Crimson Cosmos* I'd bought her. A smooth bit of cardboard peeked out of the pages. A bookmark.

"Pick a card," Tori said, "any card. . . ."

Withdrawn, it was a Rolodex card. On it, I read the name of a Fifth Avenue publishing house, the first to which I'd applied for a job in New York, and the one to which I still submitted an updated resume every year. The man's name on the card, I could no more approach than the planet Venus. Below the name was a number.

"He's been one of my best clients for years," Tori said. "I've told him about you. He wants you to call."

My wet thumb smudged the ink on the card, only confirming it was real.

"But don't call him, Brad. Make him call you. That way, you have the advantage. And he *will* call."

I stared at her. She made a cross-eyed face that scattered my dumbfoundedness.

"You were right about Skip," Tori said. "He was rich, and he taught me about winning. So, Brad, silly, are you going to invite a lady in from the rain, or what?"

~ 6

I used to collect bad writing to share with friends, mostly other bottom-feeders in genre book and magazine fiction. Six or eight of us had a regular beer night at Tad's Tap on Bleecker Street. We called it the Pen and Pitcher Club.

"Her globes suspended from her like bells on a Christmas tree, I mean the fair-sized round kind."

Collector's price guides don't produce keepers like that. I quit showing up at Tad's for being a bore. A few others made the climb to better jobs and bigger publishers. Finally, only the washouts kept the faith.

The author of "Her globes suspended . . ." may have been the best of us, after all. He had the fool's nerve to stick his pan in the stream, hoping for gold, and he dredged up mud. But it looked like gold to him.

And here I am, Tori, dipping my rusty pan into that same flow that can't convey the touch of sunlight, or the smell of chocolate, or the taste of tears, hoping for something that gleams.

~ 7

We dripped and squeaked our way up the two flights of stairs to my apartment. As my key clicked the lock, I suddenly wished the door wouldn't open.

My first apartment in New York was in the meat-packing district. I left my shoes inside the door to keep from tracking livestock blood. My second was next to a coke dealer whose clientele wasn't much on apologies for having pounded the wrong door.

This one, I'd considered a spectacular move up: three rooms, or four if you count the living room and kitchen as separate because of a shelf divider. The neighbors were reasonably quiet. The previous tenant had been entrenched there since the '60s, and must have sat a lot. The lime shag carpet was good as new.

One day, I blinked the carpet to oblivion, just quit seeing it—

Until my door swung open, and I snapped on the light to hit Tori with a sock of green that would have flattened St. Paddy.

But the carpet made no impression. "Where's Skip?" she said. *"Remember me? Where am I?"*

The toy bear. Skip was in the bedroom closet, top shelf, stuffed far in the back.

I found him quickly, though, and placed him on the dresser. Tori arranged him with the Skee-Ball between his legs. Wet-haired Tori was in my bedroom, wriggling her toes in the shag.

"Let me get you a towel," I offered.

"I'd like to use the room," she said. "I need a little more repair than a towel."

I showed her, like there was some trick to finding the bathroom, and she closed the door. I heard her open the little cupboard where I kept my mismatched towels; heard, then, the familiar creak, cry and rattle from the hot water faucet over the tub. Rustling sounds. I stood there, as she must have expected I would.

"I knew you'd have books," Tori said through the door. "You have wonderful bookcases."

"They're oak. They're what I splurge on."

Sound of the faucets turned off. Sound of body in water.

"Umm, this feels good," she said. "You should do this, too."

I glanced back to the bedroom—the neckties that hung off the doorknob, the scatter of socks and magazines in the corner, the whole disarray. I began to scoop and hide.

The bathroom door slipped open with a wisp of steam.

The dullest part of me expected to see her step out dressed and dried and ready to leave. The rest of my awful imagination conjured up, I don't know, some Botticelli Venus-in-the-hallway with discreet hands.

Instead, she stood gift-wrapped in my best white towel, still sparkling with droplets of water, as if I had this coming—as if I knew what to do with it.

"You might try kissing me," Tori said.

I moved to her, my hands finding her warm shoulders, hers finding my face, my neck, my back. The towel fell between us.

We transformed my empire's five steps between bath and bed into another promenade: the lady wearing nothing but her pendant, and her dizzy escort with the ragged knees. Tori made the ceiling light go away. We closed to kiss.

The shag carpet worked its magic on us. A stinging blue snap of static electricity sparked between our lips.

"Our friend electricity," Tori said, rubbing her mouth.

"Our friend electricity," I said, pressing mine to the sore spot on hers.

Our friend electricity joined us and melted us. We soothed. We dared. We tumbled.

Bodies and bed sheets, her hands and her kisses, we danced to the brink of a thousand little deaths. She led me on; she held me back, only to rush again. In a gasp, she called me Skip.

I tried to pretend I hadn't heard. But hard eyes shone on the dresser: Skip watching me. I tried to hide my anger, but it found a way to show.

Skip!

"Brad, I'm sorry. . . ."

Skip!

"Brad, you're hurting. . . ."

Skip!

"Brad! Brad! Brad, silly . . . Brad. . . ."

She clung to me, bound to my whim and forgiveness, but I was the one then who couldn't let go. I followed her into a soft, singing rhythm, a lullaby whisper.

"He was a long time ago—ohh!—"

In the wee small hours of later, I woke to find Tori sobbing. I kissed her neck. I kissed a warm tear. "I don't care . . . ," I said. "He doesn't matter."

"It isn't him, it isn't you," she said. "It's nothing. It's me."

"Tori—"

"They all break your heart."

I touched her nose, copying Tori's little gesture from the restaurant. "If the girl thinks my poor heart is broken right now, the girl's not too bright."

"Just hold me."

Before had been only a taste of her. When I slept again, it was the deep fall of the feasted, and it was knowing that no Annas could ever break my heart again.

I slept on the currents of Tori's breath. Above me, her eyes were the sky. "Tell me what it's like to dream about Lincoln, Nebraska," she said. I guess we talked more.

In the morning, Tori was gone. I remembered her voice like music through a heavy wall, the rhythm but not the words, not the sense of it. Not then.

She'd taken Skip and the Skee-Ball. In their place, she'd left a name card folded twice.

I didn't have to read it.

∽ 8

"Mr. Vogler, this is Sara in library reference. I found the expression you asked about, and it means what you thought. But it's short for an even older saying—one that dates back to Pliny the Elder, the Roman author. Also, it became the motto of the Malatesta family, the tyrants of Rimini, Italy, in the Middle Ages. They believed it justified the criminal behavior that kept their family in power. *Elephas indus culices non timet.* 'The Indian elephant does not fear the mosquito.'" It means, in context, 'does not fear to crush the insect.'"

So, Mr. Vogler, Mr. Important Book Editor, you with the hollow eyes in the mirror, tell me all about yourself.

Sit down and—no? All right, then, pace your cage in circles, but tell me.

You like: The color blue, pancakes at midnight, and all you really want is to hold this little card so tightly that the ink bleeds into your fingertips; that's how much you want to hold her, any part of her.

You don't like: Needles, strep throat, Coney Island. Old, happy-creepy Coney Island. Wrecked and rotted Coney Island. Tori loves Coney Island.

See these books? This shelf? All these books about New York? You've never read one. You knew these books would tell you all the ways you don't belong.

Which of these books throws the best, do you think? Way to go, sport! Hit the wall, win the lady a bear. Coney Island, pp. 139–141.

". . . by 1904, home to three dazzling parks: Steeplechase with its mechanical horse race; Luna with its elephants, acrobats and a million incandescent lights; and Dreamland, for which the lovely waltz . . ."

Tell me what it's like to dream about Lincoln, Nebraska, and I'll tell you what it's like to dream of Luna.

". . . 200,000 people a day. They came for the beach, the parks, the fun rides, the crowd. The biggest attraction of all was electricity."

Our friend electricity.

". . . time when a single bulb might have seemed a miracle or a terrible omen of change, Coney Island's electrical glow carried thirty miles out to sea."

Our friend electricity. What is it, really? Hm? Brad? Don't you wonder?

Hey, I just about wrote the book, remember? "Electricity is the flow of electrons—"

Brad, silly. Electricity is light. Light waves.

(Tori's sweet, soft hair, brushing my lidded eyes.)

Elephas non timet, Brad.

(Her lips to my ear.)

Want to ride the waves?

⌒ 9

It was noon when I began searching for her on the subway platform over Surf Avenue. I stood there, grinning for a moment, as if she might come to meet me, carrying a picnic basket with a calico cloth.

A block west, I joined the boardwalk throng. I let the crowd sweep me to the aquarium, and jostle me back to Astroland, the amusement park, and Sideshows by the Sea. The Human Blockhead had nothing to show me.

I looked for her at Nathan's Famous, where the street corner reeked of wieners and mustard. Two policemen were eating hot dogs, holding their dripping dogs at a distance like medical specimens to keep from staining their blue uniforms. Head down, I hid in the crowd.

Damned and Delighted: A Collectors' Guide to Mermaid Avenue.

Clean people tried to avoid me. They eyed me the way I had stared at losers on the boardwalk. I found a restroom and checked myself in the tin mirror. Uncombed. Unshaven. I looked drunk. I did what I could with cold water.

By evening, I knew where I'd find her, where I'd known all along. Look for mermaids in the drowning depths. Thunder snarled as if to remind me of blood and rain, and the possibility that I might have killed a man—that the next policeman I saw might be carrying a sketch of me.

Tori stood just under the Skee-Ball sign, wearing the same white dress she had worn our first time at Coney Island. Her ivory pendant gleamed white. To her side, a new attendant watched the games—watched her. He was a shirtless beanpole with his eyes opened wide like a chicken's. Tori's left hand braced tauntingly against her hip. Her right hand flipped some tiny thing I couldn't see.

She came to me with a crystal smile, a face of such delight, I felt the sting of tears.

"I won," she said, kissing the back of her closed right hand. "Take me on the roller coaster, and you can have the prize."

The Cyclone was running. I don't know how we got

there. We waited turn after turn, because Tori wanted the first car.

Finally, the train banged to a stop in front of us, and we climbed on. My hands clenched the safety bar. Tori squeezed against me, tight and warm.

"You don't like roller coasters," she said, a teasing tone that dropped to something else, something like sadness. "You don't like any of this, I know. I'm sorry."

She looked away from me. I felt her tremble as the car jolted forward. It ground its *racheta-rakkata* way up the first climb.

"Here—" Tori said, coaxing my hand loose from the bar. "What I promised you, the prize I won."

I looked at the object she'd given me. It was a rough wooden disk, with the image of an Indian's head stamped on one side. Around the head, the letters read: "Don't take any wooden nickels." A spatter of rain struck the coin.

"For luck," she said, and her tongue traced my lips. Her body, close against me, told me secrets; she had nothing else under the dress. She kissed me, hard, as we took the fall.

The coaster shook us like a mean dog. It shuddered its timbers, throwing us side to side. Once, it swooped a curve and gave us the same view as from the top of the Wonder Wheel, only better. Someone seemed to have knocked down the buildings like so many blocks. We could see the ocean.

Climb. Fall. Curve. Tori shrieked, and the nickel bit into my hand.

Climb. Fall. My face stretched back. Curve. I had a sense of shooting past a maze of towers, faces in the windows.

The last fall eased into the platform, the end of the ride. But we didn't stop. I saw the crowd, the ride attendants, as smears of surprise.

Climb. Fall. Curve. We screamed over the course again. Darkness triggered the lights, and the "Cyclone" sign crackled on. Tori locked close to me.

"They'll stop us," I said. "They have ways—" She didn't hear me.

Climb. The park washed in light. No one tried to stop us. They had no ways at all.

Fall. The towers again, become a giant's garden of lights. We cut through silver curtains of drizzly rain that whipped and stung our faces, and yet, in some crazy way, made us laugh.

Curve. We soared over the towers. Ant masses of people swarmed far beneath us. The white lights turned my eyes to burning water.

Climb. Fall. Twist. Fracture. Red. Black. Fire. Crystal. Rainbow.

Falling.

In the air, falling.

Casey would waltz
With a strawberry blonde
And the band played on.
He'd glide cross the floor
With the girl he adored
And the band played on.

Calliope music swirled through my head. I was spinning, up and down, and spinning. I clutched a spiraled pole to keep from losing balance.

His brain was so loaded,
It nearly exploded.
The poor girl would shake
With alarm

Tori! "It's all right, Brad." Tori! "I'm here." Tori! "Look at me. Look at me. Brad, silly. Please, while you can."

I tried, but the whole world kept revolving. Horses, lions, bears, swans, ran circles around me.

He'd ne'er leave the girl
With the strawberry curls—

I'd been wrong about the roller coaster. Terribly wrong. We were on a carousel.

Mine was the sterling white stallion, and Tori had mastered a gryphon with a golden head, riding perfectly side-saddle. But Tori was different.

Her hair was combed up, arranged into heavy waves under a white hat with a silk bow. Her white dress had full sleeves with lace cuffs and flounced shoulders. The satin skirt swam past her feet. The square-shaped neckline, trimmed with brocade roses, showcased her pendant. But the ivory had fallen out of it, leaving just the silver.

A question shaped my mouth, but no words fit the question.

Tori said, "This is what it's like to dream of Luna."

She reached; I took her hand. The carousel toyed with us.

"What was it you said, Brad? 'The girl's not too bright.' She finally learned the secret. She took ninety-seven times to get it right. And you know what? Right feels like dying."

The carousel slowed. I lost her touch. Riders scrambled on and off, bodies and motion between us. I stumbled to the ground, calling for her.

"Tori!. . . ." The crowd swallowed my voice, as it had my last sight of her.

Say this for madness. When madness is all around you, then madness is what you've got. You go with madness.

I accepted my new world of lighted towers, fairy-tale minarets rimmed with stars, Arabian spires circled with lights. I threw myself into a foreign crowd of women who dressed like Tori in long skirts, and some who bound themselves into breathless S-shapes, their waists cinched to nothing; boys in shorts, girls in ruffles, men wearing straw hats and bowlers, stiff collars, bow ties, suspenders, vests, watch chains, canes.

My clothes were something like that. They were like wearing my brother's clothes that I'd never have bought for myself, familiar and wrong all at once. But I seemed to fit with the crowd.

I pushed through knots of laughing strangers, searching for Tori. Someone slapped me on the back, as if I were part of a joke. I called her name, and another voice blended with mine. We sang rounds.

"Tori!"

"Lemonade! Peanuts!"

My throat caught. Sweat streamed my face. No one else seemed to feel as hot as I did. I brought concern to other faces; I may have looked sick. The air wasn't helping.

The salt smell hadn't changed, but it mingled with human and livestock scents that assaulted me, like a circus locker room.

I wandered beneath acrobats, past tumblers and jugglers. Camels and elephants thumped by. Bands played, and midgets frolicked.

Lighted signs grandly promised "THE STREETS OF FIRE!" "TRIP TO THE MOON!" "THE LAUGHING SHOW!" "FIRE AND FLAMES!" "WHIRL THE WHIRL!" "INFANT INCUBATORS!" "LUNA PARK'S WORLD-FAMOUS SHOOT THE CHUTES!"

The crowd pulled me to watch the wrestlers, the bareback riders. Then, like crows, we were off all at once, rushing to the next attraction, gaining heads and legs along the way. We jammed, we stalled, we hurried on. I strained to hear those voices around me that seemed to understand the excitement.

". . . were going to hang her, you know." "Hang? They couldn't. Would take a chain. . . ." ". . . this, instead. . . ." ". . . thunder and flash, do you think, when they give it to her?"

I pulled a man's sleeve to engage him. "I don't like it, sir, and I won't watch it," he said. His jaw set, and he bulled his way against the rush, but he lost.

We poured into an arena that smelled of dirt and animals, stronger than ever. We overflowed the tiers of seats, molding ourselves into a human wall around the open space.

"It's time, they're coming. . . ." ". . . murdering elephant, three men she's killed." "They'll make a pretty light of her."

Across the arena, a gray shape lumbered into recognition. The elephant walked passively toward the center, led by two men: one in a red uniform with gold trim and a high cap; the other, a shorter man in a brown tweed suit and derby.

The elephant's massive head came up as if she suddenly had broken the concentration of a deep thought. Her legs froze.

The man in the red uniform said something to her. I sensed it was not a command, but a comfort. His smile belonged in a hospital. He gently touched. He stroked the huge elephant's leathery trunk.

The crowd hushed. "Now, Topsy, now, now, old Topsy girl . . . ," he said, but she backed away with a start that brought people to their feet, as if to run.

"I can't do this to her, Mr. Dundy," the man said to his tweed-suited companion. "I won't let her be—"

"You w-will if you work for m-me," Mr. Dundy ordered, his stammer like nicks in the blade of his voice.

"No, sir, I won't."

The man in the red uniform stood a moment, as if he might defiantly sweep the elephant into his arms like a baby and run with her. What he did, finally, was walk away. In the crowd, some jeered at him.

Mr. Dundy wiped his face with a sharply pressed white handkerchief that he stuffed back into his lapel pocket. He motioned, and a crew of other men took the elephant keeper's place. No shiny red suits masked their business. They had sticks with nails and hooks, and they prodded and baited the elephant into the center of the arena, all the while keeping their distance from her, wounding her in the nip-and-run way of small predators. They roped her to wooden stakes.

And now, yet other men set to work on her, much to the crowd's approval.

". . . Thomas Edison's own. . . ." ". . . in from New Jersey. . . ." ". . . wires, see what they're doing, they're making what they call connections. . . ."

Thomas Edison's men attached heavy copper wires and electrodes to chains around the elephant's right front and left rear feet, and scrambled away from her.

And now, all eyes were back to Mr. Dundy. He had taken his place barely apart from the crowd, just far enough into the arena to stand out, but safely away from the elephant. Two women stood next to him tightly, possessively. He had the swagger of a rock star. His left arm wrapped a brunette with pouty, apple-red lips. His right arm—

"Tori!" Her name exploded from my throat, but she didn't hear me.

I fought the wall of backs and shoulders that kept me away from her, edging, squeezing, forcing my way into the arena. Rough hands shoved me forward. I fell through a gap in the wall, landing sideways. Something snapped in my side; I felt a tiny, sudden loss of breath, and feared I'd broken a rib. But I gathered my feet beneath me in practically the same motion.

Thinking better, I would have run the circumference of the arena until it led me to Tori. I wasn't thinking that way. I headed straight across the opening, becoming part of the show. Band music struck up as if to accompany my act.

All around the cobbler's bench;
The monkey chased the weasel

In the center, I stopped, helpless. The elephant's gaze held me. I could have touched her. I did.

From a distance, she looked weathered and hard as stone. But her skin was warm, and my hand brushed silky soft hair that was nearly invisible.

"Topsy. . . ."

Her massive front legs bent with a clatter of chains. She knelt as if to offer me a ride. Her eyes held vast secrets.

The crowd cheered. Mr. Dundy laughed his approval. He strode out to meet me, both women in tow.

"First thing we t-tried on her, we soaked her carrots in c-cyanide," he said. "She never f-felt a thing. Why, I'd just about decided she had no f-feelings at all. But y-you have a way with her."

He wanted to shake hands, but I stood there, numb, arms

to my sides, looking at Tori. She gave me not the slightest sign of recognition.

He saw my obsession. "Lillian," he addressed her, "do you k-know this man?"

She looked me up and down, but not like when I'd offered to buy her *Crimson Cosmos*. No play, no surprises. Her expression dismissed me.

"Tori, what's wrong?" I tried to take her hand.

"You are!" she said, peeling my fingers off her as if they were leeches. Her mouth pulled down to an expression she'd never worn before. "You're as wrong as I ever seen."

Mr. Dundy reclaimed her, and as he did, a dozen other men materialized from out of the crowd—dirtied workmen, some of them, and big men with clean, pressed suits and clenched hands.

"I'm a friend of hers," I said, as if somebody had to believe me.

"A f-friend, are you?" he said. "Well, here, f-friend. Take this, and g-get yourself lost."

He flipped something high into the air, where it caught the light, spinning, flashing gold. I caught it with a cold slap into my palm: a gold coin.

"Take . . . *this!*" Mr. Dundy cried in sudden recovery of his laughing mood. He hands emerged from his pants pockets with clutches of gold coins that he threw into the crowd, whirling as he let go. He made himself a fountain, spraying gold.

People *oooh*'ed, and cheered, and feet left the ground, and hands reached high. Bodies collided. Fistfights erupted. Screams. People fell to hands and knees, scrabbling after coins on the ground.

Then, laughter wove and threaded through the riot, somehow congealing into a chant, until it seemed that everyone took it up in one voice. The two women played cheerleader.

The earth may quake
And banks may break

But Skip Dundy
Pays in gold!

Whoops and laughter echoed off the bedazzled towers, until the noise startled Topsy. The elephant roused to her feet. She backed as if to turn and run, straining the ropes that tethered her legs to the ground. One of the heaviest stakes inched free.

Mr. Dundy and his women retreated. His derby jarred loose. His hairpiece slipped. He pulled the big handkerchief from his pocket again, waving it high over his head. The band broke out a drum roll, and the crowd picked up a different cry.

"Bad Topsy!" "Bad Topsy!"

Topsy lifted her enormous head to trumpet her rage and defiance. I ran from her, too. Mr. Dundy whipped the handkerchief down. The park's lights dimmed and flickered.

Billows of white smoke exploded from the elephant's feet. She stiffened in a series of shivers and twitches that tickled most of the crowd. Topsy seemed to imagine her death was only a funny feeling she could shake off.

Near me, a woman fainted. Someone cursed; someone cried.

In the end, it was like seeing a grand old building implode: that same confusion of wonder and terror, a thrill in the destruction of something huge and irreplaceable.

Topsy was dead on her feet, smoke coiling around her. Then, she seemed to lift. Absurdly, I thought of robot jets firing under her feet, blasting her high into the sheltering night.

She never reached the stars, though. She fell to her right side, her legs locked straight, as if she'd never lived at all. I felt the impact through my feet, and in the pit of my stomach like the sound of a cannon, and in my heart.

The elephant's liquid brown eyes rolled up. The current still surged through her. Her feet charred.

"C-cut the electricity!" Mr. Dundy ordered, but too late. Power hummed through the air. Blue fire crackled and arced around the fallen elephant. It snaked into the crowd. People fell back as if toppled by armies of invisible demons swinging sledge hammers.

The fire enveloped Tori.

A tendril of blue lightning snaked from Tori's eyes, connecting with mine, and I knew. I understood. I shared with her the jungle heat, the rain, the serenity, the sense of time as something soft and slow, like the rain.

And Luna Park went black.

⌐ 10

I have to tell you. This isn't the place, but you need to know. If I were editing this manuscript, I would mark an "X" here and write in the margin: "author intrusion," meaning the author has barged in like a gatecrasher, spoiling the story. But this can't wait. You'll know why.

There are mermaids in the electric ocean of time. If you glance up from your reading right now, you might see one. She could be that close.

Something in her smile, something in her eyes, makes you trust her. The deeper she takes you, the more you feel safe with her. When you trust her completely, you're already into the drowning depths.

But that's not what she wants, and that's not why she drowned all those others before you.

How many? Pick a number, any number, say—ninety-six. She cared all she could for them, and a mermaid's slightest care is more than a king's richest dream. But she didn't care enough to save them with her mermaid magic. They were all wooden nickels.

You, though, you're the one. Maybe not to another soul in the universe, but you have this one great thing going for you: You're the one she's tried so hard to find.

She drowned ninety-six, and then you came along. Or she would have drowned 960, until you came along; or 960 million, looking for you.

Numbers mean nothing to her.
But you do.

∽ 11

Luna Park fell to darkness as completely as, moments before, it had been incredibly illuminated. The cries were like
those of primitives in the grip of a solar eclipse.

Dizziness took me, but I knew it would be fatal to fall. I
would be under panicked feet. Hands clutched at me, feeling for someone familiar, for husband or mother, and shoving the stranger away.

I caught a glint of silver light, of moonglow reflected
from something familiar, the silver rim of Tori's hollow
pendant—waiting for its remembrance of Topsy.

"Brad . . ." Her breath cooled my face. "Brad, silly." She
held me. "I have something for you."

I dimly saw her touch a finger to the corner of her eye.
She lifted a tear that she touched to my lips, and followed
the taste with a kiss, and the blue fire poured into me. And
the jungle, and the rain, and the river, and the ocean.

A fly in the water stirs ripples, tiny waves; and the elephant rides. Something shifted. The ground slid beneath
me.

"I don't have the words—" Tori said.

"You don't need any."

The elephant's brain is twice the size of a person's. No
one knows how much of the universe fits in an elephant's
mind, or what becomes of the universe when the elephant
dies. But I learned enough when the current ran through
me.

I learned mermaids don't wander. They orbit. They swim
in elliptical orbits that take them farther and farther away
from where they started—from where they belong. They always return, though. They have to.

But once upon a time, there was a mermaid who swam
out too far in the ocean—so far, she couldn't get back. She

drifted, lost. She hid among people so well, no one knew she was a mermaid. But she began to have bad effects on them.

She belonged in the past, and the past infected her. She made other people long for the past, too. They cherished old pieces of times that never belonged to them, when they should have been thinking of now and tomorrow.

She needed something more than her mermaid magic to get back, and it took her ninety-seven times to find it—to find me.

"Ride the waves, Brad," she said. I kissed her for all I was worth.

I don't know when Luna's lights came back. But I know this:

When people ran home that night to say what wonders they had seen at Luna Park, it wouldn't be the lights, or the Shoot the Chutes, or that poor, dead Topsy creature they told about. It would be us.

But as the park's electrical power took hold again, Tori changed. She stood away from me. She had Lillian's mean mouth for a moment, but she smiled then, still my Tori.

I seemed to be climbing, higher and higher into a blue rain, away from her. *Racheta-rakkata.*

She faded, a white figure lost in the light.

What am I, Tori? Ninety-six, and then me, and we all loved you, Tori, and so what? Did I love you the most? The least? The fastest? The blindest? What made me any different?

I never heard the answer, but I read it. Her last gift to a reader. Her face blurred as I left her. Her image doubled, tripled, as if I were seeing her through rippled glass. I read the answer from her lips.

Oh Brad silly I love you
silly I love you
love you

>   *you*
>   *you*
>   *you*
>   *you*
>   *you*
>   *you*

Climb.
Fall.
Curve.

∽ *12*

One night, the old Pen and Pitcher Club voted the worst cliche in science fiction. *The rose in his hand* swept the field. A man goes to sleep; he dreams of a rose; he wakes up with a rose in his hand.

The Cyclone ground to a stop. I got off alone. Nobody cared.

I shambled through the amusement park, side aching, vaguely aware of something digging at my hand. And then, I remembered: Skip's gold coin.

And then, I remembered: Tori's wooden nickel.

I'd come again, always again, to the Skee-Ball emporium. The attendant who'd fought me had taken his place again on the stool. His head slumped to his chest, and he looked almost the same as before, just as dead. The only difference was the bandage under his Yankees cap.

Closer, I saw it wasn't a hospital bandage around his head. It was a rag that he might have tied himself. The spot where I'd hit him was mottled the rust color of dried blood, and the rag was greasy from whatever ointment he'd smeared on.

If he breathed, I couldn't see it. People can dic from the delayed effects of a concussion.

I rolled the object in my hand. Wood is warm, metal is cold. But everything felt cold that night. Without looking, I slid the coin onto the glass prize counter beside him, and I walked away.

What's a Skee-Ball worth, anyway?

A TEACHER'S GUIDE to
Our Friend Electricity

—Make an ACTIVITY BOX. Include a Skee-Ball, a gold coin and a wooden nickel. Challenge your class to discover how these things explain the workings of time.

—FIELD TRIP: Visit a nearby carnival or amusement park. Do the rides look safe?

—Quiz ANSWERS:

1: (A) 6,600 volts to kill an elephant; 2,000 for a man.

2: (B) TRUE. Thought is electric.

3: (C) NONE OF THE ABOVE. So far as we know, lightning strikes without a thought.

The city no longer frightened me for being old. One day, I finished the books I'd been afraid to read.

Topsy was a bad elephant, but she had her reasons. The last man she killed had fed her a lighted cigarette.

Skip died of pneumonia by some accounts, but others say it was a hat pin stabbed through his heart by a jilted lover.

Nostalgia isn't selling anymore. People want brand new. New books, new politics, new streets, new meanings, new medicines, new lives. New Coney Island.

But Tori was right about me changing jobs. The last book I candied and cudgeled through publication here made it to the *New York Times* list. The publisher said he'd called me on the recommendation of a man I'd barely known in the Pen and Pitcher Club.

There!—I felt the tug, that little slide again, that tells me I don't have to stay here. I have just enough of Tori's mermaid magic in me to go out in the ocean and swim to . . . I don't know where. But what if I couldn't get back? What if I had to love someone new in order to get back?

I see her a million times a day, in sunlight on blonde hair, in a certain smile, in every white dress, in everything silver.

Sleeping, I search for my Tori through Luna, and Steeplechase, and Dreamland, for which the lovely waltz was written. *Meet me in Dreamland, sweet dreamy Dreamland.* But the old songs are out of my head.

I have a talent. A super secret psychic talent. You tell me the name of the last one you cared about even a little. I'll tell you how much that meant to you.

It broke your heart.

They all break your heart.

—For Jan, life's exception

Social Dreaming of the Frin

Ursula K. Le Guin

Ursula K. Le Guin [www.ursulakleguin.com] lives in Port-land, Oregon. She has published seventeen novels and nine short story collections to date, and also writes poetry, mainstream fiction, children's books, and literary essays, and edits anthologies. Le Guin's work is widely read out-side the SF field, and she is widely respected as a contem-porary writer. In recent years she has published a number of distinguished short stories, and in 2001 not only did she continue to do that, but also published two books of Earth-sea: Tales from Earthsea *and a novel,* The Other Wind, *and then her ninth collection of science fiction,* The Birthday of the World *(2002). Her reputation in fantasy rests firmly on the Earthsea books, but her occasional short fantasy fic-tion is of high quality and widely influential.*

"Social Dreaming of the Frin," which was published in F&SF, *is a charming quasi-anthropological story in which people share each other's dreams over short distances. Is it about the collective unconscious? About the media? About the Internet? The story rings very true though it deftly eludes direct allegoresis.*

On the Frinthian Plane dreams are not private property. There is no such thing as a dream of one's own. A troubled Frin has no need to lie on a couch recounting dreams to a psychoanalyst, for the doctor already knows what the patient dreamed last night, because the doctor dreamed it too; and the patient also dreamed what the doctor dreamed; and so did everyone else in the neighborhood.

To escape from the dreams of others or to have a secret dream, the Frin must go out alone into the wilderness. And even in the wilderness, their sleep may be invaded by the strange dream-visions of lions, antelope, bears, or mice.

While awake, and during much of their sleep, the Frin are as dream-deaf as we are. Only sleepers who are in or approaching REM sleep can participate in the dreams of others also in REM sleep.

REM is an acronym for "rapid eye movement," a visible accompaniment of this stage of sleep; its signal in the brain is a characteristic type of electro-encephalic wave. Most of our rememberable dreams occur during REM sleep.

Frinthian REM sleep and that of people on our plane yield very similar EEG traces, though there are some significant differences, in which may lie the key to their ability to share dreams.

To share, the dreamers must be fairly close to one another. The carrying power of the average Frinthian dream is about that of the average human voice. A dream can be received easily within a hundred-meter radius, and bits and fragments of it may carry a good deal farther. A strong dream in a solitary place may well carry for two kilometers or even farther.

In a lonely farmhouse a Frin's dreams mingle only with those of the rest of the family, along with echoes, whiffs, and glimpses of what the cattle in the barn and the dog dozing on the doorstop hear, smell, and see in their sleep.

In a village or town, with people asleep in all the houses round, the Frin spend at least part of every night in a shifting phantasmagoria of their own and other people's dreams which I find it hard to imagine.

I asked an acquaintance in a small town to tell me any dreams she could recall from the past night. At first she demurred, saying that they'd all been nonsense, and only "strong" dreams ought to be thought about and talked over. She was evidently reluctant to tell me, an outsider, things that had been going on in her neighbors' heads. I managed at last to convince her that my interest was genuine and not voyeuristic. She thought a while and said, "Well, there was a woman—it was me in the dream, or sort of me, but I think it was the mayor's wife's dream, actually, they live at the corner—this woman, anyhow, and she was trying to find a baby that she'd had last year. She had put the baby into a dresser drawer and forgotten all about it, and now I was, she was, feeling worried about it—Had it had anything to eat? Since last year? O my word, how stupid we are in dreams! And then, oh, yes, then there was an awful argument between a naked man and a dwarf, they were in an empty cistern. That may have been my own dream, at least to start with. Because I know that cistern. It was on my grandfather's farm where I used to stay when I was a child. But they both turned into lizards, I think. And then—oh yes!"—she laughed—"I was being squashed by a pair of giant breasts, huge ones, with pointy nipples. I think that was the teenage boy next door, because I was terrified but kind of ecstatic, too. And what else was there? Oh, a mouse, it looked so delicious, and it didn't know I was there, and I was just about to pounce, but then there was a horrible thing, a nightmare—a face without any eyes—and huge, hairy hands groping at me—and then I heard the three-year-old next door screaming, because I woke up too. That poor child has so many nightmares, she drives us all crazy. Oh, I don't really like thinking about that one. I'm glad you forget most dreams. Wouldn't it be awful if you had to remember them all!"

Dreaming is a cyclical, not a continuous activity, and so in small communities there are hours when one's sleep-theater, if one may call it so, is dark. REM sleep among settled, local groups of Frin tends to synchronize. As the cycles peak, about five times a night, several or many dreams may be going on simultaneously in everybody's head, intermingling and influencing one another with their mad, inarguable logic, so that (as my friend in the village described it) the baby turns up in the cistern and the mouse hides between the breasts, while the eyeless monster disappears in the dust kicked up by a pig trotting past through a new dream, perhaps a dog's, since the pig is rather dimly seen, but is smelled with enormous particularity. But after such episodes comes a period when everyone can sleep in peace, without anything exciting happening at all.

In Frinthian cities, where one may be within dream-range of hundreds of people every night, the layering and overlap of insubstantial imagery is, I'm told, so continual and so confusing that the dreams cancel out, like brushfuls of colors slapped one over the other without design; even one's own dream blurs at once into the meaningless commotion, as if projected on a screen where a hundred films were already being shown, their soundtracks all running together. Only occasionally does a gesture, a voice, ring clear for a moment, or a particularly vivid wet dream or ghastly nightmare cause all the sleepers in a neighborhood to sigh, ejaculate, shudder, or wake up with a gasp.

Frin whose dreams are mostly troubling or disagreeable say they like living in the city for the very reason that their dreams are all but lost in the "stew," as they call it. But others are upset by the constant oneiric noise and dislike spending even a few nights in a metropolis. "I hate to dream strangers' dreams!" my village informant told me. "Ugh! When I come back from staying in the city, I wish I could wash out the inside of my head!"

Even on our plane, young children often have trouble understanding that the experiences they had just before they woke up aren't "real." It must be far more bewildering for Frinthian children, into whose innocent sleep enter the sensations and preoccupations of adults—accidents relived, griefs renewed, rapes reenacted, wrathful conversations with people fifty years in the grave. But adult Frin are ready to answer children's questions about the shared dreams and to discuss them, defining them always as dream, though not as unreal. There is no word corresponding to "unreal" in Frinthian; the nearest is "bodiless." So the children learn to live with adults' incomprehensible memories, unmentionable acts, and inexplicable emotions, much as do children who grow up on our plane amid the terrible incoherence of civil war or in times of plague and famine; or, indeed, children anywhere, at any time. Children learn what is real and what isn't, what to notice and what to ignore, as a survival tactic, a means of staying alive. It is hard for an outsider to judge, but my impression of Frinthian children is that they mature early, psychologically; and by the age of seven or eight they are treated by adults as equals.

As for the animals, no one knows what they make of the human dreams they evidently participate in. The domestic beasts of the Frin seemed to me to be remarkably pleasant, trustful, and intelligent. They are generally well looked after. The fact that they share their dreams with their animals might explain why the Frin use animals to haul and plow and for milk and wool, but not as meat.

The Frin say that animals are more sensitive dream-receivers than human beings, and can receive dreams even from people from other planes. Frinthian farmers have assured me that their cattle and swine are deeply disturbed by visits from people from carnivorous planes. When I stayed at a farm in Enya Valley the chicken-house was in an uproar half the night. I thought it was a fox, but my hosts said it was me.

People who have mingled their dreams all their lives say they are often uncertain where a dream began, whether it was originally theirs or somebody else's; but within a family or village the author of a particularly erotic or ridiculous dream may be all too easily identified. People who know one another well can recognize the source-dreamer from the tone or events of the dream, its style. But after all, it has become their own as they dream it. Each dream may be shaped differently in each mind. And, as with us, the personality of the dreamer, the oneiric I, is often tenuous, strangely disguised, or unpredictably different from the daylight person. Very puzzling dreams or those with powerful emotional affect may be discussed on and off all day by the community, without the origin of the dream ever being mentioned.

But most dreams, as with us, are forgotten at waking. Dreams elude their dreamers, on every plane.

It might seem to us that the Frin have very little psychic privacy; but they are protected by this common amnesia, as well as by doubt as to any particular dream's origin, and by the obscurity of dream itself. And their dreams are truly common property. The sight of a red and black bird pecking at the ear of a bearded human head lying on a plate on a marble table and the rush of almost gleeful horror that accompanied it—did that come from Aunt Unia's sleep, or Uncle Tu's, or Grandfather's, or the cook's, or the girl next door's? A child might ask, "Auntie, did you dream that head?" The stock answer is, "We all did." Which is, of course, the truth.

Frinthian families and small communities are close-knit and generally harmonious, though quarrels and feuds occur. The research group from Mills College that traveled to the Frinthian plane to record and study oneiric brainwave synchrony agreed that (like the synchronization of menstrual and other cycles within groups on our plane) communal dreaming may serve to strengthen the social bond. They did not speculate as to its psychological or moral effects.

From time to time a Frin is born with unusual powers of projecting and receiving dreams—never one without the other. The Frin call such a dreamer whose "signal" is unusually clear and powerful a strong mind. That strongminded dreamers can receive dreams from non-Frinthian humans is a proven fact. Some of them apparently can share dreams with fish, with insects, even with trees. A legendary strong mind named Du Ir claimed that he "dreamed with the mountains and the rivers," but his boast is generally regarded as poetry.

Strong minds are recognized even before birth, when the mother begins to dream that she lives in a warm, amber-colored palace without directions or gravity, full of shadows and complex rhythms and musical vibrations, and shaken often by slow peaceful earthquakes—a dream the whole community enjoys, though late in the pregnancy it may be accompanied by a sense of pressure, of urgency, that rouses claustrophobia in some.

As the strong-minded child grows, its dreams reach two or three times farther than those of ordinary people, and tend to override or co-opt local dreams going on at the same time. The nightmares and inchoate, passionate deliria of a strong-minded child who is sick, abused, or unhappy can disturb everyone in the neighborhood, even in the next village. Such children, therefore, are treated with care; every effort is made to make their life one of good cheer and disciplined serenity. If the family is incompetent or uncaring, the village or town may intervene, the whole community earnestly seeking to ensure the child peaceful days and nights of pleasant dreams.

"World-strong minds" are legendary figures, whose dreams supposedly came to everyone in the world, and who therefore also dreamed the dreams of everyone in the world. Such men and women are revered as holy people, ideals and models for the strong dreamers of today. The moral pressure on strong-minded people is in fact intense, and so must be the psychic pressure. None of them lives in a city: they would go mad, dreaming a whole city's dreams. Mostly they gather in small communities where they live very quietly, widely dispersed from one another at night, practicing the art of "dreaming well," which mostly means dreaming harmlessly. But some of them become guides, philosophers, visionary leaders.

There are still many tribal societies on the Frinthian plane, and the Mills researchers visited several. They reported that among these peoples, strong minds are regarded as seers or shamans, with the usual perquisites and penalties of such eminence. If during a famine the tribe's strong mind dreams of traveling clear down the river and feasting by the sea, the whole tribe may share the vision of the journey and the feast so vividly, with such conviction, that they decide to pack up and start downriver. If they find food along the way, or shellfish and edible seaweeds on the beach, their strong mind gets rewarded with the choice bits; but if they find nothing or run into trouble with other tribes, the seer, now called "twisted mind," may be beaten or driven out.

The elders told the researchers that tribal councils usually follow the guidance of dream only if other indications favor it. The strong minds themselves urge caution. A seer among the Eastern zhud-Byu told the researchers, "This is what I say to my people: Some dreams tell us what we wish to believe. Some dreams tell us what we fear. Some dreams are of what we know though we may not know we knew it. The rarest dream is the dream that tells us what we did not know."

Frinthia has been open to other planes for over a century, but the rural scenery and quiet lifestyle have brought no great influx of visitors. Many tourists avoid the plane under the impression that the Frin are a race of "mindsuckers" and "psychovoyeurs."

Most Frin are still farmers, villagers, or town-dwellers, but the cities and their material technologies are growing fast. Though technologies and techniques can be imported only with the permission of the All-Frin government, requests for such permission by Frinthian companies and individuals have become increasingly frequent. Many Frin welcome this growth of urbanism and materialism, justifying it as the result of the interpretation of dreams received by their strong minds from visitors from other planes. "People came here with strange dreams," says the historian Tubar of Kaps, himself a strong mind. "Our strongest minds joined in them, and joined us with them. So we all began to see things we had never dreamed of. Vast gatherings of people, cybernets, ice cream, much commerce, many pleasant belongings and useful artifacts. 'Shall these remain only dreams?' we said. 'Shall we not bring these things into wakeful being?' So we have done that."

Other thinkers take a more dubious attitude toward alien hypnogogia. What troubles them most is that the dreaming is not reciprocal. For though a strong mind can share the dreams of an alien visitor and "broadcast" them to other Frin, nobody from another plane has been capable of sharing the dreams of the Frin. We cannot enter their nightly festival of fantasies. We are not on their wavelength.

The investigators from Mills hoped to be able to reveal the mechanism by which communal dreaming is effected, but they failed, as Frinthian scientists have also failed, so far. "Telepathy," much hyped in the literature of the interplanary travel agents, is a label, not an explanation. Researchers have established that the genetic programming of all Frinthian mammals includes the capacity for dreamsharing, but its operation, though clearly linked to the brainwave synchrony of sleepers, remains obscure. Visiting foreigners do not synchronize; they do not participate in that nightly ghost-chorus of electric impulses dancing to the same beat. But unwittingly, unwillingly—like a deaf child shouting—they send out their own dreams to the strong minds asleep nearby. And to many of the Frin, this seems not so much a sharing as a pollution or infection.

"The purpose of our dreams," says the philosopher Sorrdja of Farfrit, a strong dreamer of the ancient Deyu Retreat, "is to enlarge our souls by letting us imagine all that can be imagined: to release us from the tyranny and bigotry of the individual self by letting us feel the fears, desires, and delights of every mind in every living body near us." The duty of the strong-minded person, she holds, is to strengthen dreams, to focus them—not with a view to practical results or new inventions, but as a means of understanding the world through a myriad of experiences and sentiences (not only human). The dreams of the greatest dreamers may offer to those who share them a glimpse of an order underlying all the chaotic stimuli, responses, acts, words, intentions, imaginings of daily and nightly existence.

"In the day we are apart," she says. "In the night we are together. We should follow our own dreams, not those of strangers who cannot join us in the dark. With such people we can talk; we can learn from them and teach them. We should do so, for that is the way of the daylight. But the way of the night is different. We go together then, apart from them. The dream we dream is our road through the night. They know our day, but not our night, nor the ways we go there. Only we can find our own way, showing one another, following the lantern of the strong mind, following our dreams in darkness."

The resemblance of Sorrdja's phrase "road through the night" to Freud's "royal road to the unconscious" is interesting but, I believe, superficial. Visitors from my plane have discussed psychological theory with the Frin, but neither Freud's nor Jung's views of dream are of much interest to them. The Frinthian "royal road" is trodden not by one secret soul but a multitude. Repressed feelings, however distorted, disguised, and symbolic, are the common property of everybody in one's household and neighborhood. The Frinthian unconscious, collective or individual, is not a dark wellspring buried deep under years of evasions and denials, but a kind of great moonlit lake to whose shores everybody comes to swim together naked every night.

And so the interpretation of dreams is not, among the Frin, a means of self-revelation, of private psychic inquiry and readjustment. It is not even species-specific, since animals share the dreams, though only the Frin can talk about them.

For them, dream is a communion of all the sentient creatures in the world. It puts the notion of self deeply into question. I can imagine only that for them to fall asleep is to abandon the self utterly, to enter or reenter into the limitless community of being, almost as death is for us.

Five British Dinosaurs

Michael Swanwick

*Michael Swanwick [www.michaelswanwick.com] lives in
Philadelphia, and is one of the leading writers of fantasy
and science fiction today. He is also among the most pro-
lific in short fiction in recent years. He has won and been
nominated for more awards than bear mentioning. His fine
novels come out every three or four years—In the Drift
(1984), Vacuum Flowers (1987), Stations of the Tide
(1991), The Iron Dragon's Daughter (1993), and Jack
Faust (1997). Bones of the Earth was his new novel in
2002. He published more than fifty short short stories in
2001 and 2002, and his bibliography is bewilderingly difficult to update, since he publishes frequently online.*

*"Five British Dinosaurs" appeared in Interzone, which
maintained its high level of quality in fantasy and science
fiction, though it skipped two issues during the year, publishing two combined issues. The piece is composed of five
independent vignettes ringing playful variations on the
theme of British dinosaurs, and they are light, witty, and
humorous. This is Swanwick at his most evanescently
charming.*

It was Mary Ann Mantell who discovered the first Iguanodon fossils, in the South Downs of Sussex. She was a doctor's wife and had accompanied her husband on his rounds, when she was attacked by pixies.

It was a lovely day and, since Mary shared her husband's interests in natural history and geology in particular, she stayed outside while Gideon went into a patient's house.

He'd only been gone a few minutes when two or more invisible, giggling imps began pelting stones at Mary. Small, hard pebbles struck her on the arms and shoulders. Though she could see perfectly well from whence these missiles came, there appeared to be no one there. That, and the small, wicked voices, told her what her tormentors were.

A doctor's wife in Sussex of the 1820s was no weak and simpering thing. Without hesitation, she ran to a nearby pile of gravel (the road was being graded) and proceeded to give as good as she got. Then she spotted something white in the gravel. It was a tooth, embedded in rock.

When Gideon Algernon Mantell emerged into the sunlight again, Mary had gone through the entire pile of gravel, and had a handful of teeth to show him. The pixies, capricious as ever, had stopped their barrage when she had, and were now gone about their mysterious ways.

Dr. Mantell published a description of the teeth as belonging to a gigantic Mesozoic lizard which he named Iguanodon, or "iguana-tooth," in 1825. It was a fine piece of research, and only the second dinosaur (though the term "dinosaur" did not yet exist) ever described.

Mary never told anyone of the part the Little People had played in her discovery. A new era of scientific discovery was dawning across Europe, and fairies were no longer entirely respectable.

⌒ *Yaverlandia bitholus*

Prior to our discovery, Yaverlandia was known only from a single fragmentary skull excavated from the Wealdon Marls in the Isle of Wight. Imagine our astonishment when our expedition (Chapman, Brett-Surman et al.) discovered a living specimen of this least-known of all pachycephalosaurs holding down a rather exalted civil service position in Whitehall!

With some difficulty, we obtained an interview.

"Oh, the usual," he said when Dr. Brett-Surman asked him how he made his living. "I keep my head down, I try to keep the other chaps off my turf."

"And head-butting?" Ralph Chapman asked.

"Well, I am a bureaucrat, after all."

"How do you like the modern world?" I asked.

"Things were infinitely better run in the Mesozoic," the Yaverlandia said firmly. "One associated with a better class of being. Admittedly, theropods were a bit of a problem. But mammals knew their place then."

"Are there more of your species about? Surely your existence argues that there must be a breeding population somewhere."

"I am a widower. My wife died, along with all the rest of my kind, at the end of the Cretaceous, 65 million years ago."

"But how on Earth," I cried, "have you managed to survive all the millions of years that separate the Mesozoic from the modern day?"

"I'm afraid I'm not cleared to give you that information," the Yaverlandia replied stiffly. And showed us the door.

⌒ *Altispinax dunkeri*

Like so many of Ray Harryhausen's films, the plot was unworthy of him. But when your talent is for special effects and your special genius lies in the creation of dinosaurs, you take what work you can get. Still, even for Hammer Studios, *Bertie Wooster and the Dinosaurs* was a particularly ripe notion.

Somehow, though, the movie was put into production.

Ordinarily, Harryhausen favored stop-motion animation. It chanced, however, that a friend in the Ministry of Defense knew of two experimental bipedal walking-machines that were being scrapped and could be picked up for a song. They were shaped and sized just right for a pair of Altispinax—fleet, sail-backed theropods.

He re-geared the cams to lengthen the stride, then fitted both with small, powerful gasoline engines. Lastly, he sheathed them in moulded latex, so that they looked the part of living and carnivorous dinosaurs. There was a cockpit midway down the back of each. In operation, the driver would be hidden by the sail. But for the shakedown run, he left the sails undeployed.

It was night time when he was finally done. Harryhausen turned to his assistant and, with a courtly little bow, said, "Well, young lady—care to take 'em out for a spin?"

Tess leaped into a cockpit. "Yes, sir!"

A minute later, the two Altispinax sped into the night.

It was a wild run. Cars braked wildly and slid into ditches at the sight of the two prehistoric monsters running side-by-side down Maidenstone Road. Dogs barked savagely after them. Children stared wide-eyed from bedroom windows.

The stride was smooth—Harryhausen had put a great deal of thought into the shocks—and quiet, too. Twice they ran past patrol cars, the faces of the officers within stiff and white with disbelief. They ran all the way from the studio at Bray to the steps of the British Museum. Laughing, Harryhausen drew up his beast, and made it dance in place, lifting up those great legs and setting them down with exquisite delicacy. Tess threw back her theropod's throat and, putting hands to mouth, let out a howl that would shiver spines if they decided to use it in the movie.

A paleontologist, letting himself out by a side door after a late evening's work, glanced up at the two dinosaurs and sniffed. "You're not fooling anyone, you know," he said. He pointed to the feet. "The toes are all wrong, and the hallux is reversed."

And, so saying, he went home.

ᴗ *Megalosaurus bucklandii*

Megalosaurus was the first dinosaur ever named, and one of three (the others were Iguanodon and Hylaeosaurus, both discovered by the energetic Gideon Mantell) that caused Richard Owen to create the grouping Dinosauria. Alas, the species remains something of a dustbin for large, difficult-to-attribute theropods. The original specimen, found in a quarry at Stonesfield in Oxfordshire and described by William Buckland, was fragmentary in the extreme. Which helps to explain the sculptor Benjamin Waterhouse Hawkins's reconstructions.

Waterhouse Hawkins was commissioned by Owen to create life-sized statues of his newly-named dinosaurs for the grounds of the Crystal Palace. The results—heavy, lumbering, and evil of visage—were an enormous success. A dinner party held within the body of the Iguanodon, just before its completion, was one of the great scientific social events of the Victorian era.

It was not long afterward that a Megalosaurus called upon Waterhouse Hawkins in person.

It looked nothing like he had imagined. It was a biped, for one thing, and properly attired for another. Stooping its head, so it could pass through his doorway, it entered his flat with hat and gloves in one hand, and presented him with its card. Its manners were impeccable. He had no choice but to invite it in for tea. "My dear fellow," the Megalosaurus began. "You cannot possibly imagine the distress you have caused me by your uncouth representations." It shuddered. "You have me crawling about the ground on all fours, like a common beast! The expression upon my face is that of one who is a slave to his baser emotions." It took a delicate sip from its cup. Waterhouse Hawkins could not but note how delicately it held out its third finger. "And yet, as you can see, I am quite a civilized creature."

"The difficulties presented by incomplete fossils—" Waterhouse Hawkins began.

"Yes, yes, of course. One understands, and one sympathizes. Yet consider my position. Consider my reputation! I must ask for a retraction."

"I worked, sir, with the leading comparative anatomists of Europe. Had you presented yourself while we were consulting on the designs, we should certainly have taken your self-characterization into account. However, you did not."

"But—"

"At any rate, the models were extraordinarily expensive to fabricate. There is no money left to have them redone."

The Megalosaurus stood. "You leave me with no choice but to consult a solicitor."

Waterhouse Hawkins stood as well. Coldly, he said, "I content myself with the knowledge that there is not a lawyer in London who would accept as a client a gigantic carnivorous reptile."

With an angry clash of teeth, the Megalosaurus seized his hat and left.

Waterhouse Hawkins would have taken it all for a dream, save for the fact that he saw the dinosaur once again. It was a Sunday, and he was out for a stroll when he spied the Megalosaurus coming toward him on the sidewalk. It was the exact same creature—there was no possible way of mistaking it for anyone else.

Nor could he avoid it. Common courtesy required that he smile and nod as it passed. So he did.

The brute looked at him . . . and then through him. It cut him! Waterhouse Hawkins stood trembling and outraged. He had been snubbed, by God. The monstrous beast had cut him dead!

～ *Craterosaurus pottonensis*

Our coven hired a small bus to take us to Bedfordshire, where we intended to raise the spirit of a Craterosaurus— bones of one such stegosaurid had been found there, so it seemed a good bet. We had a pleasant drive, and sang old camp songs, rather to the dismay of our driver, and then retired to our rooms to get some sleep, so we'd be fresh for the event. Midnight found us in an appropriately spooky cemetery (mood, after all, matters) with the twelve of us, male and female alike, sky-clad, and our necromancer in Druidic robes.

We had brought a rather nice trilobite fossil to sacrifice. After the appropriate ceremonies Tim, the necromancer, smashed it to powder with one blow of a hammer, and shouted the Word of Summoning.

Out from the ground rose bone after bone, assembling themselves into the complete skeleton of a Craterosaurus. Earth flowed over the bones, became muscle, and sprouted skin. The great brute shook its head and opened its eyes. It studied us a moment in silence. Then—

"You're naked," it said.

Jane Giddings blushed. (There are those who'd say that seeing Jane naked was in and of itself reason enough to join the coven, and I'd not be one to gainsay them.) "We're not ashamed of our bodies," she told the ghostly animal. And stood so straight I could hardly catch my breath.

"Oh," it said, in a tone that indicated it was beginning to find us all rather boring. "Well, I suppose you've got some questions for me. Out with them."

There was a moment's silence. I don't think any of us had prepared questions. We'd decided to raise the Craterosaurus more for the challenge of the thing than with any particular end in view. On an impulse, I said, "How did the dinosaurs die out?"

"Haven't the foggiest. After my time. When I was alive, everything was going swimmingly." It yawned. "Next question."

But neither, it turned out, did the Craterosaurus know

anything about climatic shifts or ecological issues. Nor did it know if it was warm-blooded or cold-blooded ("Define your terms," it said, and it turned out that none of us could), or whether birds were really and truly descended from dinosaurs, or who was going to win this year's World Cup. That last question was Tim's. A good necromancer, was Tim, but not the brightest bulb on the porch.

Finally, we all got as tired of the conversation as the spirit of the Craterosaurus was, and sent it back to its eternal rest. "What a stupid beast!" Ian muttered to me, as we were all getting dressed afterward. "As far as I'm concerned, this has been a complete and utter waste of time."

"Oh, I don't know." I glanced over at Jane Giddings, who was busily buttoning up her blouse. As soon as she was fully dressed, I was going to march right over to her and ask her out. "I personally learned rather a lot tonight."

The Green Word

～～～

Jeffrey Ford

Jeffrey Ford lives in Medford Lakes, New Jersey with his wife and two sons, Jack and Derek. He teaches writing and literature at Brookdale Community College. Ford is the author of a trilogy of fantasy novels: The Physiognomy *(winner of the 1998 World Fantasy Award and a New York Times* Notable Book of the Year *for 1997),* Memoranda *(a New York Times* Notable Book *for 1999), and* The Beyond *(a selection for* Washington Post Book World's *Best of 2001 list). His most recent novel,* The Portrait of Mrs. Charbuque, *was published in 2002, as was his first story collection,* The Fantasy Writer's Assistant & Other Stories. *In 2002, his short fiction appeared in* F&SF, *Sci-Fiction,* Black Gate, Lady Churchill's Rosebud Wristlet, *and* The Northwest Review, *among others, and in the anthologies* The Green Man, Leviathan #3, *and* The Journal of Pulse Pounding Narratives.*

"The Green Word" was published in The Green Man *(as were the de Lint story above, and the Bell story later in this book). King Pious tries to convert the people of the forest to Christianity or else kill them, but they resist. Their resistance is beautifully imagined, full of memorable dream-like images.*

On the day that Moren Kairn was to be executed, a crow appeared at the barred window of his tower cell. He lay huddled in the corner on a bed of foul straw, his body covered with bruises and wounds inflicted by order of the king. They had demanded that he pray to their God, but each time they pressed him, he spat. They applied the hot iron, the knife, the club, and he gave vent to his agony by cursing. The only thing that had prevented them from killing him was that he was to be kept alive for his execution.

When he saw the crow, his split lips painfully formed a smile, for he knew the creature was an emissary from the witch of the forest. The black bird thrust its head between the bars of the window and dropped something small and round from its beak onto the stone floor of the cell. "Eat this," it said. Then the visitor cawed, flapped its wings, and was gone. Moren held out his hand as if to beg the bird to take him away with it, and for a brief moment, he dreamed he was flying out of the tower, racing away from the palace toward the cool green cover of the trees.

Then he heard them coming for him, the warder's keyring jangling, the soldiers' heavy footsteps against the flagstones of the circular stairway. He ignored the pain of his broken limbs, struggled to all fours, and crept slowly across the cell to where the crow's gift lay. He heard the soldiers laughing and the key slide into the lock as he lifted the thing up to discover what it was. In his palm, he held a round, green seed that he had never before seen the likes of. When the door opened, so did his mouth, and as the soldiers entered, he swallowed the seed. No sooner was it in his stomach than he envisioned a breezy summer day in the stand of willows where he had first kissed his wife. She moved behind the dangling green tendrils of the trees and when a soldier spoke his name it was in her voice, calling him to her.

With a gloved hand beneath each arm, they dragged him to his feet, and he found that his pain was miraculously gone. The noise of the warder's keys had somehow become the sound of his daughter's laughter, and he laughed, himself, as they pulled him roughly down the steps. Outside, the midsummer sunlight enveloped him like water, and he remembered swimming beneath the falls at the sacred center of the forest. He seemed to be enjoying himself far too much for a man going to his death, and one of the soldiers struck him across the back with the flat side of a sword. In his mind, though, that blow became the friendly slap of his fellow warrior, the archer Lokush. Moren had somehow forgotten that his best bowman had died not but a week earlier, along with most of his other men, on the very field he was now so roughly escorted to.

The entirety of the royal court, the knights and soldiers and servants, had gathered for the event. To Kairn, each of them was a green tree and their voices were the wind rippling through the leaves of that human thicket. He was going back to the forest now, and the oaks, the alders, the yews parted to welcome him.

The prisoner was brought before the royal throne and made to kneel.

"Why is this man smiling?" asked King Pious, casting an accusatory glance at the soldiers who had accompanied the prisoner. He scowled and shook his head. "Read the list of grievances and let's get on with it," he said.

A page stepped forward and unfurled a large scroll. Whereas all in attendance heard Kairn's crimes intoned— sedition, murder, treachery—the warrior himself heard the voice of the witch, chanting the beautiful poetry of one of her spells. In the midst of the long list of charges, the queen leaned toward Pious and whispered, "Good lord, he's going green." Sure enough, the prisoner's flesh had darkened to a deep hue the color of jade.

"Finish him before he keels over," said the king, interrupting the page.

The soldiers spun Moren Kairn around and laid his head on the chopping block. From behind the king stepped a tall knight encased in gleaming red armor. He lifted his broadsword as he approached the kneeling warrior. When the deadly weapon was at its apex above his neck, Kairn laughed, discovering that the witch's spell had transformed him into a seed pod on the verge of bursting.

"Now," said the king.

The sharp steel flashed as it fell with all the force the huge knight could give it. With a sickening slash and crunch of bone, Kairn's head came away from his body and rolled onto the ground. It landed, facing King Pious, still wearing that inscrutable smile. In his last spark of a thought, the warrior saw himself, a thousandfold, flying on the wind, returning to the green world.

All but one who witnessed the execution of Moren Kairn that day believed he was gone for good and that the revolt of the people of the forest had been brought to an end. She, who knew otherwise, sat perched in a tree on the boundary of the wood two hundred yards away. Hidden by leaves and watching with hawklike vision, the witch marked the spot where the blood of the warrior had soaked into the earth.

Arrayed in a robe of fine purple silk King Pious sat by the window of his bedchamber and stared out into the night toward the tree line of the forest. He had but an hour earlier awakened from a deep sleep, having had a dream of that day's execution—Kairn's green flesh and smile—and called to the servant to come and light a candle. Leaning his chin on his hand and his elbow on the arm of the great chair, he raked his fingers through his white beard and wondered why, now that the threat of the forest revolt was eradicated, he still could not rest easily.

For years he had lived with their annoyance, their claims to the land, their refusal to accept the true faith. To him they were godless heathens, ignorantly worshiping trees and bushes, the insubstantial deities of sunlight and rain. Their gods were the earthbound, corporeal gods of simpletons. They had the audacity to complain about his burning of the forest to create new farmland, complained that his hunting parties were profligate and wasted the wild animal life for mere sport, that his people wantonly fished the lakes and streams with no thought of the future.

Had he not been given a holy edict by the pontiff to bring this wild territory into the domain of the church, convert its heathen tribes, and establish order amidst this demonic chaos? All he need do was search the holy scripture of the Good Book resting in his lap and in a hundred different places he would find justification for his actions. Righteous was his mission against Kairn, whom he suspected of having been in league with the devil.

Pious closed the book and placed it on the stand next to his chair. "Be at ease, now," he murmured to himself, and turned his mind toward the glorious. He had already decided that in midwinter when what remained of the troublesome rabble would be hardest pressed by disease and hunger, he would send his soldiers into the maze of trees to ferret out those few who remained and return them to the earth they claimed to love so dearly.

As the candle burned, he watched its dancing flame and decided he needed some merriment, some entertainment to wash the bad taste of this insurrection from his palate. He wanted something that would amuse him, but also increase his renown. It was a certainty that he had done remarkable things in the territory, but so few of the rulers of the other kingdoms to the far south would have heard about them. He knew he must bring them to see the extraordinary palace he had constructed, the perfect order of his lands, the obedience of his subjects.

While he pondered, a strong wind blew across the fields from out of the forest, entered the window by which he sat, and snuffed the flame of the candle. At the very moment in which the dark ignited in his room and swiftly spread to cover everything in shadow, the idea came to him. A tournament—he would hold a tournament and invite the knights from the southern kingdoms to his palace in the spring. He was sure that his own Red Knight had no equal. The challenge would go out the following morning, and he would begin preparations immediately. The invitation would be so worded to imply that his man could not be beaten, for he, Pious, had behind him the endorsement of the Almighty. "That should rouse them enough to make the long journey to my kingdom," he whispered. Then he saw the glorious day in his imagination and sat for some time, laughing in the dark. When he finally drifted off to sleep, he fell into another nightmare in which a flock of dark birds had rushed into his bedchamber through the open window.

The witch of the forest, doubly wrapped in black, first by her long cloak and then by night, crouched at the edge of the tree line, avoiding the gaze of the full autumn moon, and surveyed with a keen eye the field that lay between herself and the palace. She made a clicking noise with her tongue, and the crow that had perched upon her shoulder lit into the sky and circled the area in search of soldiers. In minutes it returned with a report, a low gurgling sound that told her the guards were quite a distance away, just outside the protective walls. She whistled the song of a nightingale, and a large black dog with thick shoulders padded quietly to her side over fallen leaves.

She pulled the hood of the cloak over her head, tucking in her long white hair. Although she had more years than the tallest of trees looming behind her had rings, she moved with perfect grace, as if she was a mere shadow floating over the ground. The dog followed close behind and the crow remained on her shoulder, ready to fly off into a soldier's face if need be. The same memory that gave her the ability to recall, at a moment's notice, spells containing hundreds of words, all of the letters in the tree alphabet, the languages of the forest creatures, and the recipes for magical concoctions, worked now to help her pinpoint the spot where Moren Kairn's blood had soaked the earth three months earlier.

When she knew she was close, she stopped and bent over to search through the dark for new growth. Eventually she saw it, a squat, stemless plant, bearing the last of its glowing berries and yellow flowers into the early weeks of autumn. She dropped down to her knees, assuming the same position that Kairn had the day of his execution, and with her hands, began loosening the dirt in a circle around the plant's thick base. The ground was hard, and an implement would have made the job easier, but it was necessary that she use her hands in order to employ the herb in her magic.

Once the ground had been prepared, she started on a circular course around the plant, treading slowly and chanting in whispers a prayer to the great green mind that flows through all of nature. As she intoned her quiet plea in a singsong melodic voice, she thought of poor Kairn and her tears fell, knowing she would soon join him.

From within her cloak, she retrieved a long length of rope woven from thin vines. Taking one end, she tied it securely around the base of the plant. With the other end in hand, she backed up twenty paces and called the dog to her with the same whistled note she had used earlier. He walked over and sat, letting her tie that end of the rope around his neck. Once the knot was tight, she petted the beast and kissed him atop the head. "Stay now, Mahood," she whispered and the dog did not move as she backed farther away from it. Then she took four small balls of wild sheep wool from a pouch around her waist. Carefully, she stuffed one into each of the dog's ears and one in each of her own.

The moon momentarily passed behind a cloud, and as she waited for it to reappear, the crow left her shoulder. Eventually, when the moon had a clear view of her again, she motioned with both hands for the dog to join her. Mahood started on his way and then was slowed by the tug of the plant. She dropped to her knees, opened her arms wide and the dog lurched forward with all his strength. At that moment, the root of the plant came free from the ground, and its birth scream ripped through the night, a piercing wail like a pin made of sound for bursting the heart. Both witch and dog were protected from its cry by the tiny balls of wool, but she could see the effects the terrible screech still had on Mahood, whose hearing was more acute. The dog stopped in his tracks as if stunned. His eyes went glassy, he exhaled one long burst of steam, and then sat down.

The witch did not hesitate for a heartbeat but began running. As she moved, she reached for the knife in her belt. With a smooth motion she lifted the exposed root of the plant and tugged once on the vine rope to warn Mahood to flee. Then she brought the knife across swiftly to sever the lead, and they were off across the field, like flying shadows. She made for the tree line with the crow flapping in the air just above her left shoulder. The bird cawed loudly, a message that the soldiers had heard and were coming on horseback. The hood fell from her head, and her long white hair flew out behind her, signaling to her pursuers.

When she was a hundred yards from the boundary of the forest, she could hear the hoofbeats closing fast. The mounted soldier in the lead yelled back to those who followed, "It's the crone," and then nocked an arrow in place on his bow. He pulled back on the string and aimed directly for her back. Just as he was about to release, something flew into his face. A piece of night with wings and sharp talons gouged at his right eye. The arrow went off and missed its mark, impaling the ground in the spot where the witch's foot had been but a second before.

Mahood had bounded ahead and already found refuge in among the trees of the forest. The crow escaped and the witch ran on, but there was still fifty yards of open ground to cover and now the other horsemen were right on her heels. The lead soldier drew his sword and spurred his horse to greater speed. Once, twice, that blade cut the air behind her head and on both passes severed strands of her long hair. Just when the soldier thought he finally had her, they had reached the boundary of the trees. He reared back with the sword to strike across her back, but she leaped before he could land the blow. The height of her jump was miraculous. With her free hand, she grabbed the bottom branch of the closest tree and swung herself up with all the ease of a child a hundred years younger. The other soldiers rode up to join their companion at the tree line just in time to hear her scampering away, like a squirrel, through the dark canopy of the forest.

The black dog was waiting for her at her underground cave, whose entrance was a hole in the ground amidst the vast stand of willows. Once safely hidden in her den, she reached beneath her cloak and pulled out the root of the Mandrake. Holding it up to the light from a burning torch, she perused the unusual design of the plant's foundation. Shaped like a small man, it had two arms extending from the thick middle part of the body and at the bottom a V shape of two legs. At the top, where she now cut away the green part of the herb, there was a bulbous lump, like a rudimentary head. This root doll, this little wooden mannikin, was perfect.

She sat on a pile of deerskins covering a low rock shelf beneath the light of the torch. Taking out her knife, she held it not by the bone handle but at the middle of the blade, so as to have finer control over it. The technique she employed in carving features into the Mandrake root was an ancient art called *simpling*. First, she carefully gouged out two eyes, shallow holes precisely equidistant from the center of the head bump. An upward cut beneath the eyes raised a partial slice of the root. This she delicately trimmed the corners off of to make the nose. Next, she made rudimentary cuts where the joints of the elbows, knees, wrists and ankles should be on the limbs. With the tip of the blade, she worked five small fingers into the end of each arm to produce rough facsimiles of hands. The last, but most important job was the mouth. For this opening, she changed her grip on the knife and again took it by the handle. Applying the sharp tip to a spot just below the nose, she spun the handle so as to bore a deep, perfect circle.

She laid the knife down by her side and took the Mandrake into the crook of her arm, the way in which one might hold a baby. Rocking forward and back slightly, she began to sing a quiet song in a language as old as the forest itself. With the thumb of her free hand she persistently massaged the chest of the plant doll. Her strange lullaby lasted nearly an hour, until she began to feel a faint quivering of the root in response to her touch. As always with this process, the life pulse existed only in her imagination at first, but as she continued to experience it, the movement gradually transformed from notion to actuality until the thing was verily squirming in her grasp.

Laying the writhing root in her lap, she lifted the knife again and carefully sliced the thumb with which she had kneaded life into it. When she heard the first peep of a cry come from the root child, she maneuvered the self-inflicted wound over the round mouth of the thing and carefully let three drops of blood fill the orifice. When the Mandrake had tasted her life, it began to wriggle and coo. She lifted it in both hands, rose to her feet and carried it over to a diminutive cradle she had created for it. Then looking up at the crow, who perched on a deer skull resting atop a stone table on the other side of the vault, she nodded. The bird spoke a single word and flew up out of the den. By morning, the remaining band of forest people would line up before the cradle and each offer three drops of blood for the life of the strange child.

King Pious hated winter; for the fierce winds that howled outside the palace walls in the long hours of the night seemed the voice of a hungry beast come to devour him. The cold crept into his joints and set them on fire, and any time he looked out his window in the dim daylight all he saw was his kingdom buried deeply beneath a thick layer of snow the color of a bloodless corpse. During these seemingly endless frigid months, he was often beset by the thought that he had no heir to perpetuate his name. He slyly let it be known that the problem lay with the queen, who he hinted was obviously barren, but whom, out of a keen sense of honor, he would never betray by taking another wife. The chambermaids, though, knew for certain it was not the queen who was barren, and when the winds howled so loudly in the night that the king could not overhear them, they whispered this fact to the pages, who whispered it to the soldiers, who had no one else to tell but each other and their horses.

To escape the beast of winter, King Pious spent much of the day in his enclosed pleasure garden. Here was summer confined within four walls. Neat, perfectly symmetrical rows of tulips, hyacinths, roses, tricked into growth while the rest of nature slept, grew beneath a crystal roof that gathered what little sunlight there was and magnified its heat and light to emulate the fair season. Great furnaces beneath the floor heated the huge chamber and butterflies, cultivated for the purpose of adding a touch of authenticity to the false surroundings, were released daily. Servants skilled in the art of re-creating bird sounds with their voices were stationed in rooms adjoining the pleasure garden, and their mimicked warblings were piped into the chamber through long tubes.

In the afternoon of the day on which the king was given the news that the first stirrings of spring had begun to show themselves in the world outside the palace walls, he was sitting on his throne in the very center of the enclosed garden, giving audience to his philosopher.

On a portable stand before him lay a device that the venerable academician had just recently perfected, a miniature model with working parts that emulated the movement of the heavens. The bearded wise man in tall pointed hat and starry robe lectured Pious on the Almighty's design of the universe. The curious creation had a long arm holding a gear train attached to a large box with a handle on the side. At the end of the arm were positioned glass balls, connected with wire, representative of the Sun and Earth and other planets. Pious watched as the handle was turned and the solar system came to life, the heavenly bodies whirling on their axes while at the same time defining elliptical orbits.

"You see, your highness," said the philosopher, pointing to the blue ball, largest of the orbs, "the Earth sits directly at the center of the universe, the Almighty's most important creation which is home to his most perfect creation, mankind. All else, the Sun, the Moon, the planets and stars, revolve around us, paying homage to our existence as we pay homage to God."

"Fascinating," said the king as he stared intently at the device that merely corroborated for him his place of eminence in the far flung scheme of things.

"Would you like to operate the device?" asked the philosopher.

"I shall," said the king. He stood up and smoothed out his robes. Then he advanced and placed his hand on the handle of the box. He gently made the world and the heavens spin and a sense of power filled him, easing the winter ache of his joints and banishing, for a moment, the thought that he had no heir. This feeling of new energy spread out from his head to his arm, and he began spinning the handle faster and faster, his smile widening as he put the universe through its paces.

"Please, your highness," said the philosopher, but at that instant something came loose and the entire contraption flew apart, the glass balls careening off through the air to smash against the stone floor of the garden.

The king stood, looking perplexed, holding the handle, which had broken away from the box, up before his own eyes. "What is this?" he shouted. "You assassinate my senses with this ill-conceived toy of chaos." He turned in anger and beat the philosopher on the head with the handle of the device, knocking his pointed hat onto the floor.

The philosopher would have lost more than his hat that afternoon had the king's anger not been interrupted. Just as Pious was about to order a beheading, the captain of the guard strode into the garden, carrying something wrapped in a piece of cloth.

"Excuse me, your highness," he said, "but I come with urgent news."

"For your sake, it had better be good," said the king, still working to catch his breath. He slumped back into his chair.

"The company that I led into the forest last week has just now returned. The remaining forest people have been captured and are in the stockade under guard. There are sixty of them, mostly women and children and elders."

Pious straightened up in his seat. "You have done very well," he told the soldier. "What of the witch?"

"We came upon her in the forest, standing in a clearing amidst a grove of willows with her arms crossed as if waiting for us to find her. I quietly called for my best archer and instructed him in whispers to use an arrow with a poison tip. He drew his bow and just before he released the shaft, I saw her look directly at where we were hiding beneath the long tendrils of a willow thirty feet from her. She smiled just before the arrow pierced her heart. Without uttering a sound, she fell forward, dead on the spot."

"Do you have her body? I want it burned," said Pious.

"There is no body, your highness."

"Explain," said the king, beginning to lose his patience.

"Once the bowman hit his mark, we advanced from the trees to seize her, but before we could lay hands on her, her very flesh, every part of her, became a swirling storm of dandelion seed. I swear to you, before my very eyes, she spiraled like a dust devil three times and then the delicate fuzz that she had become was carried up and dispersed by the wind."

Pious nodded, thought for a second and then said, "Very well. What is that you carry?"

The soldier unwrapped the bundle and held up a book for the king to see. "We found this in her cave," he said.

The king cleared his eyes with the backs of his hands. "How can this be?" he asked. "That is the copy of the Good Book I keep in my bedchamber. What kind of trickery is this?"

"Perhaps she stole it, your highness."

Pious tried to think back to the last time he had picked the book up and studied it. Finally he remembered it was the night of Kairn's execution. "I keep it near the open window. My God, those horrid birds of my dream." The king looked quickly over each shoulder at the thought of it. "A bag of gold to the bowman who felled her," he added.

The captain nodded. "What of the prisoners, your highness?" he asked.

"Execute the ones who refuse to convert to the faith, and the others I want taught a hymn that they will perform on the day of the tournament this spring. We'll show our visitors how to turn heathens into believers."

"Very good, your highness," said the captain and then handed the book to the king. He turned and left the garden.

By this time, the philosopher had crept away to hide and Pious was left alone in the pleasure garden. "Silence!" he yelled in order to quell the birdsong, which now sounded to him like the whispers of conspirators. He rested back in his throne, exhausted from the day's activities. Paging through the Good Book, he came to his favorite passage—one that spoke elegantly of vengeance. He tried to read, but the idea of the witch's death so relaxed him that he became drowsy. He closed his eyes and slept with the book open on his lap while that day's butterflies perished and the universe lay in shards scattered across the floor.

The tournament was held on the huge field that separated the palace from the edge of the forest. Spring had come, as it always did, and that expanse was green with new-grown grass. The days were warm and the sky was clear. Had it not been for the tumult of the event, these would have been perfect days to lie down beneath the sun and daydream up into the bottomless blue. As it was, the air was filled with the cheers of the crowd and the groans of agony from those who fell before the sword of the Red Knight.

Pious sat in his throne on a dais beneath a canvas awning, flanked on the right and left by the visiting dignitaries of the southern kingdoms. He could not recall a time when he had been more pleased or excited, for everything was proceeding exactly as he had imagined it. His visitors were obviously impressed with the beauty of his palace and the authority he exhibited over his subjects. He gave orders a dozen an hour in an imperious tone that might have made a rock hop to with a "Very good, your highness."

Not the least of his pleasures was the spectacle of seeing the Red Knight thrash the foreign contenders on the field of battle. That vicious broadsword dislocated shoulders, cracked shins, and hacked appendages even through the protective metal of opponents' armor. When one poor fellow, the pride of Belthaena, clad in pure white metal, had his heart skewered and crashed to the ground dead, the king leaned forward and, with a sympathetic smile, promised the ambassador of that kingdom that he would send a flock of goats to the deceased's family. So far it had been the only fatality of the four day long event, and it did little to quell the festivities.

On the final day, when the last opponent was finished off and lay writhing on the ground with a broken leg, Pious sat up straight in his chair and applauded roundly. As the loser was carried from the field, the king called out, "Are there any other knights present who would like to test our champion?" Since he knew very well that every represented kingdom had been defeated, he made a motion to one of his councilors to have the converted begin singing. The choir of forest people, chained at the ankles and to each other shuffled forward and loosed the first notes of the hymn that had been beaten into their memories over the preceding weeks.

No sooner did the music start, though, than the voice of the crowd overpowered its sound, for now there was a new contender on the tournament field. He stood, tall and gangly, not in armor, but wrapped in a black, hooded cloak. Instead of a broadsword or mace or lance, he held only a long stick fashioned from the branch of a tree. When the Red Knight saw the surprised face of the king, he turned to view this new opponent. At this moment, the crowd, the choir and the dignitaries went perfectly quiet.

"What kind of mockery is this?" yelled Pious to the figure on the field.

"No mockery, your highness. I challenge the Red Knight," said the stranger in a voice that sounded like a limb splintering free from an oak.

The king was agitated at this circumstance that had been no part of his thoughts when he had imagined the tournament. "Very well," he called, and to his knight, said, "Cut him in half."

As the Red Knight advanced, the stranger undid the clasp at the neck of his cloak and dropped it to the ground. The crowd's response was a uniform cry torn between a gasp and a shriek of terror, for standing before them now was a man made entirely of wood. Like a tree come to life, his branch-like limbs, though fleshed in bark, somehow bent pliantly. His legs had the spring of saplings, and the fingers with which he gripped his paltry weapon were five-part pointed roots, trailing thin root hairs from the tips of the digits. The gray bark of his body held bumps and knots like a log, and in certain places small twigs grew from him, covered at their ends with green leaves. There was more foliage simulating hair upon his pointed head and a fine stubble of grass across his chin. Directly in the center of his chest, beneath where one's heart might hide, there grew from a protruding twig a large blue fruit.

The impassive expression that seemed crudely chiseled into the face of the wooden man did not change until the Red Knight stepped forward and with a brutal swing lopped off the tree root hand clutching the stick. Then that dark hole of a mouth stretched into a toothless smile, forming wrinkles of joy beneath the eyes. The Red Knight stepped back to savor the pain of his opponent, but the stranger exhibited no signs of distress. He held the arm stump up for all to see and, in a blur, a new hand grew to replace the one on the ground.

The Red Knight was obviously stunned, for he made no move as the tree man came close to him and placed that new hand up in front of his enemy's head. When the king's champion finally meant to react, it was too late. For as all the crowd witnessed, the five sharp tips of the root appendage grew outward as swiftly as snakes striking and found their way into the eye slits of the knight's helmet. Ghastly screams echoed from within the armor as blood seeped out of the metal joints and onto the grass. The knight's form twitched and the metal arms clanked rapidly against the metal sides of the suit. The broadsword fell point first and stuck into the soft spring earth. When the stranger retracted his hand, the fingers growing back into themselves, now wet with blood, the Red Knight tipped over backward and landed with a loud crash on the ground.

Pious immediately called for his archers. Three of them stepped forward and fired at the new champion. Each of the arrows hit its mark, thunking into the wooden body. The tree man nonchalantly swept them off him with his arm. Then he advanced toward the dais, and the crowd, the soldiers, the visiting dignitaries fled. The king was left alone. He sat, paralyzed, staring at the advancing creature. So wrapped in a rictus of fear was Pious that all he could manage was to close his eyes. He waited for the feel of a sharp root to pierce his chest and puncture his heart. Those moments seemed an eternity to him, but eventually he realized nothing had happened. When he could no longer stand it, he opened his eyes to an amazing scene. The tree man was kneeling before him.

"My liege," said the stranger in that breaking voice. Then he stood to his full height, and said, "I believe as winner of the tournament, I am due a feast."

"Quite right," said Pious, trembling with relief that he would not die. "You are an exceptional warrior. What is your name?"

"Vertuminus," said the tree man.

A table had been hastily brought into the pleasure garden and laid with the finest place settings in the palace. The feast was prepared for only Pious and the wooden knight. The visiting ambassadors and dignitaries were asked if they would like to attend, but they all suddenly had pressing business back in their home kingdoms and had to leave immediately after the tournament.

The king dined on roasted goose, whereas Vertuminus had requested only fresh water and a large bucket of soil to temporarily root his tired feet in. Soldiers were in attendance, lining the four walls of the garden, and were under orders to have their swords sharp and to keep them drawn in case the stranger's amicable mood changed. Pious feared the tree man, but was also curious as to the source of his animation and bizarre powers.

"And so my friend, you were born in the forest, I take it?" asked the king. He tried to stare into the eyes of the guest, which blinked and dilated in size though they were merely gouges in the bark that was his face.

"I was drawn up from the earth by the witch," he said.

"The witch," said Pious, pausing with a leg of the goose in his hand.

"Yes, she made me with one of her spells, but she has abandoned me. I do not know where she has gone. I have been lonely and needed other people to be with. I have been watching the palace from a distance, and I wanted to join you here."

"We are very glad you did," said the king.

"The witch told me that you lived by the book. She showed me the book and taught me to read it so that I would know better how to wage war on you."

"And do you wish me harm?" asked Pious.

"No, for when I read the book it started to take hold of me and drew me to its thinking away from the forest. I joined the tournament so that I could win a place at the palace."

"And you have," said Pious. "I will make you my first knight."

Here Vertuminus recited the king's favorite passage from the good book. "Does it not make sense?" he asked.

Pious slowly chewed and shook his head. "Amazing," he said, and for the first time spoke genuinely.

"You are close to the Almighty?" asked Vertuminus.

"Very close," said the king.

There was a long silence, in which Pious simply sat and stared as his guest drank deeply from a huge cup.

"And if you don't mind my asking," said the king, pointing, "what is that large blue growth on your chest?"

"That is my heart," said Vertuminus. "It contains the word."

"What word?" asked Pious.

"Do you know in the book, when the Almighty creates the world?"

"Yes."

"Well, how does he accomplish this?" asked the tree man.

"How?" asked the king.

"He speaks these things into creation. He says, 'Let there be light,' and there is. For everything he creates, he uses a different word. This fruit contains the green word. It is what gives me life."

"Is there a word in everything?" asked Pious.

"Yes," said Vertuminus, whose index finger grew out and speared a pea off the king's platter. As the digit retracted, and he brought the morsel to his mouth, he said, "There is a word in each animal, a word in each person, a word in each rock, and these words of the Almighty make them what they are."

Suddenly losing his appetite, the king pushed his meal away. He asked, "But if that fruit of yours contains the green word, why is it blue?"

"Only its skin is blue, the way the sky is blue and wraps around the earth."

"May I touch it?" asked Pious.

"Certainly," said Vertuminus, "but please be careful."

"You have my word," said Pious, as he stood and slowly reached a trembling hand across the table. His fingers encompassed the blue fruit and gently squeezed it.

The wooden face formed an expression of pain. "That is enough," said the tree man.

"Not quite," said the king, and with a simple yank, pulled the fruit free from its stem.

Instantly, the face of Vertuminus went blank, his branch arms dropped to his sides, lifeless, and his head nodded.

Pious sat back in his throne, unable to believe that defeating the weird creature could have been so easy. He held the fruit up before his eyes, turning it with his fingers, and pondered the idea of the word of God trapped beneath a thin blue skin.

The ruler sat in silent contemplation, and in his mind formulated a metaphor in which the acquisition of all he de-sired could be as easy as his plucking this blue prize. It was a complex thought for Pious, one in which the blue globe of the world from the philosopher's contraption became con-fused with the fruit.

He nearly dropped the precious object when suddenly his lifeless guest gave a protracted groan. The king looked up in time to see another blue orb rapidly growing on the chest of the tree man. It quickly achieved fullness, like a balloon being inflated. He gave a gasp of surprise when his recently dead guest smiled and brought his branch arms up.

"Now it is my turn," said Vertuminus, and his root fin-gers began to grow toward the king.

"Guards," called Pious, but they were already there. Swords came down on either side, and hacked off the wooden limbs. As they fell to the floor, Pious wasted no time. He dove across the table and plucked the new blue growth. Again, Vertuminus fell back into his seat, lifeless.

"Quickly, men, hack him to pieces and burn every twig!" In each of his hands he held half of his harvest. He rose from his throne and left the pleasure garden, the sound of chopping following him out into the corridor. Here was a consolation for having lost his Red Knight, he thought—something that could perhaps prove far more powerful than a man encased in metal.

When Pious ordered that one of the forest people be brought to him, he had no idea that the young woman cho-sen was the daughter of Moren Kairn. She was a tall, wil-lowy specimen of fifteen with long blond hair that caught the light at certain angles and appeared to harbor the slight-est hues of green. Life in the stockade, where the remaining rebels were still kept, was very difficult. For those who did not willingly choose the executioner over conversion to the faith, food was used as an incentive to keep them on the path to righteousness. If they prayed they ate, but never enough to completely satisfy their hunger. And so this girl, like the others, was exceedingly thin.

She stood before the king in his study, a low table separating her from where he sat. On that table was a plate holding the two blue orbs that had been plucked from Vertuminus.

"Are you hungry, my dear?" asked the king.

The girl, frightened for her life, knowing what had become of her father and having witnessed executions in the stockade, nodded nervously.

"That is a shame," said Pious. "In order to make it up to you, I have a special treat. Here is a piece of fruit." He waved his hand at the plate before him. "Take one."

She looked to either side, where soldiers stood guarding her every move.

"It's quite all right," said Pious in as sweet a tone as he was capable.

The girl reached out her hand and carefully lifted a piece of fruit. She brushed her hair away from her face with her free hand as she brought the blue food to her mouth.

The king leaned forward with a look of expectation on his face as she took the first bite. He did not know what to expect and feared for the worst. But the girl, after tasting a mouthful, smiled, and began greedily devouring the rest of it. She ate it so quickly he barely had time to see that its insides, though green, were succulent like the pulp of an orange.

When it was finished and she held nothing but the pit in her hand, Pious asked her, "And how was that?"

"The most wonderful thing I have ever tasted," she whispered.

"Do you feel well?" he asked.

"I feel strong again," she said and smiled.

"Good," said Pious. He motioned to one of the soldiers to escort her back to the stockade. "You may go now," he said.

"Thank you," said the girl.

Once she and the soldier had left the room, the king said to the remaining guard, "If she is still alive by nightfall, bring me word of it."

* * *

It tasted, to him, something like a cool, wet ball of sugar, and yet hidden deeply within its dripping sweetness there lay the slightest trace of bitterness. With each bite, he tried to fix more clearly his understanding of its taste, but just as he felt on the verge of a revelation, he found he had devoured the entire thing. All that was left in his hand was the black pit, shaped like a tiny egg. Since the blue-skinned treat had no immediate effect on him, he thought perhaps the secret word lay within its dark center and he swallowed that also. Then he waited. Sitting at the window in his bedchamber, he stared out into the cool spring night, listening, above the din of his wife's snoring, to the sound of an unseen bird, calling plaintively off in the forest. He wondered what, if anything, the fruit would do for him. At worst he might become sick unto death, but the fact that the girl from the forest was still alive but an hour earlier was good insurance that he would also live. At best, the risk was worth the knowledge and power he might attain. To know the secret language of the Almighty, even one green word, could bring him limitless power and safety from age and death.

Every twinge of indigestion, every itch or creak of a joint, made him think the change was upon him. He ardently searched his mind, trying to coax into consciousness the syllables of that sacred word. As it is said of a drowning man, his life passed before the inner eye of his memory, not in haste but as a slow stately procession. He saw himself as a child, his parents, his young wife, the friends he had had when he was no older than the girl he had used to test the fruit. Each of them beckoned to him for attention, but he ignored their pleas, so intent was he upon owning a supreme secret.

The hours passed and instead of revelation, he found nothing but weariness born of disappointment. Eventually, he crawled into bed beside his wife and fell fast asleep. In his dreams, he renewed his quest, and in that strange country made better progress. He found himself walking through the forest, passing beneath the boughs of gigantic pines. In those places where the sunlight slipped through and lit the forest floor, he discovered that the concept of the green word became clearer to him.

He went to one of these pools of light and as he stood in it, the thought swirled in his head like a ghost as round as the fruit itself. It came to him that the word was a single syllable comprised of two entities, one meaning life and one death, that intermingled and intertwined and bled into each other. This knowledge took weight and dropped to his tongue. He tried to speak the green word, but when he opened his mouth, all that came out was the sound of his own name. Then he was awake and aware that someone was calling him.

"King Pious," said the captain of the guard.

The man was standing next to his bed. He roused himself and sat up.

"What is it?" he asked.

"The forest people have escaped from the stockade."

"What?" he yelled. "I'll have your head for this!"

"Your highness, we found the soldiers who guard them enmeshed in vines that rooted them to the ground and, impossible as it sounds, a tree has grown up in the stockade overnight and the branches bend down over the high wall to touch the ground. The prisoners must have climbed out in the night. One of the horseman tried to pursue them but was attacked by a monstrous black dog and thrown from his mount."

Pious threw back the covers and got out of bed. He meant to give orders to have the soldiers hunt them down and slay them all, but suddenly a great confusion clouded his mind. That ghost of the green word floated and turned again in his mind, and when he finally opened his mouth to voice his command, no sound came forth. Instead, a leafed vine snaked up out of his throat, growing with the speed of an arrow's flight. He clutched his chest, and the plant from within him wound itself around the soldier's neck and arms, trapping him. Another vine appeared and another, until the king's mouth was stretched wide with virulent strands of green life, growing rapidly out and around everything in the room. At just this moment, the queen awoke, took one look at her husband and fled, screaming.

By twilight, the palace had become a forest. Those who did not flee the onslaught of vegetation but stayed and tried to battle it were trapped alive in its green web. All of the rooms and chambers, the kitchen, the tower cell, the huge dining hall, the pleasure garden, and even the philosopher's hiding place were choked with a riot of leafy vine. The queen and those others who had escaped the king's virulent command traveled toward the south, back to their homes and roots.

Pious, still planted where he had stood that morning, a belching fountain of leaf and tendril, was now the color of lime. Patches of moss grew upon his face and arms, and his already arthritic hands had spindled and twisted into branches. In his beard of grass, dandelions sprouted. On the pools that were his staring eyes, minuscule water lilies floated. When the sun slipped out of sight behind the trees of the forest, the last of that part of the green word he knew to be *life* left him and all that remained was *death*. A stillness descended on the palace that was now interrupted only by the warblings of nightingales and the motion of butterflies escaped from the pleasure garden into the wider world.

It was obvious to all of the forest people that Moren Kairn's daughter, Alyessa, who had effected their escape with a startling display of earth magic, was meant to take the place of the witch. When they saw her moving amidst the trees with the crow perched upon her shoulder, followed by Mahood, they were certain. Along with her mother, she took up residence in the cave beneath the stand of willows and set to learning all that she could from what was left behind by her predecessor.

One day near the end of spring, she planted in the earth the seed from the blue fruit, the origin of her magic, that Pious had given her. What grew from it was a tree that in every way emulated the form of Vertuminus. It did not move or talk, but just its presence was a comfort to her, reminding her of the quiet strength of her father. With her new powers came new responsibilities as the forest people looked to her to help them in their bid to rebuild their village and their lives. At the end of each day, she would come to the wooden knight and tell him of her hopes and fears, and in his silence she found excellent council and encouragement.

She was saddened in the autumn when the tree man's leaves seared and fell and the bark began to lift away from the trunk, revealing cracks in the wood beneath. On a cold evening, she trudged through orange leaves to his side, intending to offer thanks before winter devoured him. As she stood before the wooden form, snow began to lightly fall. She reached out her hand to touch the rough bark of his face, and just as her fingers made contact, she realized something she had been wondering about all summer.

It had never been clear to her why the fruit had been her salvation and gift and at the same time had destroyed King Pious. Now she knew that although the king had the green word, he had no way to understand it. "Love," she thought, "so easy for some and for others so impossible." In the coming years, through the cycle of the seasons, she planted the simple seed of this word in the hearts of all who knew her, and although, after a long life, she eventually passed on, she never died.

The Comedian

<img>~~~~</img>

Stepan Chapman

Stepan Chapman lives in Cottonwood, Arizona. He has published a large amount of fiction over the last thirty years and more, from stories in John W. Campbell's Analog, in Weirdbook, and in volumes 12 and 17 of Damon Knight's Orbit, to work in many literary magazines over the years. In 2002, he published stories in Redsine 7, Leviathan 3, McSweeney's, *and* The Silver Web, *where this story appeared. His drawings and comic strips have appeared in* Eclipse, Mausoleum, NegativeInk, *and others. His critical articles have appeared in* The Comics Journal, Rain Taxi, *and* SF Eye. *In 2003, his short fiction will appear in two anthologies edited by Jeff Vandermeer,* Album Zutique One *and* The Thackery T. Lambshead Pocket Guide To Obscure and Discredited Diseases. *Some of his stories have been collected in* Danger Music *(1996), a chapbook of ten stories, and* Dossier *(2001). His novel* The Troika *(1997) won the Philip K. Dick Memorial Award.*

"The Comedian" is a fantasy about psychic powers, and a young boy whose older brother uses his telekinetic powers to become popular in high school.

That? That was nothing. Now my older brother Shell could do tricks with his mind that make *that* look like spoon bending.

You've never met my brother Shell. He's quite a character. Went through school one year ahead of me. I was a goody-goody, but Shell got into every kind of trouble. Mom and Dad never came down too hard on him, though, cause his grade average was always B plus.

No, nothing like that. He was never into drinking or fighting or drag racing or anything like that. Just got rowdy at times. His sense of humor would go out of control, and he'd play some wild prank—run a jockstrap up the flagpole or start a food fight in the cafeteria. You know the type. Teachers don't appreciate humor in their classrooms. Shell spent many hours in detention hall. Got his best studying done there, since the girls had their own detention hall. Shell was always very distractible that way.

A month before graduation, Shell came *that* close to being expelled. The school board let him off with a two-week suspension. That was the year when Bekka Wrenn broke his heart.

But I should tell you about Shell in some sort of sequence. I should begin with Shell and Peggy in fourth grade.

Shell sat in the second row of Mrs. Fernstrom's class. Peggy and her two blond pigtails sat in the desk just in front of him. Shell was fixated on Peggy, always trying to get a reaction out of her. She detested him, of course, but that never seemed to bother Shell. One boring afternoon, he collected some dead flies from the window sills. During social studies, he dropped them, one by one, down the collar of Peggy's dress, until she noticed them.

The dead flies produced a better reaction than any of his previous torments. Peggy danced in the aisle, and children

209

laughed hysterically. Shell was moved to a different desk. For weeks, he had to content himself with pestering Peggy during recess periods. Then he discovered his odd psychic talent.

It was a groggy morning in April. Shell was gazing at a dead fly on a windowsill halfway across the room. He found that if he stared hard at the bluebottle and sat very still, he could pick the fly up and hold it against the window pane, using only his mind. He practiced this maneuver for days, until he could make the flies hover in midair. Then he floated ten of them across the room, all the way to the collar across the back of Peggy's neck. Then he stuffed the flies down Peggy's dress.

Mayhem ensued again. Shell was sent to the principal's office. Mrs. Fernstrom couldn't *prove* that he'd done the deed, but she *knew*. Mrs. Fernstrom was no fool.

Since the school system had endured similar difficulties with my *other* older brothers, the principal, Miss Waxman, dealt sternly with Shell. She informed him that if he was experiencing the stirrings of some psychic power, he should play with it *at home*. He must *refrain* from taking it out and playing with it at school. At school, Miss Waxman demanded, *zippers zipped and hands out of pockets*.

Shell disliked Miss Waxman, but he followed her advice. Every day from that day forward, Shell would rush home from school and play with his psychic talent until it went limp. I watched him do it and took notes. I used to take notes on all my brothers. Each of us had some kinky telekinetic gift. These gifts were usually more trouble than they were worth, but we had a lot of fun with them. Shell could fiddle with dead animals. We conducted a series of experiments in the basement.

He couldn't budge a sugar cube or a grain of rice. He couldn't move a peach pit or a straw. But he could push, pull, bend, or levitate a dead earthworm. Not live worms, only dead ones. And given a raw chicken from the grocery, or a pound of ground beef, Shell could cause the meat to twitch. Back in grade school, he got his best effects with dead bugs. We liberated a great number of these from Dad's backlog of insect collections.

Our father not only *made* insect collections, he also *collected* collections. The older boxes gathered dust on wire racks in one corner of the basement. So Shell had lots of raw material for his puppet plays.

Shell was a natural comedian. He could make me laugh until my ribs hurt. He did this bit with a box of Japanese beetles one time . . . Invented a dozen different cartoon voices for the characters. There was the Shogun, the Empress, four sycophants, two geishas . . . Shell had me rolling on the floor. And the floor of that basement was *cement*.

We destroyed at least five collections that week, including a whole box of Bolivian Swallowtails. Thankfully, Dad never noticed.

By the time I went into the high school, Shell was a sophomore, and he could lift a dead sheep right up off the ground with his mind. Summers, we'd ride our bikes along the shoulder of the interstate, scouting for roadkills. Once we found three squashed copperheads, and Shell used them to stage a wrestling championship. The smallest snake was the referee. I told Shell that he should be on television.

At school, Shell's sense of humor made him popular. Even his teachers liked Shell. As for his talent, he kept that completely under wraps. After a certain age, Mom and Dad expected that of us.

Shell played tennis on the intramural team. Shell rode buses to other high schools with the debating squad. Certainly Shell was the most socially accepted young man that *our* household had ever produced. And popular with the young ladies too. With the exception of Bekka Wrenn, who broke his heart.

Shell and Bekka had one class in common, Fifth Level Zoology. Zoology was an advanced-placement, college-level course. It was taught by Mr. Jordan, the terror of First Level Biology, who threw erasers at freshmen when they whispered in the back row.

Bekka Wrenn sat at the lab bench next to Shell's. Her lab partner was a geek named Pamela, and both of them hated Shell's guts. But how can I tell you about Bekka?

Bekka wanted to become either a brain surgeon, or a marine ecologist, or a choreographer. She was still deciding. Bekka could have melted any boy's heart. She was unbearably gorgeous, extremely smart, and unexplainably sad. Such a sad girl she was. Everyone around her felt it. And none of us knew why. No one ever found out why. I doubt that her own family knew what made her so sad. Some people are just born sad, and being gorgeous and smart are no help at all. As for Shell, Shell didn't mind her hating his guts. Shell worshipped the girl. In the presence of Bekka, Shell stood constantly on the brink of losing all self-restraint.

He began to play silly pranks. Worse yet, he used his psychic power, during class. It began with a jug of preserved frogs.

The lab work for Zoology commenced with a basic dissection—peel, open, and eviscerate. Mr. Jordan sat on a stool beside the teacher's desk and used a pair of tongs to dole out stiff frogs, which he fished from a five-gallon jar of formaldehyde and dropped onto the steel trays presented by the students. When each student had his or her specimen, Mr. Jordan removed his rubber gloves and adjourned to the teachers' lavatory to wash his hands. The students were unsupervised for over two minutes. Since they were honors-level students, this was an intentional test of their maturity. For two minutes, Shell went completely manic.

There were five frogs still floating in the jar—leftovers. With Shell providing voices from his stool, and actions by remote control, these five frogs leaped from the jar and became Mr. and Mrs. Mucosa, their respective divorce lawyers, and a judge.

Audience response was enthusiastic and loud. Mr. Jordan reappeared scowling. As for Bekka, staging sketches with dead frog flesh did nothing to endear Shell to her. She never laughed once. She seemed to be somewhere else, far away.

"Maybe you should try stuffing flies down her dress," I suggested. "That's always worked well for you."

Like talking to a wall. I studied him like a rare specimen and filled notebook pages with my observations. I'd never seen a person fall in love before. You can learn a lot from older brothers.

After the frog disaster, Shell put the lid on his sense of humor again. With the exception of a minor incident in the cafeteria, involving some lunch meat, he played the role of a model student. He had hopes of reversing Bekka's bad impression of him. He had a snowball's chance in hell, but he lived in hope.

Bekka paid no attention to him. She had other things on her mind.

One Saturday night, when the spring rains had been heavy, the Pantano River flooded. Bekka rode her ten-speed to the middle of the Speedway overpass. She turned off her bike lamp and left the bike leaned against a guardrail. Then she tossed herself off the overpass, into the water. No one saw her do it. No one noticed.

That night, her parents called the police. On Sunday, they found the bike. On Monday afternoon, the state troopers brought in motorboats and nets and started dragging the riverbed, south of the overpass.

By this time, half of the city knew that Bekka Wrenn was missing. Someone phoned Shell and told him about the boats.

Shell and I rode our bikes down to the embankment. There was a crowd standing around, drinking pop from aluminum cans and watching the boats with binoculars. Shell stood beside me, staring at the water, knowing that he'd lost the only woman he'd ever love, and feeling himself slowly going numb inside.

The river water began to churn. The cops in the boats were shouting. Something was moving down there. Something was rising to the surface, breaking through the foam. It went on rising until it hovered, dripping, yards above the water, suspended by some invisible force from inside my brother's head. The sunshine was bright. Bekka's body wore a red jogging suit trimmed with reflective tape. Her hair was gathered back into a barrette. Her nail polish was a tasteful peach. This, apparently, was how the perfect dream girl had dressed herself to commit suicide. Whatever Bekka did, she always did it perfectly.

Shell lifted the body very high. For a couple of seconds, I thought that he would raise her clear into the sky and make her sail off like a helium balloon.

But he laid her down on the embankment. He crossed her arms and closed her eyes. Then he and I turned and went home.

The two-week suspension came a month before graduation day. Shell's test grades were slipping badly. He spent a lot of time alone, brooding. He lost touch with most of his friends. He began to act more like his brothers.

Then one night, Mom and Dad got a call from the police station. Shell had pulled an elaborate stunt in the girls' locker room. The families of the cheerleading team were threatening legal action against Shell, our family, the school district, or all of the above.

The stunt involved a megaphone lifted from a tennis equipment closet, two dozen plucked chickens from the supermarket, seven large salamis, and a gallon or so of dead worms from the dumpster of a garden supply store. The shrieks of the cheerleaders, so I was told, could be heard at a distance of half a mile from the locker room.

First there were the raw chickens running to and fro on the tile floor, causing barefoot cheerleaders to leap onto benches. Then came the shrill, amplified voice that seemed to ring out from all directions at once, pretending to be the voices of the headless poultry.

"*Run!*" sang the echoing voice. "He's coming! *This* way! No, *this* way! Help us! Hide us! Don't let him catch us! The Salami Man! The Awful Rotten Salami Man! He's after us! He's coming! *The Salami Man!*"

By now, the cheerleaders were shouting insults down at the chickens and laughing, because they had a pretty good idea of who had engineered this spectacle.

Shell burst forth from the locker where he'd been hiding. He ran up and down the length of the locker room and then sprang onto the equipment table in his telekineticized costume. He wore a wriggling wig and a squirming loin cloth composed entirely of deceased nightcrawlers. There were also the seven salamis, linked together end to end, doing their imitation of a swaying cobra with its tail tucked between Shell's legs. Shell had coated himself with blueberry pancake syrup for the occasion. He spun around on the folding table, butt naked except for the worms, the blueberry syrup, and the salami snake.

"I am the Salami Man!" he declaimed. "I am the Great Salami Man!" That was as far as he got. The cheerleaders dragged him down, buried him in dirty gym clothes, and sat on him.

The cheerleading squad had a great time. The school administrators, by contrast, were not amused. They suspended Shell. But they could have expelled him. The thing of it was, they liked Shell. Everyone liked Shell. So they gave him a chance to pull himself together, which, as it happened, was something that Shell had already done.

He salvaged his declining grade point average, dated a few of the cheerleaders, and graduated with honors.

The year after that, Shell was at college, and my own ability kicked in. I stopped filling notebooks with accounts of my weird brothers. Suddenly I had my own problems to cope with. But Shell's never forgotten Bekka.

In college, women would try to get close to him and end up wondering what his problem was. The problem was that Shell was in *mourning*. He still is. Never got married. Never even got close. I told you: She broke his heart.

He finished college. Found a career that suited him. Did the technical training and got certified. Moved north to Wyoming. Rents a furnished apartment in Sheridan. Makes good money and leads a quiet life. A solid citizen with a bald spot.

These odd talents that run in our family, they seem terribly important when you're young. But they don't *change* anything. After a while, they're just a nuisance, a false promise. You grow up, and you forget about them.

He runs a funeral parlor, actually. He embalms people.

Oh, I know what you're probably imagining now. You're thinking that he turned into some psychotic *necrophile* who secretly molests the corpses. You're so wrong.

I paid him a visit last year, and guess what? He *does* use his talent on the cadavers. And his clientele know all about it. They call him The Mortician Who Always Leaves Them Laughing. Shell has that printed on business cards. The people in Wyoming are surprisingly broad-minded about the whole thing. What Shell does is—he tells jokes to the dead people. And he makes them laugh.

I saw him do it, once. He was draining this chubby old guy named Carpinno. There were three other bodies lying around on gurneys, wearing towels, looking as though they were lounging at pool side.

"How's tricks, Mr. Carpinno?" says Shell, screwing a long needle onto a rubber tube.

Mr. Carpinno just stares at the ceiling fan.

"Got a riddle for you, Mr. Carpinno. Why did the chicken cross the road?"

Mr. Carpinno stares at the ceiling fan.

"I blame *society*," says Shell.

I didn't see the joke. But all four of the dead people laughed. Mr. Carpinno even slapped his thigh. It's a peculiar sound, four dead people laughing at a joke you don't get.

When the chuckles died away, Shell turned to me.

"You see?" he said to me. "These are the only people who appreciate my sense of humor."

The Pagodas of Ciboure

M. Shayne Bell

M. Shayne Bell [www.mshaynebell.com] lives in Salt Lake City, Utah. He has been publishing SF and fantasy since winning first place in the Writers of the Future contest in 1987. He has an M.A. in English: "I completed the first science fiction and fantasy creative writing thesis at Brigham Young University, after years of struggle. It was a collection of my short stories. The loathing for the entire genre in the English department at the time astonished me." He received a Creative Writing Fellowship from the National Endowment for the Arts in 1990. His SF novel Nicoji was published in 1991. He edited the anthology, Washed by a Wave of Wind: Science Fiction from the Corridor (1993), and has published a steady stream of short stories since.

"The Pagodas of Ciboure" is the third story in this book reprinted from The Green Man (see the de Lint and Ford pieces earlier). It uses French mythical creatures (pagodas), not much known outside of France, and is based on the childhood life of French composer Maurice Ravel.

On a day of the summer Maurice nearly died, his mother carried him to the banks of the Nieve River and his life changed forever. He was ten years old then. It was a warm day around noon in June of 1885. A gentle breeze blew off the bay, and from where they sat Maurice and his mother could smell the salt of the sea. His mother believed such breezes could heal.

"When will Papa be here?" he asked his mother.

"Any day," she said. "His letter said he would come soon."

"Will he bring a doctor to bleed me?"

"Hush," she said. She brushed the hair across his forehead. "No one will bleed you in Ciboure, Maurice. I won't let them."

Maurice leaned against his mother and slept for a time in the sunlight. When he woke, he wanted to walk along the river. Yes he had a fever, and yes he did not feel well, but he wanted to walk upstream. He felt drawn to something in that direction, curious about what might lie just out of sight. His mother watched him totter along. "Don't go too far," she said, glad that he felt well enough to do this on his own but anxious that he not hurt himself.

Maurice worked his way slowly up the riverbank. He picked a reed and swished it at the grasses ahead. The grasses gave way to flowered bushes, and the land rose gently to a forest. The water of the little river gurgled over rocks as it rushed clear and cold down from the Pyrenees.

Not far into the trees, in a wide glen, Maurice came upon the walls of an abandoned pottery. Five hundred years earlier this workshop had sold sparkling dinner plates and soup bowls to Moorish and Christian princes. After the region had passed to France, its wares had been treasured in the palaces and mansions of Paris, Lyon, and Marseilles.

But most of the wealthy family who owned the pottery had been guillotined in the Revolution. The few survivors had not returned to open it again.

The roof was now caved in. Windows in the stone walls were sunny holes. Maurice stood on his tiptoes and looked through one of the windows. He saw grass growing where workers had once hurried about polished floors.

Maurice walked around the ruined building and stopped in surprise. Three high mounds down by the river glittered in the sunlight as if covered in jewels. He had never seen anything like it. Among the daisies and the wild roses and the lacy ferns sunlight gleamed and sparkled on what looked from a distance like gems. It was as if he had wandered into a fairy treasury.

"Mother!" he called because he wanted her to see this. "Mother!"

But she was too far away to hear. Then he decided to be quiet: if there were jewels on those mounds he did not want to attract anyone else walking in the forest. He would fill his pockets first, then he would lead his mother here. If he had found jewels, they could buy a seaside mansion and he would get well and his father would come to live with them. They would all be happy again.

He walked slowly down to the mounds. His feet crunched on the ground, and he realized he was walking on broken china and glass. When he got to the mounds, he could see that that was what sparkled in the sunlight—broken dishes. The mounds were the old trash heaps of the pottery. There would be no fortune here.

Maurice scooped up a big handful of the shards, careful not to cut himself, and he carried them to the river. He held them down into the water and let the water wash away the dirt that had blown over the shards all these years. After a moment he shook out the water and spread his handful of broken china, wet and glittery, on the riverbank. Some shards were edged with a gold rim. One had a black fleur-de-lys entirely complete. Three pieces were from a set of blue china so delicate and clear he could see shadow through them when he held them up to the light.

Maurice was tired and hot. He sat breathing heavily for a time. When the breeze moved the branches overhead, sunlight sparkled on the broken china that had washed into the shallow riverbed. Maurice liked this place. Even if there were no jewels, it was nice to dream about being rich. It was nice to dream about being well again. This was a place that invited dreams.

He sat quietly—just long enough for the things that had gone still at his approach to start moving and singing again. First the birds, then the butterflies, then Maurice saw clusters of pieces of china moving slowly over the ground: one cluster, then another, then more than he could count. They moved slowly between the flowers and around the stands of grass.

Maurice sat very, very still. He did not know what was making the pieces of china cluster together and move. He shivered, but he did not dare run. He watched very carefully, hardly daring to breathe. Sometimes only three shards moved together. Sometimes a handful. The pieces that moved were bright and clean, and the sharp edges had all been polished away. One small clump of six snowy-white shards came upon the pieces Maurice had washed. It stopped by one of the blue ones, and drew back as if amazed.

It was then that Maurice heard the singing. It was an odd music, soft and indistinct, and he had to struggle to hear it at all. The simplest birdsong would drown it out. But the white china shards tinkled as they moved, and amidst the tinkling a high, clear voice sang. He thought the music sounded Chinese.

Other clusters of shards hurried up—pink clumps and white clumps and some with each shard a different color or design. With so many gathered around him Maurice could hear their music clearly. Somehow, surrounded by music, Maurice forgot to be afraid. Creatures that made music would not hurt him, he thought. They seemed to debate in their songs the merits of each piece he had washed. Maurice slowly reached out and picked up the white shard with the black fleur-de-lys. He set it down by a small cluster of terra-cotta shards and thought it made a fine addition.

All movement and song stopped. The clusters sank slowly to the ground. No one walking by would have noticed them or thought them special at all. Maurice put his hand back in his lap and sat still. He wanted them to move once more. He wanted them to sing.

It took some time for it to happen again. After the birds had been singing by themselves for a long time and when the butterflies were fluttering about Maurice's head, the terra-cotta pieces slowly drew themselves up into a terraced pattern, the larger pieces on the bottom, the smaller on top. It held the fleur-de-lys shard in the middle, as if it were a shield.

You look like a pine tree, Maurice thought.

But the more he looked at it, the more he realized it looked like a Chinese temple. He knew then what these creatures were. "Pagodas," he whispered. "Pagodas!"

His mother had told him stories about the pagodas. She'd said they looked like little Chinese temples. They were creatures made of jewels, crystal, and porcelain who lived in the forests of France. If you were good to them, they could heal you. He had thought the stories mere fairy tales.

He looked at the glittery river and the sparkling mounds and then at the shining shards around him. "Please heal me," he whispered. "I want to get better. Please help me."

He did not know how it would happen. He thought that maybe he should touch one of them. Some power might flow into him and make him well if he did. He reached out and gently touched the terra-cotta shards.

They sank down at once. He picked up each piece, then put it back in its place. He saw nothing among them. He found no hint of what a pagoda inside its shell of shards might look like. "Please help me," he whispered. "Mother's doctors can't, and I don't want Papa's to bleed me again."

Nothing around him moved now. When he heard his mother calling, he stood up very carefully. He did not want to step on the pagodas. He took off his shoes and planned each footstep before he took it. He tried to walk on grass and flowers, not the broken china. He hoped he had not hurt a single pagoda.

His mother met him at the steps of the pottery where he sat lacing his shoes. "You have been gone a long time," she said. She looked around as she waited for him. "Oh, this is pretty here. The trash heaps glitter so. You shouldn't walk barefoot to the river, Maurice—you could cut your feet on the glass!"

"I was careful, Mother," Maurice said.

She smiled and took his hand. They walked home slowly. She did not have to carry him.

That night, while the fever made him wobbly, Maurice pulled the box that held his favorite things out from beneath his bed. Inside were all the letters from his father carefully tied with a red ribbon. He set them aside. There were the thirteen francs he'd been able to save, wrapped in a note to his parents asking them to divide the money. He set that aside as well. There was the bright red, white, and blue pouch that held the set of seven tin soldiers his grandmother had sent him from Switzerland.

And there was his kaleidoscope. It was his most treasured possession. It was a shiny brass tube filled with mirrors. A person looked through one end to see the glorious patterns; the other was a chamber that could be screwed off and opened. Into that chamber Maurice would put pieces of broken glass and the beads and the strips of colored paper and string that made the intricate images in the kaleidoscope. The most common objects could become beautiful there. He could change the images whenever he wanted, and he and his mother had spent pleasant hours walking along the roadsides looking for broken, colored glass small enough to fit inside. He unscrewed the chamber and picked out three bright blue glass shards and one crystal bead. He took the tin soldiers out of their pouch and laid them in a row along the bottom of the box. Then he put the pieces of glass and the bead in the pouch.

He would take them to the pagodas, he thought. Maybe if he gave them something they would help him.

In the morning, his nose would not stop bleeding. He kept old pieces of rag stuffed up his nose and his mother made him lie down, but every time he removed the rags, his nose would bleed again.

"Will Papa come today?" he asked.

"He may, or he may arrive tomorrow morning. It won't be long."

Maurice thought about that. He wanted to see his papa. He felt better when his papa held him. But he did not like the doctor his papa took him to, and neither did his mother. The good doctors, as his mother called them, had said to keep him comfortable and to give him medicines to take away the pain. The doctor Papa had found believed he could cure Maurice if he bled him. Papa had had to hold him down while the doctor had cut his arm and let his blood drip into a bowl. It had made him dizzy and sick, and he had embarrassed everyone by crying. It was why his mother had taken him away from Paris to his grandmother's house in Ciboure.

"Can we walk to the river again?" he asked.

His mother laughed, but then she looked out the window and put down her sewing. How many mornings would he want do to something like this, she wondered? A nosebleed was manageable.

She packed them a lunch and extra rags for his nose. They walked slowly to the river. Maurice could not wait to be gone. After eating a few bites, he stuffed some of the rags into his pockets and started for the trees. His mother was glad to see him take exercise, but she could not help herself. "Be careful, Maurice," she called.

The day was chill, and Maurice wore a heavy sweater. He took off his shoes when he came to the old rubbish heaps. He stepped very carefully down to the river, careful not to crush clumps of china shards and careful not to cut his feet. He started to be able to distinguish the shards that made up a pagoda's shell: they were the shiny and polished ones, the ones with bits of color, not the ones caked with mud or dust.

He inspected the ground before he sat down, and he sat where he had sat the day before. He listened, but he heard no Chinese music. "Pagodas?" he whispered. "Pagodas?"

Nothing stirred. He looked around and saw a few clumps that he recognized: the terra-cotta shards, still with the black fleur-de-lys; the light pink shards; clumps that were all white.

"Don't be afraid," he whispered. "I've brought you presents."

He took the pouch out of his pocket and opened it in his lap. He took out one of the pieces of blue glass and set it by the nearest snowy white clump. He wasn't sure, but he thought it might have shivered ever so slightly at his touch. He waited for a time, then he set the crystal bead by the terra-cotta shards.

Slowly, shard by shard, the terra-cotta pieces rose up. He watched the bead roll along the different shards, passed from one to another until it stood balanced on the very top.

Other pagodas began to move then. They rose up and gathered warily around Maurice, keeping their distance. He could hear their tinkly music again, and all at once he understood part of what they were asking him.

"I'm Maurice," he said. "My name is Maurice Ravel."

They sang at him, and he imagined that they were telling him their names. He had never heard one of those names before. He thought the terra-cotta shards were saying "Ti Ti Ting."

"You *are* all Chinese!" he laughed.

Then he started coughing, and he could not stop coughing for a time. Most of the pagodas sank down to the ground while he coughed. But not Ti Ti Ting. It edged a little closer.

"Can you help me?" Maurice asked it. "Can you make me well? Tell me what to do, and I will do it."

All the shards grew quiet. The music stopped completely.

"I know my presents are not very valuable, but it was all I could think to bring you today."

Nothing happened. The pagodas did not tell him anything more then. After a time, Maurice could see pagodas moving all around him. The mounds were covered with them. He could see places where they were digging into the mounds—mining, he imagined, for shards to weave into their shells. In other places, they were forming what looked like protective walls four or five inches high with sharp-edged pieces of china poking out from them. He wondered what small enemies they could fear? Whatever it was, they were going about their business unconcerned with his presence.

When he heard his mother calling, he made his way barefoot back to the steps of the pottery. His mother met him there.

"Is your nose still bleeding?" she asked.

Maurice took out the rags, but no blood followed. He threw the rags aside, and he and his mother walked home.

His nose did not bleed again that day.

Before bed, his grandmother brewed him a tea from herbs she had sent for from Spain. A priest in San Sebastian had blessed the tea, and his grandmother had even paid to have the priest touch the cross of Saint Teresa of Avila to the little packet. His grandmother was sure the tea would cure Maurice. He drank the whole cup to please her. It did not taste bad.

His mother brought out her silver-handled brush from her bedroom and started brushing his grandmother's hair. She did this every night before they went to bed. He liked to lay his head in his grandmother's lap and watch her face while his mother brushed her hair. She would close her eyes and hold herself very still and lean her head back into the brushing. Sometimes Maurice fell asleep while he watched his grandmother, and his mother would have to wake him to take him to bed. He did not fall asleep that night. He lay awake on his grandmother's lap till his mother finished brushing, then she led him to bed.

"Tell me about pagodas," he asked as his mother tucked the blankets around his chin.

"Oh, they are magic creatures!" she said. "They live in crystal and porcelain cities hidden in the forests. Few people see them or their cities these days. But when I was a little girl, your grandmother told me about an evil man who had found one of their cities not far from here. He tried to steal their jewels, but the pagodas attacked him with their crystal swords. He ran away, but bore the scars on his hands and feet the rest of his life. Because of those scars, everyone in Ciboure knew he was a thief so they could watch out for him."

She stood up to go.

"Can pagodas heal people?" Maurice asked. "You told me before that they could."

She looked at Maurice, then she sat down on the edge of his bed and held his hands. "Sometimes in your sleep you can hear them singing," she said. "They weave healing spells in their music. I hope you hear their music tonight, Maurice. I wish we had pagodas in the back garden. I'd set them on your windowsill and let them sing to you all night."

When his mother had gone, Maurice touched his nose. It still was not bleeding, though it had bled most days since winter. He thought of the walks he could take now on his own, despite the fevers.

The pagodas were helping him. He was sure of it. If he could stay here long enough, they would cure him.

Maurice slept soundly but heard no music. He woke to the sound of his parents arguing softly in the kitchen. His father had come. Part of him wanted to jump out of bed and run to his father's arms, but he did not do that. Instead he lay listening to what his parents were saying. He could not hear the words clearly. He got out of bed and crept to the door. He heard his father say "doctor" and "bleeding." Then, "I want him to get well too! He's my son."

"I won't let anyone bleed him again!" his mother said.

"Does he still bruise easily? Does he still have fevers?"

"Yes, but—"

"Then Dr. Perrault knows how to help him! He uses ancient treatments for fevers and swelling, nosebleeds and abnormal bruising in children. I trust his techniques more than herbs and priests' blessings."

"Maurice is improving here. What Mother and I are doing is helping, though whether priests' blessings have anything to do with it I don't know. He is strong enough now to take walks every day. He sleeps through the nights. How could he ever sleep in Paris with all the street traffic?"

"You are wearing yourself out," his father said. "You can't do everything for him. None of us knows enough, Marie."

"I know enough not to hurt him."

"The other doctors we took him to had given up—they said to just keep him comfortable. At least Dr. Perrault had reason to think he could save him. Don't you think we should try, Marie? Don't you think we'd wonder the rest of our lives if we didn't try?"

Maurice had heard enough. He stood and opened the door. He looked out at his parents sitting at the big wooden table in front of the fireplace. His grandmother was still locked in her bedroom.

"Maurice," his father said. He stood and hurried to his son. Maurice did not want his father to touch him, but his father knelt and hugged him close. "Look at you!" he said. "So brown from the sun. Our neighbors in Paris will think I've adopted a peasant boy when I bring you back home."

"I don't want to go back to Paris," Maurice said. "Don't take me there again."

"Never go back to Paris? Who could say such a thing? Our home is in the greatest city in the world."

"I love the forest here, Papa. It's magic."

"All forests are magic," his father said.

His mother was setting out dishes for breakfast, and when Grandmother came out they all sat at the table. There was cheese and fresh bread, strawberries and milk.

"Don't ever take me back to Paris," Maurice said before any of them could take a bite.

His mother and father looked at each other. They all ate in silence for a time.

His father cleared his throat. "When do you set out on your walks, Maurice?" he asked. "May I go with you today? I want to see this magic forest of yours."

Maurice felt he had no choice but to take him. At noon that day, they set out. Maurice was nervous. He did not want his father accidentally stepping on the pagodas and crushing them. He decided not to take his father to the mounds of broken china. They would stop at the old pottery or even before they reached the trees. He'd claim to be sick, and his father would have to take him home.

His father carried a basket with a lunch in one hand, and he held Maurice's hand in the other. They passed his grandmother in her garden. She straightened up at their approach and bent her back.

"What a lovely summer this is," she said. "I find practically no slugs in the vegetables. The lettuce is free of slugs, and I found only one in the strawberries last week. Now if I could just keep the birds away."

"I'll make you a scarecrow when we return," Maurice's father said. "That should help."

She smiled and turned back to her hoeing. Maurice and his father walked to the river. Maurice was not very hungry. "You should eat to build up your strength," his father said. "Here, take more of this rabbit breast. Meat will make you strong."

"Yes, Papa," he said, and he did eat the meat. It was salty and good.

"Are those trees the forest you walk to?" his father asked, pointing.

They were soon among the trees and at the ruined pottery. They walked slowly. Maurice's legs hurt, and he was not making that up. "Can we just sit here for a time?" Maurice asked, and they sat on the steps.

His father rubbed Maurice's legs, then he put an arm around Maurice's shoulders and hugged him close. "I—" he started to say something, but he stopped. He looked away. He just held Maurice.

Maurice looked down at the mounds. They glittered, but his papa said nothing about that. Maurice looked all over the ground for the pagodas, but he saw none. That didn't surprise him. They would have taken cover at their approach.

But there were things moving on the nearest mound. Dark things. Maurice sat up straight. His father kicked at something at their feet, and Maurice saw that it was a shelled slug. It lay for a moment in the dirt where his father had kicked it, then it started crawling toward the mounds.

"Are those slugs on that mound, Papa?" Maurice asked.

His father looked where Maurice was pointing. "I think so," he said. "How odd. I've never seen them gather like that." He stood to walk over to the mound.

Maurice grabbed his hand. "Don't, Papa!"

"It's just slugs, Maurice."

"We have to be careful where we walk. We could crush things and not mean to."

"The slugs? You grandmother would be grateful if we stepped on them."

"No, you don't understand. If we walk over there, let me show you where to step."

His father sat down beside him again. "So the magic begins here, does it? What is it we're trying not to crush?"

His papa had a merry smile. Maurice knew that Papa thought this was a game he had made up, but Maurice didn't care. He had to get over to the mound to see what was happening.

"Take off your shoes and step where I step," Maurice said.

They unlaced their shoes, and his father followed along behind him. Maurice worried about his father's bigger feet, but he saw no pagodas along the way that his father might step on. None of the shards they passed were washed and polished.

The nearest mound was a frightening sight. It was covered in shelled slugs. They heaved themselves about it in a dark mass sometimes three or four deep.

"Testacella," his father said, "carnivorous slugs. They eat earthworms and other slugs. No wonder your grandmother's garden is free of slugs. If these testacella migrated through this region on their way here they would have cleaned out all the other varieties in their path."

Maurice was looking for the pagodas. Where would they have gone to escape this blight of slug-eating slugs?

"I've never seen so many in one place," his father said. "I wonder if it's their mating season?"

Maurice felt a growing panic inside him. He knew it was selfish to think only of himself, but if the slugs had done something to the pagodas or if they had driven them away and he could not find them again he would never get well.

"They seem to be trying to reach those other two mounds, but something is holding them back," his father said.

It was the pagoda walls. Maurice understood now what the pagodas feared and why they had had to build walls. But what did the slugs want here? Where were the pagodas?

Then he saw the terra-cotta shards with the black fleur-de-lys scattered on the ground on the wrong side of the wall. Three slugs were nosing among the pieces. "No!" Maurice screamed.

He started for Ti Ti Ting.

"Come back, Maurice!" his father said. "You'll cut your feet!"

But Maurice did not cut his feet. He stepped on the grass and the flowers and the slugs. He was glad to crush the slugs underfoot. He threw the three slugs on Ti Ti Ting into the river and knelt to pick up the pieces of the pagoda.

"What is it?" his father asked softly. He was standing next to him.

"A pagoda," Maurice said. He could barely talk. He

would not cry, he told himself. He would not let himself cry in front of his father.

His father knelt down next to him. "What was the pagoda?"

Maurice held out the terra-cotta shards in his hands for his father to see. He picked up the piece with the black fleur-de-lys. "I gave it this piece," he said. "And I gave it a crystal bead. I can't find the bead."

"There it is, by your right foot." His father picked up the bead and handed it to Maurice.

"I watched them building these walls," Maurice said, nodding at the low walls in front of them. "I didn't know why they were doing it."

"Your pagoda was a brave one then. He was fighting outside the walls."

Maurice saw some of the pagodas he recognized lying on the ground on the safe side of the walls: the pink one, the white one with the piece of blue glass he had given it, clumps of multicolored shards.

"We have to go, Papa. They won't stand to fight if you are watching."

His father stood. He picked up a handful of slugs and threw them into the river.

Maurice stepped forward and set the pieces of Ti Ti Ting down by the other pagodas. Maybe they could do something for him. He wiped his eyes and watched for a moment, but none of the pagodas stood up. He wished he could make them trust his papa and get up to help Ti Ti Ting or at least get up to fight the slugs.

"They've breached your wall over here," his father said. "Let's get the slugs that have crawled onto that mound."

"It's not my wall," Maurice said.

"The pagodas' wall, I meant," he said.

Maurice went after the slugs that had crossed the wall. They were nosing down among the pagoda shards on the ground in the area. They *were* eating them! Maurice knew as he stepped along that he was probably stepping on pagodas, not just slugs. He didn't know what was worse: his crushing weight or the carnivorous slugs. He threw handful after handful of slugs into the river. His legs hurt and his arms hurt, and his nose started bleeding again.

"Maurice," his father called. "Let's go home. You've done all you can do to help here."

They sat on the steps of the ruined pottery and pulled off their slimy socks. "Just throw them away," his father said. "No one would want to wash them."

They rubbed their feet on the grass, then pulled on their shoes. Maurice had to turn his head so blood wouldn't drip onto his shoes while he tied them. He found the bloody rags he had thrown away days before and stuffed them back up his nose. He could see more slugs in the grass making their way slowly toward the mounds.

"The pagodas were helping me, Papa. They were healing me."

His papa considered that for a moment. "I'm sure they were," he said. "We all want to help you. Your grandmother tries with her priests. Your mother gives you good food, rest, and quiet. I would do anything for you too, Maurice. I've tried. I'm sure the pagodas did what they could."

He took his son's hand and led him away. When they came to the road, he had to carry Maurice.

But Maurice decided he had not done everything he could to help the pagodas. He lay feverish in his bed and listened to his parents talk quietly at the table. His father was trying to convince his mother to go back to Paris in a week or so. He knew what would happen there. Never mind Dr. Perrault and the bleeding. He knew what would happen to him without the pagodas.

And the pagodas themselves needed help. He could not let the slugs eat them whether they helped him or not. No one would believe him about the pagodas, of course. They thought he had made it all up.

After his parents and his grandmother had gone to bed, and after he had listened to his father snore for some time, Maurice crept out from under the covers. He had kept on his clothes and covered up before his mother had come to tuck him in, so no one had guessed that he was still dressed. He pulled on a sweater. He picked up his shoes, opened the bedroom door, and looked around the main room. No one was up. He walked barefoot to the kitchen and set a chair carefully by the cupboard. He stood on the chair and opened the top cupboard. He took out his grandmother's sack of salt. He would give her some of his money later to pay for it. Slugs hated salt. He'd use it to drive them away from the pagodas.

He closed the front door quietly behind him and set out down the road. There was a bright moon, and the road shined clearly ahead. He had to rest by the river, but soon he was at the ruined pottery.

It was darker there among the trees. The wind sighed in the branches. It felt different being among the trees at night. Maybe the slugs had changed the feeling of the forest, Maurice thought. He hurried up to the mounds. The slugs had breached the wall again and had covered half of the second mound. He looked frantically about for the pagodas, but saw none. He looked for the pieces of Ti Ti Ting, but they had been moved from where he had set them. The pagodas he had lain Ti Ti Ting next to had all moved somewhere else, too.

He looked around for the pagodas. "Don't be afraid," he called. "It's Maurice. I've come to help you fight!"

He started scattering salt onto the slugs at his feet. They curled up quickly into little balls at the slightest touch of salt. He took a handful of salt and threw it onto a mass of heaped slugs higher up the mound by the opening of what Maurice had thought was a pagoda mine. The slugs writhed and rolled around when the salt touched them. They would pull back into their segmented shells, then stick all the way out, then pull back inside. How the salt must hurt them, Maurice thought, but he had to try to help the pagodas. There was no stopping now.

"Where are you?" Maurice called to the pagodas. "I have only one bag of salt. Show me how best to help you before it's all gone."

Then he saw a pagoda, one of the white ones—the white one with the piece of blue glass. It was standing just around the edge of the second mound. It held up the piece of glass as if in salute. But then Maurice saw that it was pointing. He looked and saw a huge mass of slugs slowly crawling over the wall and swarming over the depression between the second and third mounds.

Maurice had an idea what they were swarming over— what they were eating there!

"I'm coming!" Maurice called.

He surprised the slugs from behind. He scattered salt over the slugs massed at the wall and left them writhing there. He started scattering salt on the huge heap of slugs in the depression, but there were so many. He picked up handful after handful and threw them into the river, then he scattered more salt.

He saw more pagodas, the pink ones and the white ones and all the multicolored ones. They were standing in a defensive line at the base of the third mound—and they did carry crystal swords! Maurice saw them glitter in the moonlight. The swords were as thin as needles. He watched them stab the slugs in the mouth with them. They would wait till a slug loomed over them, its mouth gaping open, then they would strike with their swords and pull back quickly. The slugs would snap about and try to bite them, but some fell over and did not move again.

The pagodas were stabbing through the mouth into the brain, Maurice realized.

He did not see Ti Ti Ting.

"Ti Ti Ting!" Maurice called. "Ti Ti Ting!"

But he could not see him.

"Did the slugs kill him?" he asked the other pagodas, but they did not have time to sing answers to his questions.

Maurice kept scattering salt and throwing slugs into the river. He started to conserve the salt. He threw only slugs he hadn't salted into the river. The pagodas advanced on the slugs he had salted, and they could easily dispatch them with their swords as they writhed about in salty agony.

Maurice threw unsalted slugs until he had to rest. He sat down on a part of the third mound free of slugs and free of pagodas and changed the rags in his nose. His nose was bleeding steadily. He tried to stopper it up tight, though he knew the blood would soak through the rags and start dripping onto his clothes again.

He wanted to sleep. He was tired. He was feverish. But there were more and more slugs.

Then he saw Ti Ti Ting. He was drooping in a depression of the third mound. Maurice stood up to look down into that area. There were other drooped pagodas there, and some just lying on the ground. Three intact pagodas were singing to the hurt ones—he could hear the music softly. They were trying to heal their friends.

"Get well Ti Ti Ting!" Maurice said. "I know what it feels like to be sick. Get well!"

Ti Ti Ting stood a little straighter and looked at Maurice. He seemed to be trying to tell him something, but Maurice could not hear what it was. Maurice reached out and touched Ti Ti Ting softly, then he hurried off to scatter more salt.

When he ran out of salt, he filled the bag with slugs and emptied it into the river, then went back for more. He dropped unsalted slugs onto the salted ones, trying to get twice the use for the salt. He worked for hours it seemed. The night grew darker, as it does before dawn. All the wind hushed. Maurice and the pagodas had cleared the slugs from the depression between the second and third mounds. Pagodas were manning their wall again. Others were securing the second mound and the wall there, and some were advancing even on the first mound.

Maurice could do no more. His arms ached, and his legs ached so badly that he had to sit down. He lay back for a moment to slow the blood dripping from his nose.

He watched the pagodas. They were still fighting hard to save themselves, but Maurice thought they had the advantage now. He and his grandmother's salt had changed the outcome of the battle.

He knew he should be getting back before someone missed him. "Good-bye pagodas!" he said. "Good-bye Ti Ti Ting. I'll try to come back before we leave for Paris."

None of them noticed him now. They were all too busy. Maurice was tired and cold, but he decided to lie there just a little longer till maybe his legs felt a little better. He was not sure he could walk all the way home just then.

He woke with a start. Pagodas stood all around him, singing. There were more pagodas around him than he had ever seen. Ti Ti Ting stood right by his head.

The battle was over.

Maurice felt so at peace surrounded by the music he did not move. His head felt different somehow, clearer, not feverish. His nose had stopped bleeding.

A soft morning light burnished the glen and the mounds. A gentle breeze blew east off the bay. Yet it was so quiet he could hear the pagodas' music clearly.

They were singing for him.

Maurice closed his eyes. His legs did not ache. His nose throbbed, but it was not bleeding. He felt certain his body was healed. "Thank you," he whispered.

It seemed that Ti Ti Ting was singing thank you in return.

He woke again when he heard his mother and father calling his name. It was full light now. The pagodas had moved away. He could see them on all the mounds, even the first. He saw only dead slugs. He stepped carefully away from the mounds and walked steadily up to the pottery steps. He lay there waiting for his parents.

"Maurice!" he heard his mother call. "Maurice?"

"I'm here, Mother," he called.

He saw her running up the path. Soon he was in her arms, and Papa and Grandmother were there, too.

"I'm better now," Maurice said. "The pagodas sang to me last night. I went to sleep hearing them sing after we defeated the slugs, and I feel better now. They helped me."

"Oh, Maurice," his mother said.

But Maurice was right. He was still weak, and he had to work to regain his strength, but his nose did not bleed again. His legs did not bruise abnormally again. The fevers did not return. His grandmother thought her priests and their blessings had done it. His mother thought it had been all their tender care, and maybe a miracle. His father did not care how it had happened, just that his son was well again.

On their last day in Ciboure before returning to Paris, they all picnicked by the river. They let Maurice walk alone up to the old pottery.

He went straight to the mounds. The pagodas were there. None of them sank down at his approach. He looked around for Ti Ti Ting and found him standing guard on the repaired wall. Maurice knelt in front of him. He opened his tin soldier pouch and scattered the broken pieces of a dish his grandmother had dropped the day before. "I brought you presents," he said.

The pagodas all gathered around. He set down a big bag of salt in front of them. "You know how to use this," he said. "I'll bring you more next summer when we visit Grandmother."

The pagodas started singing. Maurice listened. He tried to catch a melody he could remember and hum, but it was all too different. The music seemed so foreign to him then. But Ti Ti Ting seemed insistent about something. Maurice leaned down to listen to what he might be saying. Maurice listened and listened—and suddenly he understood. Ti Ti Ting was telling Maurice that he would understand their music in time, that Maurice would write down some of it and present it to the world. They knew this about him: that Maurice would become a composer who would give beautiful music to a world that needed beauty.

Maurice sat up and laughed. "Oh, I hope so!" he said. "That would be such fun."

They said their good-byes, and Maurice made his way up the path. He met his father standing in shadows under the trees at the edge of the glen. He had an odd look on his face. Maurice just smiled and took his father's hand as they walked back to the others.

In the coming years, Maurice always took salt and bits of broken china to the pagodas when they visited his grandmother. His illness never returned, and he grew into a strong young man. In time, all the world knew the name "Maurice Ravel" because of the beautiful music he wrote. He remembered what Ti Ti Ting had told him, and when he could finally make sense of it, he used some of the pagoda music in his *Mother Goose Suite* and a ballet before that and a set of piano pieces before that. The music delights audiences to this day. Maurice hoped it might heal some of them.

One day, a letter arrived from his grandmother. She told him that a corporation had bought the ruined pottery with plans of establishing a shoe factory on the site. Maurice rushed to Ciboure. The men loading his trunks onto the train wondered why he took so many empty trunks, but when he returned they were not so empty. Maurice bought a house in the forest of Rambouillet outside Paris, and over time he purchased all the land around it. The neighbors wondered at the many happy parties the Ravel family held among the trees there, at all the tinkling lights and the Chinese-sounding music.

Maurice always donated to charities helping children with leukemia. From time to time he let his friends bring their children to his estate, if they were sick. They'd take them home well again weeks later.

The Ravels keep that forest estate to this day. It is a wild, brambly place with secret, flowered glens. No one will ever build on that land.

Other things have built there.

From the Cradle

Gene Wolfe

Gene Wolfe lives in Barrington, Illinois, and is widely considered the most accomplished writer in the fantasy and science fiction genres; his four-volume Book of the New Sun *is an acknowledged masterpiece. He has published many fantasy, science fiction, and horror stories over the last thirty years and more, and has been given the World Fantasy Award for Life Achievement. Each year he publishes a few short stories, of which at least one is among the best of the year. Collections of his short fiction (all in print) include* The Island of Dr. Death and Other Stories and Other Stories, Storeys from the Old Hotel, Endangered Species, *and* Strange Travelers. *The big fantasy news for 2003 is that he has completed the first volume of a major fantasy work,* The Wizard Knight *(to be published in early 2004 as* The Knight*), and has another forthcoming short story collection.*

"From the Cradle" first appeared in Shelf Life *(as did the P.D. Cacek story earlier in this book). It is a fantasy love story set in the future (we hope that you will not hold a few SF elements against it), about a wonderful rare book on consignment in a bookseller's window, a young clerk in the store who reads stories from the book over a period of years, and the woman who owns the book.*

A woman hath nine lives like a cat.
—JOHN HEYWOOD

The boy's name was Michael, but his father called him Mike. His mother called him Mickey, and his teacher (who was both humorous and devout) called him The Burning Bush in her thoughts and Mick when she called on him in class. His principal said "that redheaded boy," a memory for boys' names not being among his principal accomplishments.

He was in back straightening up a shelf, tickling Eppie Graph (at which Eppie smiled and purred), and looking for another book as good as *Starfighters of the Combined Fleets* when the old lady came in. She wore a navy-blue suit and shiny black shoes with heels not quite so high as his mother's, and a big gray coat that looked warm; but none of those things were of interest to Michael just then. What was of interest was the bag she carried, which was old and large and real leather, bound all the way around with straps, and plainly heavy. She tried to lift it onto the counter to show Mister Browne, but could not raise it that high until Michael helped her, scrooching down and pushing up on the bottom.

She thanked him and smiled at him; and though her hair was white, she had the brightest blue eyes he had ever seen; her smile seemed to last a long time, but not long enough. When it was over she unbuckled the straps, big black ones that made Michael think of horses. He stood up very straight then, trying hard to look like a grown-up nobody would even think of chasing away.

From her big leather bag, she took a book of ordinary size with a dark brown cover and light brown pages. Un-

240

like real books, it seemed to have no pictures; but there was a great deal of writing on all the pages; and Michael was at that age at which one begins to think that it might be better if there were fewer pictures after all, and more print.

Mister Browne whistled.

The lady nodded. "Yes, it's very old."

"You don't want me," Mister Browne said slowly. He fingered the pages in a way that said he was afraid she would tell him not to. "I'd try Kalmenoff and Whitechapel."

"I have," she said. "They don't want it. Not on the only terms I could offer it. Don't you want it either?"

"I don't know your terms." Mister Browne hesitated. "But no, I don't. It's not the sort of thing I handle. I'd want to give you a fair price." He stopped talking to rub his jaw. "I'd have to borrow most of it, and it might be years before I found a buyer."

The lady had money in her hand, although Michael was not sure she had taken it from a purse or pocket. It might have been in the black leather bag with the brown book.

"This is for you," she said. She laid it on the counter. "So you'll want it. On my terms."

Mister Browne looked at it, and blinked, and looked again. And after Michael had just about decided that he was not going to talk anymore, he said, "What are your terms?"

"This old book—" He had shut it, and she tapped the scuffed brown cover with a long fingernail as she spoke. "Was my late husband's most prized possession. He loved it."

"I understand," Mister Browne said. "I'm something of a collector myself, in a much smaller way."

"And it loved him. He said it did." The lady's voice fell. "He wasn't making a joke. Oh, yes, he made jokes often. But this wasn't one of them. We were married for almost fifty years. Trust me, I knew when he was serious."

Mister Browne nodded. "I'm sure you did."

"He told me that if he died—he was in some danger for years, you understand. He wasn't morbid about it, but he was realistic. We both were. We'd talked about the things that might happen, and what I ought to do if they did."

Mister Browne said he was sure that had been wise.

"Take the money. Now. I mean it. It's your money, and I don't like seeing it lying there."

Mister Browne did.

"He said that if he died, I was to put this book up for sale. He said that it would choose its new owner, and that I was to trust its judgment." She hesitated. "He didn't say *how* I was to put it up. I've thought of running ads on vid, but there would be a thousand cranks."

Mister Browne nodded, though Michael was not sure that he agreed.

"So I thought I'd better enlist the help of a dealer—someone who has a shop and can display it. Someone like you. My name's Caitlin Higgins. Here's a card for your terminal."

A little too late Mister Browne nodded again, his head not moving much.

"Only you must warn them I might not sell. It will tell me when the right one comes along." Caitlin Higgins bit her lips in a way that made Michael sorry for her. "Or I hope it will," she said.

When she had gone, Mister Browne put the brown book, open, in the window farthest from the door, with a sign that he had made over it. And when Mister Browne (after half a dozen nervous glances at the book) had gone as well—gone into his office above the shop—Michael went out into the street and read the sign:

INCUNABULUM
On Consignment
Make Offer

It stood open, as has been said, upon a small stand that looked very much like real wood; and Michael was happy to see that it was open to a story.

The Tale of the Dwarf and the Children of the Sphinx

A certain dwarf who wandered from place to place, at times begging and at others stealing, was driven forth from the last, a town that beholds the desert and is itself beheld by mountains far away. Not daring to return until the wrath of the townsfolk had abated, he walked very far, and when night stole over the land taking far more than he ever had, he laid himself down upon the sand and slept.

In dream, he was a tall young man, and handsome, and owned five fine fields of barley and three of millet. For long hours of the night he walked among them, seeing barley as high as his waist and millet higher even than the lofty stature that sleep had bestowed upon him.

Chancing to look toward the desert, he beheld with alarm a great spinning wind that drew sand and stones up by its force, and so had become visible, a wind that moaned and roared as it rushed toward him. His first thought was to conceal himself; but he soon noticed that it grew smaller as it advanced, so that when it reached him it scarcely exceeded his own height.

For a moment only it stood before him. Dust, sand, and stones fell to the ground, revealing a beautiful young woman, naked save for her hair. "You must force me," this woman said to him. "We yield only when forced." In his dream he seized her, smothered her with kisses, and bestowed his love upon her while she writhed in ecstasy—not once, not twice, but three times.

Then he woke, and found that he was but a dwarf, and that a great beast lay beside him. When he tried to rise, it held him; and the paw upon his chest was soft as thistledown, big as a saddle, and strong as iron.

A woman's face bent above him, and it was a face much larger than that of any true woman. "O my lover, I have had my way three times with you. Ask a gift, and if it be in my power you shall have it."

Through chattering teeth he said, "I am small and stunted."

She laughed, and her laugh was deeper than the thunder. "Not in every part."

"Spare my life!"

"I will never take it, but what boon is that once I have kissed you, and you me? Will you not ask another?"

"Then make me g-great and p-p-powerful," the poor dwarf stammered, "and small and stunted no more."

"I will," she told him, "for this night only. Suckle at my breast."

The breast she presented to him was like to that of a human woman, though greater by five. He gave suck, and at the first drop felt his back straighten. At the second he knew himself as large as she, and at the third—ah, at the third strength filled him; his thews grew thick as pythons, his body supple as a whip.

He rose, a lion with the head and shoulders of a man. He roared, and the earth shook. Roaring still, he returned to the town that had driven him forth, and his mate went with him. It was a small place now, a little cluster of wretched houses of sun-dried brick. A dozen blows from his paw would have left no brick upon brick, but he swept the roof from one such house and saw the trembling man within: a man too weak with fear to hold his spear, and his moaning wife, and the wailing children she clasped.

And he pitied them, and went away.

Then he and his mate bounded whole leagues, and raced across the desert, and reaching the mountains bounded from rock to rock there, glorying until the sun rose.

But when the sun rose, he found himself a man again, and but a dwarf, and wept.

The great sphinx who for one night had been his mate then told him how it would be with him, and left him.

* * *

He returned to the town that had cast him out, weary still, and dizzied with the memory of the night. There they told him of the storm that had so terrified them, and showed him the house whose roof had been blown away. He laughed at them for that, and because he laughed they stoned him and he fled into the fields.

Long he wandered, through many a town and down many a long road; and at length the days were complete, and in a marsh beside the great slow northflowing river he knelt in mud and water and was sicker than he had ever been, coughing and retching until at last, with a great heave that seemed that it must take his bowels with it, he coughed out an infant, a baby boy who lay howling in the dirty water and opened amber eyes. This boy the dwarf named Kalam, "pen," because his birth had been foretold, and of what has been foretold his people say, "It was written."

He would have picked Kalam up and fled with him, for he feared the crocodiles; instead he retched again, and from jaws almost burst asunder spat another infant, also a boy. This second child he named Wahl, for as he came forth he spattered his brother with mud, and it seemed to the dwarf that *Wahl!*, which means "mud," was the child's first cry.

Then would he have picked up both brothers if he could; but that affliction with which he had been afflicted held him there, and he coughed forth a third infant, a girl, whom he called Jamil, "beauty," because he saw her mother's face in hers.

Then rose he from the marsh, holding his sons and his daughter in arms scarce long enough for the task, as some other might hold a litter of kittens; and he returned to the plowlands and the grazing lands, where he found, or begged, or stole, the milk and the blood on which he fed them.

How he brought them up, and how he took them on his wanderings—how Wahl climbed the wall of the pasha's palace and returned with the pasha's roast in his mouth—how Jamil, lovely as new-minted gold though her hair was matted with dung, was pitied by the Rani, who gave her a ruby—and how Kalam, the eldest, wrote this tale with his forefinger in the dust—any one of these would make a story too long for we who must end this one.

We leave them to others. The day came when they stood at the right hand of the dwarf, with their feet upon sand and millet at their backs, and all three stood much taller than he. And upon that day he called across the desert to their mother. Small though he was, his voice was large, and held the pain of a thousand beatings and the pain of a lover who knows that love is past. All the people of all the towns that border on the desert heard him, and spoke in awe, one to another; and some said that a storm approached, and some that the earth groaned, and more than a few muttered of ghosts and ghouls and worse.

But the dwarf said, "Now, my children, you will see whether your father be mad or no. Your mother, I say, will come to my call as I have oft told you. You will see what manner of creature she is, and if you are wise you will join her, for it is the finest life in the world." His voice broke at the last word, and he fell silent.

Then Kalam, the eldest said, "How are we to join her father? You have told us many times that she has the feet of a lioness."

The dwarf affirmed that it was so.

"You have said also," Wahl remarked, "that she is large as many a mountain. How then can we join a creature so huge? We will be as ants to her."

"She is of that great size when she wills it," the dwarf explained, "but scarcely larger than an ox when she wills otherwise. Did you imagine she was of mountain size when we lay together?"

At this, Jamil said, "How could we join her, Father, when to join her we must leave you? It is you, not she, who has fed, and taught, and cherished us through all our lives. If our blood is hers, is it not yours also?"

"It is," the dwarf affirmed.

"I cannot speak for my brothers," Jamil told him, "but for myself, dear Father, I will remain with you."

"The time for choosing is not yet," the dwarf told her.

"I make no pother of it," Wahl declared. "But I will remain with you as well—should the monster come. How could I, a man, join in the frolics of such a creature?"

"And I," announced Kalam, "go. Not with the monster-mother, but out into the world of men. I have been a beggar and a thief, but there are better things. The ships in Abu Qir are always wanting crew, and it would be a rare captain who could find no use for a crewman well able to wield the pen. I wish you well . . ." His eyes softened.

"As I, you," said the dwarf, his father.

"And if you wait here all night, I will wait too with my sister and you. But when the sun rises, I go north to the docks."

"I may follow you, in time," said his brother. "I have not decided."

"If our father waits here for a year," declared Jamil, "I will wait with him, save when I go to fetch him food and drink."

"But I—" began Kalam. And fell silent, for far off, he heard the howl of a wild wind among the desert peaks. Louder it grew, and louder. The millet bowed and stood straight and bowed again.

And she came.

Kalam stepped forward. His features changed, becoming those of a man more noble than any man, though his own still. His first bound carried him so far that he was almost lost to sight; he turned and grew, so that they saw him still, and the power that was in him, and the glory. When he smiled, the love that went out from him washed over them like a wave.

Wahl passed him to stand beside their mother; and,

oh, but he was terrible and great! Even as she, and the strength of him was like the strength of the river, irresistible.

"Go," dwarf said, and he gave Jamil a push.

"I will stay with you, Father."

"But not obey me? Go!"

She did as he bid, though with many a backward glance. Ten steps, twenty, a hundred. She has not changed, the dwarf thought. Yet she had. Taller and more graceful, with hair black as a storm-cloud and tawny skin. "Go!" he said again.

She stopped instead, turned, and beckoned to him.

And he bounded after her.

Michael thought about this story all the way home, for it had made clear to him certain things about which he had wondered, but raised questions, too. At home he went to his link and called his teacher.

Her face appeared in his screen. "What is it, Mick?"

"Have I seen you anyplace else?"

"I don't know. Have you?"

"I don't know either," Michael admitted.

"I'm a simulation, Mick. There was a real teacher once, a very good teacher who looked about like this."

Michael nodded.

"Many of my programs and subroutines are based upon her. So is my face."

Michael thought a long time about that, and at last he said, "What's an incunabulum?"

in-cu-nab-u-lum in-kyoo-'nab-ya-lam   (in + cunabula L. infancy, origin)   A book printed in the Second Millennium.

Michael was working part time at the book store when R.T. Hurd came in. A friend, R.T. Hurd explained, had mentioned the brown book. He wanted to make an offer, but he would have to examine the book first. Michael switched off the motion alarm and took the brown book from the window. R.T. Hurd opened it reverently and turned its pages with care, and at length wrote his offer on a kneeboard keyboard and signal signed it.

When he had gone, Michael replaced the brown book in its window and switched the motion detector back on. R.T. Hurd's offer he carried upstairs and left on the owner's desk. It was not until he and Michael had locked the store for the day that Michael realized he had left the brown book open at a new place. And it was not until he came to work the next day that he read the pages he himself had freshly exposed.

The Tale of Prince Know-Nothing

When the world was young, there lived a certain prince who did not know he was a prince. Two thousand years before, his many greats grandfather had been a glorious king, renown for courage and wisdom throughout all the world. Many sons and daughters had he fathered; and although some had perished without issue, others had as many children as he, and two had more. Because they had been the sons and daughters of the king, they had been men and women of wealth, masters of great houses and broad lands and coffers of gold and jewels. But as the years turned to centuries, and generations were born and aged and died, the wild thyme grew up around all these things, which vanished from the sight of men; so that when Prince Know-Nothing was born, his mother did not know he was a prince or that she herself was a princess. Nevertheless the blood-royal ran strong in his veins, because his father had been a prince also, though neither of them knew it. (But someone did.)

Thus the young prince lived as other boys lived. He was strong and brave, but there were many other boys who were stronger and braver than he—or if they were not, they were at least louder in their boasts, which is much the same thing among boys. And although he was wiser than they, at his age wisdom consists largely in honoring one's parents and careful listening to the counsel of those older than oneself; thus his wisdom, though it made him well-liked and kept him from harm in a hundred ways, brought him only mockery whenever it became apparent.

"Once upon a time," said his teacher, "there was a king who had but a single child, the princess, and twelve golden plates. They were very beautiful, with knights and dragons and elves around their borders—"

"What is a princess?" asked Prince Know-nothing, and the other children all laughed.

"If everyone else knows," said his teacher, "everyone else can tell you." And she asked the girl with the pink hair-ribbon to tell Prince Know-Nothing what a princess was.

"It's a girl that's very pretty on Halloween and has a pretty white dress with a big skirt," explained the girl with the pink hair-ribbon.

Their teacher agreed that was a good definition, but she was afraid that it wasn't quite rigorous enough, so she asked the smartest boy in the whole class to tell Prince Know-Nothing what a princess was, too.

"It's the one the knight marries," the smartest boy in the whole class said at once.

"That's a good definition, too," the teacher agreed. "But princesses don't always marry knights. Sometimes they marry princes."

Here the page ended, and since the book was locked away in its window again, Michael was unable to turn it. He went home, and when the book remained in its window day after day and week after week, he knew that R.T. Hurd's offer had been refused.

Years passed, and there came a year in which he, and not the old owner, took inventory; and when it was nearly done, he got out the brown book so that he might look at it again. He was listing books by their UAISBN numbers, and he hoped to find one on it, although he did not. He considered listing it by title, but he knew only too well that there were often half a dozen books with a single title. He was puzzling over this when a young woman with bright blue eyes came in and remarked that she would like to look at the book, since it was out of its window.

"I generally leave it there, where it's secure," Michael explained. "It's alarmed, you know, and the glass filters out the ultraviolet. But I had to take it out now, or anyway I thought it did. Maybe I just wanted to touch it again." And he explained about inventory, and looking for a UAISBN in the brown book.

"You have a lot more books here than most bookstores I've been in," the young woman said. "Usually they want you to look on the screen. And then they'll print up one for you if you want it. But till you want one, they don't actually have many books."

"We can print anything you want, to order," Michael explained, "but we find we sell more books when the customer can handle an actual copy. I don't mean that we keep copies of ephemera—best sellers, and that sort of book. We don't have to. But there are a lot of very good books most people have never heard of, and we like to have copies of those, of the books we recommend."

The young woman looked thoughtful.

"Then too, we do a good deal of business in used books. You can often buy a used copy more cheaply, for one thing."

"Aren't there old editions that are nicer?"

Michael nodded. "Sometimes. Quite often, in fact. There are different papers, and for art books . . ." He shrugged. "When the plates have been produced under the supervision of the artist, that's something stores can't duplicate. Though we try."

"Can you make me a copy of this?" The young woman indicated that brown book.

Michael shook his head. "There's no number. That's the problem."

When she had gone, he returned the brown book to its

window and went back to his inventory, feeling empty in a strange, sad way, and very much alone. *I should get a cat,* he thought. *We used to have a cat. A lot of stores have cats.*

It was time to close, or nearly; and yet the inventory remained not quite finished. In the end he entered "Browne's Book—Wonders of" for the book in the window, and did the rest, turned off the lights, and pulled shut the big front door, hearing it lock behind him. Deep within the store ALARM—ALARM—ALARM flashed dimly and slowly, indicating that the system was powered, and on guard. How many times had he come out of this door?

It was not that he did not love the store; he did, just as he had loved his parents. And yet . . .

He would get a cat—a nice cat with white paws and an interesting name. (But a cat would not be enough either.)

The bus floated by. He had missed it, and there would be no more for half an hour. He inspected his windows. *The Race for Saturn's Moons* was no longer selling. It should be relegated to a shelf and replaced. Perhaps with *Fear of the Future* or *The Fall of the Republic.*

Here was the brown book again, opened at a new place.

The Tale of the Boy and the Bookshop

Long, long ago in a far-away land, there was a boy we will call Wishedfor. He had been born late in his parents' lives, after many years in which they had prayed devoutly for a son, and they treasured him above all else. One might think such a boy would be spoiled. He was not, for Allah had blessed them with a poverty not too great. He grew, and as he grew, showed himself wise and generous, strong of limb and clear of eye. He helped his mother wash and cook and sweep, and when he was old enough to assist his father, he did not cease to do so, but turned his labors from the amendment of programs to household tasks as soon as he and his father returned from the archives, for his mother was not strong.

At length she died, and his father called him to his side. "O my son," quoth his father, "thou art the light of my eyes. Not a day passes but I thank Allah for what he gave. Which is noblest, my son? Is it the gifts Allah gives to us, or the gifts we miserable mortals give to Allah, who has given us life? Consider well."

For some minutes the boy sat deep in thought; at length he said, "Gold and silks, skimmers and golights are but muck. The value of a gift cannot be reckoned from the price the giver gave or the price his gift might fetch in the market. Is that not so, O my father?"

Sadly, the old man nodded. "Proceed."

"How then is the value of a gift to be reckoned? It must be according to the heart of its giver. The most valuable gift is that given with unbounded love from a pure heart. Mere mortals, alas, are never pure of heart. Nor is our love boundless, though we may think so. Allah is pure of heart, as we are not. Allah's love is without bound, as ours cannot be. Therefore it seems to me, O my father, that the gifts Allah gives to mortals must ever be greater than those we mere mortals present to Allah."

At this the old man looked more doleful than ever. "By what means, O my son, can we poor mortals offer Allah a gift equal to those he has given us?"

Now the boy thought again, scratching his head as if he feared his mind slept there, rubbing his chin and pulling his ear; and at last he said, "O my father, I do not know. Is it possible? Tell me."

"It is, my son." The old man's gaze, which had been upon the boy's face until that time, was now upon the dust before him. "When we return to Allah a gift he has given us, we make him a gift as fine as that he gave, do we not?"

"Ah!" said the boy, and his eyes flashed like sunlight on dark pools. "Thou hast cut the knot, O my father! In all the world, is there any like to thee?"

"Many, many. My son, I would give such a gift to Allah. In the city to the north there stands a mosque like no other, the Madrasa of Sultan Hasan. Here the wisest gather to speak of the will of Allah, and His knowledge, and the knowledge of all the world. Young men come there to hear them, that they may become wise in their turn, and when they have sat long, they may question them, and so become wiser still."

At this the boy's eyes grew very wide.

"O my son, for seven years I give thee to Allah. Thou shalt go to the mosque I have named, and my blessing go with thee. Learn there. Betimes thou must labor, even as I labor at my keyboard, for the belly must be fed. As thou strain and sweat, thou must repeat in thine own ear that thou hast come to learn, and not to labor. And in seven years, if Allah grant seven years more of life, I will come for thee. If thou hast learned well, I shall die full of joy. But if thou hast not, tears and sorrow will be my lot in this life and in paradise."

"I will learn, O my father," the boy promised. And before the sun rose again, he had set out for the city; and though his heart was sad when he recalled his mother, it leaped for joy to think of the learning that would be his.

A year passed, and another, and another. The old man labored, recalling often the son he had given to Allah. Now it seemed to him that his son would surely grow discouraged upon the path of wisdom; he himself had not traveled far along it, yet he well knew how steep were its slopes and how rock-strewn the way. And now it seemed to him that within a day or two the boy would surely return, making some excuse, and he told himself ten score times that he must have hard words for the boy if it were so—and knew in his heart that they could never pass his lips. On such days he watched the road for hours. But the boy never came.

And again he imagined his son sitting at the feet of the wisest of the wise in that great mosque, the Madrasa of Sultan Hasan; and he was happy, and went about his work with increased vigor. In this way, year followed year.

At last it seemed to him that seven had passed, and more than seven, and he went to his neighbor and spoke of the boy; and when his neighbor had praised him, as all did, the old man said, "How long has it been since we have seen the light of his face? Five years, I think? I have lost track of the reckoning. Six? Has it been as many as six?"

"More," declared his neighbor. "Long and long. Behold! My picktruck that is old shone like a jewel when thy son left us."

The old man could scarcely speak, his voice shook so. "Seven? Has it been seven?"

"What is seven years to a picktruck?" replied his neighbor.

The old man left, confessing in his heart that he himself was but another such laboring machine and begging forgiveness for it. On the next day he dug up the fifteen milpiasters he had buried in his floor, and set out. The road was not short, nor was it gracious to poor travelers; yet he reached the city at last, and asking directions of those who bore kind faces, he made his way to the Madrasa of Sultan Hasan, and sat of a long afternoon hearing the wise discourse on Al Qur'an and much more, and was greatly improved thereby. Ever he looked for the boy, but he did not see him.

Betimes the light faded, and the wise departed one by one, and the old man also, to seek a place in which to lay his head.

Down one street he went, and up another, and chancing to look into a bookshop beheld one tall and lean and of serious mien, whose beard was touched with gray. Their eyes met, and both knew.

Of their embraces and the many things they said, a long tale might be made; but at last they sat together with coffee between them. Then quoth he who had been the boy, "O my father, I thought thee dead when the seventh year passed. Had I known thou still lived, I would have returned to the south long ago, and carried thee to my house in this city—the house in which thou shalt repose this night. Thou came not, and I thought, *surely he is dead.*"

"O my son," said the old man, "as each year passed I resolved to let thee remain a little longer, that thou might grow in wisdom yet more at the feet of the wise. Another year, and another year, until this. Now I feel the hand of death upon me, and I would not die as a frog in a well, by all forgotten."

"Thou shalt not die at all," he who had been the boy declared, "but bide here full many a year. But, O my father, I have sinned against thee."

"It cannot be!" the old man declared.

"It is." And he who had been the boy sat in silence while the traffic of the street clamored on all uncaring.

Until at last the old man said. "Thou canst not speak, my son. I see it. Do not speak. Let us rather rejoice, and talk of thy mother, and the days when thou wert small."

"I will not deceive thee more, O my father." He who had been the boy lifted the fragrant cup yet left it untasted. "I have betrayed thee, my father. Betrayal atop betrayal I shall not set. To this city I came worn and hungry, and thus before going to the mosque as thou had instructed me I looked first for employment that I might be fed. In this street, I beheld an old man unloading a flitter. Hastening to him, I said, 'Grandfather, thou art of years, and the boxes weighty. Permit me to assist thee.' For I hoped that he would give that with which I might eat when the task was done.

"He stood aside, and while I worked we talked. And when the last had been unloaded, he bid me carry them into this shop, and when I had carried the last, he bid me open them. They held books, such as thou seest."

He who had been the boy sighed, and the old man nodded.

"I put them in their places, as he directed me, and as I labored he discoursed upon their contents. Some came from Baghdad, some from Damascus, some from Frankish lands even to the other side of Earth, some from the stars of heaven. All were wondrous in my sight, and he saw it. He bid me sleep in the shop that night, as many a night thereafter, with a cudgel by my side to protect our wares."

The old man sipped his coffee, hot, strong, and very sweet. "There is nothing shameful in this, O my son."

"My master died. It was my loss, and all the world's, for he was both learned and compassionate. I took his shop in charge, and delivered all profit therefrom, which was never great, to her who had been his wife. Too soon she followed him. His shop became mine, and the house that had been his also. It is not large, but thou will ever find a place there, O my father."

"Nor is there dishonor in that," the old man declared, "but the contrary."

"O my father, thou sent me to this city that I might sit at the feet of the wise in the mosque. I have been there to worship many times. But I have never done as thou wished, my father. When the call to prayer came, I went—or oftimes went not. And when my prayers were done, I returned to this shop in which thou discovered me. I have done wrong, and it is no childish matter, I know. What is thy judgment? That punishment which thou decree, I will accept without murmur. It will be less than I deserve."

The old man did not speak again until he had drunk the last drop, and eaten the grounds as well, for he followed the old ways. And when the last were gone, he said only, "O my son, I must think on this."

Next morning he rose early and made his way to the Madrasa of the Sultan Hasan. All morning he sat in silence, harkening to the wise as he had the day before; but when the sun neared its zenith, "O my uncle," quoth one, "thy beard is gray. Thou hast seen much of life. Is it not so?"

The old man acknowledged that it was.

"And yet thou harken to us, and never speak. Whether thou hast come to teach us or to learn, we would hear thee."

"O revered sheikh," quoth the old man, "know that I

am sorely troubled. I am a simple man. To mere compilers and codes, to interrupts, subroutines, and iterations has my life been given. Now I must judge a weighty matter, and know not the way."

"Speak on," quoth the one to whom he had spoken.

"Upon the one hand, my son has disobeyed, O revered sheikh," quoth the old man. "Upon the other, he has done well and is deserving of approbation. Upon the first hand, I sought to honor Allah, to whom all praise. Upon the second, he confesses his fault."

"Thy voice breaks," observed he to whom the old man had spoken.

"I love him dearly, O revered sheikh, and no man ever had a better son. Yet he did wrong, and I know not which way to turn."

Others had fallen silent to listen as the old man spoke, and for a time they discussed the matter. Then came the call to prayer. All prayed, and when the prayer was done, he to whom the old man had spoken declared, "This is a troubled matter, O my uncle. Thy son hath transgressed."

The old man nodded.

"And his transgression was against Allah and thee. Is it not so?"

The old man nodded as before.

"Yet he is true of tongue, contrite of heart, and a good Moslem?"

The old man nodded a third time, and while others spoke he to whom he had spoken sat stroking his beard. Ere long, the speech of those others turned to other topics, and when that time came, quoth he, "O my uncle, there is one in this city whom we reckon wisest of the wise. Matters of great difficulty are brought to him. Let us bring thine, thou and I."

And they went, down one street and up another, and so came to a certain shop. He to whom the old man had spoken entered first, and the old man after him.

And behold!

* * *

It seemed to Michael that this story had been intended for him from the beginning. It was true that he had not remained long at the university. Money had been in short supply, and he was a member of no prioritized group. During his long wait at the bus stop, he turned the story over and over in his mind, with all that he could recall of the first two, which he had read years before.

Next morning, the young woman returned to the store. Michael looked at her, then looked again and snapped his fingers. "What is it?" she asked.

"I've been trying to think who you reminded me of," he explained. "It's my teacher, the teacher I had when I was a kid. I mean, she was really a machine, and she was older than you are, and the principal was the machine, too, like for everybody, but—but—"

"I understand." She grinned at him. "Were you sent to the principal a lot? You must have been a bad boy."

"Well, sometimes." He discovered that he was blushing, something he had not done in years. "He could never remember my name until I told him, but she called me Mick. I never could understand that. I mean, since it was all the same machine, really."

The young woman's grin had softened to a smile. "I do, Mick. May I have some of your coffee?"

"Yes. Certainly." He hurried over to show her. "There are nice chairs, and reading lights, and—and everything. Sweetener and sugar and real cream. So people can sit down and look at the books, you know. And—and everything."

"But not the big book in the end window." She was still smiling. "The brown one."

"I'd have to stay and watch." Michael decided he could use some coffee too; his mouth felt dry. He poured a cup for her and another for himself.

"Do you eat the grounds, Mick?"

"Do I . . . ? That story. You read it."

"Uh huh." Her smile had become impish.

"It's been bothering me." He smiled in return. "It bothers me more than the teaching machine ever did. Or Junior Teacher Huggins or Principal Maxwell. Will you—I feel silly saying it here, but won't you please sit down?"

She did, and accepted the coffee he had poured for her.

"Would you like sweetener? Cream?"

"Honey, Mick. I see you have honey over there."

He got it for her, and sat beside her on the sofa. "Do you really want to see that book? Are you thinking of buying it?" He tried to gauge the cost of her clothing and jewelry, and failed.

"No," she said.

"Then I can't. I mean I shouldn't. It really is a very valuable book. But just for a minute or two, while I watch."

She sipped her coffee, and smiled, and added more honey, and smiled again.

"If you read that story, it sounds like me. Like my life. Not exactly, of course, but . . ."

"Uncomfortably close."

"That's it. That's it exactly."

"The book does that, you see. That's what makes it so valuable. It's not just its age. It knows, somehow, and we were never sure whether it was just opening itself to the right place—that's what a man I knew thought—or whether it created the stories. Made them to order, so to speak, the way you print your books. I think it does both."

He was speechless for a moment, then remembered to sip his coffee, and spilled a little, and winced. At last he said, "It seems to be saying that what I'm doing—this book store—is right. But it doesn't feel right. Or not as right as it ought to. I think the man in the story . . . That he didn't feel right either, until his father came."

She nodded.

"So I thought of getting a cat or something. But I don't know." He sighed, and ran his free hand through his hair. "Only what you said about the stories, that can't be right.

There was one I read a long time ago, about a boy in class, and what was a princess? Only it wasn't all there. I could never read the end."

"Tell me," she said, and he recounted as much as he could remember of "The Tale of Prince Know-Nothing."

When he had finished, she said, "I can tell you how it ended. Prince Know-Nothing decided he should go in search of a princess; but a thousand things conspired to stop him, and he never did. At the end, a very plain girl in a very plain dress kissed him, and after the wedding he discovered that she was a princess who had gone forth in search of a prince."

"You read that one, too," Michael said.

She nodded. "Did you read any more?"

"Just one other one." He paused, not sure he remembered it at all. "It was about a dwarf and a sphinx. They had children—he gave birth to them, which used to puzzle me. And he wanted to be a sphinx like her, and at the end his children made him one, and it was wonderful."

"It was saying you ought to have children." For a moment she looked pensive. "I've never had any," she said.

"I haven't either. I mean, I'd like some, but I've never been married."

"I'd like some too, Mick." Quite suddenly she kissed his cheek; and when he turned his head in surprise, his lips. "There," she said when they parted, "and now I'm through fooling you. You've never been married."

He shook his head.

"I have. I was married for almost fifty years, Mick, but we never had children. There were reasons, but the reasons don't matter anymore, and the children do. We had love, and the love was enough, but now that's gone too, and I want love again. I want it back."

"You—you're . . ." Michael felt as though the whole world had dropped from under him.

"I'm eighty-seven now, Mick, and I used to be a teacher before I married. Don't tell me you haven't heard of cell therapy. They go in and clean up the nuclei, and your cells start dividing again, and you grow younger instead of older."

Michael managed to nod. "I've read about it. It's terribly expensive."

"It was. Fortunately, I'm terribly rich. Does it bother you that I'm so much older than you are?"

He shook his head desperately.

"It doesn't bother me, either." Her hand found his. "Because I'm not. I mean biologically. And I don't want to buy that book because I own it already. My name's Caitlin Higgins. It should be in your files."

He could not speak.

"But please don't call me Caitlin, or something awful, like Junior Teacher Higgins."

She had smiled, and he felt that he could look at that smile forever, and it would always be new, and always magic.

"My friends call me Kitty," she said.

Sam

Donald Barr

Donald Barr lives in Yardley, Pennsylvania. He is the retired headmaster of the Hackley School in Tarrytown, New York, and, before that, was headmaster of the Dalton School in New York City. Early in his career, he reviewed favorably the original 1950s publication of J.R.R. Tolkien's The Two Towers *in the* New York Times. *He was one of President Reagan's first appointees to the National Council on Educational Research. He is the author of seven books, including four educational books for children, one influential work that defends traditional standards in education—*Who Pushed Humpty Dumpty? *(1971), and two science fiction novels—*Space Relations *(1973) and* A Planet in Arms *(1981). Now he has returned to writing: historical novels, thrillers, and short crime and science fiction. A screenplay adaptation of "Sam" won first place at the Slamdance/SciFi Channel Screenplay Competition.*

"Sam" was published in F&SF. It is a fantasy based upon the eighteenth-century philosopher Berkeley, whose proposition was "to be is to be perceived." It reminds us more of the fantastic stories of Philip K. Dick than of supernatural fantasy; it is nature-of-reality fantasy. Sam is fired from his job, and just seems to disappear. There is of course a spooky psychological verisimilitude to the proceedings.

The table I write on I say exists—that is, I see and feel it; and if I were out of my study I should say it existed—meaning thereby that if I was in my study I might perceive it, or that some other spirit actually does perceive it. There was an odor, that is, it was smellt; there was a sound, that is, it was heard; a color or figure, and it was perceived by sight or touch. That is all that I can understand by these and the like expressions.

—BISHOP BERKELEY

I

When Sam Taubenseel got fired, his friends in the Principe Organization gave him a half-secret going-away party. It was a great success. Dick Trewinning and Tom Howard brought their wives and Herman Gluck did not bring his.

Mildred Gluck did not care for the guest of honor. She had made quite an oration about it, with that pejorative New York lilt of hers: "Sam Taubenseel! That's all I hear: Sam Taubenseel. Eight years now, Sam said *this*, Sam said *that*. You know what *Sam* said today? He said blah blah blah. Who told you *that* joke? *Sam*, who else? And nothing to him, *nothing*, a lightweight. Why should I go?"

"Sam has been a good friend," replied Herman sturdily. "A good friend to Acquisitions, a good friend on the outside." (Acquisitions was Herman's department.)

"He's so great, why did they fire him?"

"I—I'm not sure. Okay? You can't ask, you know."

* * *

As the party broke up, everyone said to Sam, "Keep in touch! Keep in touch!" and Sam said yep, he would keep in touch.

But he did not.

They thought perhaps he was embarrassed because he seemed to have difficulty finding a job. Hendrick ("the Shmendrick"; *Sam* had given him the nickname) Van Kleeck wrote several letters of recommendation for various kinds of employment and sent them to the agency that Sam was signed up with, but Hendrick never heard, either from Sam or from the agency, about any referrals, and he never heard from any prospective employers.

Dick Trewinning, after waiting for Hendrick the Shmendrick to hear, finally wrote to Sam at the home address on file in the Personnel Office, but perhaps he had waited too long. Everything came back "Undeliverable. Not known at this address." Sam had left no forwarding address with the Post Office. He could not have moved very far, however, because he retained the same telephone number. All his friends called him, but invariably, whether they called during the day or at night or in the early morning, they got the recording from his answering machine. It was a cheerful recording, purporting to tell them that Sam was unable to come to the phone just now but if they would leave their name and telephone number he would call them back just as soon as he could. It sounded as if Sam were about to bounce in his front door and harvest his messages and start calling immediately. They did leave their names and telephone numbers, and he never called back.

Hendrick the Shmendrick caught him at home just once—apparently Sam was expecting an important call, a business call perhaps, and answered the telephone. Hendrick had no sooner uttered the words "Ah! Sam! It's wonderful to hear your voice *live*, so to speak," when the telephone clicked and he was cut off.

Naturally, after a few months Sam's friends began to lose interest. They did not admit this to themselves. Each professed to be worried for Sam, anxious to do something for Sam, indignant at Sam's ill-treatment by the Organization; but between them they rarely discussed Sam, and if they thought about him at all, it was at three o'clock in the morning or some other ungodly hour. And after a few more months, it was almost as if Sam had never existed.

The last of Sam's friends to forget him was Dick Trewinning, but one morning Dick said to Mrs. Trewinning, "You know, I'm having the damnedest aphasia."

"What's that? What's an aphasia? Is it catching?"

"It's when you can't remember a word. You remember something but not what it's called, or some little thing happens but you can't recall when it could have been."

"My birthday? That's all right, it isn't for a month."

"I *know* your birthday. . . . This is very peculiar. I'm thinking of a person but his *name* is gone. It's as if I was looking at a stranger. You remember Sam? We went to his house that time, and he served that seafood casserole? Suddenly I can't remember his last name. Sam—Sam—I've been thinking and thinking for hours."

"Sam," said his wife, not really trying. "Sam . . . Sam . . . I can't think of his last name either. Anyway, what brings *him* up? You haven't heard from him in years."

"Months. But he's one of my oldest friends, and now . . . I must be—I must be getting Alzheimer's, I can't remember his last name."

"Oh, it'll come to you when you stop thinking about it."

But he stopped thinking about it and it did *not* come to him.

Weeks later, for no reason at all, the name "Sam" came into Dick Trewinning's head. He remembered his aphasia, and said out loud, "Sam—," trying to charge around his mental block. Wally McNeill happened to be nearby, and McNeill looked at Dick and said, "Who?"

"Sam. I think it was Sam. Or something like that."

McNeill frowned and said, "Sam who?"

Of course, Wally had never been as close to Sam as Hendrick and Dick, so there was nothing particularly sinister about it.

One day, going through a drawer full of old souvenirs and mementos, Tom Howard came across a picture of three men standing near a fishing boat. The middle one of the three was Howard himself, holding a long fishing rod from the end of which dangled a fair-sized fish. On Tom Howard's right stood Hendrick the Shmendrick. On Tom Howard's left stood the third man.

Mrs. Howard made a practice of peering over her husband's shoulder whenever he was going through mementos because she believed that her husband was keeping things from her. "Who are those men?" she asked.

"This is me, and this one here is Hendrick Van Kleeck."

"Oh yes. I met him once," said Mrs. Howard. "And the other fellow?"

"I dunno," said Tom.

Mrs. Howard sensed a certain uneasiness in his tone. "Oh," she said with bogus heartiness, "you can tell me. What's the big secret?"

"Well," said poor Tom, "he looks familiar. I—I'm not sure. . . . Well, the name escapes me. Probably just some guy at the outing."

"Yeah," said his wife, boisterously but insincerely cynical, "those outings. Why don't you take *me* along ever?"

Herman Gluck came across a telephone number scribbled in the margin of an old magazine. "Whose number is that?" he wondered, and called his wife over. "Here's somebody's number. Do you have any idea whose it is?"

"Call them and find out."

He did so. It was about three minutes to ten P.M., and he felt guilty about calling at so late an hour, but he dialed the number, and received a recorded message: "This is Sam

Taubenseel. Don't hang up. I can't come to the phone right now, but if at the tone you will just leave your name and telephone number, I will get back to you as soon as I can."

Herman Gluck hung up the phone, puzzled. The recorded voice was unfamiliar, but there seemed to be a note of desperation in it, as if the phrases *Don't hang up* and *I can't come to the phone* and *if you will just leave your name* were the pleas of a prisoner. *I will get back to you* sounded like. . . .

"Well?" said his wife.

"Guy I never heard of before. What is that number doing there?"

"It's *your writing,*" Mildred Gluck pointed out, and drew the moral: "Don't you *ever* write down a name with a telephone number? You have a bad habit of just scribbling numbers here and there and then not knowing afterward. . . ."

"I have a lot of bad habits," retorted Herman, "but writing down the numbers of total strangers is not one of them."

"Maybe you dialed it wrong," said Mildred Gluck.

Herman dialed it again. This time he got the voice of the doom operator. "Your call cannot be completed. . . ."

"You wrote it down wrong," said his wife, "that's all."

This explanation satisfied Herman Gluck, *almost*. He had the feeling that he was missing something.

Herman happened to mention this trivial episode to Hendrick the Shmendrick, by way of illustrating the truth that we are all getting older. Hendrick said, "*Hm!* Sam? Taubenseel? I can't help you there, *old man*. Ha ha. Let's look him up in the phone book. How do you spell 'Taubenseel'?"

"T-a-u-b-e-n . . . ," said Herman, without thinking.

No soap.

"Try T-o-w . . . ," said Herman.

That was no better.

"We could try the yellow pages," suggested Hendrick. "How are your *feet?* Have you been thinking about trying a podiatrist? A proctologist? A *shrink*?" he asked, becoming obvious, as he always did sooner or later. "Ha ha."

But evidently this Sam Taubenseel, whoever or whatever he was, had dropped out of Herman's universe, such as it was.

"Come on, now, it can't be important," said Hendrick the Shmendrick.

"No, it isn't, but old age is one long pain in the ass."

"Better long than short."

The Organization, like every modern organization, kept files on all its former employees. Some pension problem or legal issue might arise. The paper record—known as "the paper trail"—was too bulky to keep in its entirety. After a certain point the Organization coded the salient data and stored it in the mainframe, while the original documents were bundled into transfer files and warehoused in New Jersey.

It happened that the name of Sam Taubenseel came up during a meeting. It figured in a lawyer's notes as that of someone who might testify to a promise which had been made in the way of business—and broken in the way of business. The name was not written very clearly—the lawyer was a young lawyer—but he was fairly sure his note said "Sam Taubenseel." He asked Hendrick the Shmendrick how to get in touch with this Sam Taubenseel.

"Who?"

"Sam Taubenseel. His name is in my notes, as having witnessed the promise we allegedly made to Bergen Associates."

"Why should we want to get in touch with *him*, then?"

"We don't *per se*, but we certainly don't want Bergen Associates to get in touch with him. We can't embargo him if we can't find him."

" 'Sam Taubenseel.' I'm not sure that . . . ," said Hendrick. "Let me see that name. Have you got your original notes?"

The young lawyer rooted in his briefcase. "Here."

"It looks more like 'Sam Farben—something,'" said Hendrick.

"Now that you mention it, it isn't so clear," admitted the lawyer. "It *could* be 'Farbenteil.'" He had not noticed this before.

"I don't know who Sam Farbenteil is either," said Hendrick helpfully.

They consulted the computer. To no one's real surprise, it failed to turn up either a Sam Farbenteil or a Sam Taubenseel.

"That's strange. The name 'Sam Farbenteil' is vaguely familiar," said Hendrick. "Not the syllables. The rhythm, kind of. Let me ask Dick Trewinning."

Dick Trewinning was not helpful. "I draw a blank," he said, "but Herman might know. He's retired now, but he's still pretty sharp. Mind like a steel trap. He might just remember."

Herman was down in Maryland, doing a little consulting in his retirement. "Well," he said, "I don't . . . it doesn't really ring a bell. Are you sure you have the name right?"

"It isn't terribly clear," said Dick. "The 'r' is clear, and the 'F' is sort of clear. Well, we must have it wrong, that's all. When *I* went to school, they taught cursive. God *knows* what they teach now."

"Tell you what," said Herman. "You fax me that page, and I'll see if it calls anything to mind. . . . Well," said Herman a few minutes later, "but the 'r' isn't all *that* clear, and I'm not sure about the 'a' and the 'm'. Yes, it *could* be an 'r', but I just . . . I don't have a clue. Sorry. I know it's important to the lawyers. How's Francie?"

⌒ *II*

One night, about four years after Sam Taubenseel got fired, a young man named Bill Perlzweig, who had nothing to do with the Principe Organization and in fact had never heard of it, woke up at 3:15 A.M. Twice recently he had awakened like this in the small hours with the impression—it was hardly more than that, really—of having heard a single piercing cry, like a desperate call; it was certainly in his head, and could have been his own cry; and yet it seemed distant, somehow. Tonight was somewhat different. He had been dreaming, a curiously vivid dream, and for all of twenty seconds after he woke up, he remembered it, and then it left him, as if it had soaked into the pillow like sweat. But this time one detail remained behind: a name, "Sam Taubenseel." But who "Sam Taubenseel" was, or what he was doing in the dream—all of that was clean gone.

Bill Perlzweig was a college senior and had enough on his plate. Somebody—D. H. Lawrence or somebody—had once written that your dream is like your wastebasket, by which he meant, Bill Perlzweig supposed, that its contents are mostly rubbish of no significance, among which are one or two items of great significance which you would prefer not to keep. Bill Perlzweig dismissed the dream and went back to sleep.

He had a singularly good memory and in the morning he remembered the incident.

The next night he had a similar dream, he awoke again in the early hours of the morning, and again the name "Sam Taubenseel" stayed with him.

He looked up the name in the telephone book for Manhattan, and for Brooklyn, and for the Bronx, and Staten Island, and Queens. There was an S. Tauber, and a Samuel Tarnowski, and a Schmelke Trauerstein. He devoted the evening to ingenious investigations, pretending to be a bright young telemarketer from an investment counseling firm, but it was clear: none of these were *his* Sam Taubenseel, whoever that might be.

What strange filament of memory had retained this name? he wondered. Was he blocking out some shameful experience? Was a stranger, or a dead man, trying to communicate with him through some parapsychological or occult channel of the consciousness?

Bill Perlzweig could not afford a psychiatrist and did not want to go to the College Health Office and be laughed at.

In any case, he was reasonably certain that if his inability to remember Sam Taubenseel—the Sam Taubenseel *behind* the name "Sam Taubenseel" that he did remember—was due to "repression" of some painful experience, the name would not have outlived his dream. It would have vanished with all the other details when he woke up. He did believe, however, that the mind retained much more of one's experiences than the conscious efforts of the mind could retrieve. And he had heard that hypnotism could, under certain circumstances, get at these smothered or mislaid after-images.

He had a friend, a psych major, who was dabbling in hypnotism, having wandered into an impressive demonstration in Carnegie Hall and having then bought several popularizations of the art. Bill Perlzweig went to his friend and asked if the friend could fish out the experiences at the end of this tendril of memory.

The would-be hypnotist tried and at length was able to record on paper an experience of Bill Perlzweig's youth some five years before. It was not a shameful experience; in fact, it turned out to be a rather pleasant one.

At that time, Bill had a summer job—it was after his junior year in high school—as a messenger or delivery boy for a job-printing company. One weekend he had been given a set of proofs to deliver to the apartment of a Mr. Sam Taubenseel in Westchester, on an emergency basis. He spent too long on the phone with his girlfriend and then had some trouble finding Mr. Taubenseel's apartment house and was late getting there. He was petrified that Mr. Taubenseel would have called the printers' office and reported the non-arrival of the important packet. And indeed Mr. Taubenseel had already done just that, but he took one look at the sweaty, anxious young face at his front door and heard the stumbling account of Bill's reasons for being late, and he rushed to his phone and called the printers' office again. He told them that it was all his own mistake, that he had not heard the doorbell; the messenger had therefore gone looking for the janitor and the janitor had let the messenger boy into the apartment as far as the foyer table; that he, Sam Taubenseel, had called to complain before looking at his own foyer table, where the package was in plain view. When Mr. Taubenseel hung up he smiled at young Bill Perlzweig and said, "Now, you've got to back me up on this." "Oh sir," said Bill Perlzweig, "that was wonderful. I'll never forget your kindness!" "Nonsense!" said Sam Taubenseel. "You did your best. I got the proofs, didn't I?" He then led Bill Perlzweig downstairs and over to Constantine's Restaurant and treated him to a large dish of ice cream with a great deal of chocolate syrup on it, and sent him on his way with ten uncovenanted dollars in his pocket.

On being recalled to normal consciousness, Bill Perlzweig said, "By God, that's right! That's who it was. That was the name. Sam Taubenseel! Did you get the address?"

"Yes," said the amateur hypnotist, "I even got the address." And he gave it to him.

The following Sunday, Bill Perlzweig went up to Westchester with a three-dollar Street Map and Guide in his pocket. There was, of course, no public transportation that would get him very close to the address—Westchester having progressed not at all in five years—and he got a cab at the station. When he gave the address to the driver, the driver looked at him with a deadpan expression.

"What's the matter?" asked Bill Perlzweig.

"Nothin'," answered the driver. "Nothin's the matter."

It occurred to Bill Perlzweig that the address might be in some way notorious. He was young enough to want to assure the cab driver that he was not going to a whorehouse or a drug kingpin's headquarters or anything of that sort.

"None of my business," said the taxi driver. "Anyway, I don't know anything about that address. It's in a funny neighborhood. Gone down."

It was indeed a peculiar neighborhood, desolate; a few of the houses were abandoned, some of them with the window openings formally sealed with rusted sheetmetal. Two buildings were burned out.

The taxicab inched along the street.

"This must be it," said the driver.

Bill Perlzweig cleared his throat. "Wait here." Then he added, "For God's sake, don't leave me."

"I wouldn't leave you," said the taxi driver. "You ain't paid me yet."

Bill Perlzweig mounted the steps of what had once been a town house, and approached the front door. It was the right house, the number 319 was still legible; but there was no sign of life. What he supposed was déjà vu now occurred: he remembered the trembling relief and apprehension he had felt when he belatedly found that number five years before.

Bill Perlzweig stood on the front steps and looked toward the cab, then looked toward the door. He tried the handle. It turned freely but was somehow disengaged from any lock.

He shoved the door. It rattled but held. He looked for a doorbell and found the little round recess where the button had been. There were two wires inside the recess. Bill Perlzweig took a pencil from his pocket and pushed the corroded copper ends of the wires together. There was no spark. He moistened his little finger and thrust it into the aperture. He received no shock. He banged on the door.

As he went down the steps toward the cab, a boy on a skateboard swerved by.

"Hey, kid," said Bill Perlzweig.

The boy executed an elaborate, rocking, curling stop.

"Anybody live here?"

The boy looked at him as if he were crazy. "Does it look like it? Nah!"

"When did they move?"

"*I* dunno, nobody there in *my* time." The boy must have been all of eleven years old.

Bill Perlzweig climbed back into the cab.

"That house," said the driver. "In the last stages. A house don't get that way overnight. Gotta be ten years. Fifteen years? Twenny years, that house is empty."

"It *couldn't* have been twenty years," began Bill Perlzweig faintly. "I—"

"Look up there."

Number 319 had long ago been broken up into apartments. The front windows had once been grand, but all except two were vacant, black, some of them cracked and reinforced with dirty adhesive tape; one of the two exceptions was closed with peeling plywood and had a graceful curve scorched into its Palladian lintel; and in the one the driver was pointing to, on the third floor, the glass was dusty but reflected the dying afternoon sky, so that Bill Perlzweig could not be sure of what he saw behind it. The curtains looked desiccated. They looked as if they had been slowly shredded by gravity. For some reason the word "cerements" came into his head. Actually, though, they looked like photomicrographs of brain tissue.

Yet behind that window, only five years before, he had met a cheerful, kind, vague, garrulous, baldheaded man who took him to a diner and asked him questions about his school work while he sat eating a vast dish of Dolly Madison vanilla ice cream drowned in chocolate sauce.

And as the chocolate odor, and the prattling voice, and the shine of the afternoon light on that tanned bald head came back to him, he saw something move behind the desiccated curtains: a face came very slowly into view: it was pale, and seemed to advance into the light timidly; it looked down at Bill Perlzweig intently, and Bill Perlzweig could see the gleam of a hairless scalp as the face looked down at him and lit with a gradual smile.

Bill Perlzweig hastily pulled his head back into the cab. "Here. Thanks," and he shoved a ten-dollar bill at the driver. "Is Constantine's still in business?"

"Closed Mondays. And the food is greasy, they use that heavy oil."

"This is Sunday." Bill Perlzweig climbed out of the cab and marched up the steps of Number 319. He thrust his pencil into the doorbell aperture and saw a tiny spark as he brought the wires together.

Persian Eyes

~~~~~~~~~

Tanith Lee

Tanith Lee [tribute website: www3.sympatico.ca/jim. pattison] lives in the south of England, in a house named Vespertilio. Her fantasy and horror fiction have put her in the forefront of both genres in recent decades. Her first professional sale was to The Ninth Pan Book Of Horror Stories *(1968), and, in 1971, she published* The Dragon Hoard, *a children's novel. After receiving numerous rejections from British publishers for her adult fantasy novel* The Birthgrave, *she wrote a letter of inquiry to DAW Books, the American publishing firm founded by well-known science fiction fan and editor Donald A. Wolheim. DAW published* The Birthgrave *in 1975, beginning a relationship that lasted until 1989 and saw the publication of 28 books altogether. She is still identified with DAW fantasy, and this story is from the DAW 30th Anniversary Anthology:* Fantasy *(a celebration of writers associated with that powerful and successful imprint now under the leadership of Elizabeth Wollheim and Sheila Gilbert), certainly one of the best original fantasy anthologies of the year. Her latest book is a YA novel,* Wolf Queen: The Claidi Journals, Book 3.*

"Persian Eyes" is a supernatural horrific fantasy in the characteristic mode of Tanith Lee. The fantastic intrudes into the everyday lives of the characters in a fantasy world much like the later Roman Empire, in a fashion that is utterly consistent with their belief systems and myths.

~ I

The Roman stood looking at his slave. She was one of many, in the fine house on Palace Hill. They came and went barely noticed, across his vision, like shifting columns of sunlight, or the diurnal shadows that changed shape over the floors. But something, now, had made him see this one.

"Come here," he called. Not harshly, he was not a cruel man to his slaves, did not believe in it unless it were needed—and then a sound beating usually settled the offender. The female slaves especially he did not like to chastise unduly. Like flowers, or animals, they looked better, and were a nicer ornament to his house, if well kept.

The slave came across the garden toward him. It was the fifth hour,* late in the morning, and the sun gilded the little fountain, and the marble statue of Apollo with his lion. The slave, too, was polished a moment with light gold. And then she was in front of Livius, her head lowered.

She had black hair, plaited back and held with a thong. She wore the coarse linen tunic of her status, but of a pleasant soft cream in color. It made her honey skin look darker. She was about sixteen years old, or probably younger, for like most slaves, she would tend to appear older than her years.

Livius regarded the slave carefully. Had his wife said something about this girl? He thought so—what had it been? That she, his wife, had bought her privately, a favor to some rich friend—Claudia Metella perhaps, or Terentia. . . . *Why* as a favor?

There was nothing wrong with the girl that he could see. And if there had been, his fastidious Fulvia would hardly have wanted her, nor would he.

_____
*About 11 A.M.

"Look up," he said.

The slave looked up. For a second, a flash of her face, small and Eastern, triangular in form, the nose long and lips full. The eyes—

She had glanced down again.

"No, I told you to look up."

A slightly longer flash of face then, but not much. Obviously, she was frightened of him, the Master, thought she had done something wrong and would be punished. Maybe she had been badly treated elsewhere.

"I'm not angry. Where were you going?" This was the voice he used for a young nervous horse.

She whispered some words, his slave, which did not sound like the Imperial Tongue. Not even like the argot of the lower orders. Some Eastern muttering. But she had known enough Latin, of course, to understand his orders, if not to reply to them.

"All right. Go along, then."

She dipped her body before him, graceful, mindless, then turned and walked away across the garden.

A strange creature. Like having a tamed but shackled leopard in the house.

Livius smiled at his idea, and returned into the cool of his library.

"She has strange eyes, that slave," said Livilla to her mother.

Fulvia took no notice.

They had been having their hair dressed in the summer courtyard that opened from Fulvia's summer bedroom. Fulvia's hair, bleached by quince juice, was ornately curled and crimpled; Livilla's dark hair had been dressed more simply, as became a maiden. The slaves who had seen to this were now gone, and none of them had been the slave to whom Livilla referred.

She tried again, "Mother, that new slave—where did she come from?"

"Which slave? What? What are you talking about? Why should slaves interest you?"

"They don't. Or only this one. The one with green eyes."

"Yes," said Fulvia. She sipped her wine, mixed with the liquified pulp of roses. She looked thoughtful, considering. But said nothing else.

Livilla would not be put off.

"Mother, the other slaves dislike her. You know it can cause trouble when they get upset. They get careless. Look at how Lodia nearly burned you with the tongs—"

"Yes, yes. But I hit her with the mirror. She won't do it again."

"She was nervous, Mother. Unsettled."

"Livilla, that shade of yellow doesn't suit you. I've thought so for a long while."

Diverted, disconcerted, Livilla looked down in outrage at her yellow stola, figured with anemones. And forgot to say any more about slaves.

Fulvia, bored with the Livillan torrent of insecurities now released, in the matter of dress, hair, and skin, sat with apparent patience, offering calming words. Fulvia was used to being bored. It was her life.

Of course, she wanted for nothing, and she did not wish to change this. She did not really *wish* for anything.

Birds sang. She thought about the slave.

It had only been ten days ago that Terentia Austus had sought Fulvia out, arriving in person that morning, sitting frowning and hard among Fulvia's pretty things.

"I want," Terentia had finally announced, "you to take a creature off my hands."

Fulvia had raised her brows. Terentia was several years older, and looked it, her makeup much too heavy and her gray hair covered by an auburn wig, of a color known as *Flame*. Terentia was also powerful, the wife of an electoral candidate sure to do well, a rich woman securely fastened in a prestigious marriage. What did she want? One could doubtless not say No, whatever it was.

"A creature, dear Terentia. What kind of creature?"

The Austus family kept a menagerie, as Fulvia knew. She suspected a snappish wolf or porcupine was about to be unloaded on her.

"A slave," had said Terentia.

Fulvia was almost relieved.

"A slave. I see."

"There's nothing unsuitable about her. She's biddable and not work-shy. I'll be frank with you, Fulvia. My husband pays her too much attention."

Fulvia waited behind her polite mask. She thought that if every married woman worried about her husband's activities with *slaves*, the gods knew what would become of them all.

However, "Yes, it sounds absurd," said Terentia, seeming even more aggravated. "Why should I care? I have my sons, and besides Austus is still most attentive to me. I've no complaints. Also he keeps a woman near the Circus Gorbus. I've never had any concerns about *her*."

"Then . . ." prompted Fulvia, sensing a prompt was expected.

"This slave came to me from my sister Junia's household. She begged me to take her, wouldn't say why, or only some rubbish about the slave's being disruptive. And of course, her husband's a drunk, so one never knows."

"No."

"Then I take the wretch into our house. She does her work perfectly adequately. And then Austus—becomes obsessed with her."

"Obsessed—"

"Yes. I choose the word with care. Perhaps it's his disappointment last year in the election—"

"Oh, but, *this* year—"

"Exactly. And he must concentrate on that. So she goes. Will you accept her? A gift. I won't ask a sesterce for her. It would be unlucky."

"Well, but, Terentia—couldn't you merely—"

"No. I can't explain. Are you willing, that's all I'm waiting to hear." Terentia had risen abruptly from her seat in a flare of costly garments and clash of pearls. The severing of valuable connections twanged in the air. Fulvia did what she must. Terentia nodded. "I'll send her to you before the dinner hour."

And so the slave arrived. Looking her over, Fulvia thought her nothing much, simply an inferior from an Eastern country, which Terentia had actually said was most likely Persis. She had wondered, too, what Terentia would say to the obsessive husband, and if he would presently storm across Palace Hill after his property. This did not happen.

The girl seemed to sink into the household with very few ripples. The slaves were not notably antipathetic to her. In Fulvia's experience, they often took a dislike to newcomers, particularly females.

Her eyes were a little odd. That glassy gray-green, unusually clear in the dark skin, between the black lashes.

But there.

(Livilla had stopped lamenting, and was instead admiring herself in the silver mirror.)

Fulvia had mentioned the new slave to Livius, naturally. He had been quite uninterested, as one would predict.

They ate the evening meal in the garden, then lingered there. From beyond the house came the low rumble of heavy-wheeled traffic on cobbles, the occasional shouts of some party or other revel. Above, the sky deepened until, undimmed by the uncountable lamps of Rome, the stars were put on.

"The snails were good," said Jovus.

"No, too sticky. Cibo still doesn't know how to cook them," added Parvus, the connoisseur.

Livius listened to his two sons, neither yet a full-grown man. He had been reading, and had fallen asleep in the thick heat of afternoon, like some old grandfather. Now, leaning here, he felt curiously alert, as if expecting something. But nothing, nothing at all was expected.

A girl had brought more wine and was pouring it into his cup. Her.

He wanted to say again, *Look up.* But the eyes were downcast, she might not have had any eyes—

Outside a wild raw shout blew up. Palace Hill was a select area, but it got noisier by the night. Perhaps he should buy a farm, move out into the country among the olives and vineyards, vegetate. . . . But there was Jovus, the eldest, to secure first in a worthy career. And Livilla to marry suitably, to someone or other.

None of this, his duties, caught his attention greatly tonight. But there, the lamp was being lit by Apollo, and she was standing straight again, and the flame splintered in her eyes. How green they were. Fig-leaf green, yet cooling, like marble.

He glanced at Fulvia. She had been watching him.

"Did you like the pork liver?" she asked, solicitous, as a good wife should be. And he sensed her boredom, both with ordering the liver and its cooking, and now asking. His answer, his approval, also bored with those, as *he* was with all of it, including his children, his house, the noises of the city, the city, the night. . . .

"Delicious, Fulvia. How clever you were to think of it. Aren't the stars fine?"

Fulvia lay sleepless on her bed. It had been made in Egypt, and sloped a little, keeping her head higher than her feet, and tonight this gave her a peculiar feeling of weightless drifting, as if she might float up and out of the door, and over the high walls into the city.

What would she see? The lit porches of festive houses not her own, hung with garlands. The seven arched spines of Rome, crowded with their temples, gardens, mansions, and the dark valleys between, where the markets, dens, brothels, and slums lay twitching and surging, also sleeplessly.

Fulvia turned on to her side. At this ninth hour of the night,* it was very quiet on Palace Hill. There was only the faint stir of the plane tree in her private courtyard beyond the curtain. It sounded like the moving coils of a snake.

She had thought her husband might sleep with her here tonight. Generally she knew the signs—little attentions, a kind of heat which came from his body. She had been antic-

_____
*About 3 A.M.

ipating the visit, had taken down her hair and freshened her perfume. She no longer thrilled to his sexual attentions—all that had left her with the birth of Jovus, the first son. As if sexual pleasure (as she had) had done its duty, and so now she need no longer experience any. She had been sorry at first, then philosophical. These things happened. And she still enjoyed his arousal. The manifestation of his continuing desire, however infrequent, was a compliment.

Why had he not come in, then?

Perhaps he was tired. He had eaten a large meal, and taken a little too much wine. And it was, though the summer was so young, a hot night.

I must sleep, Fulvia commanded herself. She listened to the tree rustling, and glimpsed inside her mind a silvery snake winding through leaves, in the instant before she fell from consciousness.

Livius woke with a start.

What had disturbed him? (He listened, hearing nothing, even the noisy neighbors were silent now.) And—where was he?

Ruffled, he got to his feet. He had come back to the library and stretched out on the couch here to read for an hour before going to Fulvia. She would have realized, and he always gave her time to prepare. But again—he had slept. Now he could tell from the feel of the house, it was only an hour or so from sunrise.

Far too late to disrupt Fulvia's slumbers. He was a considerate man. It had been different, of course, when they were young. They had shared a bed every night, and kept busy.

The lamp was guttering on the desk. He trimmed the wick and took the lamp with him along the corridor. When he reached his garden, he paused between the pillars. The stars were dull now. The garden was moonless, ghostly, and the fountain shivered like a piece of silk.

As he turned into his own room, the light of the small lamp flared fierce as a torch against furniture and hangings.

Livius winced at the heavy gold, the bright inlay of ivory, the blast of scarlet curtain. How much had he drunk? Too much, it seemed. He blew out the lamp and undressed in blackness.

I'm not old, he thought, lying there. His vision seemed a little disturbed, and in the blackness, weird faces leered and smoked at him from near the ceiling. The wine, or even the pork—*I wish the gods would make me young again*, he resentfully mused. *Even five years younger.*

He thought of fig trees—he did not know why—their shade, the glow of their leaves filtering the summer sun.

We should be like that. Sleep For a while in winter, and then grow strong and new again, like leaves.

Livius smiled now at his own foolishness. He slept.

The slaves of Livius curled in their tiny cubicles tucked deep and windowless within the house. Most had a bed; that was their Master's kindness. Now and then one would creep to the privy, a dirty, stinking place, without the fitments of the rich man's easements, let alone of the lavish thermal bathroom with its sheltered terrace facing south.

Cibo met Lodia in the dark, between the privy and her cubicle. As the house cook, he had somewhat better quarters behind the kitchen, and also some power in the slave-world.

"Well, Lodia. Like a moment with me tonight?"

Lodia grinned. It was her way of saying she knew she had no choice.

Cibo guided her, and when they reached the corridor with the lamp burning, he saw the bruise on her arm. The Mistress had struck her today with the polished silver hand mirror, for carelessness. Now he joked about it, telling Lodia she was an idiot and had better watch out, or Master would sell her off to the mines.

Lodia was used to his foreplay. She said nothing. Cibo led her into the kitchen, past the man-tall pots and burned-charcoal smelling oven. He gave her a piece of bread, a leftover, smeared with pork fat. In a corner, his two assistants lay on the stone floor, snoring.

Cibo took Lodia against the wall, in a hot rush and snuffling almost-silence. He finished quickly, scowling. "All right, you can be off now. You're not so juicy as you were. Next time I'll take that new girl. The Persian."

Lodia said, "If you do, don't look in her eyes."

"Eh? What does that mean?" Lodia was once more dumb. Cibo said, "It's not her eyes that would fascinate me, Lodia. Go on back to your pit."

Jovus dreamed he was a man, and wore the Man's Toga. An augur had been taken and it foretold great things for him—though what, he was unsure. Even so, he was making a speech in the Forum, and older men nodded, and the crowd was all applause.

Then a girl walked through the crowd. She moved like a breeze through a cornfield, and the human figures swayed away from her, and back again when she had passed, but took no notice of her otherwise.

Jovus, however, lost the thread of his oration. He stopped speaking entirely, and an enormous quiet filled the Forum, and in the blue-scorched sky, another color came, as if an awning had been erected, as they did it at the circuses.

Beyond the wall, Parvus, nine years old, dreamed he was swimming in a deep green pool. He was rather anxious, for he knew that he was tiring, and the sides looked sheer.

Livilla, on her own bed across the corridor, was sobbing in her dream because she could not bear the saffron color of her stolas, and they were all like that, every one, even those she was brought that began as pink woven-air muslin, or delicate white silk—and none of them therefore suited her. She looked blotchy and too fat, unmarriageable, so she wept.

～ II

As he gazed about him, the Artifex Iudo was puzzled. But then, his clients often puzzled him with their requests—a perfectly serviceable pillar to be removed and replaced by a carved prop that made the room into a stage set; a wall with charming nymphs changed to a bacchanal of the wine god, lewd female companions, and goats.

This, though. This did intrigue him slightly.

"Yes, sir. Certainly it can be done. I have a new color that has come from the Libanus region. They call it *Sea-Wave*. Or, then, from Egypt—"

Livius said, "The color of this perfume pot, like this."

Iudo accepted the pot with its hint of nard. One of the lady wife Fulvia's, probably. It was a deep, nacreous green. He thought perhaps he would not be able to match it at all. Green was a color which so often turned, like milk. One painted it on, and as it dried, something in the plaster made it too shallow, or too strong. Which normally might not matter. But now, with this insistent instruction—

"And the subject? As I have it here?"

"Trees," said Livius absently. "Leaves. Pools. Green things."

Of course, more unusual than all the rest (than the commission for the artifex and his assistants to paint the two dining rooms, the library, and the rich man's bedroom, all in greens and variations of green) was the straw hat, such as a farmer might put on, clamped down on Livius' noble head, even here in the shade. And beneath the hat, a band of thin cotton, itself dullish green in color, perhaps to catch sweat from the forehead?

Livius' eyes were watering in the sun. They looked inflamed.

Iudo had noticed the elder of the two young sons also had this problem with his eyes, although not so badly, nor had he put on a hat against the sun.

The boy was there, now, out in the garden court, sitting on a bench, brooding the way they did at that age, whether patrician or citizenry. (Supposedly the plebian poor, in their sties, did not have time to brood in youth. They were already out pimping, whoring, stealing, cutting throats, or training in the gladiator schools. Or at the very least, standing in line for the free food the city offered.)

"Well, then. You may do it."

"Thank you, sir. We shall try our best."

"Begin today."

"Ah—very well. That may be somewhat—"

"Take this." The bag clanked heavy as a legionary's full campaign armor.

Livius sighed. He hooded his lids.

Iudo, hurrying off to organize his men and paint, did not see the rich man pull the green cloth right down over his eyes.

In the garden, Jovus *did* see this.

He stood up, nervous, his inner, nonphysical body attenuated, like the eyes of a slug standing on stalks.

Jovus picked a way across the sunny court, as if avoiding invisible obstacles, between the beds of roses and late iris, whose reds and purples seemed to be on fire.

"Father?"

Livius did not answer.

Was he asleep again? He had fallen asleep at dinner yesterday.

"Father," said Jovus, more loudly, and then his father's face turned toward him, and Jovus saw his father's open black eyes staring at him through the band of thin Egyptian cotton.

For some reason—every reason—this frightened Jovus. He was fifteen, almost a man, but he was afraid.

"Sir—"

"What is it?" The voice was weary, dismissive. Jovus knew that really all his father ever was to him now, at best, was courteous. The happy man who had played with him as a child, the grieved man who beat him when he skimped his lessons, who took pride in every achievement—that man was gone. But where?

"Which rooms are to be painted?"

Weary, short, Livius told him.

Jovus went away and slouched through the house into his own rich boy's bedroom, with its carved garment chest and bed of ebony and pine. The crimson panels painted on the walls offended him, but he stared at them until his eyes ached.

Past the doorway, then, she went.

It was just like that. As if there were no other in the house, it was all vacant but for himself, and then for her. Jovus watched her.

She *slid* along the corridor, vanishing suddenly at the turn, as if merely to turn a corner were supernatural.

He had seen his sister Livilla earlier throw a cut piece of her own hair into the flame before the household guardians in the larger dining room. But then, too, he had heard her whining about wanting to make an offering to Juno Viriplaca, to ensure her marriage.

Jovus thought the gods would not be concerned with this. They never offered help, even his family ancestors did not. Rather like Livius, they had lost—in their case with immortality or death—all involvement in the human world, save where they could be harsh in it.

The house of Junia Lallia, Terentia Austus' sister, stood behind the Gardens of Fortuna, screened by the massive poplars and ilexes. Fulvia approached uneasily and in full panoply, in the closed litter with curtains of Indian silk, with her bodyguard and two attendants.

At first, sitting in the vestibule, on a hard, gold-adorned seat, Fulvia thought that perhaps Junia might not see her, despite the delivered gifts of goose offal in honey, early-ripened peaches from the coast, and spikenard.

But then one of the house slaves conducted Fulvia into Junia's private sitting room, which opened on a courtyard garden depressing in its glory of trees, a terraced water course, tame doves, monkeys, and a peacock marred only by its rusty shrieks.

Junia was a youngish woman who scorned to bleach her

hair. Her clothes and jewelry said all there was to say on such matters.

"It's most kind of you to see me," murmured Fulvia.

"Such lovely presents," replied Junia coldly. "Is this about the elections?"

"No—no, dear Junia Lallia—I wouldn't think of bothering you, but—"

"Then it is," said Junia, staring now into space, "the slave."

"Oh," said Fulvia.

"Yes," said Junia. "The Persian woman," she added. "Her name—did anyone tell you? Roxara. Or so they called her in the market at Ostia—or again, so I understand." She paused. Then she clapped her hands. A girl came in with wine and cinnamon-water and little cakes. After the girl had served these and gone, Junia said, "It had to be faced. Of course you would come here. Terentia told me what she did. But I think she didn't tell you what *I* had done, or why."

Fulvia gave over caution. "Tell me."

Junia lifted her brows, that was all. Then she told.

"My eldest son, who as you know lived here in my husband's house when not away in Gaul, bought this slave, as men do, on a whim. He presented her to his wife, a poor virtuous little ninny with the wits of a pigeon. I suppose he liked the looks of the slave, and meant to sample her, and the poor little ninny wouldn't even have noticed, very likely. However. My son didn't sample the slave called Roxara. Instead, Fulvia, he went mad."

Fulvia felt herself whiten. She felt the blanched and rosy makeup standing out on her skin like a *separate* skin, and herself, all horror, glaring through.

Junia Lallia said frigidly, her eyes on nothing at all, "Firstly he wouldn't return to Gaul. My husband covered this up by saying our son was ill. All sorts of devices then had to be resorted to, in order to avoid disgrace. I won't tax you with those. Meanwhile physicians came and went. And my son—my beautiful son—" shocking Fulvia once more, this abrupt break into emotion, as swiftly mastered, "—lay raving in a darkened room, unable to bear the light, or any bright color, wanting the girl—not for any proper reason, but simply to *look at her*."

"To—look at her?"

"He couldn't keep his eyes from her. She had to sit in the room with him. I witnessed it day after day. She sat and looked at the ground, and then he would go to her—groveling along the floor like a dog—staring up into her face—" All at once, Junia sneezed. Having done this, she made a sign against the bad omen. She said, "We tried to keep her from him. He would cry for her. I mean he would *scream* for her as if he were in agony. Oh, then, I called priests to the house, from various temples, and other persons. Because it was sorcery, what else?"

"What else," gasped Fulvia, shuddering.

"They had some effect—mostly through drugging him to insensibility. But then they told us we must send the woman away."

"But surely—if she's a sorceress—you should have killed her—your husband, excuse me, but really, he should have killed her at once."

"He didn't dare to," said Junia. "Another strong man brought to his knees. We were afraid . . . And so—I sent Roxara to my sister, a very reasonable and sensible woman, who assured me it was all nonsense, and she would put all to rights. But, as you know, in the end my sensible sister, who fears nothing, and will walk through a cemetery on nights when the ghosts hover in the moonlight, she, too, became fearful, and she sent this evil being away to *you*. Forgive us, Fulvia. We are in your debt forever."

Fulvia thought, *So you are, but how will that help now?*

She, too, controlled herself. She said, "And your son?"

Junia turned her head, but not before Fulvia saw why she had sneezed—her eyes were bursting with tears she did not permit to fall. Junia said, "He's gone."

"To . . . Gaul?"

"No, not to Gaul."

"Then—can he be *dead*?"

"I don't know if he is dead."

Fulvia blurted "But you must know—"

"He vanished. My son vanished. When Terentia's slaves came to fetch Roxara, he was already gone, and we knew nothing. Each of us thought he had wandered to some other part of the house. Then that he was in the city. Searches were made. It was discreet. Then less so. He hasn't been found. If you have heard no rumors, that is due to my husband's connection to the Flavians."

Among the forgotten cakes, Fulvia was panting, but Junia now sat icy, stone still.

"Perhaps he will come back," Fulvia faltered at last.

"Do you think so? Now you sound like his dolt of a little wifelet. Of course he can never come back. She cast a spell on him, and it took him somewhere he can never escape and never be found, out of this world."

Junia rose.

Fulvia staggered to her feet.

"I'm in your debt," said Junia. "If I can assist in any way at all, I will do so. What will you do?"

Fulvia drew in her lips. She said, "There's only one way."

"Yes, perhaps. If you're brave enough."

The litter raced over the hills, the bearers running, the bodyguard thrusting lower citizens from its path.

At the portico of Livius' house, they came to a halt. The door was knocked upon. The doorkeeper opened it.

Fulvia got out of the litter. She was trembling, it was true, but she had crossed this threshold many hundreds of times, only once carried over it as a bride. Now, as she moved forward into the familiar house, her foot caught in the tile of a second step, *which was not there*. She felt herself falling and watched surprised as she flew out on to the mosaic floor. She heard the crack of her head against its ungiving surface, from some way off. And then nothing.

It was the Greeks and Egyptians who had thought everyone but themselves to be barbarians, as alike in their limitation as sheep. Romans, though, were also inclined to this idea—the barbarity of other races . . . the Egyptians and Greeks by now not always unincluded.

So, she was a barbarian then, from Persis, that land Great Alexander had subdued, a country of crags and brown dust and lions, of green gardens mysterious under an alien moon . . .

Livius looked about him slowly. The walls of the library were pale and painted over by green, green fruits, green leaves, green figures that danced or swam in a distance of green waves and green dolphins. The artifex and his men had worked swiftly, perhaps with not as much agility as speed. A curtain (green) hung at the yard door. The summer sun was always too bright. He found lamps were better. And sometimes he shut one eye and looked, through the spyglass of flawed emerald, at their green flames.

This amused him. But he was waiting. He knew that he was.

Once, a child, a boy, had come to the inner doorway.

"Father—the physician says—"

Something unimportant.

Who was this child, addressing him as *Father?* One of the slaves? Perhaps. In certain patrician homes, the Master was called Father.

This child-slave had been distressed, wet-eyed, and snotty. Parvus, he was called. A nickname.

Someone had told Livius his wife Fulvia (he thought they called her Fulvia) had hurt herself. He had gone to see, starting at the loud colors—raucous red, orange—in her room. He did not recognize the woman stretched out on the bed, over whom the physician bent. The smell of medicinal resins turned Livius' stomach. He did not stay there long, thinking maybe he had made a mistake, and come to look at the wrong woman.

The door curtain moved. Who would it be now?

It was her, of course, the barbarian Persian. She came in with a wine jug. She was pouring the wine. Seen through the emerald, the wine was black-green.

Livius waited for the Persian girl to raise her eyes so that he could look into them. But she would not do it.

"Sit," he said, "sit over there." She moved so adeptly, as if alive. But really he did not think she was. None of them were, nor he himself. This girl, however, although unliving, was *moved* by something live *within* her.

She sat down on the couch.

"Look up."

She raised her eyes, lowered them.

How could he ever have thought her afraid or nervous? She had no feelings or emotions, and probably no brain inside her skull, under its covering of amber skin and coarse rich hair.

"No, let me see your eyes."

A look. Gone.

He wondered if he should have her whipped for insolence. If that happened, or if he cut her with the little knife he kept here, for breaking the edges of wax seals, would she bleed green, like the sap of a plant?

Livius got up and went over and sat on the stool, gazing up into her face, and so into the lowered, half-obscured depths of her eyes.

The flames of the lamps were there in the green irises. It was like looking into a hall under the sea, lit by torches.

"Where do you come from? From Ocean? Or out of a tree—a tree nymph or a water nymph?" Her lids drooped lower. "Don't close your eyes. Obey me."

Her face—expressionless, mindless. All slaves were of this kind, unless singled out and made pets of. Would she change now, since he favored her? Livius thought she would not.

He did not want to touch her, let alone take her to him in the sexual act. He found it restful—and yet curiously exciting—simply to sit here like a boy, and stare up at her, trying to see in at the tiny glinting cracks between her eyelids.

When Fulvia opened her eyes, the room was a rippling dimness smeared by lights.

She said, alarmed yet imperious, "I can't see—"

"It will pass, madam. An effect of the drug I've had to give you. You banged your head when you fell. Your cranium is bruised but whole. And I've bled you. All's well."

"Did I fall? Where? I don't remember . . ."

"At the house door. You entered in a hurry."

"Did I? I don't remember . . ."

"You'd been visiting the lady Junia Lallia." (The physician—a know-all.)

"I don't remember . . ."

Livilla had appeared, white and terrified. She ran to the bed and made a grab for Fulvia's hand. "Mother— Mother—"

"Gently, child," barked the physician, annoyed at seeing his handiwork disarranged.

But Fulvia said quietly, "Where is Livius?"

The physician turned and busied himself at a table loaded with his salves and infusions. The air smelled of burned beetles, mint, and Greek incense.

"This doctor is Idas," said Livilla, trying to be adult, "he is the doctor Claudia Metella recommends for all things to do with the head—"

"Yes. Where is your father?"

"In his library," said Livilla. "He came in once. Then he went away."

"He mustn't be troubled," said Fulvia. She felt bitter at his lack of care for her, and resigned, because this was only what she would anticipate. Virtuously and grimly, she put him first, and did not know how thin her lips had become. But she was also sleepy from the bleeding, and the potions. "Make sure," she said to Livilla, "your father eats a good dinner."

As she slipped back into sleep, Fulvia thought, *This isn't right. I should get up and go and see to something. I know it was to be done—that was why I was in such a hurry coming in, and so I fell.* But her head ached. She thought of the thing she could not remember. *Never mind it.*

Parvus was standing behind Jovus just outside.

"Don't go in," instructed Livilla. "She's asleep."

"She's slept for days," said Jovus.

"I know," said Livilla. "But Idas says she's in no danger, and must rest."

"He's a Greek," said Parvus, a red-eyed racist, "and he may be useless, too."

Jovus put his hand on his brother's shoulder. "Hush. The Metellas sent him. He's all right."

Livilla said, "I have to go and see to the kitchen, since Mother can't."

When she had stalked off, dismayed at her (temporary) position, Parvus said, "What's Father doing?"

"What he was doing before."

They had seen him. Both had peered around the edge of the green curtain. Seen Livius, their father, a man, sitting at the feet of the Persian woman in the green darkness.

"Is she a witch?" whispered Parvus, "like the sorceress Medea?"

"It's nothing to worry about," said Jovus. He lied, wanting to be alone. "A man—does these things with his house-women. It's just some fancy of his."

Livilla entered the kitchen, and saw that it was empty, and although the day was advancing, nothing much had been done toward the main meal. Oil, onions, and herbs lay about, and some fish—one of which the cat had got hold of, dragged under a bench, and was now eating.

The girl clapped her hands, and no one came, and Livilla had a strange horrible sudden fear that all the house was as empty as the kitchen seemed to be, but for herself and the cat. Everyone was gone, the slaves, her brothers, her father, and Fulvia, too, borne off into the air.

The urge to cry ripped through Livilla, but she tried not to, for she would soon be a woman and married, and she must not let go of her dignity.

Then Lodia crept in.

Her slave's face was pale and deranged, an almost exact match for Livilla's own.

"Cibo choked," said Lodia.

"What—do you mean?"

"The cook—he choked on something. Look—he's there, by the ovens."

Livilla turned and saw Cibo's fat, impossible-to-miss body sprawled in a shadow that had somehow hidden him, and now did not. His face was turned away, and Livilla was glad.

Lodia stood swaying, holding herself in her arms. In a sort of chant she announced, "He must have tried to have her. He must have tried to." Then she sank to her knees and cowered, wondering if one of her masters would come to kill her.

But when Lodia looked up again, the Mistress-daughter had run away.

"I was glad to leave that house," said Idas the Greek. (Rather as Iudo the artifex had felt, if Idas had only known.) "Something goes on there. A great house, and full of people and slaves, and workmen, and so *silent*. And you know how now and then I see things other men are unaware of." His acquaintances in the tavern, attracted by the wine he had bought them, nodded. "Well, then, in the walls of that place—oh, at first it was aswarm with artisans painting everything green, yes, even panels in the tables and chests—I never saw the like, such a dingy, leaden color. But then, as I came from the sick lady's chamber and was passing one of these rooms, now all green-painted—and so badly—" the acquaintances waited, to see what the old romancer would bring out now, "—I saw faces in the walls, among the painted leaves. They watched me. Oh, not *painted* faces—they moved—not human faces either. The gods know what they were. Not animals—not quite that—perhaps like the faces one sees in the trunks of trees, or leaves clustered together, or in weeds under a pond . . ."

The greened house lay silent about its green courtyards. Green shadows dappled Apollo with the panther-skin of Bacchus.

No one went out. And yet it was as if they had *all* gone out. Even if you glimpsed them move there, in the rooms, along the corridors, shifting the sunlight and the hangings, even then, it was as if they were not really there. But if they were not, what was?

For a kind of energy filled all the cells. Time had passed. Some tens of days, thirty, forty. And no one called, not a single trader, and no visitors. Behind the door, in his alcove, the door-slave slept. Yet it was as if he were not there. It was as if the *house* were no longer there, merged into a green shade or green wave. Become one more grove or fountain of the decorated city.

People on Palace Hill, going by the blind outer walls, failed to glance at them, as if—the house of the patrician Livius had vanished.

⌐ *III*

At noon, Jovus went to the kitchen and took some of the olives and figs that lay on the table, and some of the stale bread. A slave—he had forgotten the man's name—had slunk out when Jovus came in, rather as the cat had been used to do, before it ran away. The slave had also scrounged some of the leftover food. Although it spoiled, there still seemed to be enough. And somehow Jovus did not think about when it would all be gone. (He had noted the body of Cibo was no longer there. Someone must have dragged it away. He did not *like* to think of *this*.)

But the house had no Master, so what could you expect of it? Or, it had one, but a Master who stayed in his library and did not move, no, not even to seek the privy or the bath. And the house had a fragile Mistress, who had been sick from a fall, and walked only a short way from her room, and back again.

The hotter colors faded from Jovus' bedroom walls, he thought, as they had faded from the flowers in the garden. Livilla's saffron stolas were now the color of soured cream.

Jovus ate the figs and bread standing in the garden, and

he looked up at the sky, which he did not think was blue, not truly, or else something came between him and the sky.

The city was deeply quiet. Occasionally he thought he heard traffic on the roads, or vague cries, but it was perhaps only the rustle of blood behind his own ears.

Moss grew in the mane of Apollo's lion. Jovus was examining this, when he heard his mother's voice from the colonnade.

"Where is your father?"

Fulvia had asked this a great deal, but then she had stopped asking, as the answer was always identical.

"In his library," said Jovus, as always. "Mother, would you like this fig—look, there are raisins, too."

"Never mind," said Fulvia.

She turned, and then she turned back. She said, her voice like pearls which had been crushed, "He isn't there. I looked. He isn't anywhere in this house."

Jovus felt panic spring in him like a tiger.

Fulvia wore no makeup. This made her seem both younger and quite old. Either way she would be no help.

Nevertheless, together they went again through the house, through room after room, into each of the courtyards. They pulled aside drapes and let sunlight into the spaces—was sunlight green? They walked through the three rooms of the bath, steamless and unheated. They searched the cubicles of the slaves. Sometimes they met these slaves, who shied, but seemed deaf and dumb, or who bolted, and this made Fulvia irritated, and so more like her previous self, a remote and pragmatic woman, offering calm words that snapped with repressed rage.

At some point, too, Livilla joined them, crying a little, but stupidly, like a small child who had mislaid what it was upset about. Parvus also appeared. He was quite naked, and very dirty, but none of them reproached him, though Fulvia clicked her tongue.

They did not find Livius.

At last, they were back in the library, where, in the curtain-dusk, the scrolls and wax tablets shone dull in their cubbyholes, like ranks of peculiar skulls.

Fulvia stood there at the room's center. She glanced now and then demandingly at the couch, the chair, then at the stool, which had fallen over. She seemed to think she might still find her husband. She tapped her fingers on her gold bracelet. (The gold was discolored.)

"It's what she told me," said Fulvia, frowning, concentrating. "I remember now. Her son. They disappear. And now Livius has done it."

Livilla sniveled. Parvus picked at a scab on his knee, embarrassed.

Jovus thought, *I don't know them, these people. Who are they?*

Fulvia thought she heard her elder son thinking this, but she did not care. She hated him really, her son Jovus, who had, with his birth, robbed her of sexual pleasure. Even the wretched, time-consuming Livilla had not done that. As for Parvus, what was he, some spawned thing, like a frog—

But there had been something Fulvia meant to do. That was it. This thing had been the reason why she had rushed home from the woman's house—which woman? It did not matter—the one who told her about a son who disappeared, as now Livius had.

What was it Fulvia had meant to do, been so concerned with that she had tripped over an unreal tile loose in a stair that was not there under her feet?

Fulvia turned to Jovus.

"Where is *she?*"

Fulvia wondered if she should go back to her husband's bedroom. She had not looked beneath the bed. Livius would not be there, but *she* might.

"Who?" quavered Jovus, but Fulvia saw the tiger of panic smoldering under his skin.

"The Persian—what was her name—*Roxara.*"

The name sounded in the room incredibly, as though it was actual, and the only thing that could be so.

And after it there followed the most subtle, silky feather of sound, the noise something might make, uncoiling over a bough heavy with leaves.

"Ah," said Fulvia. She moved quite quickly, and pulled

the curtain right down from the courtyard door, and then she put her hand on Livius' desk. She took up the little knife he had always kept there. It was only a small knife, but a young woman's neck was usually slender, and the vital vein unmissable.

Yet now Jovus was in her way. Fulvia did not care enough about her son to wish to kill him, and so she only said, "Stand aside from her." Not using his name either since she had forgotten it.

But Jovus went on lumpenly standing there, between Fulvia and the slave called Roxara, who all that while had been, presumably, sitting motionless and invisible in the room's other chair.

Then Fulvia lost patience. She struck the boy across his shoulders, and thrust him aside.

Fulvia herself stood then only inches from the Persian Creature. Fulvia could smell her. She did not smell human, but spicy, like mummia. Her head was not bowed. She was looking back at Fulvia with her opaque serpent-scale eyes, and Fulvia lifted the knife in a steady hand, because this Roxara's snake-neck was very slim, and the vein was plainly to be seen there.

And Jovus screamed, "*No*—no—Mother!" And punched her hand away. And he was strong after all, it felt as if he had broken Fulvia's wrist, there under her green-gold bangle.

"Leave me alone, you fool!" she cried. She was exasperated.

"No—*no*—" shrieked Jovus. "No—Mother—you can't kill her—you *mustn't* kill her. Mother—no—*look in her eyes!*"

Fulvia snarled like a wild beast. But even so, with the Creature's face so near to her, almost inadvertently, she did what he said.

Then she saw the eyes' real greenness, and then she saw through, to *within* their green. She stared. She stared into a limitless hall built of glaucous nothingness, like the depths of a sea. Here and there currents moved in it, like liquid winds, and faint glimmerings, like drowned stars. And

there, too, deep down and far away inside it, and in miniature, Livius was wandering—she made him out exactly, his
every detail, even to his disheveled hair and filthy toga—her
Livius, her husband. Beyond him were some other smaller
figures, farther off. She could not yet quite make them out,
although they seemed, as he did, familiar to her.

Travel Agency

Ellen Klages

Ellen Klages recently moved to Cleveland Heights, Ohio, from San Francisco, California, where she worked for the Exploratorium and developed her talent for stand-up comedy (she performs improv comedy with the Second City Organization). She is a stalwart supporter of the James Tiptree, Jr. Awards (serving on the Motherboard), and runs the infamous Tiptree benefit auction at SF conventions around the country, during which anything can happen. She has written four books of hands-on science activities for children (with Pat Murphy, et al.) for the Exploratorium. The second book in that series, The Science Explorer Out and About, *was honored with* Scientific American's *1997 Young Readers Book Award. She currently divides her time between San Francisco and Cleveland. In recent years her short fiction has appeared in science fiction and fantasy anthologies and magazines, both online and in print.*

"Travel Agency" appeared in electronic form in Strange Horizons on the Internet, and so this is perhaps its first appearance in print. This is a story that climaxes in one sharp, memorable image that literalizes the metaphor of transport by art. It is a shock-of-recognition story, in which we see ourselves.

My older sister and her daughter, my favorite niece, have come to stay with me in my house outside Boston for a few nights. Marjorie is a frequent flyer; she works for the airlines, in management. She wears stretch jeans and a white sweatshirt with glittery appliquéd gingham teddy bears. This is Emily's first visit. She's almost ten. She gives me an awkward hug, and a shy smile when her mother is not looking.

My guest room is a room that is usually the den. I have cleaned up the day-to-day clutter of papers and books, and put clean sheets on the sofabed. Marjorie frowns when she sees it. It is a little small for two to sleep comfortably.

I tell Emily that she'll be sleeping in the attic, if that's okay. The child's eyes light up as if she'd just been offered a bunk on a pirate ship. They live in a suburb, in a split-level ranch house with white carpeting. But I know from her letters that many of her favorite books seem to involve old houses with great, sometimes magic, attics. Mrs. Piggle-Wiggle's house has an attic, and the Four-Story Mistake. I think there's one in *Half Magic*, too.

Magic rarely happens in a living room, or in a basement, unless it's scary magic, which isn't the kind you want to have surround you at night.

For most of my guests, my attic is a utilitarian place. It's just a room at the top of the house, the place where the luggage lives when it's not traveling, and where the boxes of Christmas ornaments and books without bookshelf space are stored. Winter clothes in the cedar closet in July; bathing suits in plastic boxes in December.

But the child is beside herself, hopping excitedly from one foot to the other, waiting to see my attic. I am a librarian. I am neither blasé about the importance of my offer, nor alarmed at the hopping. I am actually rather delighted.

Marjorie puts a hand on Emily's shoulder and tells her to behave. The child stops hopping and pulls her ears a fraction closer to her shoulders.

The attic door opens off the upstairs hallway, between the guest room and the bathroom. It isn't one of those attics that is reached by pull-down stairs set in the ceiling. It is a proper attic, with a proper doorway and small, twisting, steep stairs. Emily turns to me and smiles when I open the door, her eyes so bright I'm amazed that the narrow stairwell isn't illuminated by them.

At the top of the stairs, we step out into one big slope-ceilinged room. It's finished in the sense that there are paneled walls and not just exposed beams and studs and lath. But it is not wallpapered or carpeted or decorated. Two-thirds of it is full of the usual attic-y jumble of boxes and trunks, lamps that don't match my new couch, and occasional tables whose occasion has come and gone. It is a place for things that no longer belong.

The far end is an open, rectangular space with a small iron cot of the same shape and vintage as the ones in the cabins of my childhood summer camp. A thin mattress lies atop springs that I know will squeak when the child sits down, or when she turns over. I have made it up with some faded green sheets and an equally faded summer-weight quilt.

The cot sits in the middle of an old, threadbare Oriental rug that holds the encroaching boxes at bay. An upturned footlocker stands at the side of the bed, topped with a green glass-shaded lamp. Next to the lamp is an offering of nine-year-old-type books that I have pulled from the dozens of bookcases that line the rest of my house: *The Lilac Fairy Book*, *The Wind in the Willows*, an Enid Blyton schoolgirl book about the fourth form at St. Clare's, and *The Phantom Tollbooth*.

A few feet above the bed, there's a small, round window, filled with the leaves of the neighbor's tall maple. The wall faces west, and the late afternoon light streams golden onto the tiny bed.

Emily stops in her tracks when she sees all of this, stops

moving altogether. I'm not even sure if she's breathing.

She looks from her mother to me and then asks, "Do I really get to sleep here?" The wonder in her voice makes one of us smile.

"For two whole nights? Just me? By myself?"

I nod. The child has her own room at home. It's not like she lies shackled to her straw pallet next to the kitchen hearth, deprived of both comfort and privacy. But this is a place that she'll remember. Years from now, she'll be able to close her eyes and recall every detail. She may no longer be able to remember where she'd been, or why, exactly, but she'll remember there was a bed in an attic, and a doting aunt who gave her the chance for a bit of a storybook childhood.

"We're going to go down and start dinner," I say, giving her a wink. "Do you want to stay up here, or come down and have a root beer while we cook?"

It is not a hard choice.

"Here, I think. Maybe I'll kind of unpack." She is already eyeing the books on the bedside table.

So Marjorie and I go downstairs and open a bottle of Chardonnay, and I begin chopping vegetables while she goes on about United, and Donald, and how they plan to landscape the yard next spring. An hour later, I excuse myself and tiptoe back up the narrow stairs.

Dust motes swirl in the last rays of twilight. As I had hoped, the cot is empty, only a small girl-shaped indentation left in the quilt. Enid Blyton is lying facedown, pages open. I smile as I close it and tuck it under my arm.

I thought it was what she'd choose. It's a lovely place for a holiday, and the girls in the fourth form are such a lively bunch this year.

A Fable of Savior and Reptile

Steven Popkes

Steven Popkes lives in Hopkinton, Massachusetts, "on two acres in Hopkinton along with his wife, son, cat and twenty-five-pound tortoise named Ibn Battuta." He has been publishing SF and fantasy for around twenty years. He's had two novels published, Caliban Landing *(1987) and* Slow Lightning *(1989), and nearly two dozen pieces of short fiction. In the tradition of most writers, his job has been what comes immediately to hand: house restorer to morgue tech to software engineer to white-water–rafting guide. Currently, he writes software for avionics systems.*

"A Fable of Savior and Reptile" is an unusual fantasy, the life of Jesus as told from the point of view of a tortoise. It appeared in Realms of Fantasy, *and is, to say the least, an unconventional point of view on the Christian messiah. Do note the word "fable" in the title.*

It was just past dawn and I was sunning myself by the side of the road when I felt the vibrations in the earth. I pulled back into the shade of a rock and watched. Three men on horses, colorfully dressed, came to the edge of the road and milled together. Two of them shouted at the third in a language I did not know—not that this was in itself unusual. There are many languages of men I don't know. Once, they threw Hebrew words at one another that were so bastardized and mispronounced I could only recognize the sound of the language but not the substance.

Finally, they came to some kind of agreement, came together, and rode off toward the East. I looked after them. For some time, I pondered: colorful garb that was out of place in this area; horses of a size I had never seen; these three excited by something in the East. I resolved to find out about it and began walking East myself.

Still, patience more than rapidity is a virtue for a tortoise. Jesus was nearly six when I found him.

From the shadows under the grapes, I watched and listened to them for several days. Humans rarely look below their knees and so I considered myself safe.

Jesus sat in the vegetables looking underneath their leaves for pests.

"Since you're just sitting there," I said in passable Hebrew, "pull off a leaf for me."

He turned and looked at me, sat back cross-legged and stared. "Did you speak?"

"Of course."

"Turtles don't speak," he said with finality.

"If God can talk through a burning bush, why can't a tortoise speak?"

"You're not God."

"It's a lesser miracle, but the principle's the same." I reached up for a leaf on my own.

He frowned. "My mother won't like you eating the vegetables."

"Then, get me something different."

The little devil did more than that. He built a cage for me quick as winking and put me in it. Not a terribly sophisticated affair, but he'd inherited a skill with wood from his father. I paced the borders of the cage back and forth and looked closely at the walls. Once around the cage a few times, I turned and started back the way I'd come, to see if I'd missed anything. Then, I repeated it to make sure.

Jesus watched me struggle to escape the enclosure. It seemed to hurt his feelings and he looked as if he wanted to cry. "Why are you doing this? Didn't I make a nice place for you? Isn't it better than the desert?"

I stopped for a moment, looked at the boy for several minutes. "It is in my nature."

Jesus sat down next to the fence. "If I let you out will you stay with me?"

I didn't reply for some minutes, thinking it through. "Ah. You wish to *bargain*." I considered further. "I came here on my own. Apparently, it is my nature to come to you. Certainly it is in my nature to associate with human beings. I've been doing that for many years. I will promise this, then. If you will release me, I will be true to my nature."

He nodded solemnly and brought me out of the cage and placed me on the ground. "I'll call you Ezen, 'cause you look like a rock."

Once I had been called a second cousin to a rock; it had not been a compliment. I nodded. "As you wish."

Jesus' birth was not sufficiently long after their marriage to be completely free of scandal. "Every baby takes nine months but the first one," as the saying goes. Even so, they seemed to be a devoted couple, both to each other and to the boy, in their rough, mammalian way. There was never any doubt as to the boy's parentage: He smelled of Joseph through and through.

Still, times were not easy for them. I had learned a great deal searching for Jesus. Sitting beneath the bushes and listening, I heard rumors of riot and vicious retaliation as Herod aged. There was constant intrigue between the priests, Herod's government, and Rome. Every few months came a proclamation in the streets for another new Messiah. Some weeks after that another man hung from a tree. This had been going on before Jesus had been born and would, no doubt, continue after his death.

Jesus and I talked often over the years. He kept these conversations secret and for my own part I preferred it so. Few are the bonds made between mammal and reptile and I had no interest in forging another. I did notice he never asked me anything about where I had been before and what I was doing with him. I did not know why. Perhaps it was because he was a child with a child's acceptance of things.

I had little contact—other than observation—with young Jesus' friends save one, his cousin John. John was several years older than Jesus and the younger boy followed after him every chance he got. Jesus would have been happier, I think, had he not been the eldest boy with all of Joseph's expectations brought to bear on him. Around John, Jesus played the role of delighted and fawning puppy. For his own part, John was a shrewd, cruel adolescent: a typical budding human male.

Jesus and I were talking when John came up behind him. I had smelled him and fallen silent but Jesus had not noticed.

"Who are you talking to?" demanded John.

"My turtle, Ezcn." Jesus reached down and picked me up and showed me to him, something I absolutely and truly detested. I mean, the boy was warm and smelled as attractive as can any mammal, but being waved about like a flag was extremely unpleasant.

"He squirms, doesn't he?" said John, watching me.

"He doesn't like to be held," said Jesus and sat me down again. Immediately, I started for cover.

"Let's get some lamp oil and set fire to him," suggested John, smiling.

I redoubled my efforts to reach the brush.

"You're not going to set fire to my turtle!" cried Jesus.

"We could play catch with him."

"No!"

I had just reached the cover of the bushes when Jesus picked me up again and pressed me to his chest. This was his idea of safety.

John did not press the matter and left soon after. I did not forget it, however, and hid whenever I heard or smelled John in the vicinity.

Things did not go well for the family in the next few years. Jesus grew like a weed, but political intrigue grew faster. Most of the commissions in carpentry had to do with the priests and Joseph was not well connected. His business suffered. Jesus had inherited Joseph's confidence with wood and helped out where he could, but Mary had ambitions for her son and sent him to the temple. This caused a little friction in the family, since they could ill afford to pay any priest to teach Jesus.

Jesus often spoke with me about the priests and occasionally asked questions. I answered if I knew anything. It was stupid of me, I know. Trouble was bound to follow.

Jesus found me sunning myself at the edge of the garden.

"You'd better hide out," he said sitting down. "Mama's upset the greens got eaten. Did you have to eat them all the way into the ground? There's nothing left but stubs."

"That's the best part of the stalk."

"Better watch out, anyway."

I looked up at him. He smelled afraid. "What happened?"

He rubbed his face. "I'm not sure. Timerphon kept me in the temple this afternoon. He and a couple of other priests asked me a lot of strange questions." He shivered. "I heard they took a whole family out and stoned them a few weeks ago."

"What kind of questions?"

"Weird things. Like, the role of Rome in the temple. And did my parents feel that the temple should be giving money to the legions of Rome. Then, they asked me some really complicated questions about the dietary and marriage laws." He thought for a minute. "One had to do with if a woman were married a lot of times, and each husband died, which one would she be married to in heaven."

"What did you answer?"

"I said I didn't know." He shrugged. "I said I didn't know anything *about* heaven. Then I tried to figure out what they were asking for. Like a test? So I said, well, one thing's for sure, if heaven was being with God, then it couldn't be much like here—this being pretty far from the heart of God, or so I've always heard. So maybe things would be different."

"What did they say?"

Jesus looked down. "They didn't like that answer. Then, they asked me if people should give money to God or to Rome. Heck, I said, God shouldn't need money. I mean, He ought to have everything He needs. Besides, the Romans mint the money; it's Rome's money, everybody says so. So, I said give them what's theirs and give God what's his." He fell silent, then burst out. "I mean, how was I to know they were talking about *taxes*! And then, they started asking me about my cousin John."

"What about John?"

Jesus gestured broadly. "Who does he talk to? Where does he go? Where does he spend his time? What does he drink? Who's his woman? As if John had only one." He shook his head bitterly and I couldn't tell if it was because of the questions or John's ways with the local women. "What color is his robe? Does he wear anything underneath?"

"What did you answer?"

"I did what he'd do for me: I said I didn't know. I'm scared, Ezen."

I thought for a long time. It grew dark. Jesus shivered but he stayed there with me. I thought until I felt myself getting sluggish as the temperature dropped.

"Listen, Jesus," I said finally. "Go inside and tell your father every word you've said to me. Leave nothing out."

"I can't do that," Jesus cried. "He'll crucify me."

"No, he won't. You've done nothing. But I suspect you will be on your way to Egypt before daybreak."

"What do you mean, we'll be going to Egypt?"

"You're not the first person to be questioned about politics. Heresy is where you find it here in Israel. You'll be safe in Egypt. You'll be able to learn things—"

"I don't want to go. Besides, you're a turtle. How would you know we're going to Egypt?"

I looked at him in distaste. "You're 11 years old. I've lived better than 50 times that. How do you think?"

I could see him laboriously working that out. "Have you ever been to Egypt?"

"Of course."

"Will you show me things?"

Boylike, he'd changed from fear to excitement. "I could," I said, starting to squirm to be let down. "But I'm not going with you."

"You've *got* to!"

"I do not. Now, put me back under the bush so I can get some sleep."

He sat next to me as I began to cool down. "Will I ever see you again?"

"It's entirely possible," I said as I began to nod off. "One of us should be able to find the other."

Near dawn, I awoke. As I was warming, armed men came and searched the house. They found nothing. Joseph and his family had gone. When the sun was higher, I left also.

* * *

"Yeah," he said as he peeled another orange. "Papa died about two years ago."

I bit into the orange he'd given me, felt the sweet juice wash my throat.

He looked at me with a smile. "I'm not boring you, am I?"

"Not as long as you keep plying me with oranges."

He snickered.

It had been six years and he'd grown some in height, but more in breadth and muscle. His beard was still wispy though his shoulders were broad and promised that in some years he would be formidably stocky.

"Mama insisted I stay with Ramo." He sucked the orange noisily.

"Who's Ramo?"

"He's a physician. Papa got him to take me on as an apprentice." He threw away the peel. "I was too good to go into carpentry," he said airly.

"So, why are you here?" I moved out of the shade to get warm. He'd found me in a small crack in the earth in Galilee. Outside, the wind was strong and cool in spite of the sun. Here in this improbable grotto, it was warm and there was a plentiful supply of greens. I'd been here two years.

"I came to say hello," he said and shrugged. "Besides, you could use the company."

"You've done that. Thanks for the oranges." I'd lost patience with the arrogant adolescent Jesus had become. I started to move back toward the spring. There was a short cave there and I could take a nap.

"Wait a minute," he yelled and put a foot in front of me. It startled me and I drew back into my shell.

"I need to talk to you," he said angrily.

I remained silent and withdrawn while he yelled at me. Pity, I thought. He had a lot of heart for a mammal.

Finally, he was reduced to kneeling in front of me and screaming at me. In a fury, he picked me up and held me as if to throw me against the rocks.

"Will you kill me now?" I asked quietly.

He stared at me, breathing hard, put me down. He leaned back against the rock.

"You were never so stubborn when I was a child," he said.

"You were never so rude."

He shrugged, stung. "John contacted me."

"Ah. That's why you're here."

"Yes. My cousin John. He went to prison for a bit. Did you know that?"

"Why?"

"For attempting to bring freedom to an oppressed Israel!"

I blinked. "I beg your pardon."

He'd stood up to say this, glanced down at me and sat down, looking embarrassed. "He joined up with the Freedom Fighters."

"Whose?"

"What do you mean, 'whose'?"

I shook my head. "Jesus, there are a hundred messiahs, heretics, and 'freedom fighters' a week in Israel. Whose crowd has he fallen in with?"

"I'm not sure." He shrugged. "He mentioned someone named Barabbas."

"Wonderful."

"Who is Barabbas?"

"Nobody important. Or effective." I stared at him for a long time. "What do you want from me?"

"Should I join him?"

"Who? Barabbas?"

"Well, join John. I guess that means join Barabbas."

"How old do you think I am?"

He grinned crookedly. "I remember when we left for Egypt—better than five hundred years, by my calculation."

"I'm probably older. But who keeps track? So, you want my advice? Why?"

" 'Cause I trust you," he said defensively.

"Why?"

"You're my friend."

"Friend!" I snorted in disgust. "I'm a reptile, second cousin to a snake. Your God put enmity between you and my cousin. You're a mammal. We have almost nothing in common. We have a bond but it's unlikely to be friendship."

"You came looking for me."

"I never said that."

He didn't speak for a moment. "It's true though. Isn't it?"

It was my turn not to speak for a moment. "I don't know. I came looking for something and found you. I'll never know if it was you I was looking for."

His face looked suddenly pinched as it did when he was a child and about to cry. I could not allow him that luxury.

"You haven't answered my question," I demanded. "Why do you want *my* advice?"

"You're the only person who has nothing to lose if you tell me the truth."

"There is no truth," I said flatly. "There is only opinion."

He stared at me fiercely. "You have nothing to lose by being honest."

I stared back at him, relaxed. "True. Toss me another orange."

He did so, laughed nervously with a sound like a sob and leaned back against the warm rock.

I considered as I ate. "There's not time enough to think about this properly."

"I can wait."

I laughed shortly, myself. As if mammals knew anything about waiting. "Here is my unconsidered opinion: I don't like John. I don't trust him. I've heard nothing good about Barabbas. And no force on earth will ever force the Romans out of Israel. They'll leave in their own good time."

He leaned forward, eagerly. "When?"

"Everything moves on eventually."

He relaxed, smiled bitterly. "I don't think I can wait that long."

"I'm not surprised. Go back to Egypt. Go back to your

mother. Become a physician. If you still feel you want to give your life for your country, give it as a living life: Come back and heal them. You'll do more than a thousand Johns."

Jesus bit his lip. "That's what you think?"

"From the depths of my reptilian heart."

It was nearly sunset and the desert was cooling fast. He brought me next to him under his blanket in the dark. I didn't protest; he was, after all, warm. But in the morning, while I was befuddled with the cold, he left. All that was left of him was his smell and a warm place in the sand.

"You should have a drink with me," Jesus said, holding out the wineskin in my general direction.

I stepped back. It smelled of spoiled fruit. "I'll pass, thank you."

"Suit yourself." He squirted the wine in his mouth. Some dribbled out the corners and stained his robe.

I'd stayed in Galilee but moved farther south, where the moist air and occasional rain had turned the desert green. It was here, as I recalled, that a great forest of Lebanese cedars had stood. Cut down, now, like every other tree in the region. The bushes and undergrowth made it difficult to farm and so few humans lived here. A pleasant trait that was sure to change in time.

We lay in the shade of some scrub bushes with the road in sight.

"God, life is good," he said dreamily. "Look at me. My parents take me to Egypt to escape being stoned and I come back a respected doctor. With a wife. And a son—a strong, healthy son. There'll be more: I'm a man with more than one arrow in my quiver."

"And your mother?" I asked.

Jesus frowned, then shrugged again. "Difficult, as she has always been. She and Rachel don't get along. But it's better now that there's a grandchild. You'd think sons appeared by virgin birth for all the attention they give me, sometimes." He wagged a finger at me. "Make no mistake, my friend. To women, men are only a means to create children. If they could do without us, they would." He laughed again.

A drunken Jesus laughed more than a sober one. I reflected on the difference and decided that the adult drunken form was marginally more likable than the adult sober form.

"I figured you out when I was in Egypt," he said. He rummaged in his pouch and brought out a pair of oranges and gave them to me. "You're a spirit come to counsel me— a sort of guardian angel, but in mortal form. Perhaps you were enlightened in a former life and this is your reward."

"Scant reward, this," I said between mouthfuls of orange.

"True," he said, placidly. "Or perhaps you sinned in such a manner that this is your penance."

I grunted, wiped my face.

"All right," he said and drank some more. "You tell me. What are you?"

"I'm old. That's all." I tore the second orange and bit into the sweetness inside. "There aren't very many of us left. There were never very many of us to begin with, but we just didn't age."

"Spirits?"

"Tortoises: Once a tortoise reaches a certain age not much can kill him. We don't die of old age."

He snorted. "That's absurd. All things have a life span— insects, elephants, man."

"All things are what they are, Jesus. We are all hatched— born in your case—live if we can, die when we can't anymore." I looked at him. "The length of that time is variable."

"The reason you talk, then, is because you've just gotten old enough to learn? That seems improbable."

I returned my attention to the orange. "I have no idea how I talk. It's not a question I dwell on."

"There must be some explanation."

"There may be. I'm just incurious about it."

"Surely—"

"Jesus!" I looked at him, impatience finally getting the better of my temper. "Humans are always looking for explanations. I'm not interested in them. Is that food over there? Is there water over the hill? Where is there shade from the midday sun and a warm rock to rest on at night? These are the important questions. Humans are mammals, that is to say they are born knowing nothing and have to question their entire lives. I was born knowing who I was. Look at the snake and the lizard, working for their food, knowing what's important. Look at the flowers, never working at all, but they grow according to their nature. I know my own nature. I need not pursue it."

"What of beauty, Ezen?" Jesus asked quietly.

"What of it?"

"Look at the flowers," he said. "They are so beautiful. Surely that is also part of their nature."

"They are not beautiful for you," I said, feeling a rare tenderness toward him. "You are merely allowed to observe them in passing."

"He was another son. I know. I delivered him myself. She, of course, was already dead." Jesus contemplated the wineskin. He had been drinking steadily for some hours. His eyes were sunken and his hands thin and fragile looking. Suddenly, the tears came again. He did not sob. He just stared across the desert.

He had found me near Nazareth. I'd wandered south, smelling out some new growth. It was an orchard and along its edges a vineyard. I had been there at least a year, maybe more.

"What of your first son?" I asked.

"Dead, also." He drank from the skin. "Puncture wound from a Roman nail. It grew septic. I cut off his leg and cauterized it. It didn't help. He died delirious and raving, calling for his mother. He didn't know me at all." Jesus looked at me. "If you are a spirit, as I have often suspected, tell me now of the other side. It is now that I need to know. Comfort me."

"I don't have much comfort." I tried to think of something but nothing came. "I know no more than breath. It comes in; it goes out. When it does not return you are dead."

"How is it you die? You live so long."

I was silent so long, thinking about his question, he had to prod me with his finger.

"Come now, no shirking; speak to me truly," he said bitterly.

"There are two ways," I said slowly. "The first is what you would expect: disease, fire, falling, the hand of man or beast. The second is less precise. Sometimes, instead of having life taken away, one just loses it. It ceases to be worth the trouble."

Jesus looked interested. "Really. What happens then?"

"One stops. Stops eating. Stops moving. Stops drinking. Eventually, death ensues. I've seen it happen. When I was younger, I thought it impossible. Now, I see more clearly."

"I see." He leaned back. The desert shimmered in a heat haze. "John has written me and asked me to come join him with the Essenes. They have need of a doctor. I think I will go to them. I have need of being needed."

He rested his hand on my back, and though it was uncomfortable, I did not protest. It seemed to comfort him.

"They are a great comfort to me," Jesus said. "I feel as if I were serving God at last."

I snorted. He had brought me oranges again. "If you brought me oranges more often, God would smile upon you."

He chuckled. "It's a good thing to feed the poor in spirit, eh? The brethren seem to like me as well. They feel I have something to say to them and they to me." Jesus grinned sourly. "John wishes to take credit for any good I might do there. He said he prophesied my coming." He shrugged. "It beats drinking. I've been sober four years."

"I see."

"He takes people down to the river and washes them and

calls them blessed. They leave him gifts." Jesus spit. "It is like watching someone purchasing salvation. He has also taken a mistress—though by rights, it is *she* who has taken *him*."

"Who?"

"Salome. The dancer. The Essenes couldn't take that. He left to live at court. I worry for him. I think he still communicates with Barabbas. Between that and lying between the legs of the King's whore, he could yet be killed."

I wiped my face. "That is not your problem."

"He is my cousin. I should do something."

"Do what? You have no army. You have no weapon—even Barabbas has more than you, and his motley crew has little enough. Perhaps if I were the spirit you have suggested, I could help. It'd cost you, though."

"Cost me?"

I intoned: "Spirits are like gods: They like followers. Look out there. All that can be yours."

"The desert?"

"But only if you fall down and worship me."

"Not the desert. Try Jerusalem. Or even Bethlehem."

"Sorry. Only the desert this week. Maybe next time."

We both laughed.

Jesus fell silent, rubbed his face. "Still, Ezen. I'm 30 years old. I ought to do something with my life."

"I met him at John's funeral," Jesus began as he gave me an orange. "He was not anything like I imagined."

"Who? John?" I left the orange. I hadn't the heart for it somehow.

"No. Barabbas." Jesus peeled another orange meditatively. "I've started a clinic among the poor here in Jerusalem. It's bad enough that medicine in Israel is so bad compared to Egypt—I've known that for some time. But it's contemptible that the poor should suffer so disproportionately. It's been very successful; good medicine is something of a miracle anywhere around here." He looked pensive. "And I've been giving . . . talks."

"Talks?"

"Yes. So much of sickness lies in people's lives, you see. Ramo taught me that. You have to cure the spirit. It's a bigger job than I imagined." He stopped. "I don't know how to say this. Hatred, loathing, and rage all have their consequences in the body. Ramo taught that the turning away from such emotions cures the body." He looked uncomfortable. "You cure a few cases of skin rot or warts and right away people are saying you're healing lepers and raising the dead. It's the condition of medicine here that's the problem, really."

"Jesus," I said, irritated. "What are you talking about?"

"Barabbas," he said. "I spoke to him at the funeral. He said that he'd heard all sorts of good things about me. How I was doing marvelous things—miraculous things—in the city. He asked me to give one of these . . . talks I've been giving."

"By 'talks,' do you mean 'sermons'?"

"No!" he said violently. Then, more quietly. "No. They're not sermons, but Barabbas seemed to think they were. Barabbas is very popular among some people. I can see why: He's very charismatic. He can speak to you of simple things and invest them with great importance. Some say he might be the Messiah, come to free Israel."

"What do you think?"

"I don't believe in Messiahs. I'd like to see the Romans out, though."

"You're thinking about joining him?"

"I don't know," he said defensively. "I don't know what role a doctor would play in an armed camp. Patch people up just to have them go out and get gutted by a spear again? It's just that when I spoke to him, Barabbas made me feel that he really is doing something for Israel. Something important. I suppose I want to be doing something like that, too."

"Your clinic is saving lives?" I asked.

"Oh, yes," he said and shrugged. Then, smiled. "We have a number of patients. I've had to recruit help—a couple of fishermen and farmers. People I can train to sew wounds and dispense herbs for simple complaints. It's belief that makes it work much of the time, though."

"I said it 20 years ago. I'll say it again." I walked over next to him and bumped his foot until he looked at me. "If you want to dedicate your life to your country, dedicate it to the living, not the dying. Stay with your clinic. Leave Barabbas alone."

I was awakened roughly by someone holding me. As I warmed, I grew aware of smells, the feeling of coarse cloth.

"Are you awake yet?" came an urgent whisper.

All I could see was shadow but I could smell Jesus. "Barely. Put me back. We can talk again in the morning."

"He's here. He came this evening. He's staying with me."

"Who?" Then, I thought. "Barabbas, of course." I shook my head and finally came awake. "Get rid of him. He's dangerous."

"I can't just put him out in the street. He'll get arrested."

"So will you if you let him stay there. Is there a reward for him?"

Jesus didn't reply for a moment. "Sort of."

"What do you mean?"

"There's this trumped-up charge of thievery against him. I think there's some kind of reward for that."

"You've both gone stupid. You have a clinic for the poor. It's in a poor neighborhood. You've recruited the poor. Now you harbor a revolutionary. Don't you think somebody's going to turn him in for the reward money?"

"Oh, God!" he cried and dropped me on the sand. I heard him running.

Aching and bruised, I dug myself slowly under a stone and waited for the light and warmth of morning.

Lying under the hedges next to the market, it wasn't hard to piece together what had happened. The soldiers had come for Barabbas and found both of them and arrested them. It was not difficult to find this out, but it had taken some days.

In another day, I found out where they were being kept.

Near dawn, I roused myself and paced the length of the building where it faced the road. After checking its length a few times, I found a crack I could squeeze and burrow through. I could smell him in the dark. It was slow, cold going.

I found myself in a small, dark room with him. I could hear him breathing. I was so cold I could barely think. I found bare skin and bit, trying to wake him up. He sat up in a cursing rage and picked me up, ready to dash me against the wall, stopped.

"Ezen?" he asked of me in his hand in the dark.

I wasn't able to reply. He held me against his chest until I was warm.

"How are you?" I was finally able to speak.

"Beaten. My right arm is broken and, also, a couple of ribs, I think." He coughed and I could feel him spasm with the pain. "Are you here to help me escape?"

"There is no escape."

"Then, what are you doing here?"

"I am being here with you."

"Ah." He did not speak for a while. "I'm going to die. They're going to kill me, aren't they?"

"So I understand. It's been the talk on the street for days."

I heard him nod in the dark. "Barabbas cut himself some kind of a deal. I don't know the details. He goes free. He wasn't able to include me." He nodded again. "He said he tried. It seems I don't have the right connections. Ciaphas and his associates want to make an example of *somebody* and I'm very convenient." He cradled me against his left arm. "I'm very glad you've come. It's very frightening in here. Alone."

I didn't say anything.

After a time, he spoke up. "I keep wondering if my life was ever any good."

"Any good?"

"Yes. Barabbas spoke a great deal of working for the common good. It was quite a thing with him. I feel so odd about it: Here it is. I'm going to die in a disgusting, painful manner and I can't quite catch on to it. I just keep thinking about Rachel and my mother and my dead son and the clinic and I keep wondering if any of it was ever any good. Do you know?"

"You're asking me?"

"Yes. I think so."

"How should I know?" I said, exasperated. "I'm a reptile for God's sake."

"You've known me nearly all my life. You've never been anything but completely honest with me. Have I lived a good life? Have I made any sort of difference at all?"

"I don't know," I answered. "I'd have to think about it."

"Don't think overlong," said Jesus testily. "If you take your usual time about it I might not be around to hear the answer."

"For all I know, I'm the oldest of my kind," I said at last. "Humans have been taking our eggs, killing us for food, and moving into where we live for as long as I can remember, and that is a long time. All of the others I once knew are dead. Some were killed and eaten. Some just decided humans smelled too bad, or the water near them tasted poorly. The habits of some were too ingrained over the years to live near humans. So, when humans finally invaded their territories, they just decided it was too difficult to continue to live. The greatest talent we have is to wait, and they waited for things to change. Things didn't and they died. It was as simple as that. People have marched along these roads as long as I can remember.

"You want to know if you did any good. I tell you, I only know this: The only good you will ever know you did is what you have seen with your own eyes. Nothing lives after you. Things you have said will be twisted and changed to fit circumstances you have never foreseen and never intended, the very words you have uttered will be reinterpreted and used for reasons unconceived by you. The deeds you accomplished that you consider most important will be forgotten and your actions that you least considered or were most ashamed of will become those for which you are remembered. There is nothing special to you that did not come to a thousand others like you, and if you are remembered at all a generation after you are dead it will be because of whim, circumstance, and random chance. Therefore, it is unprofitable to consider the impact you have on the world afterward. Instead, look at what you have done and judge yourself on that."

Jesus leaned back against the cell. "Slim comfort. What's a man to live for?"

"Only a man would have to ask that kind of stupid question."

Jesus laughed. "I cured a few people. I made my mother happy, for a while. I fed a turtle."

"For that last, your name is engraved in gold in the Hereafter."

He held me close and I did not protest.

They came for him that night. He buried me in the corner and left quietly with them. I struggled out and made my way back to the crack in the wall I had found. It was just after dawn when I found myself outside.

I walked from one end of the Jerusalem Road to the other, looking for him. It took time. I was resolved not to leave until I saw him.

I found him hanging from a tree, his arms nailed above his head, his legs to the trunk. Blood was dripping from his feet. He did not recognize me—could not see me at all. His pain was such that he saw and heard nothing else. All he could do was groan and mutter.

I stayed there another day and a night until he died, though he never became clear enough to know me. There was no one else there to be with him.

His mother claimed the body and took it away. I watched her go. Then, I began the long walk out of Jerusalem.

After that, I came here. To the edge of the desert. I found a stream and drank. I found some palm fruit and ate. The water did not refresh me and the fruit did not sit well in my stomach. The sky feels darker to me and the sun does not warm me as it once did. The taste has gone out of things and all I can smell is man.

I sit here and wait for things to change.

Comrade Grandmother

Naomi Kritzer

Naomi Kritzer [www.naomikritzer.com] lives in Minneapolis. She began publishing fiction in 1999 and has published only eight stories to date. When we reprinted her sixth story, "The Golem," in the first Year's Best Science Fiction, *we called her "perhaps the most interesting and talented new fantasy writer to emerge in 2000." No new stories appeared in 2001, but in 2002 and early 2003, her first novel was published in two volumes in paperback,* Fires of the Faithful *and* Turning the Storm. *And she published two stories worthy of inclusion here, of which we chose the shorter.*

"Comrade Grandmother" was first published in Strange Horizons, *one of the best of the electronic SF and fantasy magazines, and this is its first appearance in print. It is a provocative fantasy that combines the Russian folktale character of Baba Yaga, with her house supported on chicken legs, and the World War II invasion of Soviet Russia by the German army of the Nazi regime. A young woman saves the day.*

"—*glorious Soviet—soon* bring Hitler—complete defeat. Heavy casualties—Dnieper River—"

The voice from the radio faded into the deafening hiss of static. Nadezhda knelt to adjust the tuning dial again, but lost the transmission completely. Her temper flared and she smacked the box in frustration, then thought better of it and returned her attention to the dial. "Please," she muttered. "We need to hear this."

The other workers from the steel mill waited silently, their faces stony. Nadezhda brought in another minute or two of speech: a different voice spoke about patriotism, sacrifice, Mother Russia. Anastasya, the supervisor of their group, reached over and switched the radio off. "Go on," she said. "Back to work."

They're coming, and we won't be able to stop them.

No one dared to speak the words. Nadezhda had to bite her tongue to keep from speaking them—but it was better not to invite trouble. She retied the kerchief she wore to keep the sweat from her eyes and her hair out of the machinery. For days now there had been no real news. The official reports spoke of great Soviet victories, but these victories somehow happened closer to Moscow each day.

Nadezhda returned late to the apartment she shared, pulling off her shoes in the cold stairway so as not to wake the others. Stepping over sleeping women, she picked her way to the kitchen in stocking feet. As quietly as she could, she boiled water for tea, then sat down by the window to stare out into the darkness.

The Dnieper River was the last natural barrier before Moscow. And if Moscow fell. . . . Closing her eyes, Nadezhda could see the face of her lover, Vasily, before he'd left with the militia to fight. "We'll fight them to the end," he'd said, speaking softly to avoid being overheard. "We'll make them pay in German blood for every inch of Russian soil. But if Moscow falls, we'll be fighting a lost war." Vasily's blue eyes had been hard with fear, but he'd pulled loose her kerchief to stroke his fingers through her hair one last time before he boarded the train that would take him to the front. Vasily had no real military training—that he'd been sent to fight spoke of the Red Army's desperation far more loudly than a thousand radio broadcasts.

Nadezhda pulled her kerchief loose again and ran her own fingers slowly through her hair. She put away her teacup and took out her hidden bottle of vodka for a deep drink. Then she picked her way back through the apartment and out to the stairs, pulled on her shoes, and headed out of the small industrial city to the forests beyond.

Nadezhda was young; she lived in a world of steel mills and radios and black-market cigarettes. Her grandmother, though, was from an older time. When Nadezhda was ten years old, her grandmother had stopped telling stories—but Nadezhda had never forgotten the stories of the ancient woman who lived in the heart of every Russian forest, and how she could be found by those who weren't afraid to surrender to the darkness. As the sounds of the city and its factories were swallowed behind her in the night, Nadezhda pulled her kerchief out of her pocket, and tied it tightly over her eyes. Groping blindly with her hands in front of her, she continued down the path.

Nadezhda could hear the wind around her, the trees overhead swaying in the night. She could hear an owl nearby, its call and then the beat of its wings. Then, silence. Nadezhda pulled the kerchief from her eyes, and before her in the forest was the little hut on chicken legs, rocking back and forth, turning round and round, dipping and spinning like a wobbly gear.

Nadezhda spoke: "Turn comrade, spin comrade, stand comrade, stand. With your back to the wood and your door to me."

The house turned to face Nadezhda, and the chicken legs knelt in the soft earth of the forest floor. The door swung in on its hinges. At first there was nothing inside but moist darkness. Then the darkness thickened and deepened, and a gust of warm wind from inside enveloped Nadezhda. Nadezhda smelled cooked kasha and fresh bread; she smelled sour vodka like Vasily's breath in early morning; she smelled wet new-turned earth. As the wind swirled around her and the last of the light faded, Nadezhda heard Baba Yaga's voice.

"Russian blood and Russian tears, Russian breath and Russian bones, why have you come here?"

Nadezhda had expected an old woman's voice, cracked and rough like the voices through the static of the radio. Instead Baba Yaga's voice was young and clear, honey-sweet and eggshell-smooth, but it echoed as if she spoke from the depths of a cave.

"I've come to ask for your help, Comrade Baba Yaga," Nadezhda said. "I've come to ask you to save Mother Russia."

Baba Yaga laughed, and now she sounded old. Two shriveled hands gripped the edges of the doorway for balance, and Baba Yaga stepped down to the ground. She was a stooped, hunched old woman with thin white hair. Her eyes were sunk deep in her wrinkled face, but they were a burning ice blue, and she had all of her teeth. "For everything there is a price, Comrade Daughter," Baba Yaga said. "For everything there is a cost. We are not socialists here. Have you come to me ready to pay?"

"I have brought no money," Nadezhda said.

"I do not trade in rubles," Baba Yaga said. "You have come to ask me to destroy the German army, have you not?"

"Yes," Nadezhda said.

"You are prepared to give your life for this, if that is the price?"

"Yes," Nadezhda said, though her voice shook.

"Your life is not the price," Baba Yaga said. "The price is *Vasily's* life."

Nadezhda was stunned silent for a moment. Then she pleaded, "Name another price."

"That is the price for your salvation," Baba Yaga said. "If you will not pay, ask me some other favor."

Nadezhda closed her eyes. She was too young to remember a time before socialism, and she barely remembered life before Comrade Stalin. But growing up, she'd known that it was fear of Stalin that silenced her grandmother's stories and her father's jokes. The first day that Vasily kissed Nadezhda, they found a secluded spot in the woods. Vasily pulled her kerchief loose to touch her hair—then met her eyes with a wicked smile and said, without lowering his voice, "Have you heard the one about Comrade Stalin, Comrade Lenin, and Ivan the pig farmer?" Vasily was only a mediocre kisser, but it didn't matter. Nadezhda's heart had been his from that day on.

Vasily's life?

Nadezhda opened her eyes and looked at Baba Yaga. Baba Yaga looked at her with eyes as deep and cold as the sea. Nadezhda looked away from those eyes and said, "If we had more time to prepare, perhaps we could beat them. Turn the Germans away from Moscow."

"That's an easy favor," Baba Yaga said. "The price for that is your hair."

Nadezhda had brought a knife, and now she took it and cut off her hair. She wished that she had thought to bring scissors, because she had to saw through the thick hank of hair, and it pulled. Her eyes were wet when she had finished. Looking at her hair in her hand, she touched it once more, as Vasily had, and then gave it to Baba Yaga.

"What did you do to your hair?" Anastasya asked the next morning at the steel mill. "You look like a bobbed bourgeoisie."

"I had lice," Nadezhda said. "Picking out nits would use hours that I could be working, so I cut off my hair. It's a small thing to sacrifice if it helps our army defend Mother Russia."

Baba Yaga summoned the Fox, the craftiest of all the animals, who had fooled czars and peasants alike. "Run west to a country called Germany," she told the Fox. "To a city called Berlin, and find a little German man with a mustache."

"Do you want me to eat him?" the Fox asked.

"His bones are for me," Baba Yaga said. "I want you to whisper into his ear that there is plenty of time yet this summer to take our Moscow. Tell him that the wise course is to divide the troops headed for Moscow and send some of them north, to Leningrad, and some of them south, to the Ukraine. Do not return until you are certain he believes you."

"I will do as you bid, Baba Yaga," the Fox said. So the Fox ran west and found Berlin, and the man with the mustache, and whispered into his ear. And the man with the mustache called his generals and ordered his troops divided, some sent north and the rest south, to return and finish off Moscow later in the summer. There was plenty of time—weeks and weeks of glorious summer left to take Moscow. All the time in the world.

Fall came, and the armies returned from Leningrad and the Ukraine and moved toward Moscow again. It was possible to be executed for spreading rumors, but the rumors still spread. Nadezhda heard whispers in the mill of the death and capture of millions of Russian soldiers, and tried not to listen. She heard whispers of siege and starvation in Leningrad, and tried to think of other things. She heard whispers that there were German soldiers in Red Army uniforms, infiltrating their forces and moving toward Moscow, and she snorted in disgust—but the true rumors were bad enough.

Nadezhda thought of Vasily often as she worked. They had quarreled sometimes, like any lovers, but only once seriously. Vasily had signed up for the militia, and Nadezhda had wanted to, as well. Vasily first tried to dissuade her with humor, but when that didn't work, he became angry. "Isn't it enough that the sons of Mother Russia go to die in this war? Should we send her daughters to die as well?"

"Are you a German, thinking that a woman is good only

for bearing babies?" Nadezhda fired back. "I know as much about fighting as you do."

But Vasily refused to give up. The steel mill needed her. ("It needs you just as badly," Nadezhda said.) The militia would endure terrible hardships. If captured, Nadezhda could be raped, tortured, killed—the Germans had no respect for women soldiers. Finally, Vasily had wept in her lap and begged her not to join the militia. Nadezhda had given in, unable to bear his tears.

As the air turned chill, Nadezhda went again to the forest, to the hut on chicken legs and the old woman who lived inside.

"The Germans have returned," Nadezhda said.

"Yes," Baba Yaga said. "I did not promise that I would drive them away forever. You know the price for that."

"Name any other price," Nadezhda begged, but Baba Yaga refused. Finally Nadezhda made a different request. "Stop the German advance, at least until spring," she said.

"That's an easy favor," Baba Yaga said. "The price for that is your youth."

"I give that willingly," Nadezhda said, and felt herself grow more tired, her face grow more creased. She returned to the factory by daybreak.

"You look old," Anastasya said to Nadezhda the next morning. "Older than yesterday."

"I'm tired," Nadezhda said. "Sleep uses hours that I can spend working. A little sleep is a small thing to sacrifice if it helps our army defeat the Nazis."

Baba Yaga summoned Father Winter. "Go to the roads leading to Moscow," she said. "Bring rain to turn the roads to mud; then bring snow and ice and freezing winds. There are ill-dressed children on those roads. They do not belong there."

Father Winter smiled his cold, fierce smile and bowed slowly to Baba Yaga. "When I am through with them," he said, "they will curse every inch of Russian soil they must cross to flee my breath." And Father Winter brought rain so hard the ill-dressed children thought they might drown, first in water and then in mud. Their tanks and their trucks sank deep into the thick black muck, and would not move.

Then Father Winter blew out his cold breath over all of Russia. The ill-dressed children wore thin uniforms and light coats, without the felt boots and fur hats that the Russians wore. Some of them stumbled back the way they had come, dragging frozen tanks and trucks out of ice and snowdrifts. Their machinery and engines froze into cold, immovable blocks in the frigid breath of Father Winter, and the Russians on horses fell on the children and killed them by the thousands. The ill-dressed children cursed the Russian winter, and the Russian soldiers, and the Russian soil.

Before Vasily left, he had given Nadezhda a square of red cloth. "It's a kerchief for your hair," he'd said. He pulled loose her old kerchief and stroked his fingers through her hair, brushing her cheek.

Nadezhda pressed something cold and smooth into Vasily's hand. He opened his palm to see a rifle bullet. "My father fought for Russia in the war before the Revolution. He kept one cartridge in his pocket for good luck. He survived the war. Perhaps it will bring good luck to you, too." Vasily had closed his fist around the bullet, then wrapped his arms around her, burying his face in her shoulder. "Come back to me," Nadezhda had whispered into his hair.

Spring came again, and the German army began to rally. Summer began, and they began to move again. They weren't moving on Moscow this time, but along the Volga and into the Caucasus. Rumors spoke again of terrible losses.

In July, Nadezhda went again to the woods, to the hut on chicken legs and the old woman who lived inside.

"The Germans have remounted their attack," Nadezhda said. "We are losing again."

"Yes," Baba Yaga said. "They are moving along the Volga River, and the Red Army is falling back before them."

"Please," Nadezhda said. "Destroy the German army. Stop them for good."

"You know the price," Baba Yaga said. "Are you prepared to pay it?"

"I will pay your price on one condition," Nadezhda said. "I want to see Vasily one more time before he has to die."

"I can send you to the city where the battle will be," Baba Yaga said. "But if you go there, you may die with your lover."

"Send me," Nadezhda said.

Baba Yaga took a horn and blew three blasts. From the sky flew an eagle. "Sit on the eagle's back," Baba Yaga said. "He will take you there."

The eagle rose in the sky with Nadezhda on his back, and flew with her to the great city on the Volga River—Stalingrad. Baba Yaga went herself to whisper to the man in Berlin with the mustache, and the man in Moscow named Josef. "No retreat," she whispered to Josef. "We must make our stand now, or die trying."

At the end of July, Stalin issued a new order: "Not one step back!" Anyone who retreated without permission would be shot. Still, the Germans pushed forward, farther and farther, for Hitler had become obsessed with the city bearing Stalin's name. Nadezhda waited patiently, trusting in Baba Yaga's word that the Germans would be destroyed.

The civilian population was evacuated from Stalingrad as the German army approached. Nadezhda remained behind with the other workers from the steel mill where she had found work. "I am no soldier," she said to her comrades. "But I can kill Germans."

One of the other women spoke more eloquently. "We will die here," she said. "But we will teach the Germans something about Russian bones and Russian blood, Russian strength and Russian will. And *no one* will do to our children as the Germans have done to us."

Nadezhda clasped hands with the other workers. There were no weapons. There was little they could do. But they would not retreat. Not one step back.

* * *

The battle of Stalingrad began with an artillery attack, and Nadezhda spent the first few hours crouching in a bomb shelter with the other workers. As the artillery grew louder, Nadezhda left the bomb shelter—Baba Yaga had said that she would see Vasily again, and after that Nadezhda didn't care what happened. The others followed her out of the shelter, and soon they were able to pick up weapons from bodies in the streets. Nadezhda had never used a gun, but it wasn't difficult to learn.

Nadezhda took shelter in an apartment building, firing out the window as German soldiers marched through the streets. It quickly became clear that the Germans would have to secure or destroy every building in Stalingrad in order to take the city. They set about grimly to do just that, but Stalingrad was a vast city, 30 miles long, winding along the edge of the Volga. And the new concrete buildings that lined Stalingrad's dirt streets were not easy to destroy.

Through the months and months of house-to-house fighting, Nadezhda was never afraid. She would see Vasily; Baba Yaga had promised it. What had she to fear?

Nadezhda found Vasily one bright afternoon in the coldest part of the winter. He lay slumped behind a low crumbling wall, alone. Nadezhda ran to him and dropped to her knees, taking his hand in both of hers. "Vasily," she said.

Vasily was alive still, but would not live much longer. She could feel the blood from his wounds wet under her knees. She had tried to prepare herself for this, but in the end it made no difference.

"Nadezhda?" Vasily said. "It can't be."

"I'm here, my love," Nadezhda said. "I'm here to be with you."

Vasily turned his face toward her. "I'm so sorry," he said. "The bullet you gave me, for good luck—I used it." A faint smile crept to his lips. "I killed a German with it."

Nadezhda pressed Vasily's hand to her face. "Our sacrifice is not for nothing," she said. "The German army will be destroyed here."

Vasily nodded, but did not open his eyes. For a moment, Nadezhda thought he had died, but then he took another breath and his cold hand moved from her cheek toward the knot at the back of her neck. Nadezhda bent her head, and he loosened her kerchief and stroked his fingers through her shorn hair one last time. Then his hand fell away. Nadezhda took his hand again, to hold a moment longer. Then an artillery shell rocked the ground where Vasily lay.

Nadezhda knew she didn't have much time left, but she wanted to die fighting, as Vasily had—not mourning. Vasily had a rifle; Nadezhda took it from his body and slung the strap over her shoulder. Standing up, Nadezhda turned and saw the house on chicken legs.

"Turn comrade, spin comrade, stand comrade, stand," Nadezhda said. "With your back to the armies and your door to me."

Baba Yaga came out of her hut. Though before she had always been an ancient hag, today she appeared as a maiden younger than Nadezhda—but her eyes were still as old as the Black Sea, burning like lights in a vast cavern.

"What are you doing here?" Nadezhda asked. "I thought you stayed in your forest."

"Sometimes I must attend to matters personally," Baba Yaga said. "This was one of those times."

"Vasily is dead," Nadezhda said.

"In one week, the Red Army will crush the army of the Germans, and their commander will surrender. There will be more offensives, but the Germans will never recover from this defeat. I have granted your wish," Baba Yaga said.

"May I ask you a question?" Nadezhda said.

"Pick your question carefully," Baba Yaga said. "I eat the overcurious."

"Will Russia recover from this defeat?"

"Life in Russia will never be easy," Baba Yaga said. "But Russia will always survive. Russian blood and Russian tears, Russian breath and Russian bones, these will last like the Caucasus and the Volga. No conqueror shall ever eat of Russia's fields. No czar shall ever tame the Russian heart.

Your Comrade Josef will live another ten years yet, but when he dies, his statues will be toppled and his city will be renamed. That is what you wished to know, yes?"

"Yes."

Another artillery shell exploded nearby; the ground shook, and the house stumbled slightly on its chicken legs. White dust settled slowly over Baba Yaga and Nadezhda, like snow, or spiderwebs.

"Tell me, Comrade Daughter," Baba Yaga said. "Are there any bullets in that gun?"

Nadezhda checked. "No," she said.

"Then take this." Baba Yaga held out her hand; glinting in her palm, Nadezhda saw one bullet.

"What is the price for that?" Nadezhda asked.

"You have no payment left that interests me," Baba Yaga said. "This one is a gift."

Warily, Nadezhda took the bullet and loaded it into the rifle. When she looked up, Baba Yaga and the hut on chicken legs had vanished.

Nadezhda heard the sound of marching feet. She flattened herself against the remains of one wall, crouching down low to stay hidden. She peered around carefully, and saw German soldiers approaching.

Nadezhda knew that in the dust and confusion of Stalingrad, the men would pass her by if she stayed hidden. Perhaps she could still slip away to the woods, survive the war, live to rebuild Russia and to drink vodka on Stalin's grave.

Nadezhda turned back to look at Vasily one last time. Then, in a single smooth movement, she vaulted over the low wall that concealed her to face the German soldiers.

Russia's blood can be shed; Russia's bones can be broken. But we will never surrender. And we will always survive. "For Russia," Nadezhda shouted, and raised her rifle.

Familiar

~~~~~

China Miéville

China Miéville is currently going for a Ph.D. at the London School of Economics. A politically active socialist who listens to HipHop and Jungle, he grew up reading sf, fantasy, and horror, sports five earrings in his left ear, and also draws comics. "I've always hated Tolkien: this [his novel Perdido Street Station*] is very far from 'epic' or 'heroic' fantasy. It's sort of unheroic, unepic fantasy. I'm interested in the Weird Fiction tradition, as well as the tradition of fantasy that binds people like Mervyn Peake and M. John Harrison—a much lusher, more grotesque, and at the same time bleaker aesthetic and emotional landscape." And later in the same interview, he says, "I'm very influenced by Mervyn Peake and M. John Harrison, as I said. The whole 'other London' tradition is a strong presence for me: Michael Moorcock, Iain Sinclair, Neil Gaiman, Thomas de Quincey et al. I love the Surrealists and their precursors like Lautreamont, and the dark Modernist stuff from people like Kafka and Bulgakov. A few years ago I got into a lot of late-nineteenth/early-twentieth-century 'Weird Fiction' thing. I like Lovecraft, but I prefer William Hope Hodgson, and I like people like E.H. Visiak, Robert Chambers and David Lindsay, and precursors like Ambrose Bierce, M.R. James, and H. G. Wells, mainly for* The Island of Dr. Moreau."

"Familiar" is another story from Conjunctions: 39. *It is in the tradition of Dukas' "The Sorcerer's Apprentice."*

A witch needed to impress his client. His middleman, who had arranged the appointment, told him that the woman was very old—"hundred at least"—and intimidating in a way he could not specify. The witch intuited something unusual, money or power. He made careful and arduous preparations. He insisted that he meet her a month later than the agent had planned.

His workshop was a hut, a garden shed in the shared allotments of north London. The woman edged past plots of runner beans, tomatoes, failing root vegetables and trellises, past the witch's neighbors, men decades younger than she but still old, who tended bonfires and courteously did not watch her.

The witch was ready. Behind blacked-out windows his little wooden room was washed. Boxes stowed in a tidy pile. The herbs and organic accoutrements of his work were out of the way but left visible—claws, skins like macabre facecloths, bottles stopped up and careful piles of dust and objects. The old woman looked them over. She stared at a clubfooted pigeon chained by its good leg to a perch.

"My familiar."

The woman said nothing. The pigeon sounded and shat.

"Don't meet his eye, he'll steal your soul out of you." The witch hung a black rag in front of the bird. He would not look his client clear on. "He's basilisk, but you're safe now. He's hidden."

From the ceiling was a chandelier of unshaped coat hangers and pieces of china, on which three candles scabbed with dripping were lit. Little pyramids of wax lay on the wooden table beneath them. In their guttering the witch began his consultation, manipulating scobs of gris-gris—on the photographs his client provided he sprinkled leaf flakes, dirt, and grated remnants of plastic, with an herb shaker from a pizzeria.

The effects came quickly so that even the cold old woman showed interest. Air dried up and expanded until the shed was stuffy as an airplane. There were noises from the shelves: mummied detritus moved anxious. It was much more than happened at most consultations, but the witch was still waiting.

In the heat the candles were moist. Strings of molten wax descended. They coated each other and drip-dripped in instantly frozen splashes. The stalactites extended, bearding the bottom of the candelabrum. The candles burned too fast, pouring off wax, until the wire was trimmed with finger-thick extrusions.

They built up matter unevenly, curling out away from the table, and then they sputtered and seemed not to be dripping grease but drooling it from mouths that stretched open stringy within the wax. Fluttering tongues emerged and colorless eyes from behind nictitating membranes. For moments the things were random sculptures and then they were suddenly and definitively organic. At its ends, the melted candles' runoff was a fringe of little milk-white snakes. They were a few inches of flesh. Their bodies merged, anchored, with wax. They swayed with dim predatory intent and whispered.

The old woman screamed and so did the witch. He turned his cry, though, into a declamation and wavered slightly in his chair, so that the nest of dangling wax snakes turned their attention to him. The pigeon behind its dark screen called in distress. The snakes stretched vainly from the candles and tried to strike the witch. Their toxin dribbled onto the powder of his hex, mixed it into wet grime under which the woman's photographs began to change.

It was an intercession, a series of manipulations even the witch found tawdry and immoral: but the pay was very good, and he knew that for his standing he must impress. The ceremony lasted less than an hour, the grease snakes leaking noise and fluid, the pigeon ceaselessly frightened.

At the end the witch rose weakly, his profuse sweat making him gleam like the wet wax. Moving with strange speed, too fast to be struck, he cut the snakes off where their bodies became candle, and they dropped onto the table and squirmed in death, bleeding thick pale blood.

His client stood and smiled, taking the corpses of the half-snakes and her photographs, carefully leaving them soiled. She was clear-eyed and happy and she did not wince at light as the witch did when he opened the door to her and gave her instructions for when to return. He watched her go through the kitchen gardens and only closed his shed door again when she was out of sight.

The witch drew back the screen from before the terrified pigeon and was about to kill it, but he stared at the stubs of wax where the snakes had been and instead he opened a window and let the bird out. He sat at the table and breathed heavily, watching the boxes at the back of the hut. The air settled. The witch could hear scratching. It came from inside a plastic toolbox, where he had stashed his real familiar.

He had called a familiar. He had been considering it for a long time. He had had a rough understanding that it would give him a conduit to a fecundity, and that had bolstered him through the pain and distaste of what the conjuration had needed. Listening to the curious scritch-scritch he fingered the scabs on his thighs and chest. They would scar.

The information he had found on the technique was vague—passed-on vagrants' hedge-magic, notepad palimpsests, marginalia in phone books. The mechanics of the operation had never been clear. The witch consoled himself that the misunderstanding was not his fault. He had hoped that the familiar, when it came, would fit his urban practice. He had hoped for a rat, big and dirty-furred, or a fox, or pigeon such as the one he had displayed. He had thought that the flesh he provided was a sacrifice. He had not known it was substance.

With the lid off, the toolbox was a playpen, and the familiar investigated it. The witch looked at it, queasy. It had coated its body in the dust, so it no longer left wetness. Like a sea slug, ungainly, flanged with outgrowths of its own matter. Heavy as an apple, it was an amalgam of the witch's scraps of fat and flesh, coagulated with his sputum, cum, and hoodoo. It coiled, rolled itself busy into corners of its prison. It clutched toward the light, convulsing its pulp.

Even in its container, out of sight, the witch had felt it. He had felt it groping in the darkness behind him and as he did with a welling up like blood he had made the snakes come, which he could not have done before. The familiar disgusted him. It made his stomach spasm, it left him ill and confounded, and he was not sure why. He had flensed animals for his calling, alive sometimes, and was inured to that, he had eaten shit and roadkill when liturgy demanded, but that little rag of his own flesh gave him a kind of passionate nausea.

When the thing had first moved he had screamed, realizing what his familiar would be, and spewed till he was empty. And still it was almost beyond him to watch it, but he made himself, to try to know what it was that revolted him.

The witch could feel the familiar's enthusiasm. A feral fascination for things held it together, and every time it tensed and moved by peristalsis around its plastic cell the contractions of its dumb and hungry interest passed through the witch and bent him double. It was stupid: wordless and searingly curious. The witch could feel it make sense of the dust, now that it had rolled in it, randomly, then deliberately, using it for something.

He wanted the strength to do again what he had done for the woman, though making the snakes had exhausted him. His familiar manipulated things, was a channel for manipulation, it lived to change, use, and know. The witch very much wanted that power it had given him, and he closed his eyes and made himself sure he could, he could steel himself. But looking at the nosing dusted red thing he was suddenly weak and uncertain. He could feel its mindless mind. To have his own effluvia maggot through him with every experience, he could not bear it, even with what it gave him. It made him a sewer. Every few seconds in his familiar's presence he was swallowing his own bile. He felt its constant eager interest like foulness, God knew why. It was not worth it. The witch decided.

It could not be killed, or if it could he did not know how. The witch took a knife to it but it investigated the blade avidly, only parting and reforming under his efforts. It tried to grip the metal.

When he bludgeoned it with a flat iron it recoiled and regrouped its matter, moved over and around the weapon, soiling it with itself and making the iron into a skate on which it tried to move. Fire only discomfited it, and it sat tranquil in acid. It studied every danger as it had dust, trying to use it, and the echo of that study turned the witch's gut.

He tipped the noisome thing into a sack. He could feel it shove itself at the fabric's pores and he moved quickly. The witch drove, hessian fumbling in the toolbox beside him (he could not put it behind him, where he could not see it, so that it might get out and conduct its investigations near his skin).

It was almost night when he stopped by the Grand Union Canal. In the municipal gardens of west London, between beat-up graffitied bridges, in earshot of the last punk children in the skate park, the witch tried to drown his familiar. He was not so stupid as to think it would work, but to drop the thing, weighted with rocks and tied up, into the cool and dirty water was a relief so great he moaned. To see it drunk up by the canal. It was gone from him. He ran.

Cosseted by mud, the familiar tried to learn. It sent out temporary limbs to make sense of things. It strained without fear against the sack.

It compared everything it found to everything it knew. Its power was change. It was tool-using, it had no way of knowing except to put to use. The world was infinite tools. By now the familiar understood dust well, and had a little knowledge of knives and irons. It felt the water and the fibrous weave of the bag, and did things with them to learn that they were not what it had used before.

Out of the sack, in muddy dark, it swam ugly and inefficient, learning scraps of rubbish and little life. There were hardy fish even in so grubby a channel, and it was not long before it found them. It took a few carefully apart, and learned to use them.

The familiar plucked their eyes. It rubbed them together, dangled them from their fibers. It sent out microscopic filaments that tickled into the blood-gelled nerve stalks. The familiar's life was contagious. It sucked the eyes into itself and suddenly, as visual signals reached it for the first time, though there was no light (it was burrowing in the mud), it *knew* that it was in darkness. It rolled into shallows, and with its new vitreous machines it saw streetlamp light cut the black water.

It found the corpses of the fish again (using sight, now, to help it). It unthreaded them. It greased itself with the slime on their skins. One by one it broke off the ribs like components of a model kit. It embedded them in its skin (its minute and random blood vessels and muscle fibers insinuating into the bone). It used them to walk, with the sedate pick-picking motion of an urchin.

The familiar was tireless. Over hours it learned the canal bed. Each thing it found it used, some in several ways. Some it used in conjunction with other pieces. Some it discarded after a while. With each use, each manipulation (and only with that manipulation, that change) it read meanings. The familiar accumulated brute erudition, forgetting nothing, and with each insight the next came easier, as its context grew. Dust had been the first and hardest thing to know.

When the familiar emerged from the water with the dawn, it was poured into a milk-bottle carapace. Its clutch of eyes poked from the bottleneck. It nibbled with a nail clipper. With precise little bullets of stone it had punctured holes in its glass sides, from which legs of waterlogged twig-wood and broken pens emerged. To stop it sinking into wet earth its feet were coins and flat stones. They looked insecurely attached. The familiar dragged the brown sack that had contained it. Though it had not found a use for it, and though it had no words for the emotion, it felt something like sentiment for the hessian.

All its limbs were permanently reconfigured. Even those it tired of and kicked off were wormed with organic ruts for its juices. Minuscule muscles and tendons the thickness of spider silk but vastly stronger rooted through the components of its bric-a-brac body, anchoring them together. The flesh at its center had grown.

The familiar investigated grass, and watched the birds with its inadequate eyes. It trooped industrious as a beetle on variegated legs.

Through that day and night the familiar learned. It crossed paths with small mammals. It found a nest of mice and examined their parts. Their tails it took for prehensile tentacles, their whiskers bristled it, it upgraded its eyes and learned to use ears. It compared what it found to dust, blades, water, twigs, fish ribs, and sodden rubbish: it learned mouse.

It learned its new ears, with focused fascination. Young Londoners played in the gardens and the familiar stayed hidden and listened to their slang. It heard patterns in their sequenced barks.

There were predators in the gardens. The familiar was the size of a cat, and foxes and dogs sometimes went for it. It was now too big for the bottle armor, had burst it, but had learned instead to fight. It raked with shards of china, nails, and screws—not with anger, but with its unchanging beatific interest. It was impossibly sure-footed on its numerous rubbish legs. If an attacker did not run fast enough, the familiar would learn it. It would be used. The familiar had brittle fingertips, made of dogs' teeth.

The familiar moved away from the gardens. It followed the canal bank to a graveyard, to an industrial siding, to a dump. It gave itself a shape with wheels, plunging its veins and tissue into the remnants of a trolley. When later it discarded them, pulling them out, the wheels bled.

Sometimes it used its tools like their original owners, as when it took its legs from birds (scampering over burned-out cars like a rock rabbit on four or six avian feet). It could change them. In sun, the familiar shaded its eyes with flanges of skin that had been cats' ears.

It had learned to eat. Its hunger, its feeding was a tool like dust had been: the familiar did not need to take in nourishment but doing so gave it satisfaction, and that was enough. It made itself a tongue from strips of wet towel, and a mouth full of interlocking cogs. These teeth rotated in its jaw, chewing, driving food scraps back toward the throat.

In the small hours of morning, in a waste lot stained by chemical spill, the familiar finally made a tool of the sack that had delivered it. It found two broken umbrellas, one skeletal, the other ragged, and it busied itself with them, holding them tight with hair-grip hands, manipulating them with rat tails. It secured the sack cloth to them with its organic roots. After hours of calculated tinkering, during which it spoke English words in the mind it had built itself, the shaped umbrellas spasmed open and shut on analogues of shoulders, and with a great gust the familiar flew.

Its umbrellas beat like scooping bat wings, and the greased hessian held it. It flew random as a butterfly, staring at the moon with cats' and dogs' eyes, its numerous limbs splayed. It hunted with urban bramble, thorned stalks that whipped and pinioned prey from the air and the ground. It scoured the scrubland of cats. It spasmed between tower blocks, each wing contraction jerking it through the air. It shouted the words it had learned, without sound.

There were only two nights that it could fly, before it was too large, and it loved them. It was aware of its pleasure. It used it as it grew. The summer became unusually hot. The familiar hid in the sudden masses of buddleia. It found passages through the city. It lived in wrecking yards and sewers, growing, changing, and using.

* * *

Though it replaced them regularly, the familiar kept its old eyes, moving them down itself so that its sight deteriorated along its back. It had learned caution. It was educated; two streets might be empty, but not identically so, it knew. It parsed the grammar of brick and neglected industry. It listened at doors, cupping the cones of card, the plastic funnels with which it extended its ears. Its vocabulary increased. It was a Londoner.

Every house it passed it marked like a dog: the familiar pissed out its territory with glands made from plastic bottles. Sniffing with a nose taken from a badger, it sprayed a liquid of rubbish-tip juices and the witch's blood in a rough circle across the flattened zones of the north city, where the tube trains emerged from underground. The familiar claimed the terraced landscape.

It seemed a ritual. But it had watched the little mammals of the landfills and understood that territory was a tool, and it used it and learned it, or thought it did until the night it was tracing its limits into suburban spaces, and it smelled another's trail.

The familiar raged. It was maddened. It thrashed in a yard that reeked of alien spoor, chewing tires and spitting out their rags. Eventually, it hunkered down to the intruder's track. It licked it. It bristled throughout its body of witch-flesh and patchwork trash. The new scent was sharper than its own, admixed with different blood. The familiar hunted.

The trail ran across back gardens, separated by fences that the familiar vaulted easily, trickled across toys and drying grass, over flowerbeds and rockeries. The prey was old and tough: it told in the piss. The familiar used the smell to track, and learned it, and understood that it was the newcomer here.

In the sprawl of the outer city the stench became narcotic. The familiar stalked silently on rocks like hooves. The night was warm and overcast. Behind empty civic halls, tags and the detritus of vandalism. It ended there. The smell was so strong, it was a fight drug. It blistered the familiar's innards. Cavities opened in it, rudimentary lungs like bellows: it made itself breathe, so that it could pant to murder.

Corrugated iron and barbed wire surrounds. The witch's familiar was the intruder. There were no stars, no lamplight. The familiar stood without motion. It breathed out a challenge. The breath drifted across the little arena. Something enormous stood. Debris moved. Debris rose and turned and opened its mouth and caught the exhalation. It sucked it in out of all the air, filled its belly. It learned it.

Dark expanded. The familiar blinked its eyelids of rainwet leather offcuts. It watched its enemy unfold.

This was an old thing, an old familiar, the bull, the alpha. It had escaped or been banished or lost its witch long ago. It was broken bodies, wood and plastic, stone and ribbed metal, a constellation of clutter exploding from a mass of skinless muscle the size of a horse. Beside its wet bloody eyes were embedded cameras, extending their lenses, powered by organic current. The mammoth shape clapped some of its hand-things.

The young familiar had not known until then that it had thought itself alone. Without words, it wondered what else was in the city—how many other outcasts, familiars too foul to use. But it could not think for long as the monstrous old potentate came at it.

The thing ran on table legs and gripped with pincers that were human jaws. They clenched on the little challenger and tore at its accrued limbs.

Early in its life the familiar had learned pain, and this attack gave it agony. It felt itself lessen, as the attacker ingested gulps of its flesh. The familiar understood in shock that it might cease.

Its cousin taught it that with its new mass it could bruise. The familiar could not retreat. Even bleeding and with arms, legs gone, with eyes crushed and leaking and something three times its size opening mouths and shears and raising flukes that were shovels, the intoxicant reek of a competitor's musk forced it to fight.

More pain and the loss of more self. The little insurgent was diminishing. It was awash in rival stink. A notion came to it. It pissed up in its adversary's eyes, spraying all the bloody muck left in it and rolling away from the liquid's arc. The hulking thing clamored silently. Briefly blinded, it put its mouth to the ground and followed its tongue.

Behind it, the familiar was motionless. It made tools of shadows and silence, keeping dark and quiet stitched to it as the giant tracked its false trail. The little familiar sent fibers into the ground, to pipe-work inches below. It connected to the plastic with tentacles quickly as thick as viscera, made the pipe a limb and organ, shoving and snapping it a foot below its crouching opponent. It drove the ragged end up out of the earth, its plastic jags spurs. It ground it into the controlling mass of the old familiar, into the dead center of meat, and as the wounded thing tried to pull itself free, the guileful young familiar sucked through the broken tube.

It ballooned cavities in itself, gaping vacuums at the ends of its new pipe intestine. The suction pinioned its enemy, and tore chunks of bloody matter from it. The familiar drew them through the buried duct, up into its own body. Like a glutton it swigged them.

The trapped old one tried to raise itself but its wood and metal limbs had no purchase. It could not pull itself free, and the pipe was too braced in earth to tear away. It tried to thread its own veins into the tubing and vie for it, to make its own esophagus and drink down its attacker, but the vessels of the young familiar riddled the plastic, and the dying thing could not push them aside, and with all the tissue it had lost to the usurper, they were now equal in mass, and now the newcomer was bigger, and now bigger still.

Tissue passed in fat pellets into the swelling young familiar sitting anchored by impromptu guts. Venting grave little breaths, the ancient one shriveled and broke apart, sucked into a plughole. The cobweb of its veins dried up from all its borrowed limbs and members, and they disaggregated, nothing but hubcaps again, and butcher's remnants, a dead television, tools, mechanical debris, all brittled and sucked clean of life. The limbs were arranged around clean ground, from which jagged a shard of piping.

* * *

All the next day, the familiar lay still. When it moved, after dark, it limped though it replaced its broken limbs: it was damaged internally, it ached with every step it took, or if it oozed or crawled. All but a few of its eyes were gone, and for nights it was too weak to catch and use any animals to fix that. It took none of its opponent's tools, except one of the human jaws that had been pincers. It was not a trophy, but something to consider.

It metabolized much of the flesh-matter it had ingested, burned it away (and the older familiar's memories, of self-constitution on Victorian slag heaps, troubled it like indigestion). But it was still severely bloated. It pierced its distended body with broken glass to let out pressure, but all that oozed out of it was its new self.

The familiar still grew. It had been enlarging ever since it emerged from the canal. With its painful victory came a sudden increase in its size, but it knew it would have reached that mass anyway.

Its enemy's trails were drying up. The familiar felt interest at that, rather than triumph. It lay for days in a car-wrecking yard, using new tools, building itself a new shape, listening to the men and the clatter of machines, feeling its energy and attention grow, but slowly. That was where it was when the witch found it.

An old lady came before it. In the noon heat the familiar sat loose as a doll. Over the warehouse and office roofs, it could hear church bells. The old lady stepped into its view and it looked up at her.

She was glowing, with more, it seemed, than the light behind her. Her skin was burning. She looked incomplete. She was at the edge of something. The familiar did not recognize her but it remembered her. She caught its eye and nodded forcefully, moved out of sight. The familiar was tired.

"There you are."

Wearily, the familiar raised its head again. The witch stood before it.

"Wondered where you got to. Buggering off like that."

In the long silence the familiar looked the man up and down. It remembered him too.

"Need you to get back to things. Job to finish."

The familiar's interest wandered. It picked at a stone, looked down at it, sent out veins and made it a nail. It forgot the man was there, until his voice surprised it.

"Could feel you all the time, you know." The witch laughed without pleasure. "How we found you, isn't it?" Glanced back at the woman out of the familiar's sight. "Like following me nose. Me gut."

Sun baked them all.

"Looking well."

The familiar watched him. It was inquisitive. It felt things. The witch moved back. There was a purr of summer insects. The woman was at the edge of the clearing of cars.

"Looking well," the witch said again.

The familiar had made itself the shape of a man. Its flesh center was several stone of spread-out muscle. Its feet were boulders again, its hands bones on bricks. It would stand eight feet tall. There was too much stuff in it and on it to itemize. On its head were books, grafted in spine first, their pages constantly riffling as if in wind. Blood vessels saturated their pages, and engorged to let out heat. The books sweated. The familiar's dog eyes focused on the witch, then the gently cooking wrecks.

"Oh Jesus."

The witch was staring at the bottom of the familiar's face, half-pointing.

"Oh Jesus, what you *do?*"

The familiar opened and closed the man-jaw it had taken from its opponent and made its own mouth. It grinned with thirdhand teeth.

"What you fucking *do?* Jesus *Christ.* Oh shit, man. Oh no." The familiar cooled itself with its page-hair.

"You got to come back. We need you again." Pointing vaguely at the woman, who was motionless and still shining. "Ain't done. She ain't finished. You got to come back.

"I can't *do it* on my own. Ain't got it. She ain't paying me no more. She's fucking *ruining me.*" That last he screamed in anger directed backward but the woman did not flinch. She reached out her hand to the familiar, waved a clutch of moldering dead snakes. "Come back," said the witch.

The familiar noticed the man again and remembered him. It smiled.

The man waited. "Come back," he said. "Got to come *back*, fucking *back*." He was crying. The familiar was fascinated. "Come *back*." The witch tore off his shirt. "You been *growing*. You been fucking *growing*, you won't stop, and I can't do nothing without you now and you're *killing* me."

The woman with the snakes glowed. The familiar could see her through the witch's chest. The man's body was faded away in random holes. There was no blood. Two handspans of sternum, inches of belly, slivers of arm-meat all faded to nothing, as if the flesh had given up existing. Entropic wounds. The familiar looked in interest at the gaps. He saw into the witch's stomach, where hoops of gut ended where they met the hole, where the spine became hard to notice and did not exist for a space of several vertebrae. The man took off his trousers. His thighs were punctuated by the voids, his scrotum gone.

"You got to come back," he whispered. "I can't do nothing without you, and you're killing me. Bring me back."

The familiar touched itself. It pointed at the man with a chicken-bone finger, and smiled again.

"Come *back*," the witch said. "She wants you, I need you. You fucking *have* to come back. Have to *help* me." He stood cruciform. The sun shone through the cavities in him, breaking up his shadow with light.

The familiar looked down at black ants laboring by a cigarette end, up at the man's creased face, at the impassive old woman holding her dead snakes like a bouquet. It smiled without cruelty.

"Then *finish*," the witch screamed at it. "If you ain't going to come back, then fucking *finish*." He stamped and spat at the familiar, too afraid to touch but raging. "You *fucker*. I can't stand this. Finish it for me, you *fucker*." The witch beat his fists against his naked holed sides. He reached into a space below his heart. He wailed with pain and his face spasmed, but he fingered the inside of his body. His wound did not bleed, but when he drew out his shaking hand it was wet and red where it had touched his innards. He cried out again and shook blood into the familiar's face. "That what you *want*? That do you? You fucker. Come *back* or make it *stop*. Do *something* to *finish*."

From the familiar's neck darted a web of threads, which fanned out and into the corona of insects that surrounded it. Each fiber snaked into a tiny body and retracted. Flies and wasps and fat bees, a crawling handful of chitin was reeled in to the base of the familiar's throat, below its human jaw. The hair-thin tendrils scored through the tumor of living insects and took them over, used them, made them a tool. They hummed their wings loudly in time, clamped to the familiar's skin.

The vibrations resonated through its buccal cavity. It moved its mouth as it had seen others do. The insectile voice box echoed through it and made sound, which it shaped with lips.

"Sun," it said. Its droning speech intrigued it. It pointed into the sky, over the nude and fading witch's shoulder, up way beyond the old woman. It closed its eyes. It moved its mouth again and listened closely to its own quiet words. Rays bounced from car to battered car, and the familiar used them as tools to warm its skin.

Honeydark

Liz Williams

Liz Williams lives in Brighton, England. She has a Ph.D. in philosophy of science from Cambridge, and her anti-career ranges from reading tarot cards on Brighton pier to teaching in Central Asia. She is the daughter of a conjuror and a Gothic novelist. She has been publishing interesting novels and short fiction, much of it science fiction, for several years. She has been published in Asimov's, Interzone, Realms of Fantasy, The Third Alternative, and Visionary Tongue, among others, and is co-editor of the recent anthology Fabulous Brighton. She is also current secretary of the Milford UK SF Writers' Workshop. Her novels are The Ghost Sister, a New York Times Notable Book of 2001—a rare accomplishment for a paperback original; Empire of Bones (2002), nominated, as was the first, for the Philip K. Dick Award; The Poison Master (2003); and Nine Layers of Sky, forthcoming in late 2003.

"Honeydark" was published in Realms of Fantasy, more and more a cutting-edge magazine. The patriarch of a powerful political family in Constantinople in the 1920s decides to disappear to live out his life under less stressful and Machiavellian circumstances. But the isolated village he chooses has ancient secrets.

By the time I left Constantinople and the House of Birds I'd had more than enough of politics, what with the intricacies and intrigues of the guilds, and the resentments that burned like slow-fire for years at the heart of the Court. The war had done nothing to help, for Constantinople and its scattered retinue of states had favored neither the Austrians nor the British, and consequently the city had found itself left on the sidelines when the war's end finally came in 1921. My own daughters spent their lives in plotting: against one another, and against myself. This was the world to which I had been accustomed ever since my birth into the House of Birds, and the life that I had lived unquestioned for so long, but on my 50th birthday I woke to the realization that something had changed. I was no longer the young man I had once been, steeped in the delight of schemes. *No more,* I said to myself, *I've had enough. I'm leaving.* I should have known they wouldn't let me go so easily.

I paid off my personal servants and left my family with a set of instructions regarding the whereabouts of my fortune that were cryptic enough to keep them bickering for the next few decades. I dropped a private word into a few select ears, telling them that I intended to go into seclusion at the monastery in Irekenia, a notoriously inaccessible branch of the Attic order. Then, my preparations for disappearance being complete, I set out, slipping away in the dead of night through the streets of Constantinople. The streets were empty. This close to the end of the war, the curfew was still imposed on the city, so I kept to the shadows. I caught the midnight ferry from Pera, disembarking at Parkouri just as the sun was coming up. From here, I began walking. A man on horseback or in a vehicle attracts attention; but someone on foot is clearly too poor to waste anyone's time.

* * *

Congratulating myself on my vanishing act, I made my way across Anatolia, sleeping in the stony fields and speaking to no one. Spring came early to the hill country and I never once regretted leaving the sordid warrens of the city behind me. There was a clear brightness to the air above the plain, and asphodel was coming into flower all along the road. For the first time in my life, I could look and think, and marvel at what I had left. I had walked away from everything: from my wealth and heritage, from the House of Birds, from my battling daughters. I wondered if they would try to follow me; whether they might send janissaries, those creations of metal and dead flesh, after me. Well, I would deal with that eventuality when it came, I thought. It all seemed so simple, there beneath the winds of the high wastes. I need never go back. I could stay here in these heights with the eagle and the raven for company, more sympathetic by far than the family I had abandoned.

After a few nights in the bleak countryside, and a sharp shower of rain, the romance of this new life inevitably faded. I awoke one morning in late April, and although the sky above me was washed with light and a lark was singing up near the sun, I was as cold as the stones on which I lay and my joints ached. It was time, I decided, to seek a more comfortable retreat from the world.

The next village I came to lay on the slopes of Mt. Phrygia, in a valley overlooked by the icy crags of the Anatolian Taurus. The village was nothing remarkable: an untidy huddle of whitewashed houses around a vine-fringed square. Up on the hillside the sound of goat bells rang startlingly clear in the still air. I wandered down toward the village and sat for a while beneath the trees. Years before, someone had planted an orchard here, and the old fruit trees stretched around me, pear and plum coming into blossom in the gentler weather. It was pleasant beneath the showers of sweetness, and I was more tired than I cared to admit. The sun was hot, the air somnolent and filled with the humming of bees. Before I knew it, I had fallen asleep with my cheek resting against the soft earth at the roots of the pear tree.

I woke with a start. Something was rustling in the dry grass. I rolled over, quick as a fox, and my hand crept down to the knife that had once hung at my side. But I hadn't been armed for years: the janissaries accompanied me whenever I left the House of Birds and I was still unused to walking unprotected. Cautiously, I raised my head. I could see nothing. I rose and walked warily down through the orchard. The cloudy flowers brushed against my face. I had reached the edges of the orchard now and could see my quarry: a girl, no more than 12 or 13, standing over a hive. Her face was uncovered by the usual apiarist's veil, and the bees swarmed up her arms and into her hair. I stood very still, watching. The sight made my skin crawl.

The girl was whispering to the bees, leaning down into the hive as she replaced the celled shelves of honey. Then she straightened and saw me. She spoke a word I did not hear and the bees poured down her arms and back into the haven of the hive.

"I'm sorry," I said. "I didn't mean to disturb you. I'm just a traveler."

She said nothing.

"Do you never get stung?" I asked, uneasy at the memory of the insects crawling over her skin.

She said, with a toss of her dark hair, "No. Why would they? I'm their keeper, after all." A stray bee whirred out of a blossom and settled on the hive.

"I'm wondering—do you know if there's somewhere in the village where I might stay for a few days?" I asked her.

The girl nodded. "You can stay with us."

My uncertainty must have shown in my face, for she added with childish candor, "People often do. My aunt takes people in. She's a widow, you see, and we need the money. My uncle's army pension doesn't go very far."

"I see. Well, that would seem to solve both our problems. Where do you live?"

"I'll show you," she said.

Her name, I discovered as we walked down to the village,

was Melissa Sama. Her family had lived in this village of Eliskehir "forever," she told me. She was a serious child who took her role as beekeeper with a self-important pride. I told her that she had a pretty name, and in return for this compliment received a long, chilly stare which, I suppose, I deserved. Her aunt, Gulnara, was a handsome woman in her 40s; a little overblown, like a rose that had bloomed for too long. She greeted me cheerfully enough; I suppose I represented another few meals on the table. However much we city dwellers might romanticize the rustic simplicities, there is no denying that it's a hard life in these country districts, and often a bleak one.

Later that evening I walked back up to the orchard to watch the sun fall behind the mountains of the Taurus. The last of the light caught the icy upper slopes, turning the peaks as pink as the rosy *locum* that they sell in the Grand Bazaar, but in the valley the twilight cast the orchard into shadow. I sat down on a nearby stone and enjoyed the silence. I wouldn't have said that I welcomed company, but I found that I was pleased when the child appeared beside me. Her small face was grave.

"Have you come to watch the sunset?" I asked her.

"No, to see to the bees. You shouldn't be up here, it makes them restless."

"I'm sorry," I said, meekly.

Melissa replied, impatiently, "I can't stand here talking. I've got to see to my bees," and then she was gone. Intrigued, I rose and followed her up through the twilight orchard. The bees, perhaps sensing the presence of a stranger, stirred in the hives and I skirted the domes warily. Beneath the pear trees, it was dark and quiet. A shadow brushed past me and was gone: only a moth, sailing out in search of night flowers. I could see the pale blur of Melissa's skirt in the dusk, moving toward me through the trees. Then, she had taken me firmly by the arm and began guiding me quickly back.

"You're in a hurry," I said, amused, and she gave me a swift, uncertain glance. In the fading light, her eyes seemed huge and dark. When we emerged from the edge of the orchard, the sun was still touching the highest peak and then the light fell away.

"Isn't it a beautiful evening?" I said. Gently, I detached the girl's fingers from my arm. "I think I'll stay out here for a little while."

"No." Her face was tight-lipped and unhappy. "My aunt will worry. You have to come back with me."

Old habits die hard, and there was still reason enough to be cautious. I had no inclination to draw attention to myself. I acquiesced, and once we were back in the small, white house and I had lain down on the bed provided for me, I was thankful. I slid rapidly into an untroubled sleep and did not wake till morning.

I had intended to stay for no more than a few days, but it turned into a week, and more. I was without ambition or thought for the future, and I found that I could idle the days away very easily. Gulnara Sama showed no reluctance when I told her that I intended to extend my stay, and I paid her well enough, though not so well that she might have questioned it. I often strolled up to the orchard for an afternoon siesta, while Melissa tended the bees. The child was growing used to me: treating me with a kind of off-hand familiarity that I found refreshing after the sycophantic insincerity of my own daughters. Her tongue might be tart, but I sensed the beginning of a genuine affection.

Once, on a whim, I walked farther into the orchard to search for the inner hives, but there was nothing to be seen, only a mass of stones that suggested old fortifications. Gulnara asked me not to go up there at night, as it upset the bees: occasionally jackals came down from the heights and overturned the hives in seeking out the sweetness within. I respected both Gulnara's wishes and that of the bees, and stayed away. Instead, I took to frequenting the village square at the end of my evening walk and soon made the acquaintance of the local doctor. He was a cultured man with a long, melancholy face and a penchant for the local raki. He had been educated in Constantinople and Vienna, and I suspected that his sojourn here in this remote hill settlement was not entirely his preferred choice. However, I too had secrets to protect and it would in any case have been unpardonably rude to pry into his past. Apart from these necessary reticences, we had much in common: a shared enthusiasm for politics and an interest in the natural sciences. Dr. Akharis also possessed a considerable degree of knowledge about the history of the region, as I was to discover during the course of one of our conversations.

It had rained during the day and the doctor and I sat just inside the entrance to his house, watching the lamplight catch the drops that beaded the vine leaves. The air was freshened by the rain, pleasing after the sultry heaviness of the past few days. Akharis had reached that midpoint of inebriation: he was cheerful and expansive, but still lucid as he discoursed on the local religious practices.

"Of course, there's the new Mithraeum at Balchat, now. The old one's really only frequented by a few retired soldiers, and I suppose we'll lose those when the new railway comes, if it ever does. It's not like the city, my friend. Here, you have to plan your worship."

I laughed.

"It's true, we're spoiled in Constantinople. There's something to suit every predilection: Attic, Christian, Coptic . . . it's such a crossroads."

"Your own family are . . . ?" the doctor paused, delicately, and poured out a further measure of raki.

"Oh, well, we've always favored conventional Attic practices. . . ."

"You're in good company. The great houses principally follow the young god, so I'm told; the House of Lights, the House of Birds." He smiled. "Talking of which, they say old Petros Batrichan's gone into seclusion at Irekenia. There's a thing, eh?—a man like that, well up in politics. They say the family's in a panic; seems he took all his secrets with him and no one knows what he did with his money."

"So I've heard," I agreed, cautiously. I did not want any association to be drawn between myself and Petros

Batrichan; as far as I was concerned, that man no longer existed.

I added, "Of course, the women in our family have always followed the usual rites; they go off to the Cybelic festivities every year and so forth."

"Oh, yes, it's the same here. There's a shrine up in the mountains, but they mostly attend temple in Balchat with their menfolk. But, you know, this wasn't always the backwater it is now. There used to be a temple just outside the village, dedicated to the Lady herself a good two thousand years ago. Nothing left now, of course, if it was even there."

"I might go up and have a look. Where's it supposed to have been?"

"Ah," Akharis said, smiling at me, "I believe you're already familiar with it. They say it's located where Gulnara Sama's orchard sits."

"Really? So all those great stones lying around are—" I paused, expectantly.

"Are the temple walls. But it's stony ground in these parts, and easy to imagine things. I wouldn't get too excited. An archaeological team came all the way from Munich before the war, but they didn't find much. Mind you, that might have been because Gulnara wouldn't let them dig up her pear trees, and who can blame her?" He sighed, and his dark eyes grew moist. "What a woman. A tigress, that one, when roused." We both contemplated this unlikely description of my landlady, and then the rain began again.

That rain was the last we saw of the cooler weather. The next day burned hot and that night the little house was like an oven. I lay naked and restless beneath a single sheet, and at last I got up and threw the window as wide as it would go. I leaned out into the night air, hoping for a breath of wind from the mountains. It was very still. Through the darkness I heard a voice, quickly falling into silence, and then I saw them. They were the women of the village, coming slowly in procession down from the orchard. Their white dresses transformed them into ghosts. One of them carried a light in a jar, and the twitching flame cast Melissa

Sama's face into severe relief. I drew back from the window and as I did so, something moved across the sill. Looking down, I saw that it was a late, lost bee, perhaps a queen, for it was enormous. Against the sill it was black as coal and its wings whirred ominously. I stepped back just in time; it shot up from the sill, perilously close to my face. Then it was gone, eaten by the warm darkness.

The next morning was as hot and golden as the day before. The house was quiet. I crossed to the window, and my attention was caught by a dark smear on the sill. I looked more closely. At first I thought it was blood, but the consistency was wrong: a gelatinous crimson trail. I could make nothing of it. Fetching a cloth, I wiped the offending substance away and went in search of breakfast.

I did not see Melissa or her aunt that day. I took my usual stroll in the evening and found Akharis in his customary spot beneath the drowsy vines. The bottle of raki was only a third full, even though it was early in the evening. The doctor said, without looking at me, "Someone came to my surgery today."

"Oh?"

"A man in a linen suit. Much too good for these parts, but not out of place in Galatasaray or Pera. He had a janissary with him: all polished armor and preserved flesh." His mouth turned down in distaste. "You don't see many of those around here, not since the war."

"What did he want?" I asked, casually. My skin prickled with chilly anticipation.

"He was inquiring about strangers. Had I seen anyone new recently? He was particularly interested in a middle-aged man with, I quote, 'a saturnine clean-shaven countenance and smooth black hair.' Well, what could I tell him? I haven't seen anyone like that around here for a while." I thought of the face I had seen in the mirror that morning; sunburned and bearded, and I smiled. "So I said no, there's been no one of that description hanging around here, and I shrugged. A little verisimilitude, you see," the doctor enunciated carefully. "So he nodded sagely, gave me a tip, and he and his infernal machine departed."

"A curious business." I said.

"Most odd." The doctor fixed me with an owlish eye. "I must say, I've greatly enjoyed your company these past 10 days or so. One rarely finds anyone of refinement, or indeed anything more than bovine intelligence, in this part of the world. I should be sorry to see you go."

"So would I," I told him. We finished the raki in silence and I made my way home. I took a circuitous path back through the village, walking quickly and quietly. It proved a wise course of action.

They were standing outside Gulnara Sama's back door. There were three of them: two janissaries and the languid man in the linen suit described to me by Akharis. I knew him, of course. His name was Emet Galaray, and he was the lover of my eldest daughter Suli. It was also said that at that time he controlled half the hired assassins in Constantinople. I experienced a moment of pure and bitter regret, for the life I had lived and the kind of man I had been. If I had taken pains to be a gentler father, if I had not imbued my children with my own cynicism and taste for politics, I might have found this new peace years ago. I thought, suddenly, that I should like to do better with the c`hild Melissa. Well, there was little I could do about that now. I stepped into the shadows beneath the lemon tree and waited. I heard Gulnara Sama's bewildered voice say, "No, no, we have a guest staying here, but I really don't think—" and then the child's clear tones.

"He's been to the village, but he's not there now. I'll show you where he is."

I thought of my own daughters, who would betray me at a word, and a shiver of unaccustomed pain ran through me. The janissaries rustled and murmured. I could see their jaws moving beneath the helmeted heads: the razor edges of engineered bone. Galaray, motioning to them, followed Melissa toward the gate. I slipped from underneath the shelter of the tree and bolted for the orchard. I ran past the singing hives and in among the pear trees. Not far behind me, I heard the sound of metal footsteps. With an agility born of desperation, I caught an overhanging bough and swung myself up into the pear tree in a shower of blossom. Melissa's voice said, close and accusatory, "He's been staying with us for *weeks*. I don't like him. There's something funny about him." I kept as still as I could.

"There," the child hissed. They were below me now. I could see the top of Galaray's head and the shiny helms of the janissaries. Melissa was standing with her hands resting on top of a hive. Galaray glanced around.

"Where is he? I don't see him."

"He's here. I *told* you," Melissa said impatiently, and lifted the lid. I looked straight down into the hive. The celled cavities were a clear, translucent crimson, and they glowed as though lit by some inner lamp. Honey, as black as blood, dripped from the edges of the lid. Inside the hive, something crawled. The child spoke a word. She looked up into the pear tree and her eyes met mine, but a cloud of bees was rising between us. Then Galaray was running and Melissa, quickly as a cat, was up the tree. She flung her arms around me and I held her tightly; I thought, for her own protection. Only in the moments that followed did I realize that she was protecting me. The bees made no sound. The swarm lifted up, whirled down. Galaray fell with only a little cry. The janissaries whirred in frantic confusion. Their limbs jerked and slowed, and the cracks between their plated armor began to seep fluid, slow and dark and thick. With a hypnotic repulsion, I watched them until they lay still.

"Melissa—" I whispered.

"Be quiet! Don't you know anything?"

"But the bees—"

"Wait!"

To my shame, I found that I was shaking in the girl's grip. The orchard was gone. Through the branches of the pear tree I gazed out across a great plain, sweet with night flowers. In the distance was a river. The bodies of Galaray and the janissaries lay unmoving in the long grass, but as I watched, I saw Galaray jerkily arise and begin to walk down toward the river shore. The janissaries did not follow. The bees hummed around them for a little while and then arched up through the shadowy air. I looked up through the bony branches, and over the top of the mountains I saw the horn of the new moon rising. The silent coil of bees arched up and poured back into the hive.

"There. They'll be happy now they've fed," Melissa said, sliding down to the ground. Reluctantly, I followed her. She was standing over the womb of the hive; reaching in, she gouged out a curl of honeycomb. With a half-conscious provocativeness, she sucked her fingers clean.

"It's not for you," she told me, slyly.

"Put the lid back on that thing, for the gods' sake," I snapped. Silently, she laughed, and taking my hand she walked with me through the orchard and out under the sanctuary of the moon.

No one else has come from Constantinople to look for me. Occasionally, Dr. Akharis tells me fragments of news from the city: that my daughter Suli has been forced by the city Judiciary to marry the son of an Austrian family, and that the House of Birds no longer exists. The city seems to belong entirely to another life, and I feel safe here, among the trees of the orchard and the beehives. But then again, I have little choice. I have seen too much to be allowed to leave. My time in politics has taught me that every life has its price, as does every worship, and the bees require payment, now and again, to keep their honey sweet. Melissa has told me that it may not be for many years, but when the time is right, then all I will have to do is to accompany the women, the priestesses of the bee, up into the inner orchard. It is a more honorable end than the assassin's knife, and I suppose I should be grateful, for the mercy shown to me by the Lady of the hive.

A Prayer for Captain La Hire

Patrice E. Sarath

Patrice E. Sarath is a writer and editor living in Austin, Texas. In the years before she began to write with professional determination, she worked various odd jobs, including stable girl, short-order cook, and reporter, studied and worked in Iceland, where she added shepherd to her resume, and finally landed in Texas, where she lives with her husband and children and "writes business articles and marketing copy for one of the last dot-coms in existence." In 1993, she finally buckled down to write seriously, and six years later she sold her first story, "The Warlord and the Princess," to the small Irish magazine Beyond The Rose. *She has since been published in* Alfred Hitchcock's Mystery Magazine, Realms of Fantasy, *and* Black Gate, *where this story appeared.* Black Gate *is comparable in quality to* Realms of Fantasy, *but only published two issues in 2002. Still, it is an impressive fantasy magazine.*

"A Prayer for Captain La Hire" is a story set in France 20 years after the death of Joan of Arc, who was burned for witchcraft. It is the tale of her faithful Captain, who, along with his former comrades de Poulengy and de Metz, is summoned to the aid of another of their former band, Gilles de Rais, and finds much worse trouble than he could have imagined.

The gates of Vaucouleurs stayed opened those days, a welcome sign of peace. La Hire touched his tired horse with his heel, and the horse jogged forward amid a swirl of carts and livestock. Market day, he saw, and he turned away from the square to the courtyard. It was quieter there. A few men at arms were practicing swordsmanship, the others lounging idly. La Hire went unnoticed at first until one soldier saw him and stopped dead in mid-lunge, mouth hanging open. His partner almost skewered him, stumbling to catch himself at the last minute. Everyone turned to look, and silence descended on the courtyard. A page, cleaning armor, dropped a helmet and bolted for the castle.

"La Hire. It's La Hire." The whispers rose to the bright summer sky. The men surged forward, laughing, shouting. "La HIRE!" They swarmed around him, reaching out to touch his cloak or his sword, their eager hands almost pulling him from his horse. La Hire reined back, bellowing curses.

"Back, damn you all! Back, do you hear?"

"That's enough!" Jean de Metz, with the little page panting at his side, came down the steps into the courtyard. "Let him be. Get down, La Hire, they won't hurt you. It's not often we get heroes in Vaucouleurs. Besides me, of course." He grinned.

La Hire dismounted, wincing at the pain in his stiff back. He handed his reins to the page.

"De Metz, you ruffian. I heard you were captain here. It's good to see you."

"Good to see you too, old man. Come on in."

He could feel de Metz watching him over his cup, and La Hire looked up. He laughed at his intent expression. "So, what do you see?"

"I see the bravest man in France."

La Hire shook his head. "No more. I am an old man, de Metz. I was old ten years ago. Now I am old and fat."

De Metz raised his cup. "May we all grow old and fat."

La Hire waved his. "Hear hear." He took a swallow. "Where is de Poulengy?"

De Metz shrugged. "He's off to visit Domrémy."

La Hire set down his drink and swung his feet off the table. He stared. "The family is still there?"

"No—the father is dead, and the mother is living off a pension in Orléans. Why not? They should be grateful, after all. No, de Poulengy just goes to stare at the house. Then he gets drunk and comes home. He'll be back later today or tomorrow."

"Do you ever go?" La Hire asked.

De Metz's black eyes slid away from his gaze. "No, I—well, what would be the use of it?" He shrugged again and took a drink. "What brings you to Vaucouleurs, old friend?"

La Hire held out his cup and de Metz filled it.

"Now that the Burgundians have come back to the fold and the goddons have fled to England, I've had to take on other commissions. Gilles de Rais sent me a message, asking for my help. He didn't say what for."

De Metz stared. "De Rais? Name of God, La Hire, do you know what you're getting into?"

"Oh, not you too, de Metz. Don't tell me you believe all those stories of werewolves in Brittany?"

"No, no, of course not." The Vaucouleurs captain shifted uneasily, just barely keeping from crossing himself. "But there are other tales with de Rais' name attached to them, stories of witchcraft and murder—you've heard them too, don't deny it. And what does de Rais want with La Hire? Ten years ago you were at each other's throats."

La Hire grinned wolfishly. "Oh, he was jealous all right! I had the Maid's ear at Orléans, and not he. Thought he was going to pull his beard right out, he was so frustrated."

"She listened to his counsel too," de Metz reminded him.

La Hire snorted. "Yes, afterward, at Paris! Any fool

could have told you we could not take Paris. Tell you the truth, Jean, our little Maid was quite the soldier, but she was also a bit of a snob. If it had a title, she listened to it. Me now, just a mercenary, well, I couldn't get the time of day from her after Orléans."

"Try telling that to Dunois, or even Charles," de Metz said. He looked down at his cup, rolling it between his fingers. "Jeanne D'Arc didn't really listen to anybody, La Hire. She had her saints, and that was counsel enough. De Rais had no more influence over her than anyone did."

La Hire grunted. "Those days are long gone. And any animosity between de Rais and me can be smoothed over with coin."

"So you're going?"

La Hire eyed him over his cup. "I hoped you and de Poulengy would come along."

De Metz leaned back, his expression curious. "Us? Why?"

La Hire chose his words with care. "You know I have little faith in God, Jean, and only a bit more in myself. But I think—and don't laugh at crazy old La Hire—that I've been given a sign to go to Brittany and do what needs to be done for de Rais."

De Metz's mouth hung open for a moment. "A sign. You. From God?"

"No. From the Maid."

He presented de Metz with a small, bent ring, battered and tarnished. With a shaking hand de Metz took it and held it up to the light. La Hire watched him read the worn inscription, his lips forming the words: Jesus Maria.

"This is her ring. How did you get her ring?"

La Hire lifted his broad shoulders. "De Rais sent it with his letter."

In the name of Jesus Christ our Lord and by this token of the faith of Jeanne the Maid . . . the letter had begun. La Hire had not been prepared for the memories the little ring raised—or the uneasiness. The Maid was dead, and nothing could bring her back. If anyone betrayed her it was Charles the King, not La Hire the mercenary.

But he thought he should go help de Rais, anyway.

Footsteps on the stair caught their attention, and they could hear a voice bellowing an off-key tune. The song stopped abruptly and the door slammed open. De Poulengy stood there, arms wide, a bright grin on his lean face, his graying chestnut hair standing out wildly.

"La Hire!" he cried out, beaming. "Old friend! They told me you were here."

And with that Bertrand de Poulengy slid to the floor, out cold.

La Hire said little as they rode out from Vaucouleurs. He rode grimly, in constant pain in his hips and his knees. Drinking helped, but he couldn't ride drunk across France. He concentrated on fighting the pain. De Metz, catching his mood, kept his own counsel. Only de Poulengy seemed cheerful, once his hangover wore off. He didn't try to make conversation, sensing the somber mood of his companions, but he rode with a light expression, as if a smile waited just beneath his skin. Only once did he exclaim,

"By God, it feels good to ride again!" but he said it more to himself than the others.

The roads took them through the farmlands of Lorraine, tinted with the light green of early summer crops. The bells of sheep and cattle could be heard jingling across the fields, and here and there in the distance they could catch the gray-green waters of the lazy Meuse.

Only a few years before, those fields had been charred black, the villages ravaged by fire and war. What the Maid had wrought was, quite simply, the miracle of France's rebirth. La Hire's hand twitched to make the sign of the cross, but he held it back and instead cursed under his breath so violently that his horse started and pulled at the bit.

It was a relief to his aching joints when twilight fell and they could stop for the night, choosing a campsite along the outskirts of the Bois Chenu. The trees pressed in on them and the evening air was cold after the strong summer sun.

La Hire rolled his broad shoulders under his shirt and cracked his neck, swearing at the cold stealing into his joints. De Metz looked up from starting the fire.

"Sounds bad," he commented. La Hire only grunted sourly and de Poulengy guffawed.

"Losing your touch, La Hire?" he said cheerfully. "You used to peel paint with that tongue."

"Go bugger the devil!" La Hire snapped, and de Poulengy just laughed again. De Metz shook his head and went back to his fire building.

"So," de Poulengy said, when they had eaten and were sitting comfortably around the fire. "Do you really believe de Rais is behind these rumors of witchcraft and were-wolves in Brittany?"

"I never liked him," de Metz said loyally, glancing at La Hire. "But he was a brave knight, and he was always at Jeanne's side. Still, these rumors, spreading even into France—"

"Jeanne would have known if he was evil," de Poulengy said, crossing himself. He leaned forward earnestly. "God would have told her."

"What do you think, La Hire?" de Metz asked.

La Hire stared into the fire, dozing a little. Or not exactly dozing, but seeing behind his eyelids another fire, and inside the leaping flames a darkened form. With an effort, he dragged his attention back to the others.

"What? No. De Rais was a son of a bitch, but I don't think he is a werewolf."

They laughed, but de Poulengy persisted.

"What about the other tales, of murder and kidnapping? Something bad is happening in Brittany. And if even half the stories are true, we might find ourselves wishing for the goddons to come back."

"Might be fun to fight goddons again," La Hire said lightly. De Metz snorted.

"Speak for yourself. I'll take a Breton werewolf any day over an English goddon."

"What's the difference?" La Hire shot back and de Metz laughed.

When they sobered a little, de Poulengy said reflectively, "I know what La Hire means, though. By God, raising the siege of Orléans, then taking back the towns on the way to Rheims—we were invincible!"

The other two nodded assent. La Hire thought back to those days of triumph, following the Maid and her white banner. How her self-righteousness chafed him and the others—yet everything came out just the way she said it would.

I have been sent by God to do three things: raise the siege of Orléans; crown the dauphin at Rheims; and drive the English from France.

She had even predicted her capture; he wondered if she knew the rest of her fate, or if her saints had kept their counsel out of pity.

"Would that Jeanne were with us now," de Poulengy said finally. He ducked his head, muttering something about the smoke. The other two exchanged uncomfortable glances and waited for him to compose himself. Instead, he caught their expressions and burst out, "I know you think I'm a sentimental fool, both of you, but I'm only a fool for saying what I think." His voice went thick. "She was a good girl and a great soldier, and she was badly used by France and Charles and the rest of us. Sometimes I think she would have been better off if we had had our way with her and left her in that ditch, eh Jean? At least then she would not have come to such a wicked end."

De Metz straightened quickly. "Ho, now, Bertrand. Take it easy."

La Hire stared at both of them. "What is he talking about?"

"Nothing, nothing, we were young," de Metz said hastily. De Poulengy laughed.

"Yes it was nothing, because she shamed us out of it. When we took her to Chinon to see Charles, the plan was to take advantage of this poor, mad, innocent peasant girl. How did you put it, Jean? Put her to the test? Instead, she lay between us for ten days, La Hire, and we did nothing except cover her with our cloaks and we never touched her, because she was the Maid and was destined to save France from the English, and be burned at the stake for all her pains!"

His voice rose to a shout.

"We didn't do it," de Metz said softly. "It's all right, Bertrand."

Again there was silence, punctuated only by the snapping of the fire. La Hire thought about what would have happened if they had tupped the Maid on the road to the King. France would not have survived. He shook his head at the thought and de Metz rolled his eyes in scorn.

"Don't act so righteous, La Hire. Would she have been any safer in your hands?"

"You'll get no blame from me, de Metz. I'm just amazed you didn't try it anyway."

"We couldn't," de Poulengy said flatly. At La Hire's raised eyebrows, he went on, "Listen, we were young and cocky, like anyone, and—we couldn't. Oh, we wanted to, and I have never ridden in such painful discomfort in my life. But I couldn't even speak to her of it."

La Hire stared at him and suddenly guffawed.

"My God! I just realized that's what that expression was on everyone's faces! Especially d'Alençon's, that time he caught a glimpse of her in the baths. I used to wonder why she always wore her armor, even slept in it. I thought it was because she was so damned proud—What?" he asked at their expressions.

"He did?" they chorused.

"What? Oh, d'Alençon. Yes, you should have seen him. He was shaking as if he had seen one of her saints. He said her breasts were beautiful."

Once again there was silence as they digested this. De Metz shook his head.

"Too many revelations for one night, La Hire. I think I'm going to sleep with that image to lull my dreams."

Following his lead they rolled out their bedrolls, settling into the lumpy ground as best they could. But de Poulengy wasn't finished. From the darkness on the other side of the dying fire, he asked reflectively, "La Hire, why didn't the three of us just storm the prison in Rouen and rescue her?"

La Hire rolled over on his back, staring up at the distant stars.

"She was Jeanne the Maid, Bertrand," he said gruffly. "We all thought she'd win. Now shut up and go to sleep. We have a long ride ahead."

It was a cold August evening when they reached Château Machecoul. The twilight pressed in, mist stealing across the road in low, feathery patches. The castle loomed ahead of them, a dark presence in the forest. At their approach the portcullis was cranked up, and they rode in, their horses tossing their heads uneasily. The smell of offal wafted over them, a sweet, rotten stench that hung heavy in the air, mingled with another odor he couldn't place.

That is no midden heap, La Hire thought. But it was tantalizingly familiar. Out of the twilight a servant came forward, attended by another holding an ornate candelabra to light his way. The servant bowed.

"Welcome to Machecoul, my lords, I am Henriet, at your service." His French was heavily accented with Breton. He said something sharp, and grooms ran forward to take their horses.

The three knights looked around warily as Henriet and the servant led them through the great hall and up a narrow staircase, confining after the expanse of the hall. Shadows moved jerkily in the candlelight and La Hire thought he could hear furtive noises in the dark. He held his breath, cursing de Poulengy's heavy steps. Rats, he thought, or other vermin—he could hear rustling sounds like tiny footsteps and every once in a while a broken sob that raised the hair on his neck. Candlelight glanced off a miniature door, waist high and barred like a small cage. It seemed to him an eye peered back at them, catching the light and then disappearing into shadow. The others had pulled ahead, and La Hire lengthened his stride to catch up.

"When can we see Sire de Rais?" he called out, a little breathlessly.

"The Maréchal is at Mass and does not like to be disturbed at his devotions," Henriet said in his ponderous French. "You will attend him after the evening meal." He unlocked a door and showed them in to a chamber. A cheerful fire took the edge off the seeping chill, but the same stench that clung to the courtyard permeated the air. "You will wait here. We will bring food and drink." Henriet hesitated. "Château Machecoul is very large, Sires. It is easy for visitors to get lost. You should stay here 'til someone calls for you."

He bowed himself out. The three men looked at one another, and de Metz raised an eyebrow. He walked over and tried the door. It was unlocked; he closed it carefully, but with a look of relief.

"This commission of yours, La Hire," he said lightly. "Do you mind telling us more about it?"

La Hire eased himself down onto the bed, wincing and rubbing his knee. Hunger and pain inflamed his temper and his words were short. "You know as much as I do, de Metz. What else do you want from me? De Rais will tell us more, when he's ready." Irritably La Hire raised his voice. "Hey! Someone bring us the food and drink you promised! Damn!" The last was aimed at his leg, which was throbbing miserably.

The dinner hour passed and the chamber began to feel more like a prison. They paced and bickered, tempers flaring. At last they heard servants at the door.

"Finally!" de Metz muttered as the servants bustled in, bearing trays of meat and wine. The aroma of roasted meat pulled them all eagerly toward the table, when, coupled with the pervasive stench of Machecoul, the smell overpowered La Hire with memory.

Jeanne, weeping over the bodies of the English soldiers, burned to a crisp in the charred ruins of Les Tourelles. Their skin roasted black, their faces unrecognizable, and the smell . . .

La Hire looked down at the meat, bile bubbling up in his

throat. De Metz, perhaps prompted by the same memory, made a strangled sound. The two knights looked at each other, sick understanding in their eyes.

"Take it away," La Hire said hoarsely. The servants hesitated and exchanged frightened glances, arguing in Breton. "Damn you!" he roared, groping for his sword. "You'll understand this!" De Poulengy, in the act of sitting down, stared at La Hire in confusion. The servants didn't require another hint—they bustled out with their cargo, dropping utensils in their haste. When they finally were gone, de Metz checked the door again, this time to make sure there were no listeners at the latch. De Poulengy flung himself onto the bed, irritated.

"I don't know about you, La Hire, but it was a long time since I tasted food that good," he began heatedly.

"I hope you never did," de Metz said, his voice bone dry. La Hire shook his head.

"Oh God," he muttered. "Oh God."

De Poulengy looked from one to the other. "Afraid, Jean?" he said. "And you, La Hire, praying? My God, what was it? What was that meat?" Then de Poulengy stared at them as light dawned. "My God," he said. "My God, La Hire, what have you gotten us into?"

De Metz shook him awake after first watch and La Hire rolled to his feet without a word. He settled himself by the door as de Metz took his place on the bed and dropped instantly into sleep.

The room was cold. The fire had died down and only coals glowed on the hearth. La Hire hugged himself to stay warm, bouncing on his toes to get his blood moving and his stiff muscles to loosen up.

A sliver of moonlight through the shutters illuminated de Poulengy's face, mouth open as he drove his pigs to market. De Metz coughed and sputtered and caught his breath. Preoccupied, it took La Hire a few moments to realize he was hearing something besides his companions' deep snores. He held his breath.

A rhythmic grunting came from somewhere below their chamber, ending in two overlapping sounds, a long sigh and a muffled scream. A long metallic scrape, muted by distance, followed, and something heavy rolled. La Hire broke out into sweat.

Move, damn you, La Hire! He was numb, and for a desperate moment hoped he was still dreaming. He heard nothing more, though he strained his ears, and he wondered how long the sounds had been going on, or what else he missed before he woke. Screams? his mind remarked. Crying?

He cursed, but it only helped a little. He thought of de Poulengy and how he would have crossed himself and gotten courage from God. But La Hire had only one prayer, and it was not one that could be used when a man really needed it.

He gathered up his sword as quietly as possibly, buckling the sword belt around his waist and forgoing the rest of his equipment. Something hard pressed against his chest; running his fingers over it he detected Jeanne's ring, caught in the loose folds of the shirt. He did not remember putting it there, but he held it tightly for a moment.

Better than a prayer, he told himself, though the Maid had no patience for superstitious talismans and would have reprimanded him sharply if she had been there. Still, he felt a little better.

He limped down the long hall the way they had come up from dinner. Many of the torches had burned out, but one or two still flickered, and he snagged one to help him on his way. The stairs at the end of the hall were a descent into utter darkness. La Hire took them slowly, straining to see more than a few steps at a time, but the torch helped little to illuminate the way and only interfered with his night vision. He took a tentative step and stumbled. Grabbing at air, he windmilled desperately through the darkness into an unseen hole below.

The first thing he noticed was the pain—the next thing was the light. La Hire lay on his back on the stone floor, struggling for the breath knocked out of him. He got to his feet with difficulty. Warm candlelight bathed the room, and when he could move enough to look around, he saw it was a torture chamber, grotesquely draped in ornate tapestries. The air reeked of decay. Dried blood streaked the floor and reddened the instruments; a head, quite removed from its torso, stared lifelessly at him. Another body slumped on the rack, and La Hire saw that it was still alive, gasping shallowly every few seconds. He started involuntarily toward the victim when the tapestries swayed and a cold breeze raised the hair on the back of his neck. La Hire turned, his legs stiff and heart pounding, to meet de Rais.

The brave knight who had fought at the side of the Maid, who had argued into the night with La Hire over tactics, who was quick to anger and as quick to charm, was nearly unrecognizable. His hair and beard, always wiry, stood out in tufts from his head. His hose and tunic were as richly embroidered as always, but La Hire noted that de Rais looked like a shrunken stick inside them.

"Welcome, La Hire," he said. "Welcome to my church."

"Sire," said La Hire, his voice rusty. "I am just La Hire but I don't think this is anyone's church unless it's the devil's."

"La Hire!" de Rais said in mock surprise. "It is a miracle! You have regained your faith. Does this mean you will worship with me?"

"What do you want from me?" La Hire asked.

"Great La Hire. You are my safe-conduct to God. Or at least past the executioner. If La Hire stands with de Rais, de Rais will not burn."

"Go to hell."

De Rais laughed. "What, do you think you can stop me? You, La Hire? I traffic with forces greater than you have ever known. They have given me strength!" De Rais's voice rose to a shout. "They have given me appetites beyond anything I have thought possible, and they have given me leave to feast in ways that you cannot imagine! I burn with desire, La Hire, and I feed at will, and burn, and feed, and it is never-ending—" his voice broke.

In the silence that followed the prisoner moaned. They both looked over at him, and La Hire, his eyes adjusted to the dim light, for the first time saw that it was a boy of perhaps twelve. He felt a muscle jump in his cheek.

"No, de Rais," he said. "I can only help you by killing you, and I will do that in an instant." He moved a few steps toward the boy with the intent of releasing him, but de Rais was faster. The maréchal lunged. De Rais was wiry and strong and his fingernails gouged La Hire through his shirt. He threw the captain onto the floor and held him down. Spittle dripped from the maréchal's mouth, and his beard was stiff and pointed, so black it gleamed blue in the light.

"Kill me? I didn't bring you here to kill me. This is a church, after all. God's peace governs here. You are here to atone, La Hire."

"Go to hell, de Rais. I have nothing to atone for," La Hire shot back.

"Oh, indeed?" de Rais raised an eyebrow. His mouth opened but it was Jeanne's voice that came out.

"Save me," de Rais/Jeanne said. "Save me from the fire, La Hire." Candlelight flickered in de Rais's eyes, but the pinpoint flames turned into an inferno, and in the midst of them a young girl writhed.

"Jesus!" La Hire gasped, his eyes bulging in terror. He bucked and tried to throw off de Rais's hands.

"In God's name, La Hire, do not abandon de Rais as you abandoned the Maid," de Rais continued, still in Jeanne's voice.

"God damn you to hell!" La Hire roared, wild with fear. "I did not abandon her! I will kill you, de Rais! I will kill you, you child-eating devil, I will kill you!"

Strangling on his rage, La Hire rolled over on top of de Rais, getting one hand free and punching him so hard the maréchal's head snapped back against the floor.

It should have knocked him senseless. Instead, de Rais threw his head forward and caught La Hire in the nose with his forehead. Stinging pain exploded in his skull, and blood spurted. La Hire bellowed and shook his head to clear it, flailing to catch de Rais. The maréchal easily captured his hands again and rolled La Hire back onto the floor. With an almost gentle gesture he slid one finger down La Hire's bloody face and placed it on the captain's lips, as if shushing him.

"Did you ever wonder how I came by her ring, La Hire? I took it off her finger when I sold her to the English. Even then I knew I would need it someday. Now here it is, ten years later, and it brought you to me."

The voice was his own again. Glaring, furious, La Hire stared up at de Rais, his breath coming hoarsely.

"I will kill you," he said again, through clenched teeth. In answer de Rais leaned close to his ear, and in a soft whisper said, "No. Save me."

La Hire stared. *Stop me,* de Rais mouthed, his eyes pleading. Then cold air whipped past La Hire, raising the hair on his arms, and the room was plunged into darkness. The weight left his chest. De Rais was gone.

When he could move, La Hire rolled painfully to his feet and wiped the blood from his broken nose with the back of his hand. Damn de Rais, he thought half-heartedly, and searched for a candle.

The darkness gave way reluctantly to the feeble light and La Hire stumbled over to the rack. The boy was still breathing, but blood came from his mouth, and his eyes were staring. Fumbling with the restraints La Hire released him, and the boy fell into his arms, crying out feebly. La Hire lowered himself into a sitting position against the frame, the boy half in his lap. "Shh," he said gruffly, scraping a hand over the boy's hair. "Shh."

He started when he heard familiar voices coming from above. Torchlight winked from the stairs.

"Jean! Bertrand! Down here! Watch your step."

He heard them exclaim as they stopped abruptly at the edge of the trapdoor.

"Name of God, La Hire, what are you doing down there?"

"Not now, Bertrand! Get down here!"

They jumped cautiously into the chamber, staring around them with awe.

"Name of God, La Hire!" de Metz said, taking in the rack, the boy, and La Hire's ruined face.

"Never mind. Did you see de Rais?"

They shook their heads.

"He did this. He's mad. The dinner, now this—" he nodded down at the boy. "Who knows how many victims."

"Hundreds," croaked the boy. He clutched La Hire's shirt with weak fingers. "Sires, I can see you are men of good blood and have come to help. Go to Nantes and find Constable Labbé. He has suspected the maréchal for a long time but lacked proof. My body is the evidence he needs."

"Not your body, boy," de Metz said gruffly, but the youngster shook his head, gulping back the pain.

"No. It's too late for me. But if you can, Sires, find me a priest? And my—my mother? She lives in the village, she must be worried. If you could tell her that I will see her in Heaven—" he stopped, groaning.

La Hire tipped the boy gently into de Metz's arms and stood up. "Let's find a way out of here."

It turned out to be a mundane secret; the tapestry behind the rack hid a corridor. They followed the cold breeze coming from the outside and found themselves in the courtyard.

It was cold and pitch dark. Dawn had not yet come, and the torches had gone out. Fog settled over the open space, and they could hear water dripping loudly in the distorted air.

"Go," La Hire told de Metz. "Get Labbé and bring him back here—" he glanced down at the boy. He appeared to be unconscious. "And a priest," he finished. "We'll find de Rais and hold him for the constable."

De Metz nodded and headed toward the stables with his burden.

They found him in the chapel. De Rais knelt in front of the altar, his body still as stone and as quiet. La Hire and de Poulengy exchanged uneasy glances. They watched from the door as the dim figure bowed his head and crossed himself. De Rais got to his feet, and, still facing the altar, said, "Have you come to kill me, La Hire?" His voice was quiet, rational.

"If I must," La Hire said. De Rais nodded, as if considering that. He turned at last, his face in shadow.

"I am not a bad man, you know."

De Poulengy's laugh echoed explosively in the chapel. The other two ignored it. De Rais went on with his defense.

"I fought for France beside the Maid, as did you. God will see that. He will weigh it. And I have decided to enter a monastery. I will take a vow of poverty, you see, and I'll be good. Yes. I think it will be a good life. I am tired of this one."

La Hire and de Poulengy exchanged glances.

"I don't think that will be possible, Sire," La Hire said.

"But I am so tired, La Hire. I want to stop, but I can't. Do you think God will understand that?"

If He did, La Hire thought, it will be because there is no God, only a Devil.

"Consider yourself stopped, Sire," de Poulengy put in. He stepped forward, one hand on his sword hilt. "We've summoned Labbé."

For the first time de Rais looked directly at de Poulengy.

"You," he sneered. He stepped out of the shadow, and La Hire saw de Poulengy flinch uncertainly. "Who are you to judge me? Go back to France, little man, go back to your sad pinings for a past that never was. You are destined to be nothing but the shit under the heels of great men. First Jeanne, now me—"

De Poulengy grabbed de Rais by his tunic and threw him backward. La Hire pulled him off. "Bertrand, don't!" he said. "He is just goading you—"

Furiously de Poulengy tried to pull himself from La Hire's grip. "Let me kill him, La Hire! He is evil, he is filth—"

Pressed against the altar where de Poulengy had pushed him, de Rais watched their struggle, laughing. Roaring in frustration, La Hire threw de Poulengy aside and lunged for de Rais, catching him by a velvet sleeve just as a familiar breeze swept through the chapel. The candles flickered and the shadows swayed, but La Hire held tight, and after a moment, the candlelight came back up. Their faces only inches apart, La Hire caught the look of terror on de Rais's face.

"No!" he howled, and twisting one hand free, he grabbed La Hire's dagger and plunged it into his side.

La Hire staggered as all went still. Above de Rais's thick breathing and de Poulengy's frantic cursing, he could hear the hissing of the candle wax, even the dripping of moisture outside the chapel. He looked past de Rais to the quiet altar, and noticed for the first time the stained glass window above the crucifix. At first he thought the armored figure was St. Michael.

And then he saw who it was. The dawn must have come, because gray light filtered through the leaded glass, shining through the halo behind the armored head, black hair peeking out around the face, just as it had done in life. Her banner waved above her, and her armor, plain, unadorned, gleamed with new light. She stood on the walls of Orléans, but her gaze was not fixed on the sight of her most triumphant military victory, but upon La Hire.

"God's blood, girl," he said to her. "What are you doing here?"

"La Hire, how many times have I told you not to take the Lord's name in vain?" she scolded.

He smiled. He never thought how good it would be to see her again. "You never give up, do you? Don't you know my swearing is a hopeless battle?"

"Despair is a sin, La Hire. There are no hopeless battles where there is God."

"Even here, Jeanne?"

"Especially here, La Hire."

"He asked me to save him. To stop him from killing again."

"Then you must do so."

"Will he be brought to justice?"

"If God wills it."

"Damn you, Jeanne! I knew you'd say that."

He expected her to reprimand him again, but she just looked at him kindly, and he had to avert his gaze to tell her what he had kept pent up for ten years.

"I was in a Burgundian prison," he said at last, his voice flat. "I would have come, if I could."

She said nothing, and he plunged on lamely. "I don't know about the others. The King, D'Alençon—I don't know why they abandoned you. I suppose they thought—I suppose they thought that you were the Maid and you would win," he finished, hardly above a whisper.

He dared to look at her then, and her smile was kind, though tears sparkled at the corner of her eyes.

"But I did win, La Hire," she said.

He waited, but she said nothing more, and he noticed that the window was still again. La Hire swayed and looked down, swiping blood away from his side and staring in wonder at his hand. As de Poulengy hurried to grab him, La Hire looked at de Rais.

"I've come to save you," he said, and pitched facedown onto the chapel floor.

He woke up in a different chamber, this one streaming with morning light from shutters thrown open to the fields outside the castle. The scent of the dead children that clung to the walls of Machecoul had lessened, but La Hire knew it would never be entirely clean.

"He should have died," de Poulengy told de Metz as they stood over the bed. "I've seen wounds like that." He shook his head and went on. "But La Hire just stood there, just staring. And then he told de Rais he had come to save him. Then he collapsed."

La Hire grunted. He was still weak and his eyes kept wanting to close. "Did I say anything else?"

"No . . . at least I didn't hear anything. But de Rais said you were talking—" he looked away uncomfortably. "—to Jeanne," he finished. "And he saw behind her a vast army of knights, all stern and sorrowful, and he knelt in surrender to you."

"I didn't see the knights," La Hire said without thinking. De Poulengy looked at him.

"But you saw her?" he said quietly, his voice aching. La Hire exchanged glances with de Metz. It had never been easy for de Poulengy. The rest of them could think of Jeanne as a warrior sent from God or a boy in knight's armor rather than a girl, vibrant and spirited. A son for Dunois, a brother for d'Alençon, a weapon for Charles the King.

De Poulengy had loved all of her in equal parts, the girl, the saint, and the soldier.

"What happened then?" de Metz asked.

"While I was trying to stop La Hire's bleeding," de Poulengy went on, "de Rais tried to kill himself with the dagger, but I took it from him, and then I tied his hands with my belt.

"I didn't want to put La Hire in the hands of the servants, so we holed up in the chapel until afternoon, when I heard you and Labbé in the courtyard."

"The boy's evidence was all that Labbé needed to get the warrant for de Rais's arrest from the Bishop of Nantes," de Metz said. "He told his story to Labbé before he died."

La Hire wondered if the boy had seen a priest before dying. He hoped so. Despite himself, his eyes closed. He heard the two knights leave and the door close behind them. With the last of his strength he fished out the little ring from his shirt, the ring that had brought him to de Rais, not to save him from the executioner after all, but to save him from himself.

The ring was too small to go on his broad fingers, so he held it between his hands as he began to pray.

Origin of the Species

James Van Pelt

James Van Pelt lives in Grand Junction, Colorado. When he is not writing, he teaches high school and college English at Fruita-Monument High School and Mesa State College. His fiction and poetry have appeared in a variety of magazines including Asimov's, Analog, Realms of Fantasy, Talebones, *and* Weird Tales, *and in several anthologies. His stories have been nominated for Nebula, Hugo, and Stoker awards. In 1999, he was a finalist for the John W. Campbell Award for Best New Writer. His first collection of stories,* Strangers and Beggars, *was published in 2002, and was named by the American Library Association a Best Book for Young Adults. In addition, he published at least half a dozen excellent new stories in 2002, a significant achievement in a generally strong year for fantasy and science fiction.*

"Origin of the Species" is from Weird Tales, *the finest of the magazines of dark fantasy and horror. But it is a humorous, pleasant, witty story with a good solid psychological underpinning, about the teenage feeling that there is some kind of beast inside you. The answer is, there is.*

Romulus stood under an elm in the moon-washed shadow of the long, green sward between Grey Mountain Golf Course's ninth fairway and the Grey Mountain Country Club, listening to the tinny dance music of Pinehurst High's prom. He absently pried chunks of bark off the tree with his fingernail; but his focus was on the building, pink light leaking from the windows, a hundred shiny windshields catching the moon in the parking lot beyond, and the sad-leafed whisper of the wind.

Shadows passed between the light and the windows, couples dancing, heads close together, gliding by during the slow song; and Romulus wondered which one was Fay with her date, what's-his-name, the troll.

He looked through the leaves at the moon, three days short of being full; and he scuffed the ground in disgust. Since September, when Student Senate scheduled the dance, he'd known. All the full moons were marked on his day-planner, mixed in with deadlines for college applications, baccalaureate, Senior Academic Awards night, and graduation. There it was, a perfectly circular moon on the Tuesday after prom, and he'd known he would be standing outside, skin a little itchy, jaw aching, watching the dance.

When Romulus was a freshman, Dad told him it was regressive genetics catching up. They'd sat in his bedroom, Romulus' wildlife posters covering the walls, Dad, a little embarrassed, telling him the facts of life.

"You're getting to that age, son." Dad pressed his hands on the tops of his knees and locked his elbows straight, clearly uncomfortable.

"I know, Dad." Romulus scooted farther away on the bed. Dad's weight pressed the mattress down; and no matter where Romulus sat, he felt like he was an inch away from tumbling into him. And Romulus *did* know. He'd known for years, listening to his parents talking late at night, marking their calendars, Dad slipping out at dusk the nights of a full moon. What kid wouldn't know?

"You're going to start noticing girls more. You're a sensitive boy," Dad said.

Romulus blushed. It was true, he did. They'd walk by him in the halls, their backpacks hanging off one shoulder, intent on conversations with each other; and he'd catch himself staring at the almost invisible hair on a naked wrist, the curve of muscle in a neck. But most of all, it was their smell. For the longest time he hadn't known what it was. Once a month or so, depending on the girl, he'd catch a stray whiff beneath the shampoo and perfume and hair spray; and his muscles would tense. He hoped to God that Dad wasn't going to say anything about that. That would be too much. He'd rather jump out the window than listen to Dad fumble his way through an explanation of the smell.

Instead, Dad launched into an oblique reference to evolution and the origin of the species. "The genes mixed, son. I know what they told you in your science classes about where man came from, but they don't know the half of it, the magical half."

Romulus let out a relieved sigh. Dad wasn't going to talk about girls after all. Instead he talked about elves and harpies, goblins, giants and humans. "The dominant breed won out and all were assimilated. Everyone's human, more or less, but sometimes a regressive gene rises to the surface. Do you know what I'm trying to say?" He put his hand on Romulus' knee. "You're a special kid. There are others like you, some just like you, some from the other races, a little bit of old ancestry, the old mythologies, in everyone, more or less."

"Sure, Dad. Thanks for clearing this all up for me. I've got to do my homework now. Okay?"

"Oh, good." Dad let out a noisy sigh, like he'd just set down a great weight. "So you know why things are the way they are?"

"Yeah, I got it."

Then Dad left. Romulus didn't do his homework, but lay in bed instead, his hands clasped behind his head, staring at the ceiling, thinking about smells.

So he started paying attention to the lunar calendar his freshman year. As time wore on he grew a few inches, filled out in the chest, found he needed to shave; and the week of the full moon he didn't schedule anything at night. He wondered, *Was Dad right? Was* everyone *descended from mythological creatures?* Sometimes he wandered the halls during passing period, or he sat in class and tried to figure where the other students came from. Was the cheerleader part elf? Was the junior class president's great, great, great, great (and so on) grandmother a gorgon? She was frightening enough, and there was a snakyness to her hair when she stood in the wind. He sniffed her, but she smelled purely human. He'd never identified anyone's deep ancestry until he smelled the troll in the boy who liked Fay, and that was a pure scary fluke. They'd bumped the hall. The troll shoved him off, and in the shove Romulus had smelled him. A line of associations clicked—an instinctive recognition—but so strong that for a second the boy's hands were twisted claws, and his incisors hung from his mouth like stout tusks.

Romulus hadn't known whether to run or snarl. And what bad luck! Of all the boys in the school, the troll had to ask Fay to prom.

It wasn't his fault the stupid Student Senate decided this date for the dance. He leaned against the tree. Fay hadn't understood, really, when he told her he couldn't go to the prom. She'd smiled. Was sweet about it. Maybe she even believed him when he stammered his excuses. So she made the date with the troll. Romulus squeezed his eyes shut in frustration. The music changed to a faster beat. Shadows bounced against the window. A couple boys slipped out the doors and walked to their truck, avoiding the security cop in the parking lot. Even from a hundred yards away, Romulus smelled the beer. They only stayed in the truck for a few minutes, then headed back to the dance.

Romulus left the lawn and walked the neighborhoods,

choosing streets randomly. He hid from cars—it was long past curfew, and he didn't want to explain to a policeman what he was doing. Sometimes a dog chained in a back yard caught wind of him and howled. He didn't howl back, didn't even growl; but he wished one would break free. They could run the blocks together, or they could stand face to face, teeth showing in the moon. "This is mine," their postures would say. Maybe the dog would leap, go for his throat. Romulus closed his eyes and felt the night air on his cheek, the stony road beneath his shoes. Or maybe *he* would leap and the dog's throat would be in *his* teeth. He could almost feel the pulse in his mouth.

It seemed for hours that he walked, often with his eyes closed, not paying attention to where he was, trusting his nose to lead him. When a car turned the corner ahead of him, and he dove into a bush, he was surprised to find he was directly across the street from Fay's house. The car parked. It was the troll's convertible, top down, looking low, black, and ominous in the moonlight. Fay and the troll walked to the porch.

"I had a nice time," she said, her hands in his between them.

"Me too." The troll wore a letter jacket over his tux. Even from the bushes across the street, Romulus could see the multiple brass bars glistening in the porch light, bars that showed how many times he'd lettered in football, wrestling, and track. A thick-necked, thick-wristed, thick-headed wunderkind with perfect balance and the fast twitch muscles of a cheetah. A vague suggestion of Harrison Ford in his chin and smile. A careless black lock of hair that fell across his forehead in an unkempt way that some girls found charming.

Romulus was loath to think Fay could fall for this, but as the two talked, their faces came closer and closer together like an inevitable collision, two lambent planets closing on each other in the night sky, until they were kissing; and Romulus turned away, a bitter tear in each eye.

Later, after Fay went into her house and the troll drove away, Romulus walked back to Grey Mountain Country

Club. Other than empty beer cans and broken glass in the parking lot, nothing remained of the prom. He wandered onto the golf course, fell asleep on the third green, and when he woke in the morning, stiff from tiredness and the cold, he saw his own dew-drawn silhouette in the grass.

In the hallways that Monday, Romulus moved listlessly from subject to subject, avoiding Fay until finally he ran into her between Calculus and Mythology, a class they shared.

They talked outside the door. "Did you do your homework?" she asked.

He nodded. They were supposed to write a report on a character from Camelot. He'd chosen Uther Pendragon. As always, he found himself staring. Her complexion fascinated him, absolutely exquisite, like polished silk, pale and smooth, dark-blue eyes, a hint of copper in her blonde hair. He thought about a willow wand swaying on a river bank. Looking at her was like listening to water dance over rounded rocks, all foam and bubbles and deep, still pools.

Fay glanced into his eyes, then looked away. "I don't think teachers should be allowed to make assignments on Prom weekend."

"You didn't get yours done?" His palms sweated just talking to her.

Fay shook her head.

"You can have mine. I've got an *A* in there already without it."

Fay smiled. "Really? You'd do that?"

Embarrassed, Romulus put his head down. "It's no big deal."

She put her hand on his arm. "That's the nicest thing I think anyone's ever offered to do for me, but I better face the music on my own." She stood on her tiptoes, kissed him on the cheek, then slipped around the doorway into the room.

Students streamed past him, intent on beating the tardy bell, but Romulus didn't move. Slowly he brought his hand up to his face and brushed his fingertips where she'd kissed him.

During class, Romulus barely listened. He focused instead on Fay, who sat a row over and two seats in front of him. The troll sat beside her. Halfway through class he passed her a note. She read it quietly, wrote something on it, and passed it back. The troll nodded and put the note in his folder. Mr. Campbell talked at length about the search for the historical King Arthur. In despair, Romulus turned his attention to Campbell. "The real King Arthur, if there was one, may have lived in fifth century England, a hero because he drove out barbarian invaders. Much of our knowledge of King Arthur came from a historian, Geoffrey of Monmouth, who in the twelfth century set down the reigns of British kings. He made most of it up, evidently. But it's through Geoffrey that we first learn of Merlin."

Romulus wrote names and dates disconsolately until Campbell said, "The death of Arthur and disappearance of Merlin are the end of wizardry in the world. Belief in mythological creatures fades with every passing century." He said it within another context, but the words reminded him of what his dad had said about evolution and magic. Romulus wondered if the biology classes ever touched on this alternate explanation for changes in the species.

Quickly, Romulus wrote his thoughts below Campbell's facts: "What if Merlin's disappearance *caused* the downfall of mythological beings?" He thought he'd ask Dad about it later.

Fay concentrated on her own notes. The troll wrote something on a slip of paper, and with a husky whisper, handed it to the boy behind him, a freshman who somehow had been assigned this senior-level class—Romulus had stepped between the boy and a pissed-off football player earlier in the year, but other than a grateful "thank you," they didn't talk—he gave the paper to Romulus, muttering, "Pass it on." Behind Romulus sat one of the troll's wrestling buddies. Romulus often found himself a courier for their stream of letters, mostly directions for the weekend's parties. The torn paper sat, message up, on the desk. The troll hadn't bothered to fold it. It read, "I'll nail her tomorrow night." He'd scrawled a lopsided happy face below, its eyes two squashed circles. Romulus' fingers curled up, revolted by the thought of touching it.

Something whacked the back of his head.

"Hand it back, dog breath," hissed the wrestler.

Romulus grabbed the note, twirled in his seat, and banged it on the desk. The wrestler leaned away, a startled look in his eyes. He said, "Hey, I was just joking."

After a few seconds, Romulus broke his glare and faced forward, and he heard a sigh of relief behind him.

"Boys?" said Campbell.

"Sorry, sir," said Romulus.

For the rest of the period, the note ran through his brain, "I'll nail her tomorrow." The happy face looked more and more evil in his memory. He opened his text to the illustrations, and wasn't surprised to see a resemblance between that lopsided face and the book's woodcut of a troll.

After class, in the hallway once again, Romulus pushed his way through the crowd until he caught up with Fay; but once he reached her side, he was not sure what to say. The certainty he'd had in class faded. Maybe the troll was talking about someone else. How could he ask her what she was doing tomorrow night? She carried her books against her chest, her chin down, as if she were mulling over something.

"Fay?" he said.

She looked up, smiled at him. "Hi, Romulus. Isn't your next class the other way?"

He blushed, he could feel his face heating, and the heat embarrassed him even more. It was all he could do not to turn away, but he had committed himself now. He had to know.

"I wondered if you wanted to go to the Senior Choral Recital. It's tomorrow at seven." As the words slipped out, he knew he'd never be able to keep the date. At seven the sun was still up, but it was a two-hour concert.

Her expression fell. "Oh, I'm sorry. I can't. Not tomorrow. I . . . have other plans."

In the pause he heard the truth. The troll's note was about her. And he knew where they'd go too, Chaney Park, a spot on the bluffs overlooking town. It's where the troll always took his dates. His activities there were legendary.

Fay smiled again, her face perfect in the bustling hallway. Her eyes glistened. Even as his heart ached, he marveled at her eyes that were brighter than they should be, as if they reflected a crystal light no one else saw. Then he caught a hint of her smell. Like everyone else, she smelled of shampoo and deodorant, but underneath was her own essence, a spring-drenched forest, nothing fleshy at all.

"I'd like a rain check, though," she said. "Ask me again another night."

Romulus blinked in surprise, and she was gone. Just kids bumping against each other, making their way from room to room.

That night the moon rose in Romulus' window, white and fat and unblinking. His lights out, he sat on the edge of his bed, breath short, skin on fire. Inside he was all pressures and cramps, legs trembling. Dad would know what to tell him, but Dad had stolen out the back door when the sun went down. The moon had never seemed so large; it was larger than the window, and the light had never seemed so potent, so penetrating. Romulus scratched at his chest, popping buttons. Where the light touched felt better, not cooled, but caressed in warmth.

Romulus whined, biting in the sound he really wanted to make. He pulled his clothes off. A part of him worried his mother would come to check on him, and what would she think, him standing naked in the pale, moonlit square in his room? She'd caught him in the bathroom the other day, staring in the mirror.

She'd said without pausing, "Your father plucks his, you know."

"What?" he'd said.

"Most people have two eyebrows." She leaned past him, buffed a spot on the counter, then left.

Confused, he'd looked at himself again. Although he hadn't been thinking about it at the time, he'd always considered his eyebrows his best mark, in a lupine sort of way, and the shadow between them a distinguishing feature. Dad plucked his?

Of course, he was his father's son—she would not be surprised to see him naked in the moonlight either. Still, he worried she might come in. The other part, though, saw himself leaping through the window. He thought, *I must go to the forest.* Already the trees quivered, waiting for him. And in the trees they would expect him, the entire panoply: elves, fairies, goblins, and giants. The other creatures lost in mythical, evolutionary time.

But there would be trolls there too, and dragons. All the old maps said so: in the unexplored areas, *Here there be dragons.*

From the moon-tinted hills beyond town, a thin howl rose in the light. Very lonely. Very far away.

Romulus tried a howl back, a tentative utterance that couldn't have made it past their front gate.

He did it again, louder. It hurt tearing through his throat that wasn't quite shaped for it, but it felt good too. Once more.

A door popped open across the street, and a neighbor stuck his head out. Romulus buried his head in a pillow. No way Dad heard that, he thought; but he didn't try it again. When the moon rose high enough so the light was not so obvious, he curled on the floor to fall asleep.

The day passed miserably until Mythology, where he hoped he could figure a way to warn Fay; but no matter how he thought to phrase it, his message sounded unbelievable. In the classroom's afternoon mugginess he doodled at the bottom of his notes. Fay split her attention between Campbell, who moved meticulously through the history of the Knights of the Round Table; and the troll, who smiled slyly at her when she turned toward him.

"Many re-tellings of Arthur's legend say that after the boy king took the throne at fifteen, and under Merlin's tutelage, he rid his country of monsters and giants," said Campbell.

Romulus sketched a sword rising from a lake. If he had Excalibur, he thought, he would rid this classroom of a monster himself.

When the bell rang, Fay continued writing her notes. The troll stood beside her, put his hand on her shoulder, then spoke softly in her ear. Romulus scrunched his toes in his shoes to keep himself from springing from the desk.

That evening Romulus finished dinner, told Mom and Dad he needed to take a walk, and went out the back door, but not before he caught a knowing glance between them.

Chaney Park was a six-mile hike up a gravel road that rose too steeply the last three miles to bicycle, and Romulus figured he could be where kids parked by 8:30 or so. There was no question about using the car. He shuddered to think of himself behind the wheel, driving a two-thousand-pound vehicle, and the moon pouring through the windshield like a million biting ants.

The houses on his street were new brick and crisply painted bi-levels, but a block over was an older neighborhood, where the roofs rose to steep peaks, and every house sported a single attic window, a lone eye watching him trudge toward the edge of town. Behind him the sunset flared orange and yellow, but before him only the bluffs' tops caught the last pale sliver of daylight, and they didn't hold that long. The woods below already swam in shadows.

He crossed the railroad tracks; the blacktop changed to dirt; and soon, thin-trunked trees, rustling with spring growth lined the path on both sides. He trudged up a long hill. At the crest he looked back. The town spread out behind him, stretched along the river, a tiny fiefdom at this distance. Streetlights could just as well be campfires; the baseball stadium glowing on the other side of town, a castle. He turned and walked into the dale beyond, losing the town and the day's final glow at the same time. A few stars twinkled in the sable blanket.

Romulus took deep breaths. He hadn't walked at night out here before. He felt keen, sharp. Another breath. Oak. Old oak that had started growing before the town existed. There were other smells he recognized too; fox, a shy one who must have crossed this path only seconds before he came into sight; and squirrel; and damp ferns dripping into moldy leaves, some so deep in shadow that winter's frost was only inches below.

In the distance, wheels crunched through gravel; and engine noise rose above the murmuring forest. Romulus loped off the road and into the brush, around a great ball of roots from a fallen tree. He gripped two gnarled, woody wrists and peered out. A moment later a car roared by, radio blaring a steady rap thump. A snatch of laughter, then a beer can clattered against a rock. Then dust.

He waited until the air cleared before stepping from behind the tangled dead-fall. In the hills above, the car's rowdy passage rose and fell. Hands jammed deep into his pockets, he continued his walk, thoughtful now that the car had gone. What if Fay wanted to be with the troll? There would be nothing to warn her about. This trek to Chaney Park could be seen as little more than stalking her. There wasn't much he could do anyway. Still, he pushed onward, leaning into the road's steepness, taking each hairpin turn with measured deliberateness. His legs buzzed pleasantly, and he felt as if he could go forever if he had to. With his eyes closed, he imagined trotting along through the forest, tireless, behind deer maybe, waiting for one to drop from exhaustion. He smiled at the image. Several more times he leaped into the covering woods as more cars drove by. He didn't see the troll's car.

Finally the road leveled; but the trees surrounded him thicker than ever, leaning over the road and blocking the stars. It wasn't until he reached a clearing and the forest opened before him that he realized he'd made the top. The moon sat on the horizon, a bloated egg, rich and ivory and huge again, as it had been on Sunday in his room; but now there was no window between him and it.

A full moon in the height of its glory. Romulus had never felt its light so intensely. A breeze swept through the tree tops and the oaks creaked. He looked around for a high place, then saw one, a jumbled pile of boulders that made a miniature mountain to his left. He ran to its base, his wavy, gray shadow flowing over grass and brush and branch. Up he clambered, hands down, like feet, fingernails clicking, leaping from rock to rock until he gained the summit. No forest blocking the moon now. He howled. Not self consciously, but a full-throated paean to the night sky. "Oh," he said afterward, and he crouched so his hands took part of his weight. *Is this the way it is for Dad?* thought Romulus, *or am I even closer to the past than he is? Could I actually* change?

He felt the animal shape beneath his human one moving about. Then the sky darkened as a cloud crossed the moon's face. Romulus shook his head to clear it, and he looked about him for the first time. To the east there was no sign of the town, but he knew if he walked a little bit farther along the road, he'd be at Chaney Park, where the bluff offered a view of the entire valley.

A car's headlights cut through the trees below; and in a few seconds, the car itself passed, turned toward the park, and vanished into the forest, its tail lights glimmering long after he'd stopped hearing it. The moon was a hand's-width above the horizon. How long had he been on the promontory? Moaning, he ran down the boulders, careless of injury, hit the road at top speed, and raced toward Chaney Park.

Three cars and a van rested on the picnic area's lined asphalt, noses pointed toward town, but none of them were the troll's convertible.

Romulus crossed the back of the narrow lot in the tree's shadows. From one car a muffled conversation mixed with the wind. A sticker on the van's bumper proclaimed, "If we're rockin', don't come knockin'."

Past the parking lot the road turned to dirt again to wind up the hill. Every fifty feet or so a private picnic area opened on the left or right, complete with a split-log table and iron charcoal pit. The first one was empty; a rusted pickup occupied the second. Romulus stayed low, just off the path, walking in the soggy remains of last year's leaves, his nose telling him as much as his eyes. The breeze caressed his face. Other cars waited ahead; he could smell them, the still warm engines, their tires, cigarette smoke. Then he caught it, a distinct whiff of the troll. He growled. A girl's quivery voice in a car ten feet away said, "What was that?" Romulus crouched even lower in a run, his hands nearly touching the ground.

Then, ahead, clearly in the forest's silence, he heard Fay. "Don't!" she said. "I don't want . . ."

The road rose. At the crest he saw the final picnic spot in the clearing fifty yards below, the troll's car in the middle, top down, bathed in moonlight. He paused. Where was Fay? He could smell her perfume, and he smelled troll. Romulus spotted them in the back seat, the troll's dark letter jacket blending into the shadow; he was struggling, holding Fay down beneath him. Her hand rose above him, like a drowning person. Cloth ripped.

Romulus charged toward them, his lips pulled away from his teeth in a noiseless snarl; but everything suddenly felt underwater and syrupy. It took an hour for his foot to hit the ground and an hour for the next. Fay's hand froze in the air like a marble statue. Slowly, it seemed, so slowly, he came closer.

The troll laughed, the throbbing sound coming to Romulus almost too low to hear. More cloth ripped. A button, a fine pearl-colored disk, flipped lazily into the air. Only ten yards away now, but every step seemed to cover less distance.

Then the air about the convertible changed. Even in his urgency, breath tearing through his throat, his teeth aching to bite something hard, Romulus slowed. The air changed, centering on Fay's hand. A circle of moonlight ten feet around slid toward her. It was as if the light wasn't light at all, but a thin coat of paint, funneling to her hand. For a moment it seemed as if the stars themselves swarmed, each touching her hand until it shone with potency, and her palm turned down. Her elbow crooked as if she were about to embrace the troll. Romulus stopped, nearly touching the car. Now he could see it all. The troll had pushed her back, trapped her legs with his own, pinned her with his weight, one arm stuck behind her, his lips pressed against the side of her face. Her eyes were closed, but not in fear—Romulus had time to study her—she was concentrating. The light flowed down her arm, filled her face. She glowed from within, like a porcelain night light. Then all the brightness emptied from her hand in a cascade of sparks, slamming into the back of the troll's head.

He stiffened.

Romulus stepped back, covering his eyes.

When he opened them, he had to blink away a black spot in the spark's shape to see Fay, now sitting up. She'd rolled the troll onto the car's floor, and her feet rested on his back.

"Dang," she said. "Just look at my blouse." She pulled the torn front together, then zipped her jacket.

She turned to Romulus and said in a voice no different than if she'd run into him in the mall, "What brings you to Chaney Park this time of night, Romulus?"

Her face still glowed, and something glimmered in the back of her eyes, very sharp and ancient. She combed her fingers through her hair. Romulus noticed her ears. They were distinctly pointed. He'd not seen that in her before.

"It seemed a good night for a walk," he said lamely. The troll snorted beneath her feet, then settled into a comfortable-sounding snore. "What *are* you?" Romulus said.

She stood on the back seat, brushed her hands down her pants in short, brisk strokes. "Fairy, I think. At least that's what my mother says. And you?" She jumped out of the car to land beside him.

Romulus tried to answer, but all his words had been sucked out of him. He attempted to speak a couple of times, but nothing came out.

Understanding came into her eyes. "It's the moon thing,

isn't it?" She looked into the sky. "That's why you couldn't go to prom. Oh, I should have figured it out earlier. But I still don't know why you're here tonight."

Finally Romulus said, "I couldn't sleep." His voice rose at the end, as if it were a question.

Fay glanced at the troll, then back at him. She shook her head. "You're sweet, Romulus." She looked thoughtfully into the car for a moment, then pulled the keys out of the ignition and threw them into the forest. "Would you like to walk me home? I think I've lost my ride."

Romulus nodded dumbly, so happy that if he had a tail to wag, he would wag it a thousand miles an hour.

They started toward town, leaving the sleeping troll and his car behind.

Romulus took a deep, deep breath of night air. He could smell everything, all of it, leaf, branch and tree.

Fay cleared her throat. "You're not going to try to bite me, are you?" She sounded only half-joking.

Romulus let the air out in a relieved rush. "Oh, no! Not you."

"Good," she said. "That would make it tough for us to date." She moved next to him.

They walked down the winding dirt road, hands not touching, but very close, both so full of moonish power they thought they'd burst.

Tread Softly

Brian Stableford

Brian Stableford [freespace.virgin.net/diri.gini/brian.htm] lives in Reading, Berkshire. He is a writer of international prominence and has a worldwide reputation as a literary historian of fantasy, horror, and science fiction, and is a leading critic and reviewer. A sociologist by training, he was a lecturer in sociology at the University of Reading until he quit to write full time in 1988. His main reputation is as a science fiction writer, but he is also a translator of fantasy and a major contributor to the great Encyclopedia of Fantasy, as well as the author of a significant number of fantasy stories. His 2002–2003 publications include the SF novel The Omega Expedition; translations of Lumen by Camille Flammarion and Nightmares of an Ether-Drinker by Jean Lorrain; three essay collections, Slaves of the Death Spiders, Space, Time and Infinity, and The Devil's Party; and two short story collections, Complications and Other Science Fiction Stories and Salome and Other Decadent Fantasies.

"Tread Softly" appeared in Interzone. It deals with one of the traditional images of Oriental fantasy stories, the magic carpet, with an original twist. We particularly like its convincing antiquarian plot details and atmosphere.

It was Pemberly who told me about the shop just off the Barking Road where magic carpets could be bought. He should not have done so, according to his own principles. He was not only breaking a confidence but setting a lure before me that could only lead me into trouble—but it was the greatest stroke of luck I ever had.

I met Pemberly in the convalescent hospital at Kimmeridge in August 1917. He had been shipped home from Durban, having stepped on a mine while serving in the King's African Rifles. Surgeons there had amputated his left leg above the knee, and the cauterized stump had become infected. The infection brought back a feverish madness that had first possessed him in Tanganyika. My younger brother had lost a leg at Ypres, and had not survived his own battle with decay even with the assistance of a barrage of sulfa and a battalion of friendly maggots, so we had something in common even before we discovered our shared interest in the Mysteries of the East. I had been wounded myself, of course, else I should not have been in England either, but the burns had only cost me the use of my right eye and the ability to smile.

I have no idea how Pemberly had fetched up in the KAR, having spent 15 years before the war working for the government in Rajputana, but he must have been far from the ideal civil servant and I dare say that his superiors had been only too glad to let him go, especially to another continent. His father was a baronet and his maternal uncle an earl, but as the youngest of four sons he had been surplus to requirements at home, and must have stepped into the role of black sheep with a certain stylish wantonness. He was inclined to look down on a mere vicar's son—who was not even an officer, having been pressed into the RAMC as a conscientious objector—but he was grateful for the care

404

that brought him gradually back to sanity. It was the strength of his constitution as much as treatment and care that enabled him to fight off the blood-poisoning, but I played my own part.

It was while he was delirious and raving that Pemberly mentioned the dream-weavers of Kharshahar, and there was not another man in the entire Medical Corps to whom the words would have had meaning—but my great-grandfather had been a Company man until the '57 mutiny put paid to all that, and his diaries had been passed down to me with his paltry heirlooms. I, unlike my direly pious father, had not merely read them but had taken them seriously, so I knew of the existence of the Secret Trade, although I had always assumed that it had not survived into the era of Dalhousie's railways.

Such investigations as I had been able to make at a distance of 6,000 miles had suggested that Kharshahar, a settlement precariously situated in the northeastern hills of the Thar Desert, had been obliterated by one of the calamitous monsoon failures that led to the founding of Blanford's Meteorological Department. I had assumed that the art of dream-weaving had died with its famine-stricken population. When I related the history of my own researches to Pemberly, however, he felt obliged to demonstrate the superiority of his own knowledge.

"At least two families of dream-weavers survived," he told me. "Had to go a long way in search of succour, mind. Fetched up among Mohammedans in the Sulaimans. Found it much harder to sell their wares once they were settled. Nothing in the world can persuade a follower of the Prophet that there's any kind of Hindu magic but black.

"I arranged the export of half a hundred carpets myself, but it was a dicey business even before the formation of the Muslim League—impossible now, I should think, even if the craftsmen still have the art. Old Ruscoe complained that more than 30 of them were feeble, and half a dozen spoiled, but I reckon he and Radland were glad to have them anyway. Sold them all, I dare say—except perhaps the ones that were spoiled. Might have one or two of those still tucked away."

How could I not plead with him to give me the address of his London agents? "You'll get nowhere unless you mention my name, mind," he informed me, loftily, "and maybe not then—but if old Ruscoe is still alive, he'll surely remember me."

When I went up to London on my next leave I found the address that Pemberly had given me easily enough, no more than half a mile from the East India Docks. It was more warehouse than showroom, and its gloomy interior was manned by an equally gloomy caretaker, who could not have been a day under 75. He was alone; the shop did not seem to be doing enough business to warrant keeping the place clean and decently lit, let alone properly staffed—but that was only to be expected. War stimulates demand for many things, but exotic rugs are not among them.

"Mr. Ruscoe?" I asked.

"Radland," he replied curtly—slightly intimidated, as many people are, by the sight of my face. "My former partner died two years ago."

He knew Pemberly's name, though. "Is that old rascal back in England?" he asked, as if he found the notion astonishing.

When I explained that Pemberly had left his left leg in Africa, but that the rest of him was safe in Dorset, the old man's response was a sardonic smile.

"Well," said Radland, "I suppose he still has his stamping foot—though it won't be much use to him without a fulcrum. If he sent you here in search of money or opium, I've none to offer him. The firm is one step short of ruination and the navy's taken over the other business."

"It's not for him that I'm here," I explained. "He said that you might have a magic carpet in stock."

"Then you're a fool who's been had for a mug," was the prompt retort. "The Turks will lose Baghdad to Allenby before the year is out—best wait until the boys bring their trophies home. Plenty of flying carpets among them, I dare say, if you can only find the formula that will make them take off."

"I'm not talking about fantasies from the Arabian Nights," I told him. "I'm talking about the produce of the dream-weavers of Kharshahar. My name is Arthur Wouldham—as was my great-grandfather's. He was a Company man before the mutiny. If you cast your mind back, you might remember rumor of his name."

Had I not had that second name to conjure with, the old man would never have admitted that he knew what I was talking about—but he had heard of Arthur Wouldham, and seemed to think more kindly of that name than he thought of Pemberly.

"Those were the days, according to my father," he said meditatively. "Kharshahar carpets had quality then—but the art went bad after the second great drought of the '60s. The stuff Pemberly sent us was rubbish. Too much hunger, too little hope. Worthless as luxury items, not much good even as collector's pieces. My grandfather sold dream-weaves to the likes of Byron and Wellington, and my father sold them to Carlyle and Davy—but nothing we had after the Mutiny could have helped men of that caliber. Oscar Wilde asked for one back in '91, and Yeats after him, but I'd have been ashamed to sell them Pemberly's merchandise."

"So you still have some of them in stock?" I asked.

"We shipped most of them to America," Radland informed me. "No more than half a dozen stayed in England. Ruscoe got what he could for them, but there were some we should have burned. Only one buyer demanded his money back, though. Ruscoe gave it to him, I believe. Reputation of the firm to uphold."

"And Ruscoe took the carpet back?" I said.

It is conceivable, I suppose, that Radland had never bothered to ask that question, of Ruscoe or himself, before I raised it. In retrospect, it seems unlikely, but at the time I was fixated on the possibility of acquiring a magic carpet. It required ten minutes to make Radland admit that Ruscoe was not the kind of man to hand a customer's money back without reclaiming the goods, and a further 20 passed before he condescended to work out where it might have been stored—but that interval seemed small by comparison with the time it took to root around the basement storage-racks until the rug materialized out of the shadows, rolled and wrapped in oil-cloth.

Radland needed little encouragement to spread the thing out—he was understandably curious to see the design—but making the purchase was another matter entirely.

I'd never seen a dream-weave before, but I'd read my ancient namesake's account of them. I knew that the only colors the dream-weavers used were red and black, symbolizing blood and darkness, and that the pattern would be an amazingly intricate maze, but I was unprepared for the shape of the carpet, having expected an ordinary rectangle, and for the fact that the lines making up the maze were hectically curved rather than straight.

"I told you it was spoiled," Radland said. "I never saw a perfect square or circle, of course, but this . . . I do believe it's worse now than when Ruscoe first sold it. It's not supposed to be sensitive when rolled, or capable of growth in the absence of light, but London's a city of six million souls, and spoiled rugs acquire a certain saprophytic quality . . . metamorphic self-cannibalism. Ruscoe should have burned it. I should burn it."

"I want it," I said.

"Then you're worse than the idiot who believes that carpets can fly," he told me, "and I'd be worse than Judas if I took your money." I could tell that he intended to try anyway. I knew that there was no use in bargaining. When I had persuaded him to name a price, I would not have been able to pay it.

"In that case," I said, "I'll steal it."

I didn't hit him. I'm not a violent man. I could hardly be a conscientious objector if I were. Even when he came at me with the carpet-knife, I didn't intend to hurt him. It was his own excitement that killed him, and his own carelessness in tripping over the edge of the carpet. It wasn't my fault. But I had to have the carpet, and he could not have named a price that I could afford to pay.

*   *   *

There are turtles which live for hundreds of years, and trees that live for thousands, but there are microscopic parasites which are effectively immortal, provided that they never meet with a fatal accident. They even multiply themselves, by dividing in two, so that even if thousands meet death by fire, drought or poison there are thousands more that live on and on. There are creatures in the microcosm which have lived for millions or billions of years, comfortably housed within the huge assemblies of plant or animal flesh which are their manifold Utopias, their multitudinous self-renewing cataracts of milk and honey.

My great-grandfather knew nothing of such things, so his account of the carpets of Kharshahar was steeped in superstition, but I am the child of enlightened times. I see everything more clearly than he did.

Agriculture and animal husbandry have been blessings to mankind—but imagine what boons they were to those populations of tiny immortals whose paradise was composed of the husk of the wheat, or the wool of the sheep! There are many, I do not doubt, that are consigned to oblivion by industrial processes—but within the clothes that we put on every morning, and the plush of our settees, and the litter on our stable floors, there are invisible empires.

For the most part, those empires ignore ours just as ours ignore them—but not invariably.

There was a time when all human craftsmen and artisans were magicians, although the steam-engine, the lathe and the dye-factory have put an end to that. All manufacture is mechanical and sterile now, save for the fabrications of a few fugitive communities remote from the deadening hand of civilization. Even there it is dying, because every enclave of human society is part of something infinitely vaster, and the whole oppresses all its parts. The old magic is all but gone. This war will surely put an end to it—but its memory is not yet vanished. Nor are the last of its products.

I know, although my namesake could not, that although the carpets of Kharshahar are not alive in any gross sense, they are host to immortal and invisible empires. The nature and organization of those empires, devastated fractions of which are all that can be glimpsed on microscope slides, is beyond our understanding, but it is conceivable that they too harbor their artisan-magicians, who once used the dream-weavers for their own arcane purposes even as the dream-weavers used them. For whatever reason, though, the carpets of Kharshahar are responsive to dreams, and the dreams of those who walk upon them are sensitized in their turn. It is a trade, of sorts: the secret trade supporting the Secret Trade.

A Kharshahar carpet is sensitive to daydreams as well as those that visit humans by night, but there is no way to know which are held more precious by the dwellers in the weave. In the same way, the emanations of the carpet affect the reveries of the day as well as the visitations of the night. A man who owns a Kharshahar carpet will not only find his sleep enriched but his consciousness too. The dream-weavers of Kharshahar are merchants of hope, ambition and creativity as well as vendors of hallucination.

But I should not be writing in the present tense. The dream-weavers are extinct and the virtue in a Kharshahar carpet is not eternal. That virtue may survive one owner—perhaps "collaborator" would be a better word—and perhaps two or three, but it cannot last forever. This is not because the invisible empire within the weave is ever annihilated, but rather because its constitution changes. Perhaps its need for human dreams is essentially temporary—an appetite to be sated or a resource to be surpassed—and perhaps there is some other cause, but the consequence is clear. In time, even the finest dream-weave becomes enfeebled, and a Kharshahar carpet becomes a carpet like any other. All my revelations regarding the wonder of such possessions ought, therefore, to be written in the past tense.

The carpets of Kharshahar *were* capable of absorbing and influencing the dreams and daydreams of their owners. They *were* capable of enhancing hope, ambition and creativity—but even the best of them is inert now. Even the one that I owned must surely be inert now.

* * *

I never told Pemberly that I had the magic carpet. So far as I know, he never heard of old Radland's death, and it was probably not considered suspicious in any case, but I did not want him putting two and two together.

I am not a fool, and I knew exactly what Pemberly and Radland meant when they said that a carpet was "spoiled." They meant that it was more likely to enhance despair than hope, sloth than ambition, destructiveness than creativity. They meant that it was a source of nightmares, offering more glimpses of hell than anticipations of heaven. I understood why the man who had bought the carpet from Ruscoe in the 1890s had demanded the return of his money. I understood why its shifting colors, whose mazy pattern reflected its transactions with the mind of its possessor, had been twirled and twisted into a puzzle that the human eye could barely follow, let alone aspire to solve.

I understood all of that, but I wanted the carpet anyway. Nor did I want it for anyone's use but my own. Kharshahar carpets are useless as weapons because anyone unwary enough to accept a spoiled specimen as a gift would simply conceive a strong distaste for its appearance, roll it up and throw it away. A man who has such a carpet, whatever its proclivities, can only obtain the full benefit of its potency by establishing a careful and conscious relationship with its invisible inhabitants; the magic is a matter of exchange and sympathy, of a mystical union of interest and involvement.

I wanted the magic carpet for myself because I believed— or, at least, hoped—that I could redeem it. There was a sense in which I had desired a spoiled specimen even more fervently than I could ever have coveted a perfect one, because it offered more of a challenge, more of an opportunity. I had deduced from my great-grandfather's records that all such artifacts begin as reflections of their makers, but that once they are sold their owners become their masters. If the maker and eventual master are in spiritual harmony, the transition is easy; if not, hard—but I firmly believed that no matter how disadvantageous a carpet's relationship with its maker might have been, a good owner ought to be able, eventually, to superimpose his own personality upon the invisible host within the weave.

I knew that the carpet I obtained from Radland would be a difficult beast to tame, but I believed that I could do it, because of the quality of man that I am.

I do not mean by this that I am an unusually virtuous man, rather that I am an unusually sane one. I am the son of a clergyman, but unlike my brother I had the strength of character, even as an adolescent, to become a freethinker. I am in the midst of the greatest and worst war that has ever afflicted the world, but unlike my brother I had the strength of character to remain a man of peace. Lest anyone think that "conscientious objector" is synonymous with "coward," I ought to record that I was at the front for six months, which included the first battle of the Somme. The burns that spoiled my face and half-blinded me are ample evidence of the fact that stretcher-bearers are in no less danger from shellfire than those who carry rifles with bayonets fixed. I have always prided myself on being a man who sees things clearly, even in my dreams; the loss of half my eyesight may have rendered my perception two-dimensional, but has not clouded it at all. Other men have seen me differently, since my injury if not my schooldays, but they have never broken my conviction, or my faith in myself.

That was why I had to have the magic carpet, as soon as I knew that it existed—but I knew that I would have to be patient, if I were to lavish the care and attention upon it that it needed or deserved. I had to put it away until the war was over.

The hospital where I spent the latter half of 1917 and the early months of 1918 was a fair way inland from Kimmeridge Bay, but it was sited on a hill to the east of the village, and the sea was visible through Gaulter Gap from the attics where the orderlies were lodged. The view was delightful when the sun shone, sublime when storms hurried up the channel—but for the last year that I spent there, I was incapable of feeling anything but a desire to be gone. The sea became the stream in which Tantalus stood, its horizon a mocking invitation. When the armistice was signed at last, the more intimate contest began in earnest.

My father's vicarage in Stukeley had been closed to me before the war, but I would not have gone back there even if I had been welcome. In 1914 I had been living in Clevedon, near Bristol, tending the machines for a printer named Priestland and lodging over the shop. I did not expect to find the position still in existence, let alone that he would have held it for me, but I found the old man eager to readapt his business to the opportunities and demands of peace-time, and moved almost to tears by the sight of me. I only had to help him clear four years' worth of accumulated junk from my old room to reclaim it. Mr. Priestland even apologized for the fact that the carpet had been ruined and the bed broken, and would certainly have offered to find me replacements had I not assured him that there was no need. I settled in with alacrity. The situation seemed ideal; my daily labor was sometimes hard but not intellectually demanding, and left my soul free for higher and more difficult work.

I had not noticed any change in my dreaming while the carpet was rolled in its oilskin in a storeroom at Kimmeridge. I had had nightmares, but they were no different in kind or intensity from those I had had ever since the first day on the Somme. My daydreams were entirely taken over by expectations of my use of the carpet, but that required no supernatural influence.

At first, when I spread the carpet over the floor of the room above the print-shop, I was so exhilarated by the enjoyment of my possession that I could hardly sleep at all. Had it been summer I might have slept naked on the carpet without so much as a sheet to compromise my interaction with it, but it was the dead of winter and I had no alternative but to wear a thick nightshirt and seal myself in a sleeping-bag. It was not until the third night that I contrived to fall deeply asleep, and to immerse myself in a dream which owed nothing at all to my memories of the Somme.

I dreamed that I was a bloodstained corpse wrapped up in the carpet, whose fibers were drinking from my veins, having already imbibed the fluid that flowed from numerous knife-wounds about my torso and abdomen. Dreams will not recognize paradoxicality, so I felt nothing odd in being conscious of being dead. I was interested to observe from within the decay and dissolution of my tissues. The experience was not terrifying; indeed, it was quite calm and strangely reassuring.

"What hope can a man have," my father had once shouted at me, "if he has none of Heaven?" Even in 1910 he thought the world a vale of tears without relent.

"The hope of enlightened life," I had replied then—but the carpet taught me that even the oblivion of death is not something to be feared. It is something that lies beyond fear, in being outside time. I have not forgotten that lesson.

Perhaps the carpet had been used at one time—presumably in India—to hide and transport a murdered man. If so, it had also been used to hide a living child, for I dreamed a few nights afterward that I was wrapped around by the carpet yet again, taxed this time by tears instead of blood. There was fear a-plenty in this vision, but none of it was mine. It reminded me somewhat of the fears of my own childhood, but I was sufficiently detached from it not to enter into the experience or be subdued by its pressure. Its principal effect was to remind me how far I had left childhood behind.

My dreams became less claustrophobic thereafter, and their impressions vaguer. At times I dreamed that I was exceedingly hot, at others exceedingly cold; sometimes I felt myself so heavy as to be made of lead, sometimes so light as to be hurled giddily about by the lightest wind. I was threatened on numerous occasions by monsters lurking in the shadows, all the more horrible while they could not be clearly seen. Once I felt that all my teeth were becoming loose, crumbling and falling out. More than once I looked into a mirror and saw that my entire face was now burned, and felt the sight of my remaining eye blur and fade as its humors congealed. Once I was in a graveyard when all the graves began to open and a uniformed army of the dead struggled upward through the fertile mud.

I could understand how innocent dreamers might have found these experiences profoundly disturbing, but I was ready for them, and prepared to meet them with a level head. They were not pleasant, but they did not disturb me. They did not make me doubt my purpose. I was glad to move through them, because I knew that in so doing I was moving toward a worthwhile conclusion, and that I was helping the carpet to cleanse itself of all infection.

Things did not go quite as well by day. Mr. Priestland's two presses had been old in 1914, and they had been busy all through the war with official forms and notices. They were coming to the end of their useful life, and were suffering the consequences. Whenever one or the other broke down I contrived to repair it, but time is money to a printer and Mr. Priestland could not help becoming vexed. Typesetting was his responsibility, not mine, so the mistakes made because his hands were not as agile as they had formerly been could not possibly be laid at my door—but the fact that they were made, and work returned to be re-done, did not improve his temper at all.

"Sometimes," he told me, at the end of January, "I feel as if the war had never ended. Nothing has gone rightly since."

"You would not say that if you had been at Kimmeridge," I told him, "or anywhere else that the war's human wreckage fetched up. The world is spoiled, but it is not irredeemable. It requires time, and goodwill, but everything will be well again."

"You're 25 years old, Arthur," he told me bitterly. "You'll not say that when you're 55."

In March Mr. Priestland had to hire a boy named Tom Hurley to set the type, because his hands would not be still, but he would not replace either of the presses.

"They'll see me through to the end," he said—and so it proved, but only because the end came much more swiftly than he had anticipated.

* * *

On the fourth of April 1919 Mr. Priestland suffered a fit in the shop and had to be taken up to my room while he waited for the doctor. It was the first time he had been in there since we had cleared out all the clutter, and the first time he had seen the carpet unrolled.

"My God, Arthur!" he said, when Tom and I let him down on to the chair. "How can you live with that appalling rug? That pattern is enough to drive a man mad!"

I was surprised, for I had not merely grown accustomed to the mazy swirl but had come to feel entirely comfortable in its contemplation.

"It's beautiful," I told him. "And very, very rare."

By the time the doctor arrived he was dead. The room was full of the stink of his shit—but when the body had been taken away, and the window thrown wide open, the air was purged with remarkable rapidity.

I was anxious lest I lose my lodgings, although Tom and I kept the machines going and the work moving out—but Mr. Priestland's solicitor praised my efforts, appointed me "Manager" and told me to keep the business going as well as I possibly could, until he could find a buyer. I cannot say that it thrived under my authority, but I managed to maintain a sufficient flow of income to pay the suppliers and the boy's weekly wage—and I did not despair.

The carpet had been spoiled, according to Pemberly and Radland, but I did not become melancholy, or slothful, and I certainly did not become destructive. I did my daily work, and I did my nightly work, with all the precision I could muster.

Nor was Mr. Priestland's opinion of the carpet unchallenged, for Tom had been far more impressed with its intricacy. He began to make excuses to come up to my room in order to look at it, and set out more than once to try to trace a route through the maze with the steel-capped toe of his boot, although he always lost the track within a couple of minutes. When he asked me where it came from I told him that it was from an empire far away. He guessed that I meant India, and I was content to confirm the guess.

When Tom died of the influenza in May I could not suppress a pang of relief, because the weekly extraction of his wages had left the takings too short. I had to do the type-setting myself now, but I set about it with a will and found it not too hard, even for a man with one good eye. By the time one of the presses broke down irreparably I only had work enough to keep one going anyway, so it was by no means a disaster.

My mother died in June, also of the influenza, and I had to leave the carpet behind while I returned to Stukeley for a few days. My father's hostile attitude neither astonished nor hurt me. "Still doing the devil's work?" was his derisive greeting, but I did not take the trouble to discover whether he was making a play on words, having misunderstood the significance of a "printer's devil," or whether he was labor-ing under the misconception that I had been apprenticed to a pornographer.

When I returned to Clevedon, my dreams were haunted more by grief than any apparatus designed to produce ter-ror, but that was only natural. It is a well-known fact that grief sometimes takes odd forms, so I was not surprised that my mother did not figure in them at all. Nor, for that mat-ter, did my former employer or my little colleague. The im-agery of the dreams was far more amorphous, featuring bleak and desolate landscapes and black abyssal depths, windswept ruins and baleful swollen moons. I rarely expe-rienced any physical presence of my own in these dreams, but was present in the way that a discreet narrator is pres-ent in a story: invisible and intangible and yet all-wise. Sometimes, I felt that I was the mind of the world—not the world in which I actually lived but some other, which had already ended in any meaningful sense, all life having been annihilated upon its surface, abandoning its creator to the burden of an infinite loneliness.

By day, I was far more cheerful. I threw myself into my work even more fervently than before, taking pride in every line and every sheet. Although the print-shop had been twice as noisy when both presses were still active, it now seemed constantly abuzz with a musical clatter, whose ca-cophonous surface hid plangent cadences and apiary melodies. I always wanted to sing as I worked, and often did, although every time I caught myself doing it and stopped, I could not remember a single syllable that my throat and lips had formed.

Life was not easy, but I was content. And now that the spring was turning into summer I could discard my sleeping-bag and nightshirt at last, and stretch myself out naked on the carpet's cunning maze. The caress of its fibers on my own coarse hide was as tender as it was luxurious, as sensuous as it was welcoming.

It was on the 13th of July that Mr. Priestland's solicitor concluded the liquidation of Mr. Priestland's estate by finding a buyer for the print-shop. Unfortunately, the buyer—a Mr. Horrocks—was not a printer, and he told me as soon as he was introduced to me that the shop was to be closed immediately. He requested that I vacate the premises within a fortnight, and demanded to be shown my room so that he could see what might be made of it.

Unlike Mr. Priestland, Mr. Horrocks was immediately taken with the Kharshahar carpet. "That's an interesting item," he observed. "I presume that it's included with the fixtures."

"Of course," the solicitor said.

I protested, but in vain. The solicitor was armed with an inventory which included a carpet in my room, and a bed—for whose removal Horrocks suggested that I ought to be charged. Mr. Priestland had made no record of the originals being spoiled. Nor, of course, had I any receipt to prove that I had purchased the carpet, or even any account to offer of exactly where and when I had obtained it. I might have found witnesses to testify that I had put a carpet in store at Kimmeridge, and that I had taken it with me when I left, but that would only have led to further inquiries as to its origin.

I had no alternative but to take it away without permission, knowing that the removal would be calculated as a theft. I knew that I had to go a long way to avoid the possibility of pursuit, arrest and imprisonment, so I headed north and did not stop until I came to Cumberland.

I dared not look for work as a printer or a medical orderly, so I became a general handyman and kitchen assistant in a hotel in Keswick in return for my board and a weekly pittance. It was enough; all I wanted was a place to lay my magic carpet so that I might complete its redemption—but such was my anxiety that my dreams turned from misery to terror once again. Their hard-won amorphousness was replaced by materials of an intensely personal nature.

I dreamed that I met Pemberly, and that he stamped upon my face with his army boot, no less forcibly for the want of a fulcrum. I dreamed that I met Radland, and that he stabbed me in the guts with a carpet-knife. I dreamed that I met Priestland, and that he shit all over me and turned my flesh putrid. I dreamed that I met Horrocks, who brought policemen and bailiffs to carry out his furious orders. I dreamed that I met my mother . . . and had far rather it had been my father, even if he were leading an army of wrathful angels.

I did not know, at first, whether this was merely another phase in my redemption of the carpet or a setback in my mission. Eventually, I was forced to admit that the latter was more likely—but that only made me determined to redouble my efforts. I began to answer my phantom persecutors, not with active resistance but with calm, counsel and forgiveness, but dream-Pemberly continued to rain his impossible kicks upon me, and dream-Priestland continued to decay before my eyes, and my dream-mother wept so fearfully that . . . all of which would have been nothing but a temporary setback, I feel sure, if . . .

Everything would have worked out perfectly had I not looked into a mirror one day in September, while fully conscious and about my legitimate business, sweeping the corridor on the second floor, and realized that my face was blurred.

I had to put my nose to the glass to see the clouding that had begun to overtake my left eye. Some mysterious blight had spread from its useless counterpart.

I continued to ply my broom as best I could, but when I came to wash the dishes after dinner I broke three glasses, and had to confess to the cook that I was no longer competent to do my work.

That night, for the first and last time, I tried to trace the carpet's maze with my finger. I held to the track for three full hours, but I could not complete the course. My dreams that night were all of color, fire and glory, but when I woke in the morning I was blind to the actual world.

The hotelier wanted to be rid of me without delay, and there was only one thing I could do. I gave him leave to write to my father—who is, after all, a Christian. While I was sighted, the Vicar of Stukeley had refused even to look at me; now that I was blind, he could not refuse to take me in. Nor did he, although he would not come to fetch me.

I begged the hotelier to send my carpet with me when I set out on my journey home, and he promised faithfully to do it. Something certainly traveled with me, rolled and wrapped in an oilskin, and I am certain that I never took my hand off it, in the trap or on the train, even when I fell asleep—but I was cheated somewhere en route, more likely at the beginning than the end.

The hotelier swore, of course, that he had done exactly what I asked of him, and when my father was called upon to judge the carpet that was rolled out in my room he swore by God and all the angels that it was exactly as I described it to him—but they could not fool me. I am blind, but not an idiot.

"It's hideous, Arthur," my father said, "fit only for the company of a blind man." But he did not know what he was saying.

My father insists to this very day that the carpet on which I sleep is the one that I brought from Keswick, and that the carpet I brought from Keswick was the carpet I took to

Keswick, but I know differently. I know that the carpet which sits beneath my bed is not the same, in shape, in texture or in quality as the marvel I had been briefly privileged to own. I know that the weaver of my dreams, laboriously repaired upon the loom of my soul, has been stolen, and that all the magic of my life has been stolen within it.

There is nothing remotely tender or sensuous in the caresses of the carpet that lies beneath me now—perpetually, for I never go out anymore. There is no more luxury or promise in that coarse indifference than there is in my father's bleak resentment of my presence in the world.

My father says that he does not hate me now that I am all that is left to him, and that he has forgiven my betrayal of everything that he and God hold dear. It is not true, but I cannot care. Nor can I dream, by day or by night. There is nothing in my sleep but the moonless night of forgetfulness, and nothing in my days but an awareness of my own futility. Once, I lived in the borders of a great empire, to which I brought a kindly light. Now, I live in the margin of the world of horrid men, in which I am nothing.

I know that I could have reversed the spoliation of the Kharshahar carpet if only I had been given the chance to continue my efforts. Blindness of the sort that now afflicts me would have been no handicap. Such work is the work of a lifetime rather than a year, but it can be done; all it requires is the right man and a proper sense of purpose. I am that man, and have not the slightest hesitation in writing in the present tense. I am as sane as I ever was, as the continued ire and spite of my pious father will readily testify.

My face is spoiled, and my eyesight too, but the man who dwells within a shell of flesh is master of a realm where there is neither ugliness nor incapacity. If my soul is hurt, it is because I have lost my magic carpet and the opportunity to cure its malady. The wounds inflicted by the war could not have diminished me at all, if I were only able to weave my dreams with art and authority. In my mind's secret eye I see the truth more clearly than you could ever believe—and that truth would surely set me free, if only I could summon the empires of the carpet to my relief.

There is no longer magic in the weave of my life. I move mechanically through my sterile days. Once, I could have imagined no Hell worse than living as I now do. But I remember very vividly the days and nights when I had one good eye, and was able to tread so softly upon the gentle pile of my magic carpet. I am grateful for that memory, and I live within it as much and as best I can.

How It Ended

Darrell Schweitzer

Darrell Schweitzer lives in Philadelphia. He is the co-editor of Weird Tales, *and his principal reputation has been as a fantasy and horror writer, editor, critic, and poet. He has been a familiar figure at SF conventions since the early 1970s, as a book dealer, panelist, and huckster of his own (mainly small press) books. His nonfiction includes books on Lord Dunsany and H.P. Lovecraft, a number of non-fiction anthologies (*Discovering Classic Horror Fiction, *etc.),* On Writing Science Fiction: The Editors Strike Back *(with George Scithers and John M. Ford), and numerous interviews. He is the author of three published fantasy novels,* The White Isle, The Shattered Goddess, *and* The Mask of the Sorcerer. *He has published more than 250 stories, some of them collected in the following volumes:* We Are All Legends, Tom O'Bedlam's Night Out, Transients, Refugees from an Imaginary Country, Nightscapes, Necromancies and Netherworlds *(in collaboration with Jason Van Hollander), and* The Great World and the Small.*

"How It Ended" was published in Realms of Fantasy. *It is at heart a weird tale of supernatural discovery, perhaps in the tradition of Clark Ashton Smith's Averoigne stories. It represents medieval consciousness and attitudes well and in this regard is an interesting comparison to the Sarath story earlier in this book. An elderly knight, Jehan of Auvergne, at the end of a long and happy life, dreams that there is something wrong with the picture of his life. And there is.*

Jehan, a knight of Auvergne, who had been called the Brave in his youth after he had taken up the Cross and served in the holy wars, and now was called Jehan the Good to his face and Jehan the Placid or even Jehan the Fat behind his back, stirred awake on a winter's morning.

He sat up in bed, shivering. His breath came in white puffs. He reached over to the nightstand, broke the ice in the fingerbowl, then wiped his face.

The sharpness of the cold air on his wet face was good. It reassured him.

Yet he sat with his knees raised up under the covers, his arms locked over his knees, and he was not reassured.

"The dream again?" The Lady Asenath stirred beside him. Her gray hair had come undone and streamed all over the pillow, yet her face was still marblewhite and beautiful. It made her look, he thought, like something cast away among leaves and vines.

"It was the dream."

"Vapors of the mind. Forget it."

But he could not forget how he had dreamed of a slain knight lying in an empty field, beneath the sun and stars. All his short life this young knight had served God and the cause of righteousness, and yet now God and righteousness seemed to have tossed him aside like so much rubbish. Seasons pressed gently yet relentlessly upon him, first the dry leaves, then frost gleaming off his shattered hauberk (for he had been struck with a spear through the breast); and then snow covered all. In spring, flowers grew between his bones, birds took the last strands of his yellow hair to make their nests, and his great helm was made the habitation of worms.

Jehan dreamed these things in the night, and in the morning the dream was not quite over, lingering even as he regarded his wife sleeping beside him, as he thought of his three sons, as brave as ever he had been, all of them now gone to the Holy Land to fight for God with great distinction. The youngest, knowing he would inherit no lands, had even carved out a dukedom for himself by the Sea of Galilee, in the very homeland of Our Lord.

Should he, Jehan, not then be content?

Yet he was afraid as he regarded the age spots on his hands, as he thought how the top of his head was bald and his whole body grew gross and decrepit. These were the first touches of the grave, he knew. He thought it even as the dream did not end, but continued while he sat awake, in his memory like an echo *and the soul of the slain knight lingered, and could not rise up to Paradise nor slide into the Pit, but struggled to get free like an animal caught in a trap. It cried out in a voice that was no more than a faint breeze rustling last autumn's leaves, but a voice nonetheless, filled with sorrow and longing and bewilderment that all his courage and chivalry had brought him to this.*

Jehan looked at his spotted hands and wept softly, for something he could not put into words, a truly nameless dread.

His wife got up, wrapped herself in a robe, and came around to his side of the bed. She kissed him gently on the forehead, then tugged him by the arm.

"Come here."

He let her lead him to the window, where he stood in the bracing cold and beheld his own lands, untroubled by war and witches all these years, stretching as far as the eye could see. True, he held them in trust for a duke, who held them for the King, but for all practical purposes they were his, and he had grown fat on the profit of them.

The fields lay brown and still beneath a steel-gray sky. He could smell snow in the air. Crows soared above the stubble of last year's crop.

He saw the mill by the river, near the castle gate, and beyond, a new cathedral rising up, one tower complete, the other half-built; and houses clustered like piglets around a great sow. His wife said, "Look. This is *not* a dream."

It must have been in a dream then, still dreamed while he stood there awake, *that the slain knight heard a voice calling his name, out of the darkness on the first evening of summer. Dared he hope to awaken from the nightmare of death? Dimly, his mind came to itself. His limbs stirred. With a great heave, he stood up. Worms tumbled onto his shoulders.*

And a voice sang to him, beautiful beyond words, it seemed, and he dared further to hope that it was a voice of an angel, summoning him to Paradise. Yet he did not rise above the earth . . .

"Be thankful for what you've got," Jehan's wife said. "God has been very good to us."

"How can I be certain?"

Playfully, half-angry, she buffeted him on the temple. "Ah, you've got worms in your head. They've eaten your common sense."

Clumsily, groping, like a player impersonating his way through a play when he has completely forgotten his part, the dead youth walked, his armor rattling, mud pouring out of the joints, scraps of rusting metal trailing behind. Yet he found some semblance of strength, as bone came together unto his bone, and the mud and rotted leaves and few scraps of flesh remaining fused together in imitation of life.

He opened his eyes.

And the voice sang in his mind, as if in a dream that lingered even when he stood there awake; and the voice was not that of an angel, for there was an edge of sorrow in it, but it called him nonetheless; and he could almost make out the words.

But Jehan's wife only laughed and said, "Do me the favor of remaining alive for a while. We have work to do." She put her arms around him from behind, placed her chin on his shoulder, and nuzzled her cheek against his. "Besides, I still love you. What would I do without you?"

What indeed? Therefore he rose and dressed, called for his servants and his breakfast, and went about the business of the day, some dull matter involving rents and tenants and an inconsistency in accounts.

All the while, as he endured these things, listening to stewards complain about one another and about the burghers, and to the burghers complaining about the stewards, Jehan the Good, the Gracious, Generous, Caring, or Reasonable (called thus to his face) otherwise known as Jehan the Old, the Inert, Stingy, Bald-Head, or Sluggard realized with the force of quiet revelation that he could not be absolutely certain that he had ever awakened from his dream at all. He could just as readily be a dead man dreaming himself alive.

It was like the first piece of plaster falling from a ceiling, a tiny speck, but the beginning of the end nevertheless.

Adventures came to him. As a knight, he turned toward adventure like a plant toward the sun. A demon swooped down out of the sky, its black, swirling wings blotting out the sky like ink spilled on an illuminated page. Stars shone faintly through it, and a face like a leprous, pale moon rose and spoke to him, bidding him to lie back in his grave, to rest and be still.

"I cannot rest," said the dream-knight, for the music within his mind would not let him rest, nor had he any grave.

The blackness darkened, the stars gone. Only the moon-face remained, rising slowly above the horizon, saying, "Tarry then, and despair until my master Satan fetches thee."

Yet again a maiden's voice, sorrowing and beautiful beyond words, called the knight by his name. Therefore he did not despair, but with greater urgency drew his rusted sword and struck. The demon's blood poured down through the sky like an aurora, and the leprous face vanished.

He walked more surely now, beneath a summer sky filled with brilliant stars.

The afternoon was better. Jehan's groom brought a new stallion for him to ride. He could still do it. He still felt young in the saddle. He trotted the horse around the yard, faster and faster; and within his mind he heard that infinitely haunting song all the while; and his doubts increased, like plaster falling; and he saw *the dead knight in the worm-filled helmet, walking amid wolves, which closed around him, then drew away, disturbed, but able to dismiss him as carrion too far gone to be worth devouring.*

The earth trembled. A dragon reared up, filling the sky, its flaming breath roaring over him. Yet he divided the fires with his sword as a ship's prow divides the ocean, and the dragon fell away, and the sword was made new and strong by the heat of the flames, and the fire was the slow and gentle sunrise, and still he heard that voice within his mind.

He startled the groom by spurring the horse suddenly and riding out of the castle yard, through the gate, down the curving path past the mill, over the bridge until he drew up at the rectory behind the new cathedral and pounded on the door, while the townspeople gaped and remarked that old Jehan (whatever they called him) had not moved like that in 20 years.

In his mind, more plaster fell from the ceiling. In his mind, the earth shook. In his mind, he heard, still, that bewitching, yet not at all comforting, song he could just about make out as, in his continuing dream of memory, *he came to a town, where all fled before him in terror, but for one dirty-faced child, who spoke with the voice of prophecy, saying, "Your lady awaits." But a mounted knight waited for him in the middle of the road, beyond a ruined bridge at the edge of the town. There was no challenge. The knight lowered his spear and charged; and the dead youth in the worm-filled helm caught hold of the spear with more than human strength. He yanked the horseman out of the saddle and swung him shrieking down onto the ground, like a thresher threshing wheat; and the rider died in the roadway, his neck broken, his ghost stirring in confusion like a little whirlwind amid the dust, before it found its way either to Paradise or the Pit.*

Yet the young knight who had arisen from the dead had no such relief. He seized the terrified horse, holding it to his will. He mounted and galloped, as memories rose in his mind like bubbles from the depths of a dark pool, summoned by that song he constantly heard, beautiful, terrible, almost resolving itself into words of infinite mystery and power.

Jehan pounded on the door, which opened. He sent

novices scurrying to fetch Father Giles, a learned and holy man. He spoke to the holy man in a torrent of words, a great tempest of sputtering fears which ended over and over again in the question, "What if—? What if—"

And Father Giles took him aside, into a great hall, where massive books were kept chained to desks. He opened a volume of chronicles, pointing to the pictures and running his fingers slowly over the words as he read how Jehan the Brave, in the 18th year of his life, had put on the Cross and journeyed to the Orient, where he won great worship as a servant of Christ, riding at the side of the hero Godfrey of Bouillon into Jerusalem when the city was taken and the streets ran with blood of slaughtered pagans up to the knees of the horses, all for the glory of God. This was all written down. It was certain: the deeds of Jehan, his return, his marriage, the births and exploits of his sons.

But Jehan told how he had dreamed of a young man who took up the Cross, yes, but also carried his lady's glove beneath his surcoat, thinking on her when he should have been thinking on God; how he was killed over some trivial point of chivalry before he even got to the Holy Land and left like a heap of rubbish in a field, rotting and rusting while his soul was caught like an animal in a trap.

"These doubts are like scabs," said Father Giles. "Don't pick at them."

Yet Jehan felt the cold earth upon his face. He felt the wind and the leaves and the frost upon his bones. Nervously, irritatedly, he brushed his shoulders.

He fled from Father Giles and leaped onto his horse, riding back up the long, curving road to the castle in the evening twilight—for the day had somehow fled all too fast—and he felt the stones become an avalanche in his mind, the plaster gone now, the edifice of his life and sanity collapsing. He saw a dragon rearing up behind the castle. He saw the leprous moon above the towers, calling out his name; and the stars were blotted out as if ink had been spilled over them. He reared up his horse and called out a challenge, yet no one answered him, save for that singing voice he still heard within his mind, beautiful, shrill, bewitching, horrible, telling him in words he almost entirely understood now, that at long last he had *awakened*, that what he had thought to be real life was a dream and his dream was reality.

He trembled. He wept. Like a player who has forgotten all his lines and has to pretend, fooling no one, he dismounted and entered the great hall of the castle.

There a dirty-faced servant child stood before him and spoke with the voice of prophecy.

"The Lady Asenath awaits you."

Now he heard the music of his dream clearly, and he understood the words without any doubt. When he confronted his wife, her eyes widened, and she *knew* that he knew and with a long, despairing wail, she fled from him.

And the dead knight, returning home from the wars, greeted the Lady Asenath whom he still loved, and he removed his great helm, scattering worms. She screamed and screamed. And her scream became a kind of music, the echo of it a song just at the edge of understanding; and she did not sing alone, but joined her voice with another, one who cried out in anger and pain and the despair of utterly lost hopes.

There was, in this castle, a certain room Jehan was not allowed to enter, far below in the vaults, a room kept barred with heavy bars, chained and locked, blocked with stones, forgotten in the darkness and damp. It had been Asenath's castle before it was his. Her father had died without a male heir, and he gained the place through marriage, having proven his worth in the wars of the Cross. But he married and gained the castle on the single condition that he never go down into that vault, unbar that door, or discover the secret of that room.

At the time he had laughed about it. "I don't have to know everything," he'd said. "Just let it stay where it is and I will stay where I am, and all will be well."

And his bride Asenath, who loved him, laughed and agreed.

But now she turned from her flight and followed after

him. She shrieked and clung to him, and fell to her knees, begging that he remember his promise, that he just leave things alone and let all go on as before.

"If you love me—" she cried. "If you love me—"

He did love her, still, but he could not stop. It was too late. He had awakened. The singing voice inside his mind revealed all. Outside that barred door, he heard that voice, not in his mind but with his ears, like any other sound.

His wife shrieked and no servant dared stop him as he hurled away the stones. He had but to touch the door and the heavy bars, the locks, and chains all fell away like dust. The door swung open, and there within, revealed by some unnatural light of vision, was a harp set upon a stone coffin. The harp was made of human bones and strung with golden hair. It played itself and sang with the voice he had heard all these years in his dreams. And as he looked there rose up from out of the stone coffin the ghost of a maiden who sang and played upon the harp now, where before it had played alone.

Jehan turned to Asenath and demanded in astonishment, though he already knew the answer from his dreams, "What is this?"

She fell to her knees, sobbing, and said only, "I did it all because I loved you."

He listened as she told how she had drowned her own sister, Eleanor, down by the mill.

"But you didn't have a sister."

"You could not remember her, for she was not part of the new thing I made by—"

"By what?"

"By witchcraft." And Asenath told him how her younger sister foolishly loved Jehan the Brave also, though he was betrothed to the elder. When word came back that Jehan was killed in a duel, and the younger dared mock the elder, all else followed: the murder; the frenzy of the younger sister's absurd, twisted love, her anger, and pain bound into the harp by Asenath's great magic; the harp commanded by Asenath to call Jehan back, to alter the very course of time and turn their lives in another direction.

"This was surely a great sin," said Jehan. He drew his sword and struck a blow, smashing the singing harp. In profound silence, the spirit of the murdered Eleanor drifted up. It gazed upon Asenath in terrible reproach, but only for an instant. Then that gaze turned to things beyond the living world, and the spirit passed through the stone ceiling and was gone.

In silence, Jehan beheld his wife, on her knees before him, her face wet with tears.

"It was for nothing," she said softly.

In the final instant of the dream, Asenath recovered her composure. She stopped screaming and spoke calmly, saying, "Welcome husband. I have waited long for your return." And trembling, she accepted his embrace.

Old Jehan knelt down and raised her up. He realized that he should be angry. He should condemn. Yet he could not.

He got out her glove from beneath his clothing, where he'd always kept it as a love-token, and pressed it to his face as if it were the sweetest smelling of roses.

A worm fell onto his shoulder, and another.

She looked at him, wide eyes brimming with tears, but silent.

"I cannot judge," he said at last. "I can only say that these things are for God and that from God you should seek forgiveness, not from me. A true knight must defend and succor his lady always, or else he is not a knight." He took her by the hand and said in a low voice, "Hurry, I don't think we have much time."

He led her upstairs into the great hall. He commanded that a feast be set and that all make merry. But he and his wife took their supper in their own chamber while the household celebrated, uncertain what was being celebrated.

He ate little, gazing into her face all the evening. Once a worm fell into his wine cup. Discreetly, he spilled it out.

While he still had the strength (which was failing fast), he led her to their bed and lifted her onto it. He lay beside her. They did not touch, but merely lay there, on their last night together, speaking of the love of two young people who lived long ago. Was it not expected, he put to her, something you read in the chronicles anyway, that a knight's love for his lady should transcend all things, even morality? Did it not follow, she rejoined, that hers should do likewise?

He supposed that it should. "Let God sort it out."

Later, he held her hand in his, though his hand was no more than bone and a few scraps of flesh and old leaves. He was afraid. He asked her to comfort him, to tell him that yes, somehow, they really did have three brave sons, that such sons would be possible, born out of illusion, begotten by a corpse, and still be living sons.

"Let God sort it out," she said. "I think so."

"Truly ours is the greatest romance in all the annals of chivalry," he said.

"I think so."

"I love you," he said, but he did not say, *more than God*, nor did she say it.

And so it ended.

In the morning, then, the servants found her kneeling by her bed, weeping before some old bones which had somehow come to be there. This was a great prodigy, they knew. Father Giles was sent for. Asenath confessed to him, and gave over all her riches and lands to her sons. She put on the veil, spending the rest of her brief life as a penitent, beseeching the forgiveness of God, and of Jehan, and of her sister Eleanor.

But that same morning, just before dawn, Jehan saw the leprous, devil-faced moon crumble into sparks and shooting stars. He saw the sun rise. His soul broke free, like an animal out of a trap, knowing that the quest of his life was complete, that his knightly task had been nothing less than to draw Lady Asenath back from the brink of the Pit.

He had done it, by the grace of God, and he gave thanks. His soul leaped up. The angels caught hold of him.

Cecil Rhodes in Hell

Michael Swanwick

Michael Swanwick [www.michaelswanwick.com], as we said in the note to his story earlier in this book, has been publishing a very large number of short short stories since 2001. In 2002, he continued a series of fantasy and SF pieces appearing online at SciFiction.com, Michael Swanwick's Periodic Table of Science Fiction, short-shorts inspired by the periodic table of the elements. Element 45 on the table is Rhodium, and this story features the imperialist Cecil Rhodes, for whom the country Rhodesia was named.

"Cecil Rhodes in Hell" is a moral revenge fantasy, an incendiary political satire that runs up to you, lights a fire to your tie, and disappears. If you choose to relate it to contemporary politics, it still has the moral force of a particularly brutal fairy tale. This is perhaps its first appearance in print.

Cecil Rhodes is remembered today as a statesman, an industrialist, and a leader of men. If you're white, that is. The inhabitants of the lands he seized and exploited remember him differently.

Cecil John Rhodes was 17 when he arrived in South Africa. By age 25, he was a millionaire, a founder of the De Beers diamond company, and the beneficiary of myriad sharp dealings with local farmers.

But his goal was not wealth. He was an imperialist. He wanted to make all of Africa—and the former American colonies too, if possible—part of the British Empire. In 1888, he met with Lobengula, a leader of the Ndebele, and through deceit and deliberate mistranslation got him to agree to British mining and colonization of lands between the Limpopo and Zambezi rivers. The land grab was on! Rhodes and his private army marched northwards, making their own laws and declaring their own government. By 1895, Lobengula was dead, the Ndebele were a defeated people, forced labor was a commonplace, and the country was known as "Rhodesia."

In 1902, at age 49, Rhodes died. At his request, he was buried atop a mountain near his estates that he neither knew nor cared was sacred ground to the Ndebele. For his sins, he went directly to Hell.

As a matter of policy, the denizens of Hell are normally kept ignorant of all events on Earth. There are always exceptions, however. Years after his death, a panel of historians met in solemn deliberation and decided that in terms of brutality and sheer mindless savagery, Rhodes was the second worst tyrant that Europe had ever imposed upon Africa. The first, of course, being King Leopold II of Belgium.

The Devil heard the news and gleefully told his imps to cease their tortures long enough to pass it along.

When Rhodes heard that he had only placed second, his agony was redoubled.

435

Hide and Seek

~~~~~

Nicholas Royle

Nicholas Royle lives in London. He is the author of four novels—Counterparts, Saxophone Dreams, The Matter of the Heart, *and* The Director's Cut—*in addition to more than 100 short stories, which have appeared in a variety of anthologies and magazines. He has edited eleven anthologies including* A Book of Two Halves *(Phoenix),* The Tiger Garden: A Book of Writers' Dreams *(Serpent's Tail),* The Time Out Book of New York Short Stories *(Penguin), and* The Ex Files: New Stories About Old Flames *(Quartet). Characteristically, his stories are horror.*

It was a way to pass the time and keep the kids happy. Kids. When I was a kid myself I didn't like the word. I didn't like being referred to as one of 'the kids.' It seemed unrespectful, dismissive. I preferred to be one of 'the children.' When my own kids were born, I consequently referred to them always as 'the children,' never 'the kids.' In fact, to qualify that, it was when the first one was born that I stuck religiously to that rule, which lasted until just after the second one came along. The second and final one, I might add. Nothing I've ever done in my life drains the energy quite like having kids. Don't get me wrong: I wouldn't go back. I wouldn't unhave them. My life has been enriched—immeasurably. Practically anyone who's had kids will tell you the same. Apart from the abusers, the loveless, the miserable. So no, I wouldn't go back, but nor would I have any more. I'm shattered as it is; plus, how could I love another one as much as I adore the two I've got? Mind you, I thought that after the birth of the first one.

Harry, our firstborn, is a handful, as naughty as he is adorable. Good as an angel one minute, absolute horror the next. Would I have him any other way? The standard answer is no. I wouldn't want him any different. The standard answer sucks, however. Doesn't take a genius to work that one out. Sure I'd have him different. I'd have him good all the time. It would make life easier, that's all. However, he's lovable the way he is and if making him any less naughty made him any less lovable, then, no, I wouldn't have him any different.

He's funny. He makes faces and strikes poses I wouldn't have thought a four-year-old capable of. He's a mimic in the making. I love him like—well, there is no like. I love him more than anything or anyone I've ever loved. Before his sister came long. Now I love her the same way I love him.

I'm nuts about her. If our relationship is less developed, less complex than the relationship I have with Harry, that's only because he's got two years' head start. Our dialogue is less sophisticated, but we still talk. In fact she's talking more and more all the time. For months, while other two-year-olds were chattering away, Sophie remained silent. She'd point and she'd cry, but she didn't have much vocab. Then it started to come in a rush. Now she knows words I didn't know she knew. Every day she surprises me with another one. The longest sentence she can speak gets longer every day. She's also the most beautiful little girl you've ever seen (takes after her mum—my wife—Sally), but then they all say that.

Sometimes when I'm out with the two of them somewhere I forget that while Harry's walking beside me and holding my hand, Sophie's sitting on my shoulders, and I briefly slip into a dizzying panic. Where is she? Where have I left her? Will I ever see her again? Sure you will, she's on your shoulders, you dummy. It's like forgetting you're wearing your glasses. Don't tell me you've never done that: searched for your glasses for a good quarter of an hour, only to realize eventually they're stuck on the front of your head.

But those moments, those moments when I forget she's there and I don't know where she is, they remind me of when Harry was little. I mean really little, three months or so. When having a baby was still a novelty, when you turned round and saw him lying in his Moses basket and gave a little start because you'd forgotten, you'd forgotten you'd got a kid—or a child.

I had this fear that one day I'd look in the Moses basket and he wouldn't be there. Not that he could climb or roll out of it, he couldn't, but that he just wouldn't be there. That somehow I would have reverted to that pre-parental state. Gone backwards at speed. One minute I had a child, the next minute I didn't. It didn't make any sense, of course, but a lot of stuff goes through your head in those early months that doesn't make any sense.

I was looking after both the kids. Sally was working late, attending a meeting. Harry kept going on about Agnes, one of his little friends. He wanted her to come round. Or to go round to hers. We couldn't do that, I explained, because Agnes's parents had invited us round to theirs the other day. You have to be invited, I explained to him. You can't invite yourself.

Agnes's parents were our closest friends and they lived just two streets away. To stop Harry going on about it, I called them to invite them over. It turned out Agnes's mum, Siobhan, was at the same meeting Sally was at. They worked in the same field. So Agnes's dad, William, was looking after Agnes on his own. Looks like the tables have been turned, he joked. Our wives are out at work and we're left holding the babies.

Then he explained he was trying to finish some work of his own and needed to make the most of Siobhan's being out at the meeting. He was going to try to get Agnes into bed early. Instead, I offered to look after Agnes while he got on with his work. I'll bring her back after an hour or so, I said. Are you sure? He asked. No problem, I said. She's a very easy child.

William dropped Agnes round and she ran into the house, all excited at spending time with Harry and Sophie. William called after her, hoping for a goodbye kiss or hug before he went back home, but she was gone. I saw his crestfallen face, knew how he felt, but knew also that he'd be feeling relieved to have offloaded Agnes for a bit, so he'd be able to get some work done, or just have a break. I locked the door after him: my kids knew about not leaving the house unattended, and no doubt Agnes did too, but it didn't pay to be careless. So there I was now with three of them to keep happy at least until Sally got home. No problem, I'd said to William. No problem, I thought to myself. I loved Agnes almost like my own. Almost. There's always that almost. The love you have for your own kids is different. It's instinctive, fiercely protective. With someone else's kids it's less visceral, more of an affectionate responsibility.

Let's play hide and seek, I suggested. Yes! they all shouted, jumping up and down. Hide and seek. Hide and seek.

Who wants to hide first? I asked. Me! they chorused.

When Harry first started playing hide and seek, when he was two and a half, perhaps, or three, he'd tell you where he was going to hide. I'm going to hide under the bed, he'd say, and you'd try to explain why that wasn't really going to work. Later he would just close his eyes, believing that if he closed his eyes, not only could he not see you, but you couldn't see him either. Eventually he got the hang of it and became quite proficient at the game. He got so that you genuinely couldn't find him for two or three minutes. It was pretty much the only time, apart from when he was asleep, that you could get him to keep still and quiet for more than ten seconds. For this reason we encouraged the playing of hide and seek.

Sophie was still only learning, like Harry had been at her age. And Agnes—well, I was about to find out how good Agnes was at hide and seek.

Who's going to hide first? I asked, as if I didn't know. All three shouted 'Me!' and put their hands up, but I knew from experience that if it wasn't Harry, then it wasn't going to work. He'd go into a sulk, wouldn't play properly and everything would start to fall apart. OK, Harry first, I said, raising my arms and my voice to forestall protest. The rest of us count to ten.

Twenty, he shouted as he bounded up the stairs.

I counted loudly enough to drown out his retreat and the girls joined in. Sophie was jumping up and down with excitement. She had just learned how to jump and liked to do it as much as possible whenever there was a situation that seemed to call for it. Twenty, we concluded at the tops of our voices. Coming ready or not. Dead silence from the rest of the house. That's my boy.

Shall we look in the kitchen first, I suggested, in case he managed to sneak past us while we had our eyes shut?

The girls both nodded and I led the way into the kitchen,

which smelled of onions and fried minced lamb. Still steaming on the hob was the big pan of chilli I'd made earlier for Sally and me to enjoy in front of the TV when the kids were in bed. The fridge door was a collage of art postcards, Bob the Builder yogurt magnets and photo booth pictures of me and Sally with the kids. Over in the corner, a stereo was playing Porcupine Tree's *Lightbulb Sun* album for about the twenty-third time that day.

No sign of him here, I said. Shall we look in the dining room?

The knocked-through dining room and lounge looked like it usually did when both kids had been home for more than half an hour. Like a cyclone had ripped through the boxes, crates and cupboards filled with toys. A riot of Thomas the Tank Engine, Buzz Lightyear and Woody, Teletubbies and Barbie. Scott Tracey and Lady Penelope masks. Bob the Builder construction vehicles. Britains models and Matchbox Super-fast cars (handed down from father to son). Teddy bears, rag dolls and dozens of assorted soft toys. Full marks to the kids for having out-Chapmanned the Chapman Brothers, who would have been proud of the maelstrom of miscegenation and mutilation.

No sign of him here either, I said, checking under the coffee table and behind the settee. Shall we look upstairs?

Yes!

Upstairs we looked in Sophie's room. We'd recently taken the side off her cot. As a result she could get out of bed and wander in the night, which was marginally preferable to one of us having to go to her if she started crying. Let her come to us instead.

Harry wasn't in Sophie's room.

Sophie and Agnes had already checked out the bathroom. Next was Harry's room. Harry had recently become keen on coloring in and cutting out and sticking down. His masterpieces covered every available inch of wall space. On the floor was a little pile of jagged scraps of paper from his most recent session with the kiddie-proof scissors. I quickly looked under his bed, but could only see his plastic Ikea toy crate-on-castors that I knew was full of dressing-up gear, Batman costumes, old scarves and so on. He wasn't in the walk-in cupboard or the walnut wardrobe.

By now the girls were shouting his name, enjoying the fact that we couldn't find him. We had a quick but thorough look in mine and Sally's bedroom, but he wasn't in there either, so he had to be upstairs again. The top floor held my office, another bathroom and the spare bedroom. As soon as we'd looked in all three I began seriously to wonder where he might be. It occurred to me that, although I couldn't imagine how he might have done it, there was the tiniest of possibilities that he could have slipped past us while we were in his room and nipped downstairs. So I ran downstairs and rechecked every possible hiding place. It didn't take long; I knew where they all were by now. I made my way back upstairs like a cop with a search warrant, clearing rooms as I went, mentally chalking a cross on the door, one stroke on the way in, another as I left. Back at the top of the house, I finally admitted to myself that I was anxious.

Harry was good at hide and seek, but not this good. How was it possible, in a house I knew so well, for him to vanish so completely? I forced myself to be calm and to stick to a methodological approach. He couldn't have left the house—the front and back doors were locked, as were the windows. The door to the cellar was kept bolted. The door leading to the crawlspace that was all that was left of the loft after its conversion was not locked, but it was inaccessible behind the ratty old settee in my office and neither of our children had ever shown the slightest interest in it. I looked down at Sophie and Agnes. Their eyes were wide with excitement. Sophie was jumping up and down, shouting Harry's name.

Follow me, I said, something having made me think of triple-checking his favorite hiding place. In Harry's bedroom I got down on all fours and pulled out the plastic toy crate from under his bed. There he was, in the far corner, still as a statue, scarcely breathing. His eyes met mine and he started to smile.

He crawled out and I hugged him so tightly he protested that it hurt.

I'd lost my appetite for hide and seek, but naturally the kids hadn't and Sophie was insisting on hiding next. I knew if I stopped the game there'd be trouble, so we counted to twenty while she toddled off. It took us less than another twenty seconds to find her, a telltale giggling lump under the duvet in mine and Sally's bed.

In fairness, I now had to let Agnes go off and hide despite overwhelming tiredness on my part and a growing desire to head back downstairs, open a beer and listen to the news on the radio while allowing the kids to veg out in front of Cartoon Network. I couldn't expect either William or Sally for another fifteen minutes.

. . . eighteen, nineteen, *twenty*!

The first place Harry looked was under his own bed. I think we might have heard if she'd hidden in here, I suggested, but in fact we hadn't heard anything at all. She'd managed to slip out and hide without leaving us any clues.

Let's look in Mummy and Daddy's room, Harry urged.

Sophie instantly copied what he'd said in her more condensed delivery, in which all the words ran together and could only be decoded by remembering what had been said before.

Agnes wasn't in Mummy and Daddy's room. The three of us climbed the stairs again to the top floor. Spare bedroom, bathroom, my office—all clear. Back down to the first floor. Bathroom, Sophie's room—both empty. We trooped downstairs, Harry running on ahead, wanting to be the one to find Agnes. There was no sign of her in the lounge, dining room or kitchen. Back in the hall, I noticed her shoes at the bottom of the stairs. She'd taken them off just after coming into the house.

I checked the locks on the doors and windows, then we ran back up to the first floor. I looked under each of the beds, behind all the curtains, in every cupboard. I added my voice to those of Harry and Sophie. I shouted that her Dad was due to collect her and he'd want to get straight back. It was time to come out. She'd won. (*No, I won!* Harry protested.) Come on, come on out, Agnes!

I ran up to the top floor without waiting for Harry and

Sophie. I shoved the settee in the office out of the way and yanked open the door to the crawlspace, shining a light inside. Fishing tackle, rolled-up film posters, Christmas decorations, stacks of used padded envelopes, suitcases full of old clothes I couldn't bear to throw away—but no little girl, no Agnes. I looked under my desk, behind the oversize books on the bottom shelves of the bookcases, in the corner between the radio and the radiator. Running back out of my office I collided with Sophie on her way in. She fell over and started crying, but I ran on, into the spare bedroom. I ripped the sheets off the bed, hauled the TV away from the wall. In the adjoining bathroom I tore aside the shower curtain.

As I took the stairs three at a time back down to the next floor I could hear that both children were crying now. In our bedroom I emptied the laundry basket, fought my way through the dresses in Sally's wardrobe. I made myself stop and stare into the room's reflection in the full-length mirror in case that revealed any hidden detail I had somehow otherwise missed. I ran into Sophie's room and climbed up onto a chair to open the door to the linen cupboard.

I had checked everywhere, every possible hiding place, and she wasn't to be found. She'd gone.

The door bell rang. Sophie's room was just at the top of the stairs, so I could see right down to the front door. Through the frosted glass I could see that it wasn't Sally. Anyway, she would have used her keys. It was William.

Death in Love

R. Garcia y Robertson

R. Garcia y Robertson lives in Mt. Vernon, Washington. His novels to date include The Spiral Dance *(1991),* The Virgin and the Dinosaur *(1996),* Atlantis Found *(1997),* American Woman *(1998),* Knight Errant *(2001), and* Lady Robyn *(2003). His stories have appeared in* F&SF *and* Asimov's *with some regularity for the last fifteen years and are characterized by their broad range of concerns, stylistic sophistication, and attention to historical detail. Garcia has tended toward time travel or historical settings for both his fantasy and SF stories. Some of these stories are collected in* The Moon Maid and Other Fantastic Adventures *(1998). Another collection is overdue. In recent years, he has published several stories set in the fantasy world of Markovy, which is something like Russia and Eastern Europe in the late middle ages, except of course that magic works, the supernatural beings of mythology inhabit the landscape, and there's always a lot happening.*

"Death in Love" is from F&SF, *and is one of two fine Markovy stories published there in 2002. It is an interesting contrast to the Kritzer story earlier in the book, which borrows from some of the same traditions.*

Eros grimaced, as cute as only the God of Love can be, his gloved hand hovering over a glass box full of hissing adders. "M'Lady knows how I hate being a hero."

Lady Kore nodded, all too aware of her page's limitations. Eros might be a demi-god, but he was young, flighty, and male, never pretending to be brave, or strong, or the least trustworthy. True godhead lay beyond his grasp. Still, he had his uses, and he was family—Kore's first cousin. "No one expects heroics from you," she assured him. "Just stand alongside me looking sweet."

Eros brightened visibly. "Or better yet, behind you?"

"As you wish." She smiled at the idea of this strapping blond demi-god, trying to find cover behind her tiny body. Lady Death was small, even for a woman. "Now I need another snake," she told him. "A big one."

He hesitated, his gloved hand inches above the snakes, whose bright green scales gleamed like polished jade beads in the sunlit air. Perched atop Seagate's second-highest tower, the white marble serpentarium had tall glass windows overlooking the sparkling green Sound with its purple islands fading one into the other. Black ships rode at anchor below, their masts rising like a thick pine forest on the sea. "You could do this so much easier," Eros complained.

"True," Kore admitted. She had grown up handling poisonous snakes, and at twelve she could lie still and naked in a bed of vipers, or kiss the nose of a striking cobra—yet her handsome cousin-german had to get over his fear. "But handling snakes is good for you," she pointed out.

"How so?" Sweat beaded on his cutely knit brow.

"Snakes teach still attention," she explained. "And instant reaction, both qualities we shall shortly need. It would be better if you took off your gloves."

Eros grimaced again. "You said that I need only look sweet," he reminded her. Drawing a deep breath, he snatched at the box.

His hand came out holding an adder just behind the head. Staring in queasy arm's-length fascination, he brought the twisting snake slowly over to her, its tail lashing his mailed sleeve. With enemies at the gate, even Love wore armor. "Will this one do, pretty cousin?"

"Perfect." Saying a swift protection spell, she reached past the fangs, taking the venomous snake in her bare hand. Shining brown-green scales felt cool and familiar between her fingers. Like most witches Lady Kore was left-handed, and her white sacrificial gown buttoned tightly from wrist to elbow with carved child-bone studs. Loose sleeves led to horrible mistakes. She carried the struggling snake to the milking table, intoning a sonorous chant adders found soothing. Spring sunlight streamed onto the tabletop, reflecting off a venom cup standing amid vials, powders, and potion rings. A flat throwing knife in a tooled leather scabbard lay at the end of a short strap, looking like a doll's sword and belt. Alongside it sat an apple.

Holding up the snake, she spoke softly to the blunt hideous face, "I am sorry to scare you. We mean no harm, but we need your power, some of your innocent deadliness. I will try to do good with it."

Beady eyes glared back at her, not at all mollified. Too bad. Kore knew how the snake felt, boxed in by enemies and beset for no reason. Black ships dotted the Sound below—many more than were welcome—and Seagate was besieged by men Kore did nothing to harm. Sea Beggars had descended on the Narrows, spreading woe in their wake. Kore knew the tall carrack in command, the *Mermaid*, infamous from here to the Far Isles. Two smaller carracks, *Nymph* and *Tempest*, watched over the seaward approaches to the Narrows. Row barges, barques, and light galleys led by the galeass *Scorpion* had cut Seagate off from the Sound. Any of these vessels would have been unwelcome; taken together they were a catastrophe. The Sea Beggars had captured the docks and water gate, and breached the outer bailey. An attack on the inner ward had just been turned back—leaving Kore no time to get this snake's permission.

Hooking the adder's long fangs over the lip of the venom cup, she milked the poison glands with her fingertips. Twin gleaming threads of amber venom ran into the cup. Eros shuddered. "Moments like this make me glad I am a man."

"Playing with snakes and poisons does not appeal to you?"

"Not the least."

"Come, you've been in battle. That cannot be much better. What is it like to stand in the front rank, thrusting your boarding pike at some hulking wild-eyed berserk trying to slash you in half?"

"That is when I wish I was a woman," he replied primly.

At least Love did not lie. When she had enough venom, she handed the adder back to Eros. "Here, find him a rat. But carefully, he still has plenty of bite."

Eros took the serpent gingerly, fairly radiating caution. By the time he returned she had refilled her pearl venom ring, and had the viper's tongue in her hand. Touching the steel tip into the venom, she drew back on the stopper, watching as the amber liquid disappeared into the hollow steel shaft. When she had drained the cup, she picked up a pinch of cork and stuck it onto the needle sharp point, careful not to prick herself. Latching the silver stopper, she slid the viper's tongue under the crescent-moon comb in her hair.

Wiping the cup out with her finger, she touched it to her own tongue, feeling the tingle of fresh venom. As Demi-Goddess of Death, she had venom in her blood, given to her in small doses ever since she was a child. She held her finger out to Eros. "Here, try some. It numbs the tongue."

Eros shivered at the suggestion. "I will take M'Lady's word."

She laughed, slipping potion rings onto her fingers. "Come, the Sea Beggars are waiting. You will shortly wish you were back juggling adders. Blindfolded."

Her page bowed. "Without a doubt." Eros never deigned to hide his concern. Lady Kore liked that, hoping to tap that well-honed sense of self-preservation. Taking the flat throwing knife and scabbard from the table, she lifted her white sacrificial skirt, strapping the knife to her thigh. Eros looked on in grim amusement, "Does M'Lady need a hand?"

She smiled at the compliment. Cousin Eros could keep his hands to himself. Cousin or not, he was still a man, young, good-looking, and the God of Love, and from what her serving women said, very athletic in bed. But Kore had long ago given up playing under the blankets with boy cousins. Female descent and male ambition led naturally to ritual incest. Cousins married cousins, and sisters slept with brothers to keep family keeps and castles from passing to strangers. Eros had no sisters to seduce. If he wanted to claim any of the family holdings he must marry one of his cousins—preferably Kore, or her little sister Persephone. Or face being a homeless deity. Having no sisters meant all his mother's holdings, even the castle Eros was raised in, would one day come to Kore, something Eros never forgot.

Standing up, she let her skirt fall back down to her ankles. Stretching out her arms and fingers, she could feel the knife on her thigh, the rings on her fingers, and the silver viper's tongue in her hair. There was even a spring-loaded blade in her left boot. She shivered. Being decked from head to foot with blades and potions was not a pleasant sensation, but she was the Demi-Goddess of Death, Dark Daughter to the Goddess-on-Earth. Her own mortality was always before her, and she accepted her death, hoping only to have a daughter one day to raise in her place. Now she must go down to the breach to parley with the besiegers, where she could not count on chivalry to protect her, not from Sea Beggars. Witches were beyond the pale. No promise made to witches need be kept. No flags of truce need be honored. If the Sea Beggars seized her, they could sell her to some local landgraf for burning. Or throw her into the Sound with an anchor stone tied to her ankles. And no one could lift a hand to save her, not even dear cousin Eros, who found her so pretty.

So Kore must see to her own safety. She took the apple off the table, slipping it into a secret pocket, and saying to Eros, "Order the bowmen to hold their fire. Then meet me at the gate." Bowing obediently, he opened the big bronze door for her. Serving women waited outside the serpentarium, ready to help her into the stiff cloth-of-gold surcoat that fitted over her white gown. Kore's personal arms were embroidered on the front—on a field gules, a vulture sable vorant a child—a black vulture on a red field devouring a child. Too gaudy for ordinary wear, but perfect for greeting barbarians at the gate.

Standing still, she let them dress her, knowing she was their hope and protection, the Dark Daughter that women turned to in the face of death. Word went swiftly through a keep full of women; everyone knew who came and went, what plans were made, what omens were told—while constantly recasting their personal horoscopes. Right now all fortunes looked bleak. Already these women were virtual prisoners. As they worked, she touched each in turn, drawing their fear into her dark core. Some were much older than she, others heartbreakingly young; all were scared. If Sea Beggars sacked the keep, any woman who survived would see her life get worse—far worse. To emphasize that point besiegers used women and children hostages in the last attack, driving them forward at spear point as human shields. It had not worked, but it showed what to expect.

Yet their fear came from clinging to life, while she had given herself over to death, putting her in cool command. "Dinner must be served at the usual time," she reminded them, "not a jot later—unless you hear from me. Understand? And no heavy cooked dishes. Cold meats. Smoked ham. Fish and cheeses, served with figs, apples, scones and salted butter. Is there any fresh herring to be had?"

They shook their heads. "The herring fleet never arrived." And was not likely to.

"Salt fish will have to do. And beer. Cold beer from the cistern, in big buckets."

They grinned at that.

"That's good. Be brave, bring beer, and all will be well.

Dead or alive." They laughed at that too. No one could serve Death daily without developing a sense of humor. Liveried guards in her vulture crest saluted as she descended the spiral stairs and crossed the inner drawbridge leading to the gate. Eros met her at the outer portcullis, with a white satin sheet tied to a herald's gold staff. Heralds were sacrosanct, but Kore saw he still had mail under his ermine and velvet surcoat, and doubtless a folding crossbow up his flowing sleeve. Having no scruples himself, Eros lacked faith in others. She asked, "Did you warn the archer?"

"I told him to cover us. And if anyone fires at the wrong time, I promised to strangle him with his own bowstring."

"I suppose that must do." She waited for the portcullis to rise. This inner gate was a miracle of military engineering, built around an inner drawbridge, with a portcullis at either end, and openings above allowing all manner of noxious substances to be poured over intruders. Narrow arrow slits with round firing ports at their bases covered her from three sides—soldiers had an amusing name for these deadly stone slits—one referring to female anatomy. Though she learned it as a girl, no one now dared use it to her face.

When the portcullis clanged to a stop overhead, Eros stuck his white flag out the gate, waved it energetically, then made an after-you motion. "Lead on, M'Lady."

Even people who hated and despised her thought it must be fine to be Dark Daughter to the Goddess-on-Earth, Demi-Goddess of Death, Lady of Seagate, heiress to castles and keeps. And a witch as well. Perhaps it was, though Kore had nothing to judge it by, since this was the life she was given. Now she must prove her worth—be Death incarnate, or share the fate of any hapless serf girl stoned for having the evil eye. Or for playing with snakes.

She stepped out onto the stone flags of the inner ward, a flat triangle jutting from the base of the keep. Towering clouds topped the peaks to the west, and sunlight shone on the water around her. Eros followed her out, dutifully waving his flag. Seagate stood atop a rock spur ringed by water, separating the Narrows into two channels—called the Gullet and the Windpipe. Stone bridges connected Seagate's inner ward to the adjacent headlands, but the main entrance was the water gate at the base of the rock, now in the hands of Sea Beggars. No ship could now pass the Narrows, nor approach the keep. Nor was there a friendly fleet big enough to break through to Seagate.

Women and children cowered against the outer parapet, huddled just below the wall walk, staring wide-eyed at her, Death herself walking their way. These were the hostages the Sea Beggars had driven before them. Kore signed for the women to keep down. First task was to somehow get these innocents inside the keep—but a general rush for safety would only provoke a massacre. Sea Beggars crouched just behind the battlements in the outer ward—crossbows cocked, heads hidden, but still hoping the hostages would block up the keep's elaborate gate defenses.

"Not a promising picture," Eros concluded. Kore nodded, seeing the open ward littered with bodies, surrounded by spent arrows and catapult balls. The body closest to her stirred, breathing, but unable to get up. Kore went down on one knee beside a Sea Beggar in a bright blue brigandine jacket studded with nailheads. A melon-sized catapult ball had crushed his leg; he also had a crossbow bolt in his boot and a couple of arrows in his armored jacket—but those hardly counted. She doubted he even felt them.

"Does it hurt?" she asked.

The bearded pirate winced. "Like fire, M'Lady."

"This will help." She told Eros, "Get out your horn and cup." Her herald produced a drinking horn, pouring water into the shallow cup that served as a cap. Opening a potion ring, she mixed in sleeping powder, then gave it to the man. He immediately downed the potion—a wound like his produced a powerful thirst. Then he sank back, breathing softly. Sea Beggars did not flinch at being tended by a witch, happily taking whatever you had to offer—and more.

She went from body to body, saying a prayer each time. All the other Sea Beggars were beyond help, save for a beautiful blonde boy with a big javelin clear through him. Hitting too low to kill outright, the iron spear tore through the boy's intestine, severed his spine and spilled buckets of

blood—doing everything but killing him. That was left to
Kore. Soothing the boy, she told Eros to give him water,
then she drew the viper's tongue out of her hair, slipping off
the cork. This was her most feared aspect, though it was
merely the dark side of healing. Seeing him taste the water,
she slid the needle into his neck, saying a prayer and pressing the stopper. She held his head, singing softly until he
was dead. Mother-Lover-Destroyer, with him until the end.

Women and children huddled below the wall walk,
watching Death work up close. None of them were
wounded. Horrified and frightened for sure, but not physi-
cally harmed—so far. Archers atop the keep knew their
business, shooting over the heads of the hostages, neatly
dropping everything from crossbow bolts to catapult balls
onto the Sea Beggars behind them, who now crouched behind makeshift barricades studded with arrows.

She slid the viper's tongue back into her comb, having
done what she could for the dead and wounded, turning
her attention to the live and whole—a much harder task.
Head-sized stones landing on a man's leg made him much
more manageable, piteously glad for a woman's touch.
Hale and hearty Sea Beggars holding the outer ward were
not so easy to please. Motioning for Eros to follow, she
strode up to the breach the Sea Beggars had made by throwing a wooden footbridge over the gap between the outer
and inner wards. Helmeted heads peeked up to take a look
at her. Her white silk gown and scarlet surcoat were picked
to draw attention—meant to make her look more like a
prize than a target. Saying a short protective spell, she
stepped up onto the wall walk, an easy mark for any arrow,
Eros's white flag waving behind her.

Sea Beggars in steel helmets and studded jackets
crouched at the far end of their short footbridge, which
bristled with arrows. Boarding pikes poked across the gap.
Rising onto her toes, Kore called out, "Hallo, the outer
ward. Who calls at Seagate keep?"

Slowly an unkempt captain in dented half armor rose to
greet her. Under less trying circumstances he would have
been handsome, with a strong hawklike face, a trim beard,

and deep-set eyes—but now he just looked haggard, like he had lost sleep, with a fresh cut over his eye, and an arrow hole in his salt-stained hose. Between them lay five yards of arrow-studded bridge, flung across the gap between the two wards, a forty-foot-deep rock trench separating the inner and outer wards. Stepping up onto the footbridge in worn sea boots, the Sea Beggar doffed his steel pot-helm and managed a sweeping bow. "Stefan Ryschov of the *Mermaid*, at your service."

"Lady Kore of Seagate," she replied, neglecting her other titles—right now this was the one that mattered. Last she heard the *Mermaid* was commanded by Le Suisse, but among Sea Beggars ownership is a sometime thing. She stepped up onto the bridge, putting them on the same level, asking, "Why have you come here, disturbing our peace?"

"Because we have no choice, M'Lady. We are fleeing for our lives, and you were merely in the way. Believe me, we do not wish to be here, but this is our sole way into the Sound."

Where they were thoroughly unwanted. She tactfully pretended they had a chance of getting in. "Ships enter and leave the Sound every day. You could have anchored here, asking leave to pass in civilized fashion."

Captain Stefan scoffed at the notion. "And be wiped out while you listened to our pleas and sobs, in civilized fashion? No, M'Lady, we have women and children aboard our boats. We had to see them safe before settling down to talk."

Admirable sentiments. It was hard to hate such a reasonable-sounding villain. She made a sign to Eros, signaling him to get ready. "What is this you fear so much?"

He smiled ruefully. "Something so terrible it has me knocking on Death's door."

Not just knocking, but darn near breaking it in. She studied the brigand intently, trying to see the man behind the dented half-armor and stained hose. His men were afraid of her, literally cowering at Death's door. Even his Ensign barely poked the mermaid banner over the parapet. But handsome Captain Stefan Ryschov stood atop the breach, a target for the entire keep, boldly answering her back, trying to better see the curves behind her vulture surcoat, treating Death herself like a woman. Whatever this man ran from must be truly frightening. "What could be worse than Death?"

"Black Sails." He said it softly, as though he feared they would hear.

"Black Sails?" She, however, had never heard of them.

He nodded, not liking to say the name again.

She signaled with her hand, saying, "Suppliants at Death's door deserve to be fed." Eros dipped his truce flag twice, and smiling women in flowing white dresses emerged from under the iron portcullis carrying smoked hams and baskets of figs and scones, along with bags of apples, tubs of butter, and big cool buckets of beer. Helmeted heads rose up along the far parapet, revealing smiles on haggard faces—a ragged cheer came from the Sea Beggars.

Women came bravely forward, holding the food in front of them, stepping around the bodies by the breach. Sea Beggars stood up, gesturing wildly, calling to the women, "Come here, Honey. Is that beer? Bring it, we have a horrible thirst."

Encouraged, the women came right up to the breach, laughing and making a game of passing beer and food across the gap, throwing figs and scones over to the men, sticking hams on spear points, looping bucket ropes over their pikes so the beer would slide down the pike shafts to them. Kore stepped farther out onto the bridge, ignoring the dizzying drop, drawing the apple from her secret pocket, offering it to Captain Stefan. "Here. You too are a guest of Seagate."

He did not take it, staring hard at her, not liking the way his men had dropped their guard to welcome her women. But he knew it was no use ordering them back. She stepped closer, still holding out the apple. "Afraid to eat from the hand of Death?"

"You have used poison on one of my men already." He meant the dying boy.

"He could be helped no other way." She took a bite of the apple, finding it cool and tart. Then she offered it again to him. "Your own case is not nearly so hopeless."

"So you say." He took the apple, turned it in his hand, and bit where she had bit. That was Eros's signal. Shielded by the women joyously handing out food, he hustled the hostages across the inner ward and under the portcullis into the keep. Men at the breach were much too busy swilling beer and calling to the women to think of trying to stop them. Task one was a *fait accompli*, at the cost of turning her besiegers into dinner guests.

To keep Stefan's attention on her, she asked, "Who are these Black Sails?"

He took another bite of the apple, calmly accepting the loss of his hostages; after all, he now had her within easy reach. "They came from the east, from north of the Great Wall, killing and burning, emptying villages to make room for their cattle. Without warning they fell on the coastal cities, sacking Ustengrad and Zransky. Ustengrad resisted and they slaughtered everyone, even the dogs and cats. Zransky opened its gates in abject surrender, but they still killed everyone taller than a wagon wheel, saving only the children to sell as slaves."

Ustengrad had its temple to her, so did Zransky; she appointed the head priestesses herself, loving competent women committed to care for the sick and dying. Kore said a silent prayer for their souls. "What of Tskova?"

Captain Stefan waved his apple at his men in the outer ward, happily eating and drinking. "We are what is left of Tskova. Those you see here, and their families aboard ship. Our homes are gone, along with our livelihoods. We sailed across to Korland, thinking the broad sea reach would save us—only to find them there ahead of us. Nordgorad and Lulavik were already in ashes; what survivors there were joined us, leaving nowhere to go but here. Or to the Far Isles."

Nordgorad and Lulavik as well. Every seaport north of the Sound gone, swept away before she heard there was even trouble. She had celebrated Solstice in Lulavik less than a fortnight ago. "How is that possible?"

"Hell alone knows, M'Lady." He very much meant it. She saw handsome Captain Stefan could barely compre-

hend how he came to be standing here, hundreds of leagues
from home, a half-eaten apple in his hand, bargaining with
a witch at Death's door. "Until now I had seen nothing like
them. Black Sails worship only the wind which fills their
sails, taking them where they want to go. Nothing stops
them, not city walls, nor open sea. Fearing nothing, they
give no quarter, falling out of nowhere like a steel typhoon,
wiping the sea clean in their wake."

She shook her head, barely believing this could happen
without her knowing. She had heard sea tales aplenty of
course, enough to know Captain Stefan was a cunning
ruthless pirate, running for his life along with his women
and children, and willing to throw men and ships against a
stone fortress that had stood scores of sieges—if he was not
running from these "Black Sails" then it had to be from
something equally bad. She asked, "Are they human?"
That at least would give her an edge; she was still Demi-
Goddess of Death.

"Perhaps," Stefan shrugged armored shoulders. "They
do not look like us, having leathery skin and slanted demon
eyes. At Zransky they raped the younger women before slit-
ting their throats. Does that make them more or less human?"

She saw his point; but humans had human weaknesses,
giving her some hope. Her women bid happy farewells to
the men across the gap, blowing kisses and tossing the last
of the apples, then skirting the bodies and heading for
safety. Men clamored for them to stay, calling out endear-
ments, reaching into the gap, begging, "Come finish the
beer with us!"—but making no concerted attempt to stop
them. Only a shower of arrows could keep her women from
reaching the keep, and that was out of the question—no
one wanted to turn the party back into a battle.

Now she alone had to be extracted, standing on—and
blocking—the makeshift bridge over the rock trench between the two wards. Keeping her gaze fixed on Captain Stefan, holding his attention, she asked, "What do you want?"

He smiled insolently over the apple, flirting with Death
for a moment. "To eat, to breathe, to make love to women.

Beautiful ones if possible. Nothing that out of the ordinary." Then he nodded over his shoulder. "It is not what I want—it is what the Black Sails want that matters. They will be here, sooner than you think."

"How soon?" Less than an hour ago she did not know these Black Sails existed; now they might top the horizon at any moment.

"We feared they might be here ahead of us, like at Nordgorad and Lulavik."

"And now that you have beat them here?"

"We have no time to waste." Captain Stefan deftly ticked off demands. "After sending our families to safety in the Sound, we can unite to defend the Narrows, doubling your garrison and adding a fleet of warships. Together we might have a chance to hold them off, a tiny one it is true, but a chance."

How like a man. Breaks in her door, strews bodies on the inner ward, and instead of apologizing he wants to move in. Captain Stefan could use a lesson in humility. "Do you not fear to make a deal with Death?"

He shrugged again. "Death we can bargain with, but not the Black Sails."

Pity. But there would be no bargaining, not now anyway. Captain Stefan could keep what he had won, and not a jot more. She told him, "This most important message you have brought must be taken at once to my mother, the Goddess-on-Earth, if you are to find safe haven in the Sound." One very huge "if"—absolutely no one in the Sound wanted Sea Beggars settling in—she foresaw that without any spellcraft. "Until I return with her answer, make free with the outer ward, which is yours to use so long as you are here. Water and provisions will be provided from the castle cistern and stores. Your man with the broken leg should live—if you lack a reliable bone-setter, I will provide, for you are my guests and under my protection."

His grin returned, "But that is not near good enough. I need you to open up your keep, and give assurances."

"You have my promise of protection," she reminded him.

"Hardly reassuring," he retorted.

"Alas, it is the best I have—now I must consult with the Goddess-on-Earth. I look forward to seeing you again, for this has been most pleasant." Lifting her skirt, she turned and started back toward the inner ward, mindful of the arrows sticking in the bridge.

Captain Stefan cried, "Stop!"

She turned to him, arching an eyebrow. "What for?"

"I did not give you leave to go." Stefan's men looked up, surprised to find things suddenly amiss.

"Then pray give me leave, for I am going." She stepped down off the bridge and started walking across the inner ward toward the gate.

Again he shouted after her, "Stop! I must have access to your keep."

She turned, smiling apologetically. "You have been excellent company and provided a most valuable warning—putting me doubly in your debt—but if this warning is to make a difference, I must go at once, for your benefit as much as anyone's." No one could say Death was not polite.

"Wait!" he demanded. "My archers can cut you down before you get halfway to the gate."

"Do what you will," she told him primly, turning her back on the bows. Death left all such decisions up to the living, taking each soul as it came.

"Halt!" he shouted, angry to have given away his hostages for ham and beer. "I vow if you take another step, I shall have them fire."

Thank Hecate she made a small target. She continued walking toward the gate, silent and implacable as her namesake. Let them shoot. Kore lived every moment of her life ready to die—the only way for the Demi-Goddess of Death. How could she ask others to let go of their lives gratefully, if she was not always ready to give up her own? Secretly, however, she did not think Captain Stefan would have his men shoot; killing the one person who offered him shelter was not a good bet for a buccaneer. Completely out of character in fact. And it was doubly unlikely his archers would obey—only a bold Sea Beggar would drink and eat at Death's door, then shoot his witch-hostess in the back.

Sailors were far too superstitious. If Captain Stefan meant to kill her, he would have to do it himself.

But he did not. When the portcullis rang down behind her, handsome Captain Stefan still stood at the breach, holding his half-eaten apple.

~ Hawking

Lady Kore went hawking to be alone. The pastime's very nature insured privacy. As soon as she put on her fleece-lined hawking jacket over harem pants tucked into soft leather boots, and climbed past the palace dovecotes into the dimly lit mews, she entered a world of limitless freedom and exhilarating solitude, a world denied to everyone but falconers and their birds. And right now she needed solitude, to be alone with her problems, ordering her thoughts in private, before meeting with Mother. In Seagate under siege, everyone's eyes were on her. Women attended her waking needs, then watched over her while she slept. Dwarfs peered up at her. Stone gargoyles glared down. Guards gawked in silent fascination as she passed, knowing their life lay in her hands. In a crisis she was supposed to be as implacable and unfeeling as death itself, and dared not share her private fears with any of them, not even cute cousin Eros.

Moreover, hawking was a woman's pastime, not as practical as needlepoint, nor as dangerous as childbirth, but not safe or frivolous either; a pastime where patient sensitivity counted for more than size and strength, where for once Kore's light weight and small frame were actual advantages. Hawking took infinite care, an even temper, and calm alert daring—all qualities Kore needed to nurture. Big as a barn, and perched on the topmost tower of Seagate keep, the high gabled mews had tall double doors at each end. The mews-boy met her at the trap entrance, touching his forelock, asking, "Which bird does Your Highness wish? Will it be Havoc?"

Havoc was her favorite hawk, a huge purebred Barbary roc. "Make it Ripper," Kore decided, "the young griffhawk in training. We can both can use the exercise." Already things were simpler.

Bowing, the boy hastened to obey, leading her to the griffhawk's perch. The smaller birds—merlins, goshawks, gyrfalcons, peregrines and golden eagles—had their roosts high up along the wall, with long ladders leading to them. The larger birds—rocs, griffhawks, and giant condors—had tall perches spaced along the floor, high enough to keep their sweeping tail feathers from touching the coarse clean sand. With a low whistle, Kore caught the griffhawk's attention, talking calmly and gently while the boy used a ladder to saddle the *falcoform* six times his size and weight. As she tightened the breast straps, Kore told the hawk what fun they would have. "This is a day for flying. Just you and me. Free as the air."

Cocking her hooded head, the huge bird-of-prey looked fiercely back at Kore through the eye holes. A full-grown griffhawk stood ten feet at the shoulder, and could spear you with her talons, or take off your head with her great curved beak. Hawking was not a pastime for the timid. Or foolhardy.

Which was why Kore hand-raised her hawks, never trusting a bird she did not know. Most birds in the mews were her nestlings, but only the griffhawks were native to Markovy, coming from beyond the Iron Wood, where they lived off steppe antelope and straying cattle. The giant condors were bred from a single pair, sent to the Goddess-on-Earth by a distant potentate. Rocs came from Far Barbary, where hillmen risked their lives climbing crags to steal their eggs. A single egg was worth a fortune, if the hatchling was female—males were too small for flying, fit only for breeding and bringing down deer. Hand-feeding her hawks from the time they hatched, Kore talked to them, and got them accustomed to her touch, taught them simple commands. As they grew older, she trained them to take the hood and empty saddle, and to follow a lure. Weight was added as they matured—until the day when the hawk could carry her. "Come," she told Ripper, " 'twill be an adventure."

Climbing onto the hawk, she lay down on the saddle, strapping herself in and taking up the hood reins, telling the boy to untie the leash and open the great double doors. Flocks of pigeons from the dovecotes wheeled through the noon sky. The griffhawk followed them with her eye. Kore leaned forward, whispering, "Go."

Spreading wings as long as catapult levers, the griffhawk sprang from her perch. Soaring out the double doors, she swooped low over the inner ward, gathering speed. Lying prone in the saddle, Kore felt the heart-pumping surge of takeoff. Women cooking on rooftops or hanging out wash looked up. Children waved. Walls flashed past, then sea and rocks rose to greet her. "Up, up." She shifted backward in the saddle, saying, "Lift and soar."

Ripper obeyed, catching the updraft off the keep walls, soaring upward. As they rose, Kore pulled harder on the hood reins, banking to the right, to search for the broad standing wave where the prevailing west winds rose up over the eastern headland. Turning through a shallow three-quarter circle, she felt for the updraft, urging the hawk to go higher. Again the griffhawk obeyed. Young and new to the game, the hawk still enjoyed flight as much as Kore. Catching the wave of air breaking over the sea cliffs, they spiraled upward into morning sunlight.

Looking back over her shoulder, she saw Seagate falling away behind her, ringed by scattered rocks and white reefs, its twin bridges reaching out to the east and west headlands. Seagate divided the Narrows into the Gullet, and the narrower Windpipe; these two channels were the only passage between the Sound and the White Sea, an inlet of the Arctic Ocean that separated northern Markovy from the polar ice cap. Two massive underwater chains kept ocean-going ships from using either channel without permission—but the Sea Beggars had slid their galleys, barques, zebecks and row barges over the chains into the shelter of the sound. Only their big seagoing carracks were blocked from entering. *Nymph, Tempest,* and the flagship *Mermaid* were moored in the mouth of the Gullet amid a half-dozen captured merchant ships, safe from wind and sea but unable to enter the Sound—hopefully Captain Stefan was swinging in his hammock, taking his ease until she got back.

But whatever devilment the Sea Beggar planned, she prayed it did not hatch until she returned, or there was bound to be yet more mayhem. Being Demi-Goddess of Death was not as soft as some folks imagined; accepting her own death did not make the death of others any easier. Mere mortals clung pitifully to life, like that boy in the inner ward, his guts speared and spine cut, his body useless, but still he sobbed at her breast, clutching her gown, wanting to live. And now whole cities full of them had been massacred. Or so the Sea Beggars said. Way too much depended on the doubtful word of a buccaneer and smuggler trying to bully his way into the Sound. For all she knew the Black Sails were just a sea story like sirens and lost Atlantis. Korland and the northern ports might be basking in the long warm days after solstice, enjoying peace and plenty while she was put into a panic by a smooth-talking pirate.

Hoping handsome Captain Stefan was making a complete fool of her, she steered her hawk along the high eastern headland, riding the long wave of air curling over the mountain spine bordering the Sound. When the east shore sank down into rolling foothills, she turned inland toward the Iron Wood, catching the hot updraft off the black barren expanse of metal trees. Spiraling upward in this massive thermal, she took the griffhawk higher than any bird would ever go, until they were alone in the vast sea of air. Here was hawking at its most lonesome, woman and bird surrounded by miles of open sky.

Saying a prayer to the winds, she turned Ripper back toward the cloud-wracked Sound, putting the hawk in a shallow stoop, gathering speed. By the time they broke through the clouds they were winging over water, with Fair Isle just ahead—her mother's home, sanctuary to the Goddess-on-Earth. Lying under the Peace of the Goddess, Fair Isle had no guards, no garrison, and no edged weapons, unless you counted scythes and turnip knives. Tall natural cliffs forced all boats to land at a single small wharf, where people and cargo were lifted up the cliffs in oversized baskets. Otherwise Fair Isle was unapproachable, except by air. She brought her griffhawk down inside the temple precinct, landing in her mother's private garden, telling the startled nymphs to feed and care for her hawk. Death is always informal, arriving when and where she pleases.

Ripper happily preened herself, pleased with her flight. Everyone else did Kore instant homage—not as unnerving as you might imagine—but she much preferred the informality of Seagate, where people wore her livery without dropping to their knees whenever she appeared. Open adoration showed how much these people feared her. Fair Isle lived on what her people grew, and on milk from their flocks—all with very little discord. Any crimes or accusations were judged by the Goddess herself, under threat of banishment. Theft was rare, rape unheard of, and there had never been a killing of any sort. No one even ate meat, and the only animals slaughtered were goats fed to her griffhawks. Kore alone was allowed to bring weapons and killing to Fair Isle.

Mother met her in the innermost sanctuary, a square court open to the sky, where they could kiss and hug, and talk in private—though everyone knew the Dark Daughter had come unexpectedly, and everyone feared the worst. Mother wore her silver regalia, the cloth-of-silver gown, crescent moon headdress, and white polar bear cloak of the Goddess-on-Earth. Kore still had on her leather flying jacket, over harem pants and hawking boots, making her feel less like death incarnate, and more like a child, running in all disheveled and dressed for play, telling her Mother a terrible story. And her tale was terrible, sounding worse each time she told it. Eros at least was openly scornful—claiming Sea Beggars would say anything for a chance to loot the Sound—but that was male bravado, unwilling to admit to problems Love could not solve. On peaceful undefended Fair Isle, Captain Stefan's story sounded ten times worse. Mother was properly horrified, saying she had never heard of these Black Sails. "Cathayans speak of 'barbarians' north of the Great Wall, but claim they are of no account."

Kore smiled grimly. "We are all no account barbarians to the Cathayans."

"Exactly," Mother agreed—though she never left Fair Isle, the Goddess-on-Earth had vast knowledge of people and places. "And Tskova has long been a troublesome nest of smugglers and privateers." Neither Sea Beggars nor Cathayans could normally be trusted. "Men will most likely call it a lie. . . ."

"Eros already has," Kore told her.

Mother nodded, ". . . meant to ease their way into the Sound."

"So Eros said."

"Cousin Eros is a valuable window into the male mind," Mother observed, "never deigning to hide his thoughts, no matter how prurient or self-interested. Yet he remains open to reason." That could hardly be said for the rest of the Sound's floating population of fisher clans, Norse traders, Flemish merchants, monks, sealers and the like—loosely ruled by quarrelsome Markovite boyars farther south. Only fear of Kore and awe of the Goddess-on-Earth kept them in check, without making them the least bit trusting. Mother swiftly foresaw their reaction. "First they will deny the danger, thinking only of the Sea Beggars and their threat to the Sound."

Kore agreed. "It would take gem-hard proof to convince them." Boyars and landgrafs were more likely to burn witches than listen to them.

"And if we do convince them, they will want to fight," Mother pointed out. "First the Sea Beggars, then the Black Sails." Keeping Death awfully busy for the foreseeable future. Kore agreed that unreasoning denial followed by blind aggression were the most likely reactions. Even Captain Stefan knew better than that—offering an immediate alliance against the Black Sails—desperate enough to die defending someone else's home. "We can only hope the Sea

Beggars are lying," Mother concluded. "If they are, and Seagate holds, then these buccaneers cannot get their big ships into the Sound—keeping the combatants apart."

With Seagate in between; Death did the dirty work, so Fair Isle could stay pure. "As long as there are no Black Sails," Kore pointed out.

The Goddess-on-Earth eyed her intently. "Do you think these Black Sails are real?"

Kore nodded, "Yes, I do." She wished it were not so, but she did.

"Why so?" Mother asked.

As Demi-Goddess of Death, Kore had a worst-case mentality that came from accepting the most terrible outcomes—but that was not why she believed the Black Sails were real. "I could see it in Captain Stefan's eyes. He was not telling a sea tale; he was frightened. And he is a man not easily scared."

Mother arched an eyebrow. "And is he handsome as well?"

"Moderately so." Kore had no designs on Captain Stefan, no matter how handsome. Death must be a maiden, or a crone, never a mother. She could not both raise a child and be always ready to die. Someday she would give up her post to have children, but not now, not today, not with Sea Beggars in the Sound and Black Sails bearing down on her. "But good looks could not hide his fear. The Black Sails are real and dangerous. They may not be as bad as Captain Stefan says, but they are bad."

"We must have more than a Sea Beggar's word on this," Mother pointed out. "And we must know more than he has told you. Who are these Black Sails? Where did they come here from? And why?"

It was Kore's task to find out, since Death got all the difficult cases. To rest her griffhawk, she flew one of Mother's rocs back to Seagate. Bigger than griffhawks, rocs could be ridden sitting up, and the Goddess had a half dozen pairs in her mews, though only her daughters and granddaughters flew them. The giant birds lived by hunting deer and antelope on the mainland, observing Fair Isle's ban on killing for food.

Skimming low over the shore, Kore caught the hot updraft off the Iron Wood, spiraling slowly upward, giving herself time to plan. She had to go to Korland herself to see if Nordgorad and Lulavik were really in ashes, and search for some sign of the mysterious Black Sails. But first she must keep the Sea Beggars from making mischief behind her back—maybe even forge a truce with Captain Stefan. It was in the Sea Beggars' self-interest to confirm their story and scout the movements of the Black Sails, assuming they existed. Flocks of snow geese flew alongside her in big honking V formations, headed for summer feeding grounds on Korland.

Riding the standing wave along the eastern ridgeline, she saw the black mass of Seagate ahead, silhouetted against the tarnished gold glow of a high latitude summer sunset. It had been a long, long day—that began before dawn, with Sea Beggars bashing in the water gate and seizing the outer ward—and she could use whatever rest the short night had to offer.

No such luck. As she neared the keep she made out tiny black specks in the sunset glow, hanging about the Gullet Tower like wasps in amber. War kites. Instantly awake, she leaned forward, putting her roc into a stoop, flashing over the Windpipe to take a closer look. Damn, she could not leave for even half a day without some new disaster. Circling above the keep, she saw that the Sea Beggars had brought row barges towing war kites into the Gullet, anchoring just upwind of the Gullet Tower, which sat at the west end of the inner ward, serving as a gatehouse for the bridge spanning the Gullet. But that was not why the Sea Beggars had attacked the Gullet Tower; they picked it because the tower housed the mechanism working the chain guarding the Gullet. By taking the tower the Sea Beggars could bypass Seagate, bringing their big ships and merchant prizes straight into the Sound.

Landing her roc on a wall walk out of range of the kites,

she told the startled sentries to fetch Eros, "And have him bring my scythe!"

Sentries dashed off to do her bidding, making her glad to be back where she was obeyed instead of worshipped. What should she make of this second Sea Beggar attack? Was it proof Captain Stefan had lied, merely seeking to loot the Sound? Or was he just desperate to escape the Black Sails? Either way, he must be turned back as quickly and cheaply as possible—just to prove that force would not work. Then they could negotiate. She wished she had called for Havoc as well as her scythe, but there was no time to change rocs in mid-battle.

Eros brought the scythe, a big beautiful one with a black handle and a long shining steel-alloy blade shaped like a sliver-thin moon. He had his own Love God's bow as well—a gold-chased double crossbow with a telescopic sight. Handing over the scythe, he made his report, saying Sea Beggars had indeed anchored kite barges in the Sound. "They cleared the top of the Gullet Tower with arrow fire, then landed men from one of the box kites, who let down a line to more men waiting on the seaward side of the tower. Luckily that is all they have taken, but they are trying to fight their way down to the chain mechanism. So as long as their kites fire down on us, we cannot mount a counterattack or direct adequate fire on the tower."

"How many kites?" she demanded, determined to do something before they lost the light.

"Two big box kites, and a dozen smaller ones." Eros pulled a clip of six hypodermic quarrels from his belt, sliding it into the bow; springs in the clip fed the quarrels two at a time into the double bow, which was already bent.

Kore grinned at him. "Make love not war?"

"Naturally." Eros smiled back, closing the bolt, locking in the quarrels.

She took off, again wishing she were aboard Havoc, urging her borrowed roc upward into the fading light, her scythe shining blood red in the sunset. Heading for the nearest kite line, she swooped down, picking a spot where she could not be fired on from the barges or by the archer lashed to the huge kite at the end of the line. As her hawk plunged past, she caught the silk line with her scythe, slicing it neatly.

Half the line dropped down into the Gullet and the other half shot off as the man-kite was borne away downwind. She said a prayer for his soul. If he came down in water the fellow was a Sea Beggar and presumably could swim—if not, Death had small sympathy for someone who made his living as a sniper.

She cut a second line and a third, one by one getting rid of the kites along the west wall of the keep. Archers strapped to the kites and firing powerful recurve bows kept Eros and his men from advancing along the wall walk toward the Gullet Tower. As she severed a fourth line a spear flashed past her; looking up she saw a big four-story box kite with a basket beneath it. A windlass on a barge below was winding the box kite down, and two men in the basket were throwing heavy javelins at her, trying to spear her borrowed bird.

Banking hard to avoid the next spear, she made a pass at the cable connecting the box kite to the barge, slashing as she flew by. But the box kite cable was too thick, and she nearly lost her scythe and her seat. Saved by her saddle strap, she put her roc in a stoop to gain speed, then flew back up along the wall, with black night wind rushing through her hair. Ahead she saw more silk kite lines to cut, standing taut in the last of the light. Eros and his men were on the wall walk, shouting and waving to her. She waved back with her scythe. Eros had his double bow out, aiming it her way—which she could not understand. What was he trying to say?

As she pondered her cousin's strange behavior, a heavy weight hit her from behind, knocking the wind out of her. Arms closed around her chest, and she lost her scythe, along with her grip on the reins. Seeing a flash of steel, she expected to feel a stab in the back, or a blade through her throat. Instead the knife cut her saddle strap, and her roc fell away.

Feet kicking in empty air, she was no longer flying, but being held aloft by whoever had her—if he let go, she would fall to the rocks below. Twisting about, she grabbed one of the kite straps, though the man showed no sign of releasing her. Looking up, she saw the huge rounded outline of the kite bowed by the evening wind, and beneath it a familiar face, grinning back at her.

"Lady Death, we meet again." It was Stefan Ryschov, Captain of the *Mermaid*, lashed to a man-carrying kite and looking almighty pleased with himself. And rightly so. He had dipped his kite down as she sped past, catching her from behind—a neat bit of maneuvering, showing Captain Stefan and the men on his barge were masters at kite flying—putting her at his mercy.

Almost. Turning in his arms, she braced a boot against the kite and grabbed his shoulder with her left hand, her killing hand. Her venom ring was inches from his neck. "Quit struggling," he told her, "or I will have to drop you."

She could feel herself dropping already, rapidly being reeled down by the crew of the row barge—veteran fishermen hauling in their catch. Her heart sank further with each turn of the winch. Men waited on the deck below to seize her; in minutes she would be in their hands, and killing a few of them first was not going to make her chances any better.

Suddenly a golden crossbow quarrel hit her captor in the shoulder, seeming to sprout magically out of his bicep, inches from her face. His arms tightened convulsively, pulling her closer to him. She recognized one of Eros's arrows, with its needle-thin point and hypodermic body, designed to deliver an injection on impact. For a dizzying moment she hung there, locked in Captain Stefan's arms, holding tight to the kite strap, staring at the little golden arrow.

She felt a stab in her buttock, followed by the burning surge of an injection. Eros's second shot had hit her. She opened her mouth in protest, but before she could get a word out Captain Stefan leaned down, covering her mouth with his. He was kissing her, and in a moment, she was kissing him back.

* * *

⌒*Black Sails*

Damn Eros and his arrows. She was in love, head-over-heels, crazy in love with the Sea Beggar busy carrying her off. Clinging to his whip-hard waist, she felt his hand on her back, pressing her harder to him, breast to chest, hip to groin. And all the time they kept kissing, exploring each other's mouths in midair. Exciting and intimate, thrilling even, with nothing beneath her but black air. Kore had never been in love before—not like this at least. Death was no blushing virgin, nor was she as experienced as people supposed, especially if you did not count kissing cousins. Few men pounded on Death's door demanding a date, and most who did had mixed motives, like handsome Captain Stefan here.

Totally new to mating on the wing, she found her new soulmate surprisingly adept at it, feeling him reach around and roll down her pants, keeping their lips and bodies locked together. She felt the stab of pain as her hypodermic dart came out, falling down into the dark Gullet. His was still in his arm. Letting go of his lips, and the kite strap, she pulled the golden shaft from his bicep, dropping it after its mate. Then she kissed the wound it left, licking up blood and aphrodisiac.

Deft as Captain Stefan might be aboard a kite, he could not get her harem pants down fast enough. They were still tangled around her knees when the barge deck slammed into her flying boots, nearly spilling her onto the wet wood. Fortunately sturdy Captain Stefan helped break her fall, as did the overloaded kite, snapping silk butterfly wings in a crash of splintering bamboo. Keeping her feet, she stepped sideways out of the wreckage, half-naked and totally disheveled, but shamelessly happy. Being Demi-Goddess of Death meant never having to blush. Her advent stunned the Sea Beggars around her. Rowers sat open-mouthed at their oars, and even the men who had wound her down stood frozen at the windlass, waiting to see what happened next.

Shedding the remains of his war kite, Captain Stefan shouted to the amazed men at the windlass, "Up anchor!"

Then he called to the startled rowers, "Back oars. Get us out of the Gullet while we still have the light." Stefan turned to a tall picturesque Sea Beggar wearing hip boots, silk pants, a steel breastplate and a green-turbaned helmet, telling the pirate, "Signal withdrawal. Two yellow rockets. Take your launch and see to the retreat. Keep the other kites aloft until our men clear the tower, then meet me back aboard the *Mermaid*."

Bowing, the armored Sea Beggar disappeared over the side into a waiting launch. Captain Stefan turned back to her, bowing courteously. "Lady Death, welcome aboard the *Salamander*. If you will follow me."

"Kore," she told him, pulling up her pants. Since they were going to be intimate, best to start out on a first-name basis. "You can call me Kore."

Captain Stefan's smile widened, looking very much like a man in love, who was about to get what he wanted. "Will M'Lady Kore come with me?"

"Of course." She nodded amiably. He would get his way, because Kore was in love as well, horribly so. There was no fighting Eros's arrows. Stefan's approving smile sent sharp pangs of happiness shooting through her. Heavens, he was good-looking and amazingly bold, even for a pirate. And he was hers, every handsome ruthless inch of him, hers to have and to hold, to love and nurture, for as long as Eros's spell lasted. Warm feelings welled up within her. Death almost never got to be tender and maternal, unless you counted moments like this morning with that dying boy at the breach.

He led her to a red silk tent at the rear of the row barge, lit from within by soft yellow lantern light. This crimson love nest was already occupied by three women and a handful of startled children, whom Captain Stefan immediately ordered to leave. Surprised but obedient, the women gathered up children and possessions, then left, taking the lantern with them, knowing she and Stefan would not be needing the light. Pushing children's dolls and women's things off the dark bed onto the deck, she realized this must be the barge master's tent, and his family was being kicked out to make room for her. Not that it mattered. Nothing mattered except feeling Stefan's tense lean flesh against hers, forgetting all their fears and differences, forgetting everything but their shared desire. Stefan was vastly delighted to discover her thigh knife, "Must Lady Death drag weapons into bed?"

"Who dragged whom here?" She had three more ways to kill him hidden about her naked body, but was way too busy to disarm completely—any man who bedded Lady Death did it at his own risk.

When desire was spent, she lay listening to his breathing, becoming slowly aware of the world beyond their bodies. Wet silk sheets smelled of sweat and sex. Waves lapped against the barge's black hull, gently rocking the bed. From outside she could hear the splash of oars, propelling them through the night. Men were moving on deck, talking in low tones, and a child cried fitfully, no doubt wanting her bed back. "Are you all right?" a voice asked. It was Stefan, awake and up on one elbow, warm and comforting in the darkness.

"Absolutely wonderful," she murmured, slipping closer to his big hard body. How had she managed so long without love? It hardly seemed possible that she had survived without someone to care for her, to share her problems with.

"Me too," Stefan admitted. "Who would have thought that bedding down with Death could be so marvelous?"

Who indeed? Not even the demi-goddess herself, who was completely surprised to be so transported. She ran her finger over the naked curve of his chest, saying, "Blame it on cousin Eros."

"Cousin Eros?" Stefan sounded surprised.

"It was his dart I pulled from your arm."

"What does that have to do with it? I have been in love with you from the first moment you stepped up onto the breach and asked for a parley, facing our arrows without flinching."

"Is that why you did not have me shot?" She remembered her long walk to the keep portcullis, expecting that at any moment she might get a shaft in her back.

"Of course." He pulled her tight against him, letting her feel his renewed excitement. "I wanted you here with me, like this, not all punctured with arrows. Together we can work miracles."

"Let us hope so." She laughed. Love had given her new heart, but had not solved all her problems.

"You shall see." Stefan brimmed with male self-confidence. "With my fleet and your fortress, we have half a chance against the Black Sails."

She laughed lightly at that suggestion. Love had not made her take total leave of her senses. "I cannot just let you into Seagate." Into her body yes, but not her fortress keep.

"Why not?" Stefan sounded wounded. "How can you not believe me? I swear I would not lie to you, in fact I have never lied to you; there has barely been time, since we only met this morning."

"But I do believe you," she assured him. "Alas, every bit of evidence points to your telling the absolute truth." Even the borrowed bed she lay on, with its rag dolls and baby baskets, was added proof—Sea Beggars would not bring their women and children into a night action unless they were desperately short of deck space, and frantic to break into the Sound.

"Since you believe me, we should start at once," he suggested. "Your keep and my fleet gives us a fighting chance. What more can a man ask for?"

"Women want a good deal more," she informed him, fearing they were headed for their first fight. "Men think that dying sword in hand somehow makes a difference—it does not. Take Death's word for that. The dead are dead, believe me, I know. And it matters not if you go down boldly giving blow for blow, or blubbering for mercy on your knees."

Stefan sounded taken aback, asking, "What does matter?"

"Life," she told him, sliding her bare body against his, knowing how best to avoid a fight, "living better and happier, while putting off dying as long as you can."

"Strange thing for Death to say," Stefan observed, stirring with pleasure.

"I am a strange sort of demi-goddess, one who must see these Black Sails for herself."

"Whatever for?"

"Because I must," she insisted, not used to giving anyone reasons, least of all some Sea Beggar in a borrowed bed.

Stefan groaned. "Death, I see, is going to make a difficult mistress."

"Absolutely." She kissed him, thinking the sooner Captain Stefan got used to that the better.

Oars ceased splashing, and someone barked orders, followed by a hail from across the water, then a bump and a thump as the row barge came to rest against some bigger object. Bare feet beat on the deck boards. Stefan sat up, announcing, "This will be my flagship, the *Mermaid*."

Helping Kore out of bed and back into her clothes, he led her out on deck. The *Salamander* was flush up against a high-sided carrack, a big black mass blotting out the stars, lit by torches on the quarter-deck and fire pots hanging from the forward yard ends. Stefan answered another hail from above, and torches moved to the main deck, illuminating the ladder. Climbing toward the light above, she could tell this was Stefan's ship, infused with his spirit, alert but informal, ready for anything, yet not afraid to look relaxed. He led her past the astonished deck watch, past sleeping families camped on the main deck, to his great cabin on the quarter-deck with its sweeping glassed-in stern galley, glittering oil lamps, and big canopied bed. Gilt and glass threw back the light, making the cabin seem to sparkle. Stefan spread his arms, asking, "What do you think?"

She surveyed his opulent quarters, thinking of the families huddled in the hold. "Some Sea Beggars sleep better than others?"

"Of course." Stefan pulled back the bed curtains to show off his broad feather bed. "What would be the use of being a Sea Beggar if there were no chance of improvement?"

Waking next morning alone in Stefan's big canopy bed,

she heard loud calls from the half deck above. Pushing back the fur coverlet, Kore spread the curtains and stared out the wide stern windows, seeing nothing but wave tops stretching toward the watery horizon. Then a broad gray shadow swept past the windows.

Instantly she was out of bed, wrapped in silk sheets and stepping out onto the stern galley. Wet sea air greeted her, cool and salty. Stefan's mermaid flag snapped in the breeze above her, flying from the stern post. Seeing the big shadow wheel about, swinging back by the ship, she gave a falconer's cry. Havoc answered with a cry of her own, dropping low to skim over the wavetops astern of the ship. Her favorite roc had come looking for her, wearing a flying saddle, complete with a bow and quiver. Cousin Eros's work.

Captain Stefan burst into his cabin, not looking the least surprised to find her standing in the open stern galley, wearing one of his bed sheets, talking with a huge roc. "So you know this bird?"

"Certainly." She called for Havoc to come to her. Shouts erupted from the half deck above as a huge roc came down to rest on the long stern boom that supported the bonaventure stays, perched two stories above the water and peering into the stern galley. Havoc had come looking for her mistress, and was living up to her name.

Stefan admired the giant falconiform. Hawking had an aura of the supernatural, and was as suspect as witch's flight, but he acted intrigued. "Is that the bird I plucked you from?"

"No, that was a borrowed roc. Had it been on Havoc, you would never have gotten hold of me."

Stefan laughed, though it was only the truth. Havoc was a wonder of nature, who would never have let some kite-flyer swoop down on her. Just having Havoc here restored the balance between her and Stefan. Eros's arrows kept them from harming each other—but did not stop him from holding her captive. In fact he had excellent reasons to want her with him. Yet with Havoc here, Kore could leave anytime. She asked Stefan, "Will you come with us?"

He looked from the roc to her. "With you? Where?"

"North to Korland," she reminded him, "to hunt the Black Sails."

Stefan rolled his eyes. "They will find us soon enough. Are you so in love with death that you must hurry it along?"

"No, I am not the least in love with death," she replied primly. "I am Death. You are who I am in love with."

"Which makes me the one in love with death." Stefan shook his head in dismay. "But I suppose I have known that all along."

"Why else would you have come pounding on my door?" She kissed him, to show that having death for a mistress was not all danger and heartache.

Stefan could not bear to see her head north alone, nor could they go on the *Mermaid* with her hold full of refugees, so he transferred his flag to a low sleek zebeck, the *Sparrow*, with lateen sails and seats for twenty oarsmen. Favored by smugglers and corsairs, the zebeck had no half deck, and no great cabin and stern galley, just a lean-to tent on the quarter-deck for the captain and his demi-goddess. Havoc rode on the grating deck, a rakish stern extension of the quarter-deck. Hugging the coast, they headed north, aiming for the Korland Strait. Kore meant to take a look in at Lulavik, at the southern end of the strait, where she had celebrated Solstice only a fortnight ago—hoping against hope to find this was all a hoax.

Four days north of the Narrows, she saw her first sign of the Black Sails. Sailors called from the masthead, pointing out a black speck low down to windward. Stefan put the tiller about to run straight downwind toward the tiny speck, while she took Havoc aloft to investigate. Eros had stocked the roc's saddlebag with fresh potions, and the arrows were drugged; tied to them was a note:

Alas, these are not true love's arrows, and will only put you to sleep—but mayhap you and your new bedmate will be needing some rest.
Love

Shredding the note, she dropped the pieces into the White Sea, then turned Havoc toward the speck downwind. As she approached the dot grew slowly in size, becoming a huge gas-inflated black parasail, floating along several hundred feet above the wave tops. Hanging from the gas-filled sail was a black boat-shaped hull, with a small cabin in the stern. Oddest of all, the boat hull had big iron-shod wagon wheels, looking utterly useless so high in the sky over water. Keeping clear of arrow range, she flew Havoc completely around the flying-boat, trying to see who was aboard.

Apparently no one. Close up, the dangling boat hull looked abandoned, having the distinctive smell of death about it. Flocks of white-black arctic terns flew by, headed for summer feeding grounds. Kore coaxed her nervous roc into making a landing on the foredeck, but the bird's weight made the flying-boat dip, losing altitude alarmingly. Ocean rushed up to greet her.

Seeing ballast bags lining the rail she slit several open with her thigh knife, and sand tumbled into the sea, bringing their fall to a halt. Happy not to be crashing into the wave tops, she surveyed the flying-boat's bamboo deck, finding it virtually empty, just some stray rope ends, the ballast bags, and a dozen arrow quivers lashed to the rails. She sniffed the air, finding the death smell came from the small cabin. Inside was the crew, three of them lying on their mats wrapped in blankets, still wearing gray tunics faced with fur and blue cavalry pants. But for the smell they might have been sleeping.

Here was where Lady Death earned her name. Kneeling on the bamboo, she said a short prayer for their souls, then stripped their bodies bare, going over every inch of skin, searching for a cause of death. They were short wry men with weather-beaten oriental faces, who had all died within a day of each other, several days ago. None of them had bodily wounds, aside from old scars long healed; one had broken his leg as a boy, and the other two had old arrow wounds. None showed clear signs of poisoning. All were alarmingly thin, but not starved, and they all had tiny red blisters on their bodies, mostly on the hands, face, back, and forearms. Two were badly pocked, but the other had hardly any blisters at all. Seeing he was wearing a ring, she pulled it off and found a solid red band of pustules. Weird but not unheard of. Examining the ring, she noted it had Cathayan characters, then slipped it back on the man's finger. He had been the first to die, and the ring had probably killed him—but it was not up to Death to judge, the ring might have been important to him.

Aside from clothes, money, and weapons, they had scant personal effects, a wind shrine, simple jewelry, paper lanterns, leather water bottles, fishing line and hooks, needles and thread, rice, millet, sesame oil, sulfur matches, a cooking pot and several cups, one carved from a human skull. And not a scrap of writing. No orders, no letters from home, no favorite poems or recipes. No prayer strips or religious texts. Not even someone's initials carved on a sword or cup. All signs that the Black Sails were illiterate. There was a messenger pigeon cote on the stern, but it was empty.

Having searched the entire boat, she collected all the burnables, including underclothes, chopsticks and some Cathayan paper money; piling them against the cabin wall, she doused the whole mess with cooking oil, lit a paper lantern and tossed it on top, starting a brisk fire. Going back on deck, she released the sand ballast, sending the flying-boat soaring upward. She made sure she was taking nothing from the burning ship as she climbed back onto Havoc and took off. While she glided back down toward the *Sparrow*, she watched the flying-boat drift off downwind, dwindling as it got higher. When the flames reached the inflated sail, the gas inside exploded, leaving a black blotch in the sky while the burning hull plummeted toward the sea trailing a plume of smoke.

Alone with Stefan in the yellow-striped quarter-deck tent, she told him about the flying-boat, asking if it matched the ones used by the Black Sails. Stefan said it did. "The big black sail is filled with a light gas that keeps the boats afloat. By adjusting the trim of the boat and the pitch of the sails they glide great distances downwind. Tethered to a fixed line they can rain death on any fortress or cities. Black

Sails are implacable, having no writing nor philosophy, worshipping only the wind in their sails. Cathay feared they would cross the Great Wall. Now they have come our way instead."

It sounded ghastly, even to Death. "What are the wheels for?"

"When the winds are wrong, or there is no flying to be done, the sails are deflated and the hulls are hauled along behind the Black Sail's yurts."

"There is worse," she admitted. "These Black Sails died the Red Death."

"Yikes." He stepped back, taking his hands from her. "Great Goddess in Hell, the Red Death! Do you mean smallpox?"

She acknowledged his compliment, the Goddess Hell being one of her ancient names, hardly used nowadays except in oaths. "Sometimes it is tough to tell the poxes apart, but the deadlier ones are my specialty, and there is scant doubt."

"And I thought Black Sails were the worst we would find." Stefan did a worried turn around the tent, never having wanted to come north in the first place. "Let the men hear this and it will be mutiny."

"Do not worry, I am immune and not a carrier." She showed him the vaccination scar on her arm. "And you cannot get Red Death from a roc."

"My men are not likely to believe you," he pointed out.

When faced with smallpox, even the word of Death herself was not good enough. "So we must be silent," she told him. "But there can be no landfall now. Havoc and I will have to do the scouting."

Standing out to sea, Stefan made for the Korland Strait by dead reckoning, hiding behind the curve of the Earth. When they got close enough, Kore took Havoc aloft for her look in at Lulavik; as feared, she found the little port city at the southern tip of Korland destroyed. Turning north she followed the east coast of Korland, the great island separating the White Sea from the Arctic Ocean. Fishing villages and sealing camps had vanished, replaced by nomad yurts and cattle brought over from the mainland. Farther up the strait she spotted a big ship sheltering in a Korland cove. Dipping down to investigate, she found a prosperous broad-beamed merchant ship anchored placidly amid the plague and devastation. Strange behavior, which she promptly reported to Stefan on the *Sparrow*'s quarter-deck.

"Damned odd," was Stefan's response. "Why a merchant ship, when there is no one to do business with but the Black Sails and the Red Death?"

It did sound daft. Stefan suggested it was some corsair's prize, fancifully hoping a fellow pirate had gotten lucky. She pointed out there were no other ships around to have captured her. "And what pirate would leave a valuable prize where the Black Sails could fall on it?"

"Not a wise one," Stefan admitted, asking her to describe the ship.

"It looked Cathayan," she decided, "broad-beamed, blunt-bowed, with steep tumble home to the sides, and at least five masts. Strangest of all, there was a tiny cabin atop the main mast, not a crow's nest, but a little bamboo house with a basket hoist to supply it. Very curious. I must have a closer look, when the crew is asleep."

"Is that wise?" Stefan wondered, with worry in his voice. Worry for her, which was terribly touching. She was not accustomed to people fearing for her—just being afraid of her.

"Maybe not wise," she admitted, "but necessary. So far this ship is the only thing that does not fit, making it worth a closer look. When facing disaster, look for anything that points in a different direction."

"If you say so." Stefan deferred to her superior knowledge of death and disaster.

She flew over Korland to come down on the cove from the north, seeing the sun set on nomad yurts and herds. Black Sails had crossed in force, bringing not just their flying-boats, but their flocks and families as well—a whole nomad horde out of nowhere was now jammed onto the subarctic island, living heaven knew how. They could not stay here long without starving, and they had crossed the Korland Strait, so water would not stop them; they could come swarming down onto the Sound as soon as a north wind blew. Thankfully winds had been steady from the east, which would blow them to the Far Isles, or even Finland. But that could hardly last. When the sun set she turned south, feeling her way down the dark coast, guided by the white line of breakers and the sound of the surf. Stefan had described the approach in detail, being intimate with every nook and cove in the South Korland coast. Too bad he could not be here.

Finally she saw a light ahead, dim and flickering, but it did not go out. She flew toward it, until Havoc suddenly had to swerve to keep from hitting it. Looming out of the night was the ship, and the light was a paper lantern in the little bamboo house atop the masthead. Landing Havoc on the mainyard, she sat silently in the roc's flying saddle, looking through the window of the little bamboo house, seeing a single silk-lined room where a black-haired young woman dressed in white sat reading from a scroll. Strange, but perhaps to be expected. Death could not help but see the dark side.

Dismounting, she made her way along the mainyard to the window, seeing nothing of the boat below but lights on the bow and stern. Making sure the young reader was alone, she slipped inside, shocking the occupant senseless. Death does not come calling every night, not silently through a window several stories high, carrying a hypodermic bow. Before the startled young woman could cry out, Kore nocked an arrow. "Be silent, I only want to talk and look. Do you know who I am?"

Nodding, the woman sat rigid, holding her scroll in her lap, hands still, not knowing it was only a sleep arrow. Long black hair hung all the way to her hips, and her dark eyes were wide and staring.

"Then you know your life is at stake. Whose ship is this?"

"The Karakhan's." By that the woman meant the ruler of Black Cathay, the land of tea and spices that lay beyond the Great Wall. Which put this ship far from home, having come by way of Korea and the Arctic Sea. "We are carrying the Karakhan's ambassador to Korland."

"And what are you called?" Kore asked.

Staring down at her lap, the woman answered softly in a southern-sounding accent, "Autumn Rose."

"Always?" Kore asked. "Did you have a different name as a child?"

"I was called Ah Toy."

"Cantonese?" That explained the southern accent. "Do you belong to the Karakhan as well?"

Autumn Rose nodded yes to both. Too thin and withdrawn to be a courtesan, she seemed of scholarly bent, sitting with an open roll of poetry in her lap. Kore recognized T'ang dynasty script; Li Po, an excellent choice, amusing and insightful, perfect for passing the time. More scrolls poked from neat little pigeonholes. Why would the Karakhan send this female scholar on an Arctic expedition? "What are you doing so far from Cathay?"

Autumn Rose smiled slightly, saying, "I am a gift for the Black Sail Khan, who is in Korland."

Why not jade earrings? Or a silver pagoda tea set? Both would be more useful than this frail poet. She told Autumn Rose to stand, and when the woman did, she ordered her to strip, "I must see what the Black Sail Khan is getting."

Pursing her lips, Autumn Rose objected, the night was cold, and none of this is necessary. . . .

Kore nodded at the invisible boat below. "And no one is going to shinny up the main mast in the middle of the night to save you from Death's arrows." This woman was kept high on the masthead for a reason. "Obey and I promise to leave you alive. Give me trouble, and I will be inspecting your body."

Without further protest Autumn Rose stepped out of her white robe, then shed her undergarments, standing naked, hands at her side. Taking the paper lantern, Kore went over the woman, telling her when to lift her arms and spread her legs, looking for pock marks, or scabs, or the little white scars left when the scabs fell off. She found none of them, just smooth skin, pale from seldom seeing the sun. Finishing with the woman's face, she asked, "Have you ever had the pox?"

"No, never." Autumn Rose shook her head decisively.

"But it was in your village."

"When I was a girl," the woman admitted. "And again when I was grown."

"But the second time it mainly took children."

"How did you know?" Autumn Rose asked.

"I know the disease." And she had seen enough. "When will you be presented to the Black Sail Khan?"

"When the Khan is ready to have me. His highness is hunting, and I am but his humble gift, to be taken at his majesty's leisure."

Humble and more. She slipped back out the window, leaving Autumn Rose to dress alone, making her way to Havoc's perch on the mainyard, telling her roc to return to the *Sparrow*. There she told Stefan, "I must speak with the Khan of the Black Sails."

"There are better ways to commit suicide," Stefan suggested. "Just as sure and not near so painful."

"Perhaps, but this is the one I have chosen."

"How can you even find the Khan? Korland is big, and the nomad camps are bound to be scattered around the island to get the best grazing."

"I hear he is hunting. Where is there game to be found in Korland?"

Stefan snorted, "At this time of year? Only on the north of the island, away from the ports."

"Then there is where we must head for." North Korland was a great rolling sweep of grass and tundra, sprinkled with wildflowers and virtually treeless, aside from dwarf willows that lived as ground plants. Taking advantage of a south wind, Stefan steered north through the straits, hugging the Korland coast, using his smuggler training to see without being seen. The Khan's great hunt made no attempt to hide; all of North Korland was being scoured by a huge line of horse archers stretching across the island, backed by flying-boats tethered to trains of wagons. Every beast and bird was being driven toward the northernmost tip of Kor-land using fireworks, blunted arrows and padded lances. Herds of elk and reindeer, ground squirrels, geese, swans, lynx, lemmings, wolves, and arctic foxes, were all jammed into a broad peninsula, pinned in on three sides by the sea, and blocked on the landward side by thickening lines of cavalry. Trapped animals ran back and forth between the horsemen and the shore, unable to escape or find shelter. Frantic wolves and foxes ignored their normal prey, too frightened to hunt. So far none had been harmed, since the honor of the first kill always went to the Khan.

"Here is your chance," Stefan told her, standing safely out to sea. "I have seen these nomad hunts. Tonight they will light a line of fires to keep the animals from escaping, then at dawn the Khan will go in alone to make the first kills. Until then not a weapon will be fired, not even at your roc. It is *lèse majesté* to kill before the Khan—even to save his life."

Kore nodded. "Any Khan that cannot cope with trapped beasts, or a woman on a bird, hardly deserves the title."

"Exactly." Stefan nodded. "And believe me, Black Sails take such things seriously."

Over-seriously one might say; having destroyed or driven off Korland's human population, they were now going after the animals, right down to the ground squirrels and grass voles. At dawn Kore had Havoc aloft, riding the wave of air where the sea breeze rolled over a headland, waiting for the Khan to enter the killing ground. Reindeer huddled on the headland, along with a lone elk, eyed by a polar bear on the beach still hoping to turn calamity into a free meal. When the line of armored cavalry parted, the Black Sail Khan strode bow-in-hand straight for the beach and the polar bear, ignoring startled arctic hares and snow geese.

Kore brought Havoc down on a bare stretch of beach, right between the two most dangerous northern predators, feeling extra small and happy to be atop a roc. Seeing her alight, the man nocked an arrow and bent his bow, taking a defensive stance, while the polar bear dived into the Kor-land strait, striking out for the mainland. No free meals today. She did not bother with sleep arrows, since the last thing she wanted was a fight, calling out in Cathayan, "Do you know who I am?"

His highness nodded tersely, looking very much like the men in the flying-boat, only better fed, with fat on his body and sleek oiled hair. He wore fur-lined boots, lacquered armor, and a grim smile, and though he was only average height, that might be tall for a Tartar. "You are Lady Death who dwells by the Western Sea. We know no human gods, worshipping only the winds."

"But you do know Death. It was the Red Death that brought you here to Korland."

"Yes," he admitted, relaxing the pull on his heavy recurve bow. "The Red Death's reach proved longer than we supposed, so now we have put the sea between us and the pox."

"It will do you no good," she warned.

"We shall see," replied the Khan blandly.

"You shall die," she assured him. "Believe in me or not, but you will not escape this pox, because it is carried by people."

His majesty nodded. "Before any clan or family comes over to Korland they must spend a month apart on the mainland, proving they are pox free."

"Nevertheless you will die." With some people it paid to be relentless.

Arching an eyebrow, the Khan asked, "Then there is nothing we can do?"

"Put yourself in Death's hands," she suggested, getting an outright laugh from the Khan, dry and mirthless. Ignoring his levity, she insisted, "I am your only hope. People call me Kore, and Korland is my country. You have come to me, and I am the only one who can save you from the Red Death." She had flown all this way for a reason; apparently this was it.

"How?" The Khan of the Black Sails looked skeptical.

"Certainly not for free." No one believed in a cure that cost nothing.

Keeping his bow nocked, the Khan asked warily, "What do you want to free us from the Red Death?"

"If I free you from the pox, you must promise to abandon all of Korland." She swung her arm to indicate the surrounding shore, where frightened lemmings scurried about the rocks, nerving themselves for the suicide leap into the sea. Big ground-dwelling bustards bobbed about the beach, never having flown over water and not liking the thought. "This lone island will not support your herds and people. Right now you are destroying half the animals in a summer single hunt. What will you eat when winter comes and the grass is gone? Can you and your herds live on moss and lichens?"

"We know that," complained the Khan. "We saw at once this island was too small even after we destroyed the settlements and drove away the people. Only the pox keeps us off the mainland."

"Exactly. So if I free you from the pox, you must abandon Korland, returning it completely to the original inhabitants."

"It shall be theirs," the Khan agreed, "as we will not be needing it."

"And the people you have driven from the mainland must be allowed to settle here." Stefan's Sea Beggars needed somewhere to live.

His highness shrugged. "Where they go matters not."

"And you must free all local children taken as slaves," she added.

"Death drives a hard bargain," the Black Sail Khan observed.

Kore smiled. "I have a reputation to uphold."

"So be it," the Khan declared. "Save us from the pox and you will have Korland back, and whatever slaves we have taken here."

"Then I will give you the secret of the Red Death. Smallpox is not caused by bad water, or evil spirits, it is a living entity, passing from person to person by contact, or through the breath. Breathing through cloth masks can actually slow the spread. It lives mainly in people, and less often in animals; in fact the pox cannot survive long outside a person, though it may live for a time in corpses, and on things that recently came from the sick, or dead. Where did the disease first hit you?"

"In the Inner Lands along the Great Wall. We fled westward onto the steppe, but the pox seemed to follow us, though we abandoned our sick and dying. And not just the sick but their families as well, and any who had spent time with them; we were utterly ruthless."

No doubt. Yet ruthlessness had failed for once. She told him about finding the flying-boat, and the corpse with the Cathayan ring on his finger. "The Cathayans are seeing you do not escape the pox. Fearing your flying-boats, they are using the disease to drive you away from the Great Wall. Right now an embassy is waiting for you to finish your hunt, and on their ship is a carrier named Autumn Rose, who will bring the disease to Korland, hopefully putting it right in your yurt."

"How can this woman carry the pox?" the Black Sail asked suspiciously. "Would it not kill her?"

"What you see as the disease, the fever, the blisters, the scarring, is not really the smallpox, it is your body fighting the disease. Some people—like me—are immune to the disease. My body easily destroys the pox, so I can sup with the sick and dying, without even breaking a sweat."

"How lucky for you," observed the Khan.

"Luck had nothing to do with it. My immunity was given to me as a girl when I trained to be demi-goddess. Other people are carriers; the disease lives in them without killing them, and their bodies do not fight it. Autumn Rose has no pocks or scars, yet she can give the disease to others, so the Cathayans keep her in a tiny room atop the masthead."

"Until she can be given to me." The Khan of the Black Sails shook his head. "They told me she was so beautiful she had to be kept safe from the sailors."

"No, the sailors were being kept safe from her." Kore thought of the frail scholar reading poetry in her little room. "Death is not always great and terrible. Sometimes it appears meek and mild, or even pretty."

"Like yourself." The Khan of the Black Sails relaxed his

bow, slipping the arrow back into his quiver. Then he bowed his head, saying, "Lady Death, you have saved me and my family from terrible fates."

As terrible as the fates of Ustengrad, Zransky, Nordgorad, and Lulavik? Not likely. Men like him made her hate the living. Still she took it as a compliment, saying, "There is more. Luckily for you, my immunity can be reproduced." She showed him the scar on her arm. "I can show you how to produce the immunity; a harmless form of the disease may be gotten from cattle—called cow pox. Those who are given cow pox never get smallpox."

"That seems like a miracle." The Khan was a man of action, not medicine, more accustomed to spreading death than curing it.

"Yet here I am." She rose in her roc saddle. "Living proof the immunity works." Complete willingness to risk death always imparted the ring of truth.

Bowing his head, the Khan who knelt only to the winds thanked her. "You have given my people life when even the winds could not save us. We are a scrupulous people, and you have given much, asking for little in return. This is wise, for we are now in your debt. And to have the good will of the Black Sails is no small thing."

"Fine." She modestly accepted his thanks. "Now release all these animals."

"These animals? But why?" The Black Sail Khan looked as bewildered as the lemmings at his feet.

"They are also original inhabitants," she pointed out. "Free to live here unmolested by you."

His smile returned. "Death too may be scrupulous, it seems." She could see the Khan was pleased; the more painful the cure, the more the patient believed, and the Black Sail Khan needed to believe. If she was lying, he faced very unappetizing choices.

But she was not lying, not about smallpox at least, and in less than a month she was headed home in triumph aboard the *Sparrow*, running down the Korland Strait before a brisk northwest wind. Halfway down the strait, they passed the Cathayan ship hove to in a high-walled mainland cove, waiting out the wind, which had to veer more to the west before they could head home to Cathay. Seeing the ship, she told Stefan she still had one more task. "Make it a short one," he advised. "This wind worries me."

"Why?" she asked. "It is fair for home."

"Too fair." Stefan seemed determined to fear something—survivor's syndrome—Kore had seen before, when so many die that the living feel guilty, foreseeing their own deaths.

Urging Havoc into the air, she flew across to the Cathayan ship, creating a commotion when she landed on the mainyard. Leaping off her roc, she fairly ran along the yardarm to the window. Autumn Rose was there, scroll in hand, looking astonished. Kore told her, "I am heading south to safety. There is a place for you there, and a cure for your condition. Come, live, and be with people, otherwise I fear you will soon die."

Autumn Rose spun about and started grabbing scrolls. "Not too many," Kore advised. "I have a fine library, including Li Po and Tu Fu." Nocking her bow with a sleep arrow, she kept an eye on the ship below, but the crew just stared back in horror, watching Death drop out of the sky to carry off their prisoner-cum-plague-case on the back of a giant bird of prey. Hardly an auspicious omen.

Autumn Rose emerged with an armful of scrolls, and Kore hustled her along the mainyard and onto the roc. Two small women on one big roc would be hard; fortunately the *Sparrow* lay downwind, and if need be she could always dump the scrolls. Catching the wave of wind rolling over the southern headland, she worked back and forth to gain altitude. Looking back, she saw black shadows lifting off from Korland, the last of the Black Sails headed for the mainland. Yurts and herds had already been ferried across the straits, but the flying-boats had stayed behind, awaiting a favorable wind—until now.

At the top of the climb, she watched as the flying-boats swept low over the straits, headed for the cove where the Cathayans were sheltered. She saw what Stefan meant about the wind being too favorable; it was blowing from just the right quarter to let the flying-boats leave Korland,

and keep the Cathayans penned in the straits, unable to escape into the Arctic Sea. Just the wind Black Sail shamans would pray for. Coming in low and in a line ahead, the flyingboats made masthead-level attacks, each releasing a single big round ball at the ship below. Then the lightened flyingboat would soar upward, passing easily over the south headland, so close she saw the crews wave and smile.

Half the missiles missed, plunging harmlessly into the water alongside the ship, but the half that hit exploded in great balls of fire. She had seen these bombs back at the Black Sail camp, big glass balls filled with naphtha, and within each ball was a bottle of oxidizer—so when the bomb hit, ball and bottle shattered, mixing the contents and igniting the naphtha. By the time a dozen had hit, the Cathayan ship was aflame from stem to stern. Succeeding Black Sails dropped ballast instead, saving their naphtha balls for another time—while Autumn Rose wept for her scrolls.

With the wind at her back, Havoc bore her double load straight to the *Sparrow*, and Kore was finally home free. The *Sparrow*'s crew were the first ones inoculated—to show suspicious Black Sails that the serum made from cow pox was safe—so there was no need to cage Autumn Rose on the masthead, and for the first time in years the scholar walked freely among other people, making up in part for the loss of her scrolls.

Running back down toward Seagate, with Stefan beside her, Kore felt torn. High summer was here, the short season when everyone got ready for winter, and Stefan's Sea Beggars would be resettling Nordgorad and Lulavik. Shrines must be rededicated, and priestesses appointed, and there were many dead to pray over. Yet when summer was gone, where would she winter? At Seagate of course, but would Stefan be with her? Not if he was settled in Korland. Life was becoming far more complex than death had ever been. Hopefully, she could convince Stefan to winter the *Mermaid* at Seagate, where stores were ample, giving Korland fewer mouths to feed—but it was hard to have to count on someone else's wishes. And children by him would mean added wishes to consider. Death was an accomplished abortionist—in complete control of her body—but she wanted children, especially children with Stefan. Eros was to blame for all this, Eros and his arrows.

She got her chance to give Eros his dressing-down when they arrived triumphantly at Seagate, announcing the return of Korland, and the retreat of the Black Sails. Calling her wayward cousin in for a private audience in her presence chamber, she upbraided him for daring to shoot her with one of his arrows.

"It was all I could do," Eros protested. "You were facing certain capture, probable rape, and imminent execution; I had to shoot him to protect you. Since that made rape even more likely, I had to shoot you too."

Turning it into consensual sex. Eros was nothing if not neat. "Damn you, what if I have children by him?"

"Mad because you might no longer be Miss Iron Drawers, Maiden Goddess of Death?"

"Demi-Goddess," she corrected her smiling cousin.

"Look, you have nailed this Death Goddess role, no one will ever do it better, but now you need to move to something new, like raising your replacement." Eros pursed his cupid's bow lips. "Having children is not so bad. So you might have to train Persephone to be Dark Daughter— what of it? You would still be Lady of Seagate, while Persephone would love the task, and could surely use the training. Start her out easy, make her Killer of Children, then let her work her way up."

"You have always had eyes for Persephone," she observed.

"Love smiles on everyone," Eros replied blandly. "So you cannot be both Death and Mother at the same time—things could be way worse. Look at me, I must go about seducing lovely innocent maidens and begetting beautiful bastards. No one ever asked if I wanted to, it is just expected of Love. Yet do you see me complain?"

"Thou art an inspiration to us all." She could see the interview going nowhere; as usual everything was up to her.

"Naturally," Eros beamed happily. "Love is all you need."

Story Copyrights